Books by Elisa Braden

RESCUED FROM RUIN SERIES

The Madness of Viscount Atherbourne (Book One)
The Truth About Cads and Dukes (Book Two)
Desperately Seeking a Scoundrel (Book Three)
The Devil Is a Marquess (Book Four)
When a Girl Loves an Earl (Book Five)
Twelve Nights as His Mistress (Novella – Book Six)
Confessions of a Dangerous Lord (Book Seven)
Anything but a Gentleman (Book Eight)
A Marriage Made in Scandal (Book Nine)

There's much more to come in the Rescued from Ruin series! Connect with Elisa through Facebook and Twitter, and sign up for her free email newsletter at www.elisabraden.com, so you don't miss a single release!

A Marriage Made in Scandal

ELISA BRADEN

This is a work of fiction. Names, characters, places, and incidents are products of the author's imagination or are used fictitiously and are not to be construed as real. Any resemblance to actual events, locales, organizations, or persons, living or dead, is entirely coincidental.

Copyright © 2018 Elisa Braden

Cover design by Kim Killion at The Killion Group, Inc.
Couple photo by Period Images, Inc.

All rights reserved. No part of this book may be used or reproduced in any form by any means—except in the case of brief quotations embodied in critical articles or reviews—without express written permission of the author.

For more information about the author, visit www.elisabraden.com.

ISBN-13: 978-1-72-446784-3
ISBN-10: 1-7244-6784-0

Prologue

"Winter is also beautiful. One is wise to keep one's distance, however, lest you catch your death."

—The Dowager Marchioness of Wallingham to Lady Berne in a prescient conversation about the Countess of Holstoke.

January 7, 1797
Primvale Castle, Dorsetshire

Hoarfrost, shaggy as an old man's beard, coated the castle's long drive. A gust made the horses attached to his father's coach lower their heads. The wind made Phineas close his eyes, too, but only for a moment. The tips of his fingers had gone numb.

His father reached the castle's bottom step and trudged along frozen gravel. It crunched beneath his boots. He did not stop to pat Phineas's head, as he'd always done. He was as white as the frost.

Inside, Phineas shook. Papa was going to Bath, they'd told him. He was going to take the waters. Phineas had not understood. Surely the baths at Primvale would do for Papa. Surely he did not have to go away.

Then, his tutor, Mr. Cox, had shown him a map and explained how the waters of a town called Bath were quite beneficial to those who had taken ill.

Papa was very ill. He scarcely recognized Phineas any longer.

One of the horses shook its head, and its mane scattered frost in a cloud.

Phineas held himself still, his hands clasped at his back the way he'd seen Papa do. Another gust. Now, his toes were numb, too.

One of the footmen braced Papa's elbow, helping him the last few feet to the coach. The footman opened the door, and Papa turned. For a moment, his eyes found Phineas. Papa's eyes were light, like Phineas's eyes. His hair was black, like Phineas's hair. And, while Papa was tall and Phineas was small, his nurse, Miss Banfield, said he would grow just as big one day.

Papa looked at him now and blinked. Frowned. His eyes did not see Phineas. They did not know Phineas. They seemed confused.

The footman helped Papa climb the coach's step. Then, Papa disappeared and the door closed. The footman blew into his gloved hands before climbing up to sit with the coachman.

Frozen gravel crunched as the coach pulled away.

Phineas could not feel his hands any longer.

"Come, my little lord," said Miss Banfield from behind him. "Let us find a pleasant spot where we might have a biscuit and practice our mathematics. Mr. Cox will arrive soon."

Phineas turned away from watching the coach disappear. He was careful to keep his gaze lowered until he glimpsed the castle steps. A flash of blue silk entered his vision. Blue, like the sky. He tried not to look. Quickly, he blinked and focused upon the steps. But she stepped into his sight. Broke his concentration.

He raised his gaze. She was like glittering frost. White-gold hair piled high. White-pure face far more beauteous than Miss Banfield's or any of the paintings he had seen. Her eyes matched her gown, which billowed out from her waist and forced itself into his vision.

Phineas froze. Dropped his gaze to her shoes. They were gold.

"Inform the master gardener I shall require his plans within the hour," she said to the butler. "One minute longer, and he may find a new position."

Her voice held Phineas pinned in place as another gust battered him from behind. It was best if she did not notice him.

Her skirt fluttered and halted. One gold shoe rested on the first step. "Miss Banfield," the cold voice snapped.

"Aye, my lady?"

"Keep the child out of my sight."

"Of—of course. As you wish, my lady."

Miss Banfield's voice trembled the way Phineas's stomach trembled whenever his mother was near.

Gold shoes climbed the steps. Blue silk disappeared.

Phineas tried not to turn his head, but he couldn't help it. The rim of the fountain was closer than he'd thought, and it brushed his arm as he sidled away from where his mother had been.

Another gust. Frost rained down upon him from the top of the fountain. He shouldn't look up, but he did. He blinked, his chest starting to pound.

The snake was killing the bird-lion. Its teeth were in the bird's throat.

"There, now, my little lord. Let us go round to the east

entrance. 'Tis too cold to stay out here any longer." Miss Banfield moved away from the fountain toward the side of the castle.

Phineas could not stop looking at the bird-lion. He could not move. Only shake.

"They are nothing but stone, little one," he heard in his ear. A shawl draped around his shoulders. He could no longer feel his legs. "Come, now. You must try to stay hidden from her ladyship, do you understand?"

Miss Banfield tied the shawl around him and nudged him forward. He stumbled at first because his feet and legs were numb, but she pressed his back, and soon they were inside the castle then the nursery, where a fire warmed the chamber.

Mr. Cox arrived just as Phineas finished his tea. His fingers prickled after the cold. Now, he only felt numb on the inside.

"Holstoke finally took my advice and went to Bath?" Mr. Cox asked in a half-whisper. Phineas's tutor and Miss Banfield often whispered to one another when they thought he couldn't hear. They also kissed when they thought he couldn't see. Phineas found the kissing strange, so he paid it no mind.

"His lordship's been so very ill," said Miss Banfield. "I pray the waters help. Most times, he cannot even recognize his own son."

"If he dies, you must find a new position, Frances. Promise me."

"I cannot leave the boy with her. I will not."

"You must think of yourself. Until we marry—"

"He is a little ghost, George. He rarely speaks. Often, I find he's been in a room with me for an hour or more, and I haven't noticed, he sits so still. Everything worsens when Lord Holstoke is away. His father is all he has."

"He has you, and that is no small thing."

"And you," she said.

Phineas thought perhaps they were kissing now. He rose from the desk chair and moved to the window. The wind was stronger. It blew frost through the air in glittering swirls.

Phineas liked the shapes. He traced the line of frost upon glass panes. Ice spread outward like leafy branches.

He liked how frost and trees were similar. He liked how shells and flowers were also alike. Natural things had patterns, and he found them beautiful.

Not beautiful like his mother. But, rather, beautiful all the way through.

"When Holstoke returns, unless he is very much improved, I shall recommend the boy be sent to Harrow," murmured Mr. Cox.

"He is too young."

"His intellect is not. I have instructed boys ten years older with less capability. He defeated me at chess not three days ago."

Miss Banfield sighed. "I wish ... I wish we could take him away with us."

"You know we cannot. The school will do him good. Being around other boys. Order and tradition. He will like the routine of it, I expect."

They whispered to one another for a while longer, but Phineas did not want to listen. So, he slipped out of the nursery while they were kissing and went to the library. It was his favorite room, the place where his father had taught him to play chess. The place where Papa wrote his letters while Phineas read about how seeds became wheat and eggs became hens.

Now, in the dark room where he remembered Papa best, he closed the door and leaned against it.

They wanted to send him away.

He knew what he'd done wrong. Inside the numb place, it bloomed like hoarfrost. Except it was not white but black.

His breathing was too fast, so he covered his mouth. Closed his eyes. He tried to picture the patterns. Focused upon them until the black frost stopped spreading. He went to the shelf and selected a book. He carried it to Papa's desk and withdrew paper from the drawer. Then, he took up a pen and began his work. The squares helped him think, helped his chest feel lighter.

A long while later, when the windows had turned gray, he blinked. Replaced the pen. Sprinkled sand upon his notes and blew it away.

Then, he gathered his stack of pages into a pile and opened the library door.

"Say it again, Mary."

He halted. Froze. His stomach hurt.

A small whimper. "I—I should have taken more care with the bucket, my lady."

"Again."

The maid repeated the words. His mother demanded she say she'd been wrong over and over. Phineas counted twenty times before Lady Holstoke let her go. Mary was sobbing by then. His mother looked on with a queer smile.

Blackness bloomed wider inside Phineas. He shuddered and tried to make it stop, but the patterns didn't work this time.

She must not see him. Miss Banfield would be punished as Mary had been. Worse, even. She might be sent away. He closed the door carefully and listened. He could scarcely hear past his pounding chest.

Was Lady Holstoke gone? He reached for the knob. Twisted. It slipped inside his hand. Finally, he inched the door open the barest crack.

The corridor was empty, he thought. Quiet.

He slipped out the door, clutching his papers to his burning chest. That was when he spied it.

Silk the color of the sky. Her back was to him as she examined something in her hands. A sketchbook, he thought.

Mustn't be seen. Mustn't be seen. The words chanted in his head.

Without breath, he began to walk backward. Chest pounded harder. Watching the blue silk. Shaking and shaking.

Blue silk shifted. He spun. One of his pages flew from his hand.

Mustn't be seen. Mustn't be seen.

He ran. Rounded a corner. Saw the great doors open as a footman carried an empty bucket inside. He ran again, out into the cold. Down the steps.

The bird-lion stared down at him, covered in ice and forever dying.

He ran farther. Faster. His papers were damp now, but it didn't matter.

Mustn't be seen.

The waves grew louder as the sea grew near. The wind grew stronger and the ground slickened beneath his feet. He slipped and gripped dirt. Frost-coated grasses lashed his cheeks. Yet he ran. Found the edge. The trail down the cliff was steep. If he could, he would make it into stairs. But he could not. Not until he was bigger, like Papa.

The trail wound down the great, gold-and-white cliffs of sandstone and chalk like a long scar. The wind battered him. Numb feet slid on the wet, but he focused upon the next step. Braced a numb hand on a wall of rock. At last, he reached the bottom, where pebbles lay in deep, soft sand. They crunched and squished beneath his shoes as he circled along the edge of the beach until he found his place—the great boulder beside the great arch.

He looked back at the trail. Saw only the high cliffs and no blue silk. Breathed and felt his papers fall apart in his hand. He dropped the sheets like leaves. Then, he sat right where he stood, sinking into pebbles and sand. The waves rolled and rumbled, clawed their way ashore. The wind blew away his papers, turned everything to ice—especially Phineas.

He leaned against the boulder. Hugged his knees and rocked. Shaking. Shaking. Shaking.

The black frost grew. He focused upon a seashell, the infinite pattern.

The black frost grew. He remembered his papa as he'd been before the illness.

The black frost grew. He laid his cheek upon his knees.

This was why they must send Phineas away.

No boy should hate his mother. No boy should wish her dead.

Miss Banfield thought him afraid of the bird-lion or the snake. But in Phineas's nightmares, *he* was the bird-lion. He hated the snake with every beat of his black heart. And, rather than the snake sinking its teeth into his throat, he tore the snake into pieces and scattered them at sea.

He squeezed his eyes closed. The black frost was everywhere, freezing until it burned. In time, everything went numb. Then warm. That was when he decided the black frost might never go away. He could not destroy it. He'd tried. But he could freeze it.

Behind his eyes, he pictured squares. Boxes to keep things orderly and understandable. He imagined the frost gathered into the boxes. He imagined the boxes filled with water and sealed up tight. He froze them in his mind until the black frost lived inside the ice, motionless and trapped. Then, when the frost was contained, he pictured the squares coated in white like the fountain. Shaggy and crusted like an old man's beard.

Nothing grew while it was frozen.

Not even this.

He was warm now. Sleepy. He could not feel anything—not his hands or his feet or his cheeks or his belly. Some might think it unpleasant, but Phineas was floating as the sea sighed his name.

"... little one. We'll get you warm soon ..."

He blinked. Someone carried him. He smelled wool and chalk and the sea.

"... must take him away from here, George."

"... to Harrow. I shall send a message to his lordship at once. We cannot wait for his return. With you gone, I don't know what she'll do ..."

Phineas was floating. Up the trail. Into gray mist and frozen grass. Beneath white-bearded oak branches. Onto gravel. Past the bird-lion who was dying. Always dying.

But not dead. Frozen, perhaps. Wounded.

The snake thought it had won. Phineas rested his cheek against the wool of Mr. Cox's coat and smiled.

The snake thought wrong.

Chapter One

"The word 'extraordinary' may be taken in two ways, Eugenia. One implies awe. The other implies you have crossed the bounds of decent society into realms best unexplored."

—THE DOWAGER MARCHIONESS OF WALLINGHAM to Lady Eugenia Huxley in reply to said lady's assertion that turbans should never have fewer than three feathers.

May 7, 1825
Mrs. Pritchard's Millinery Shop, London

"WHAT POSSESSED YOU? MRS. PRITCHARD HATES RED FLOWERS." The words wafted toward Eugenia Huxley on a low hiss. "She'll give you the sack this time, for certain. And none too soon, you ask me." Along with the odor of poorly cleaned teeth, the woman's loathing formed an unpleasant fog in the cramped workroom.

Genie stabbed her long needle through her newest leghorn straw creation and spared a glare for her fellow millinery assistant, Nancy Knox—or, as Genie had dubbed her, Fancy Nancy.

A keen bit of sarcasm, of course. Weathered fence posts had more imagination than Miss Knox.

Plucking a purple ostrich plume from the basket beside her chair, Genie glanced toward three finished hats resting upon a shelf at the rear of the room. One was dyed indigo and adorned with the forbidden red silk roses. Another was swathed in emerald damask, accented with pleated ivory lining, and topped by five majestic peacock feathers.

The third was brown.

Plain. Dull. Brown. With darker brown binding around a modest brim and black velvet ribbons to tie beneath the wearer's chin.

If a lady had a sudden need for half-mourning, Fancy Nancy's handiwork was the answer.

Genie raised her chin and tucked the purple plume inside a brocade band. Turning the bonnet this way and that, she *tsked*. "More color, I think. Ah, yes. I know just the thing." She stood to fetch a length of red silk. Slanting a grin at Miss Knox, she returned to her chair and began folding ribbon into petals. Briefly, her eyes landed on the other woman's piteous attempt at a yellow cap.

"Lace?" she gasped. "Your boldness shocks my very senses, Miss Knox. Why, next thing you know, you'll be dabbling in witchcraft."

Miss Knox's glare flashed with anger. At least, Genie thought it was anger. Fancy Nancy's eyes were both brown and dead—like mud, but with added spite.

Another foul-smelling hiss floated her way. "The *sack*. Mark my words, you insolent—"

Mrs. Pritchard entered with a swish of the striped curtain that separated workroom from storefront. "Mrs. Herbert requested five turbans by tomorrow morning," she said, her smile at odds with her tight expression and tighter hair. "I suggest you retrieve the white plumes, Miss Huxley."

Long before Genie had arrived to plague her employer with rebellious red flowers, Mrs. Pritchard had been defeated by her own mediocrity. The wheat-haired milliner often smiled and tittered like a silly girl at Almack's, but her pleasantness poorly compensated for what she lacked—talent and intelligence. To Genie's eye, tight lips, scraped-back hair, and careworn creases bespoke two decades of disguised ineptitude. Mrs. Pritchard might smile like a society miss making her debut, but she was a dreadful milliner.

Genie had no intention of suffering the same fate.

"Scarlet, this time?" she quipped under her breath. "Or will it be jonquil?"

Mrs. Pritchard's smile flattened and pursed as though she'd swallowed a spoonful of vinegar. "You will make them precisely how she prefers." A new smile emerged, bright and false. "Precisely."

Genie held the woman's gaze for a moment then dropped her eyes to the red ribbon in her hands. "Of course. Gold with white plumes."

"Plume, Miss Huxley," The response was low and vexed. "I shall not repeat it again. Add two as you did last time, and that will be that."

That will be that.

Her stomach filled with cold lead.

Fancy Nancy had been right. Genie was about to be dismissed. Given the sack from an east Oxford Street milliner. One who catered to miserly, middle-class matrons. One who had hired Fancy Nancy, of all the talentless wretches in London. One who, last week, had insisted the three of them take tea while fourteen orders remained unfinished.

Because Mrs. Pritchard preferred things pleasant. Nothing was more pleasant than tea in the midst of a hectic workday, apparently, when one departed at six rather than ten. No, working into the wee hours was for assistants—*junior* assistants, to be precise.

Genie examined Mrs. Pritchard's expression, gauging her seriousness. Her coif was so severe, her brows arched in permanent surprise. Or alarm. Or wakefulness. Genie had never quite decided, but it forced the creases from her forehead, which was likely the point.

Genie's stomach grew heavier as an unlikely furrow formed between the woman's brows. "Gold satin. One white plume," Genie murmured, setting her red rose aside and plucking a white feather from the bottom of the basket. "Straight away, Mrs. Pritchard."

Acquiescence was *not* surrender, she assured herself, but tactical retreat. She needed this position. She needed to learn how to run a shop—or how *not* to run one, more to the point. She needed to know she could do this work and that her life was not over.

The curtain swished as Mrs. Pritchard disappeared into the front of the shop, where she would wait for the barest trickle of customers to woo with Fancy Nancy's plain, dull creations.

"Told you, didn't I?"

Genie answered Miss Knox's utterance with a taunt she knew would fall on uncomprehending ears—which only made it sweeter. "Ah, yes. A prophecy worthy of *Macbeth*. Witchcraft suits you, Miss Knox."

Two hours later, after the other two women had departed and the light through the tiny window had dimmed to a yellow haze, Genie fastened a single white plume into place on her fourth turban. All she could see when she blinked was gold satin, white feathers, and tiny stitches. Her fingers ached. Her back burned. Her stomach growled.

And she had run out of gold satin.

Rising, she groaned, rubbed her lower spine, and examined her work.

Identical to the last three, it was an elegantly arranged series of silken folds. It begged for a band of pearls, perhaps a plaited cord, and at least two more plumes. But, because Genie wanted Fancy Nancy's prophecy to be wrong, it was precisely as Mrs. Herbert preferred. She sighed and removed the turban from the hat block before placing it gently on a shelf alongside three others.

Returning to the table, she sifted through tiny scraps of gold satin. She needed more. She didn't have it.

But Mrs. Pritchard's husband did.

Drat.

A hat-maker far more skilled and far less pleasant than his wife, Mr. Pritchard ran the adjacent shop, Pritchard's Fine Hats. The place served strictly male customers, of course, but men's hats required lining. And she happened to know Pritchard favored the same gold silk Mrs. Herbert fancied.

Genie tapped one fingertip against the table and another against her lip. She eyed the door connecting the two workrooms.

She shouldn't, of course. Mrs. Pritchard had forbidden her assistants from borrowing Mr. Pritchard's supplies. But she had also declared, "That will be that."

Genie took such a threat as permission to do what was necessary.

Before she could think better of it, she inched the door open and peeked inside. Then she rolled her eyes and cleared her throat.

The portly young man currently hunched over a book jerked. Booted feet dropped from the table to the floor with a thud.

"What have you there, Mr. Moody?" she teased.

Rounded cheeks reddened and a sheepish smile came her way over Lewis Moody's shoulder. "Only one of me stories, Miss Huxley." He set the book beside his hat block. One freckled, pudgy hand stroked the cover before he stood and gave her a bashful nod. "What brings ye visitin'?"

Mr. Moody was Pritchard's assistant, and the hatter allowed him to manage the shop in the late afternoons when business slowed.

She shot him her best grin, which made his color deepen, and pointed toward the bolt of gold silk on the table behind him.

He swiveled. "Right. Mrs. Herbert again, is it?"

"Fully five turbans this time." She shook her head and clicked her tongue.

"Identical to the last lot?"

She nodded.

"Puzzlin'."

She chuckled. "Heaven knows what she does with them."

"Some do favor things of a single kind."

Yes. Some did. Those who lacked vision. "Might you spare a bit of the gold silk? Mrs. Herbert requires her identical headdresses to be delivered promptly."

Mr. Moody laughed and nodded. "Certainly. I'm glad to give ye whatever ye require, Miss Huxley. More than glad."

The glint in his eyes spoke of a double meaning, but she ignored it, patting his elbow as she squeezed past him. "That is why you are my favorite of all Mr. Pritchard's assistants," she teased. The two other assistants were sourer than Fancy Nancy. By comparison, Lewis Moody was positively dashing.

As she bent over to cut the silk, she thought she heard him squeak, but concluded it was the front door of Pritchard's shop. Bells chimed. Boots rapped.

"M-Miss Huxley, I must tell ye," Mr. Moody began, "how much I admire your ... that is, I been meanin' to ... "

Hearing his tone—low and earnest—Genie's hands slowed. Her heart sank.

Drat. She hoped he was not about to—

"Do ye suppose one day soon—not today, o' course, but one day—that ye might ... with me, I mean ... perhaps we could—"

A distinct rap from a boot heel striking plank floors echoed through the curtained doorway.

Pretending nonchalance, Genie resettled the silk and smoothed it for cutting. "Sounds as though you are needed, Mr. Moody. Mustn't tarry on my account."

A sigh. "Right." The squeak of boots and the swish of a curtain signaled his departure.

Genie straightened and bit her lip. Her eyes drifted to Mr. Moody's abandoned book. *Ivanhoe*.

Her second-oldest sister, Jane, was a reader, constantly nattering on about this novel and that. Genie rarely paid much mind, but even she had heard of Sir Walter Scott's tale of medieval adventure. Given Lewis Moody's lot in life, she imagined escaping into the past, picturing oneself as the hero of the piece, was a welcome diversion.

Drat again. She liked Mr. Moody. He reminded her a bit of Jane, actually. Shy. Good-natured. Hoarding every spare farthing to spend at the circulating library.

He'd likely object to the comparison. Jane was female, after all—a mother of five and wife to the formidable Duke of Blackmore. But apart from that, they might as well be twins. Cousins, at least.

Genie must dissuade Lewis Moody from developing a *tendre* for her. She liked him entirely too much.

With a sigh, she resumed cutting Mrs. Herbert's silk, hoping to finish before he returned.

"... did it take on such damage, m'lord? If ye don't mind me askin'."

"Does it matter?"

Genie froze, the shears half-open in her hand. That voice. Clipped. Patrician. Low and flinty.

"Suppose not. I shall have it for yer lordship first thing tomorrow morn—"

"Why can it not be repaired now?"

Oh, yes. She recognized that voice. It had been years, but she knew it instantly.

"The damage is ... well, there is quite a lot of it, isn't there?

Nothin' beyond repair, mind. But it might take an hour or more."

"I shall wait."

"Beg your pardon?"

Silence.

Genie remembered those, too. Long, curious silences between brief, clipped sentences.

Lewis Moody cleared his throat. She could almost hear the young man turning red. "As you like, sir. I mean, m'lord."

The curtain swished. As she'd surmised, Mr. Moody's cheeks were crimson and his hands shook. He frantically gestured toward the doorway with a misshapen hat. It appeared to have teeth marks in the brim. "You'll never believe it," he whispered, eyes wide. "It's—"

The Earl of Holstoke. Yes, she would believe it. He'd almost been her brother-in-law.

"—an *earl*, Miss Huxley. Never spoke to one of the quality before. Not more'n a 'yes, sir' or 'pardon me, sir,' at any rate."

In truth, he *had* spoken to one of the quality on numerous occasions. An earl's daughter, in fact. But he didn't know that, and she preferred to keep matters as they were.

"Well," he said, tilting the wrecked hat toward his worktable. "Best get to it."

She nodded, folding Mrs. Herbert's gold silk and squeezing past Mr. Moody. On her way to the connecting door, she glanced at the curtained entrance, a curl of curiosity wending up her nape.

"He elected to wait, I take it," she said.

"Hmm? Oh, aye."

"Bound to grow impatient." She tapped a fingertip against the silk. "The quality often do."

A pause and a clink as one of Mr. Moody's tools was exchanged for another. "Suppose so."

Curling curiosity wormed deeper. Dug in. Demanded.

"I shall keep him occupied for a while," she murmured,

drifting toward the curtained doorway. "Give you time for the repairs."

"Oh, no. That is, certainly you may do as you like, Miss Huxley, but ..."

She was no longer listening. She'd shouldered past the curtain and entered Mr. Pritchard's shop where few females ever set foot—even Mrs. Pritchard.

Holstoke stood with his back to her, one hand clasping the opposite wrist behind him. A waning shaft of light gleamed a streak across black, short-cropped hair. He was tall—an inch or two above six feet. She recalled craning her neck to speak with him, though it had been years.

"Lord Holstoke. It has been an age."

His shoulders stiffened. Were they broader than before? They were, she thought. Heavier, too, as though both muscle and bone had thickened.

His head tilted and he began to turn. First came the cheekbone, high and prominent. Next the nose, long and straight. Finally, the eyes.

Ah, the eyes. Like green ice, pale and piercing. She'd nearly forgotten how they made one shiver. Eerie, one of her sisters called them. Others termed them ghostly. Genie simply thought them an unusual shade of green.

Genie was not one for poetry.

"Lady Eugenia." Low and deep, his voice resonated like metal. Unblinking eyes slid along her torso, pausing where she clasped the gold silk before returning to her face. "Six years."

She moved past the counter toward the window, where he stood as still and expressionless as she remembered. "Is it six? I had thought five."

"Six."

"No matter. It is splendid to see you again. My sister mentioned you were in town for the season."

"You have four sisters. Perhaps you could be more specific."

Her mouth quirked in a sympathetic smile. "Lady Dunston,

of course."

Silence. And a long, green stare.

Genie forgave the moment of awkwardness. A natural thing, really. He had courted her third-oldest sister, Maureen, ardently before having his marriage proposal rejected in favor of Maureen's real and only love, Henry Thorpe, the Earl of Dunston.

Turning, Genie laid her silk upon the counter and moved nearer the man many found intimidating if not frightening. His features had a spare quality Maureen had once called "ascetic." Genie wasn't certain what that meant, but the high cheekbones, bladed nose, and lean jaw enhanced the chill of his strange, expressionless eyes. And yet, he was tall. Trim. Wealthy. An earl. And, unless he had changed a great deal in the past six years, a man of stunning intellect.

By all rights, Phineas Brand, the Earl of Holstoke, was a splendid catch. If one overlooked his peculiar nature.

Curiosity—one of her abiding weaknesses—struck again. But she could not simply ask him the question burning in her head, so she began with an easier inquiry. "What happened to your hat?"

He surveyed the empty shop as though wondering how she'd made her way there from Bedlam. "Lady Randall."

"Lady Randall ate your hat?"

She'd said it to make him laugh. Or smile, at least. But she'd forgotten how rarely he did either.

"Her dogs."

She grinned, chuckled, and rolled her eyes. "Little devils. She never could control her pugs. A shame, really. Yours was a very fine hat. Exquisite beaver."

He did not reply.

"So," she continued, feigning blitheness. In truth, curiosity was eating at her like one of Lady Randall's pugs on a slice of ham. Or a very fine hat. "You are in town. After six years rusticating in your Dorsetshire castle."

Glancing down at his gray wool sleeve, he retorted dryly, "Observant of you."

"Oh, come now." She stepped closer. "Do not play coy. How goes the search?"

"My hat was damaged less than an hour ago. I have not yet sought a new one."

"You know very well I meant—"

"Yes," he said softly. "I know."

Any other woman would have heeded the warning in his voice. Genie had never been any other woman. "Well? Tell me, then. We were friends once."

A hard light glinted inside icy green.

"After a fashion," she clarified.

His expression remained stony.

"Very well, *acquaintances*. My family is fond of you, Holstoke. We should like to know whether you have found a suitable bride."

"We?"

She sighed, conceding his point. "*I*. I should like to know."

"Why?"

"Matters were left ... rather a mess."

His jaw hardened and tilted. "Quite the contrary. Lady Maureen became Lady Dunston. Matters were made extraordinarily clear."

Yes, she supposed that was true. And he had been hurt. Genie had hated it, for Holstoke was a fine man who had pursued her sister honorably. He'd even shown generosity to Maureen's two fractious younger sisters, bringing Genie and Kate along on several excursions, including a lovely day at Astley's Amphitheatre.

"Regardless," she said. "I should like to see you make a good match." She raised a brow and eyed him teasingly from beneath her lashes. "A lady capable of coaxing a smile from those lips now and then."

Something strange flashed in Holstoke's eyes—stranger

than normal, that was. A kind of fire. Perhaps he was angry.

Quicker than a blink, his gaze dropped to her mouth then came up again, cold as ever. "Six years is a long time. Whatever our prior connection, Lady Eugenia, my present circumstances needn't concern—"

She abandoned pretense. "Yes, but I am *dying* of curiosity. You must tell me."

His silence was long and probing. She wondered if he was remembering the time she had astutely advised him to wear an emerald pin with his silver cravat, or the time she'd wheedled a surprised chuckle out of him as they'd departed Astley's. To her recollection, she had been quite helpful. Perhaps he would take pity upon her and satisfy her craving.

After long seconds, he did. "I've yet to locate a suitable wife."

Just as she'd suspected. He'd run aground in the marriage mart. In this, at least, she might be useful. The marriage mart had proven rough waters for her, as well.

"You are not unattractive," she began, assessing level black brows and flat lips.

The comment earned her a blink.

"Not handsome either, mind. And even you must admit to having a rather peculiar nature."

This produced a small frown.

"Still." She propped one elbow on her opposite wrist and tapped her lip with her finger. "Attractive, in your way. Maureen doubtless would have accepted your suit had she not been mad for Dunston. By all rights, you should be besieged by ladies eager to be made a countess."

It was true, and yet she sensed it displeased him greatly.

"*What* are you doing here?" He snapped the first word and glided over the rest.

Her finger paused. "I am employed here. The milliner's shop, rather. Next door. I am here to fetch silk for a customer who wishes to add to her collection of identical turbans." She shook her head and snorted. "Speaking of peculiar."

Green eyes calculated and probed as though she were a complex equation. "Why?"

"My question precisely. Is she part of a secret society in which gold turbans with a single white feather are required for entry? Or is the reason more sinister? Dreadful taste, perhaps. But if that is true, she might aim for variety at the very least—"

"No. Why are *you* working here?"

She blinked. "Where else should I work?"

"I shouldn't think you would be working at all, *Lady* Eugenia. I assumed you would be wed by now."

"Wed?" She laughed, shaking her head.

He tilted his head as though she'd made a jest he didn't understand.

"The scandal?" she prompted, sighing when his response was another inscrutable stare. "You've been away from London too long."

"I know about the scandal. Whatever your indiscretions, you should not be reduced to"—he glanced around the tiny shop—"this. You're an earl's daughter, for God's sake."

"My employer does not know. To her, I am Miss Huxley, lately of Nottinghamshire. I came with excellent references." Her lips quirked. "The Dowager Marchioness of Wallingham, no less."

"Patently ridiculous. Someone should marry you and stop this nonsense at once."

Sniffing, she folded her arms beneath her bosom. "You and my mother are in agreement. And yet, despite her efforts, three years on, no man has tendered an offer. Disgraced brides are in low demand, evidently."

"I saw your mother several weeks ago outside Almack's. She mentioned nothing of this."

"Mama has reinvested her hopes in my younger sister, Kate. For my part, I simply stay out of sight and attempt to keep my scandalous vapor from spoiling the husband hunt."

Again, his head tilted. "Do you always speak so bluntly?"

"Candor spares us all a good deal of meaningless prattle, wouldn't you agree? As for my employment, working here is preferable to wandering about the grounds at Clumberwood Manor." She had done that for nearly two years. It had felt like prison.

A perplexed cleft now shadowed the bridge of his long, straight nose. "Your father can be none too happy."

"Papa would prefer I remain in the country, rotting away like some old, forgotten rodent in the corner of the stables. Here, at least I shall learn a useful trade. That is more than most spinsters can claim."

"Making hats."

She stiffened at the implication in his tone. "I have a talent for it. Hats are an integral element of a lady's fashionable ensemble. A veritable proclamation of—"

"So, you are a milliner."

She sniffed. "Assistant. Milliner's assistant." At his raised brow, she straightened her shoulders and tried to forget Mrs. Pritchard's ominous assurance: *That will be that.* "Only for now, whilst I learn the trade," she hedged. "One day, I shall open my own shop."

"Huxleys do not open shops. Particularly …" Green eyes dropped to her apron-covered skirts then returned to her faded blue bodice. "Female Huxleys."

Her hands propped on her hips. "Well, this one shall."

He moved mere inches away, his gaze now disconcertingly focused.

At this proximity, she felt the weariness in her neck, a disturbing shortness of breath. He was taller than she'd previously estimated. Perhaps three inches above six feet.

"Your older sisters have borne twelve children between them."

Four. Definitely four inches. The man *loomed*. "Your point?"

"Huxleys breed. A lot." He muttered the words to himself, though his eyes never left her.

Amusement tugged at her lips. He truly was a most peculiar fellow. "Some do."

"But not you?"

Amusement shook and dissolved. "Breeding is best done with a husband. Or so I have heard."

"Rather than a footman." Again, he murmured the words to himself like a scientist puzzling out the structure of an exotic insect, unconcerned with the insect's feelings on the matter.

A footman. She wanted to laugh and cry at once, felt both urges shuddering in her chest. No, a footman could not be her husband.

The scandal had ravaged her family. Mama had wept for weeks. Papa—kind, loving, good-humored Papa—had not spoken to Genie for a fortnight. Finally, when he had, he'd quietly explained that if she wanted Kate to have a chance at an acceptable match, she would leave London and remain in the country until the scandal receded. Genie had left for Clumberwood the following day.

Even now, some in the ton still whispered about her, crass epithets and lewd snickering. She didn't care, so long as the cruelties did not touch Kate. It was why Genie needed employment. Needed to finish Mrs. Herbert's silly gold turbans. Needed to endure the false smiles and forced cheer of Mrs. Pritchard.

Her family had borne the Great Burden of Genie too long.

"Well," she said briskly, raising her brow at the man whose eyes pinned her like a silk rose to a straw brim. "I believe we have solved the mystery of your difficulties in the marriage mart, Holstoke. A bit of subtlety might help. Perhaps even a jot of politeness."

"*You* were neither subtle nor polite."

"Yes, but when I am blunt, it is bold and charming. When you are blunt, it is offensive and annoying."

"That is hypocrisy."

She shrugged. "Call it what you will. I do not make the rules."

"Newton's third law of motion is a rule. Your statement is an assertion."

"A correct one." She sighed and reached out to pat his elbow, ignoring how he stiffened. "Listen carefully, Holstoke, for that is the only way you will find success among the matchmaking mamas. You are odd. There is simply no way round it. The less you say, the more the ladies will fill in the gaps with their own suppositions. Begin with polite flattery. Practice it. Then, do not—whatever you do, do *not*—deviate from your script."

His gaze fell to where her hand rested on his arm. "Among my oddities must be forgetfulness." Pale green came back narrowed and sparking. "I don't recall asking your advice."

She withdrew. "Very well. Ignore me, then. But do not complain when you must return next year to dance the same tedious dance."

Head rearing back, he flared his nose in disgust.

"Indeed," she said with satisfaction. "No man wishes to enter this farcical exhibition twice. Or, in your case, thrice."

He'd spent his first season courting Maureen, of course. For a proud man, the rejection must have cut deeply. Then had come revelations about his mother. Little wonder he'd avoided London all this time. Even six years later, the embers of that particular scandal smoldered throughout the ton. In fact, Genie would wager Holstoke's mad mother in part explained why he'd not yet found a wife. Lady Holstoke might be dead, but she'd been a murderess on a grand scale.

It was hardly an argument for perpetuating the bloodline.

"My family will help," she assured him. "Mama will delight in the challenge. She always was fond of you."

"Unnecessary," he answered, his frown returning deeper than before. "I am perfectly capable—"

"Of course you are." She patted his elbow again, grinning.

"But *you* are not a mother who has successfully launched four daughters."

His head lowered until she felt his breath upon her nose. He smelled of mint and lemons. Those pale eyes lit gold in the late-day sun. "Five."

Suddenly, she could feel what others complained about. Shivers. Breathlessness. She swallowed and licked her lips. "I was a scandal. I do not signify."

"I think you do."

Her reply was stopped short by an ominous, overly pleasant voice. "Miss Huxley, you may return to your work. Now."

Genie's heart thudded. Her stomach cramped. Her eyes slid closed for a long moment.

Drat. Drat, drat, *drat*. She'd been certain Mrs. Pritchard had left already.

"Of—of course, Mrs. Pritchard." Retreating a step, she gave Holstoke a wobbly, regretful smile before turning to face her employer. "Straight away."

Mrs. Pritchard had been tippling the vinegar again. Her pursed lips and pinched nostrils resembled a caricature with that tight coiffure.

"I expect Mrs. Herbert's order to be complete before the morning," the milliner snapped. "Is that very clear?" The words were low, spoken as Genie gathered her gold silk and headed for the workroom doorway.

She nodded, not wishing to further antagonize the woman.

"*Speak*, Miss Huxley, so that I know you understand."

Genie halted, her skirts brushing the curtain, her fingers clutching the silk.

There it was. The viper beneath the pleasant façade. Others imagined it did not exist.

Until it bit them.

Genie had always known. A woman like Mrs. Pritchard possessed only enough competence to eke out a feeble enterprise, and only enough intelligence to resent those with more. Ever so slowly, the milliner was failing, the flow of customers down to a trickle, her shop propped up by her husband. Shortly before Genie had arrived, a string of assistants had either left or been dismissed. Once Genie had seen Fancy Nancy's handiwork, she'd understood why.

Mrs. Pritchard liked things plain and pleasant. She did not favor being shown she was wrong.

Contrarily, Genie preferred progress above pleasantness. Her creations had attracted dozens of new customers. Another milliner might have viewed her as a boon.

Instead, Mrs. Pritchard had assigned Genie more orders like Mrs. Herbert's five turbans and suggested fashionably minded ladies might be better served on Bond Street.

Bond Street. The very idea of rejecting new customers out of hand had sparked Genie's outrage, and she'd redoubled her efforts, using Mrs. Pritchard's love of pleasantness against her. Red silk roses had been the least of it.

Genie had felt the noose of dismissal more than once, but never more than this moment. She straightened and regarded the other woman's face. Mrs. Pritchard would not meet her eyes, half-turned and fully puckered.

"I understand," Genie answered. "Mrs. Herbert will have her turbans, precisely as she requested, before the morning."

A sharp nod signaled the end of the interchange. Mrs. Pritchard pasted on a false smile and approached Holstoke, who scowled in Genie's direction.

He was about to protest. Perhaps even inform Mrs. Pritchard of Genie's rank. She felt it coming like a storm on the horizon. She met his eyes over the other woman's shoulder and shook her head, pleading for him to keep silent. After a long moment, his nostrils flared and his shoulders flexed as though anger were moving him against his will. Then, he gave a slight nod.

She smiled and mouthed, "Thank you," before rushing past the curtain. Waving away Mr. Moody's round-eyed stare, she returned to the millinery workroom.

Sinking into her chair, she closed her eyes and felt the silk between her fingers, the noose around her neck. Drat, drat, drat. She should have ignored Holstoke, stifled her everlasting curiosity, and hurried away to finish Mrs. Herbert's tedious turban collection.

But, then, she wouldn't have seen him again or learned of his struggles on the marriage mart or rediscovered the strange kinship she'd always felt in his presence.

Somehow, she would repay him, she decided, spreading the silk upon the table and retrieving a white plume from the basket at her feet. It was the least she could do. He would keep her secret, after all. This she knew without question.

For, even when he said nothing, the Earl of Holstoke could be relied upon to keep his word.

Chapter Two

"Fortunately, wealth matters far more than handsomeness. Or charm. Or a gaze which does not freeze a lady's slippers. Despair not, my boy. With wise counsel, you may yet claim victory, despite many shortcomings."

—The Dowager Marchioness of Wallingham to the Earl of Holstoke in a letter expressing optimism for his matrimonial prospects.

Phineas Brand read triumph on his sister's delicate features a bare second before she took his bishop with her knight. Briefly, he considered letting her win, but the last time he'd done so, Hannah had explained with devastating care that treating her like a child was not kindness but condescension.

"In my life, I have borne a good deal more than the loss of a game, Phineas," she'd said softly. "Pray, allow me the dignity of a fair fight." Her eyes had been brittle as frosted leaves.

Indeed, she had borne more. Unspeakably more.

He hadn't let her win since. He didn't intend to now. "Are you certain—"

"I have taken your bishop," she crowed, a black curl tumbling against her white cheek as she leaned forward in her chair. "Prepare for defeat."

He sighed. Plucked his watch from his waistcoat pocket. "I should be off."

"No. I shall have my victory at last."

His father's daughter was a beauty—soft-featured and striking with hair black as a night sky and eyes the same as his. Had she not been a by-blow, titled suitors doubtless would be flooding Holstoke House at this very moment, begging his permission to marry her. She *should* be married. She should be playing chess with a husband, not losing to her brother every night.

"Do not look at me that way," she said, her natural dignity slumping as she began to suspect her long-awaited victory was not, in fact, at hand. "Phineas. I have won." She perused the board, her fine, black brows drawn together in puzzlement. "I have."

Gently, he slid his rook into place. "Check."

"But ..."

He stood, stretching his neck side to side. Evenings such as this tended to end in a headache. "Lady Randall's fete began a half-hour ago. If I wait any longer to arrive, she will think me unforgivably rude."

"Why should you care what Lady Randall thinks of you? Her dog ate your hat."

Indeed, the fattest of Lady Randall's seven pugs had pounced without hesitation. Phineas had been standing outside an apothecary shop on Oxford Street, arguing the proper application of grafting with Lord Gilforth, who had refused him entry into the Horticultural Society of London.

Lady Randall's escaped horde of pugs had trotted by, promptly entangling their long, loose leads around both his and Gilforth's ankles. As Lady Randall's shouts had shrilled along the street, Gilforth had gone down, Phineas had wheeled away to avoid being pulled down with him, and his best hat had rolled across eight feet of cobblestone. The walleyed little beast had snatched the "exquisite beaver" hat between its jaws, shaken it viciously, slobbered and gnawed, growled and grunted, then sprinted away with the crown dragging along the pavement. Fortunately, the dog's girth dragged in a similar fashion, slowing its pace considerably. Phineas retrieved his hat in a few strides, but not before much damage had been done.

Lady Randall had been first mortified at her dog's misbehavior, then aghast when she'd realized whose hat her "beloved Dicky" had purloined. As she'd recognized Phineas, her apologies had stuttered, her mouth working like a fish's. Her face had drained of color. Finally, she'd issued a reluctant invitation to this evening's fete.

He assumed the overture had been meant as compensation for his inconvenience. She'd likely hoped he would decline. He probably should have. But offers like hers were rare—at least, for him.

The trickle of invitations Phineas had received at the start of the season had been granted out of curiosity. In time, even those evaporated. Few hostesses desired the son of the Primvale Poisoner at their tables. Understandable. Among his mother's victims had been some of the ton's own members.

Glancing down now into Hannah's eyes—slightly tilted, pale and serious, so like his own and their father's—he wished for the thousandth time he had been the one to remove his mother from this world. But he hadn't realized the depth of Lady Holstoke's evil until it had been far too late.

Until his fragile, innocent sister had been tormented. Hunted. Forced to defend herself in a way that had added to her scars.

God. He pivoted and made for the parlor door, an unwelcome black tide rushing up to choke him. "I shan't be too late getting back," he said, forcing his voice to steady.

"Phineas."

He pulled the door open, the knob creaking inside the pressure of his fist. "Do not wait for me."

She followed him into the corridor. "Phineas." Her gentle voice was a plea.

He slowed.

"Why must you put yourself through this absurdity?"

For you, he thought. He could not say it. She would be wounded. She would object that he must never make sacrifices for her. But, in truth, he was "dancing this tedious dance," as Lady Eugenia had put it, for Hannah's sake. To show her it could be done.

Ten years of Hannah's life had been a horror, imprisoned by a madman named Horatio Syder, who had used a young, innocent girl as a bargaining chip against Phineas's mother. It had made his sister bitter toward men, fearful of being in their control. She trusted Phineas, of course, but few others. He was heartened that she had improved since they'd discovered one another's existence six years earlier. Constant nightmares, weeks of silence, fearful starts at the slightest clatter—all had diminished in both severity and frequency. Only last week, upon spying his old walking stick, she had remained seated, calmly cradling her teacup. A year ago, she would have gone bloodless and fled to her bedchamber.

Hannah was healing. Yet, despite being two-and-twenty, she refused to consider marriage. As her brother, he must see to her happiness. She deserved to know what having a family meant. She deserved to know marriage was not some leg trap waiting to bite into her flesh. No matter how he tried, he'd been unable to explain these things to her satisfaction.

No, he needed a wife—a proper, suitable wife to establish a proper, suitable family. Which was why he continued thrusting himself into the marriage mart, despite ample evidence he was unwelcome.

He gentled his voice. "It is time for me to marry, little one. You know this."

Her nose flared in vexation. "They are unkind to you. *You.* After everything you did to set things right."

"They fear me." He sighed, rubbing at the ache behind his right temple. "Reasonable reactions, given—"

"Stay. Let us finish our match."

He glanced back toward the parlor and raised a wry brow. "Our match is finished."

She frowned. "I could still win."

"Only if I suffered an apoplexy and lost my senses."

"I am an excellent player, you know."

"Or the rules altered so that castling is permitted whilst your king is in check. Come to that, one must still assume the apoplexy."

"Do not even speak of such things."

"Alas, none of the aforementioned scenarios is likely to occur. Therefore, our match has concluded. Study the board. You will see."

"Stay."

He bent to kiss her cheek, taking care to move slowly and keep the contact brief. Hannah still struggled with being touched. "I shall return in a few hours."

Gently, he withdrew, striding the length of the corridor to the main staircase.

"I am an excellent player, Phineas," she called after him. "One day, I shall even be better than you."

A half-hour later, he entered Lady Randall's drawing room with a pounding head and a marked sense of doom. The room teemed with bright silks and dark tailcoats. Wealthy, milk-skinned misses murmured in low tones, casting him fearful glances from behind their fans. Like a school of fish, mothers and chaperones clutched their charges and guided them away from his position near the archway to the music room. Behind him, two ladies performed a duet of pianoforte and harp. Each note drove another dagger through his right temple.

This evening would be abominable.

Still, it was not the worst he'd endured.

"One hopes you have a better plan than freezing them all with your gelid glare." The sonorous female voice, raspy with age, approached from the music room. Its small, white-haired owner came to stand at his left side.

He glanced down. Many called her a dragon. To him, she had always resembled a bird. Not some delicate finch or wren, despite her size. No, she was a falcon. Bird of prey. A species known for its bold females.

"Lady Wallingham."

"Lord Holstoke." She raised her quizzing glass to one sharp, emerald eye. "You have not answered my letters."

Returning his gaze to the crowd, he noted Lady Randall calming one of her guests as the woman sent him furtive glances. "No."

A sniff from beside him. "Never took you for the daft sort. Mad, perhaps. Peculiar, certainly."

He opted for silence. It did not help.

"What else should one conclude?" Her voice was a snap. "You refuse my assistance when it is most desperately needed. Daftness is heritable, you know."

"My father was not daft. He was poisoned."

"Yes. By your mother." The dowager shifted, raising her quizzing glass again to assess the crush. A ring of empty floor wreathed their position as though he were a noxious weed known for giving young ladies a rash. "Have you considered conducting your wife hunt in Scotland? Perhaps news of your unfortunate pedigree halted at the Roman Wall."

The throbbing inside his temple grew. "I was in Edinburgh earlier this year."

"Ah. Walls are not what they used to be, then. Ireland?

Nothing but sheep and rain, but one is bound to find more biddable wifely stock than in Scotland."

He rubbed at the bitter ache behind his right eye. "Lady Wallingham, your advice is ..." He wanted to continue. Intended to.

But he could not. Because, in that moment, a laugh he had not heard in six years reached his ears. Joyful and tumbling, it spanned a room full of revelers and musical cacophony. It bridged six years and a lifetime of distance.

Maureen. Instantly, he knew.

He found her standing near blue draperies at the edge of a far window. Golden-brown hair fell in perfect, looping curls around her sweet face. She was older, of course, her cheeks a bit fuller, but as lovely as he remembered. Radiant and flushed, she lightly stroked the arm of her lean male companion.

That man wore a black coat, scarlet waistcoat, and a rapt expression.

Phineas watched him caress Maureen's lower back and grin down into her eyes with both longing and possession.

"Dunston refuses to abandon his penchant for preposterous waistcoats. I have told him a father of five children should show greater dignity."

He frowned. "Five?" It was four. Maureen had four children.

"Perhaps you should have read my letters."

Phineas's gaze flew to where sun-hued silk flowed over Maureen's belly. Was she rounder there? He looked at her face. Glowing. Shining for the man she had married.

After declining to marry Phineas.

"Three months along, I'd wager." The old woman beside him stared across the room through her quizzing glass. "Of course, you would know this if you were not suffering from rampant daftness."

The towering plume extending from the old woman's

turban brushed his chin. He swiped it away and cleared his throat.

"I read your letters," he said. He had. All seventeen of them. She'd made no mention of Maureen expecting another child. He would have remembered.

"And yet, no reply. How are we to solve your intractable problem if you do not *engage*, dear boy?"

He had no answer, for he did not understand her interest. Lady Wallingham was an interfering busybody, true. But she had no particular connection to him. Her bosom friend happened to be Maureen's mother, Lady Berne, so perhaps that explained her relentless focus upon Phineas's matrimonial prospects. Otherwise, it confounded reason.

Recalling another female who had recently offered unsolicited advice, he nearly shuddered. Was he the topic of discussion at the Huxley dinner table? Did they all amuse themselves by debating his prospects and lamenting his failures?

Good God, what a nightmare. The thought of Lady Berne, Lady Wallingham, and Lady Eugenia pitying him over parsnips and lamb was enough to turn his blood cold. Imagining Maureen as part of the conversation made his head throb with renewed fervor.

In fairness, Lady Eugenia was different. He was damned if he could make sense of it. The woman's presumptuousness was nearly the equal of Lady Wallingham's, and yet the dowager vexed him far more.

Eugenia Huxley had long treated him with a perplexing degree of familiarity, as though they'd known one another from the cradle. They hadn't. She'd been sixteen and he seven-and-twenty when he'd begun his courtship of Maureen. While Maureen had affectionately called her "brat," he hadn't found her bold, forthright nature exasperating so much as a curiosity. He'd never met another female quite like her.

His frown deepened as he recalled their encounter in the hat shop. The scandal had taken its toll. Her cheeks were slimmer, her jaw gaining delicate definition. Her eyes had acquired new shadows. For a moment, he hadn't recognized her. Perhaps it had been the context. She was *working*. In a hat shop. On the end of Oxford Street most ladies of quality avoided. Furthermore, she answered to a harpy who could scarcely blink for the tightness of her hair, and, unlike the Eugenia he remembered, she'd silently begged him to let that harpy treat her like a servant.

Bloody outrageous.

Of course, not all the changes he'd observed were for the worse. Eugenia's eyes sparked with the same challenging humor, yet inside, they were steadier than he would have predicted. Her wit was sharper, wry and unapologetic. Her hands were slender. More ... womanly.

Her bosom was fuller, too. Round. A lush counterpoint to her hips. He shouldn't have noticed, but he was male and not currently blind.

Still, her circumstances had deteriorated abominably, and it irritated him like a thorn inside his boot. Quite why, he did not know. Perhaps he should speak with Lady Berne. Something must be done. An earl's daughter should not be treated with such condescension.

"What about Miss Froom?" The crackled voice of Lady Wallingham pierced his thoughts, adding to his headache.

"Who?"

Her plume bobbed in the general direction of the punch bowl. "The plump one, there. Resembles a canary."

He blinked. Looked. Miss Froom did, indeed, resemble a canary. Yellow gown. Sharp, short nose. Small, dark eyes. "What of her?"

A *tsk* of impatience. "Have you bothered to approach–"

"Yes."

"And?"

He glared down at the diminutive dowager. "She swooned when I said, 'Good day.'"

"Bah! You surrender too easily."

"Then screamed for her mother upon awakening."

A sniff. "The young are prone to dramatics."

"Her mother likewise screamed and subsequently swooned. I believe the pattern might have continued in perpetuity had my salutations persisted."

An emerald gaze narrowed upon him. "Hmmph." Returning to her perusal of the crowd, Lady Wallingham and her quizzing glass spotted yet another candidate. "Ah, yes. Lady Theodosia." She nodded toward a gaunt woman whose elbows could sharpen knives. Come to that, so could her chin. "Eight-and-twenty. To be on the shelf, she would first have to be removed from the attic. Truly a desperate—"

He sighed. "At her father's insistence, we took a turn about the park."

"Promising. Go on."

"She spent the entire interlude in silence."

"Some men appreciate a quiet woman."

"Yes."

"Have you asked her to dance?"

"No."

"Whyever not?"

"Her butler relayed her request that I make no further overtures. Evidently, Lady Theodosia is smitten with Lord Muggeridge."

White brows dropped low over sharp green. "Muggeridge? He is riddled with gout and drowning in debt. Good heavens, is she mad?"

"No," he answered absently. "Fearful."

Letting his attention wander across the room to the woman he'd once thought to marry, he paused. Why had he never noticed the lack of resemblance between her and Lady Eugenia? They were Huxleys, so naturally, both were curvaceous and petite with hair and eyes in shades of brown. But the two sisters must have branched from opposite sides of the same tree. Maureen's nose was shorter, rounder, like Lady Berne's. Eugenia's was slim and straight like her father's. Maureen's eyes were rounder, too. Eugenia's were more cat-like—impish and rich. And while Maureen's hair was light brown, Eugenia's was the color of polished mahogany. An uncommon shade. Dark and deep. Lustrous and silken.

"Cowardly chits," Lady Wallingham scoffed. "Given their hysterics over a few measly murders, one would suppose plump-pocketed earls were as plentiful as the hairs in Lord Muggeridge's ears."

How he despised the marriage mart. Every calculating part. Even if the matrons and their charges had clamored for his attention rather than fleeing from him, he would still have a bloody headache. Only one person had appeared to understand his position, and she'd been consigned to work in a milliner's shop where she was treated no better than a scullery maid.

He glared down at the Dowager Marchioness of Wallingham. "If you are so keen to wield your influence in someone's favor, perhaps you could begin with Eugenia Huxley."

The quizzing glass slowly lowered. A white brow arched. "Lady Eugenia made her bed. Beside a footman, no less."

"She is employed."

"Yes. Much to her mother's dismay, I assure you."

"You are one of the most influential—"

"I am *the* most influential, Lord Holstoke. Make no mistake about it."

True enough. Lady Wallingham wielded astonishing power among the ton. Enough to sway opinions from one pendulum peak to the other. Enough to have eased a scandal involving an earl's daughter and a footman, had she chosen to do so.

"You should have helped her."

Assessing eyes sharpened. Glinted. "I did. I gave her a reference, didn't I?"

He waited.

"The girl was caught wearing a footman in place of her skirts," she snapped.

His stomach tightened. He did not like picturing Eugenia that way. Perhaps because she was Maureen's sister. Perhaps because he'd known her when she was but a girl of sixteen. Perhaps because he admired her family—enough to want something similar for himself. Regardless, he now had a gut ache to match his headache.

"The incident was witnessed by two Almack's patronesses, two gossipy lords, and Lady Gattingford for good measure," the dowager continued. "Foolish girl. She did not even have the decency to dally with her *own* footman, instead choosing one of Lord Reedham's. God Himself could not have spared her, dear boy. I did what I could."

"Not enough." His words were low and cold.

Lady Wallingham's gaze grew calculating. "We were discussing *your* prospects, not hers. And while yours are scant, hers are nonexistent." The quizzing glass resumed its duty. "Now, then. Clearly, the waters in which you have cast your line are sparse, Holstoke. Either bait your hook with something more desirable than last year's stale pudding or move on to slower fish."

He glanced across the crowd. He could plead thirst, he supposed. Escape to the punch bowl. Greet Miss Froom again and watch her swoon like a downed canary.

"I should leave," he muttered to himself, his fingers digging into his temple.

"Widows."

"What?"

"A more *seasoned* pool of candidates will prove less skittish, I daresay."

Hannah had been right. He could have played out their chess match. Gone to bed. Awakened early for a ride. Purchased a new hat.

He could have avoided every word of this conversation.

"You know, my son married a widow. They said she was barren, but Charles takes after his father in *many* respects." The old woman chuckled. "Have I mentioned I have three grandsons? *Three*, Holstoke." Her plume swiped his jaw as she trained her quizzing glass on the far corner of the room, where a broad-boned, black-gowned, ruddy woman with massive hands stood conversing with Lord Randall's niece. "Ah, yes. Mrs. Steventon. A bit long in the tooth, perhaps."

He rubbed his eyes with his thumb and forefinger. "She recently buried her sixth husband."

"Precisely. A history of unexpected deaths will not send her dashing for the smelling salts, will it?"

"She is in mourning."

"A technicality. Where other men hesitate, a clever one finds his advantage."

Yes, leaving was the best idea he'd had all day. He pivoted toward the music room, bowing briefly to his unwanted companion. "I fear I must bid you good evening, Lady Wallingham."

Ten feet after the dowager's "hmmph" followed him through the archway, he heard the sweet voice he'd once imagined would awaken him every morning. Now, it halted him as surely as ropes.

"Holstoke? Is that you?"

Her scent was different than before, though still laced with vanilla.

"Lady Dunston," he said, closing his eyes briefly before turning on his heel.

She gazed up at him with a dawning smile, warm and affectionate, her dimples on full display. "It *is* you. Oh, how splendid. Hannah has visited several times, but I was beginning to despair of seeing you before Henry and I return to Fairfield." She tilted her head. "How have you been?"

Apart from being the prettiest of the Huxley sisters,

Maureen might also be the kindest. She'd long reminded him of daffodils—cheerful and domesticated and sweet. A welcome answer to winter's desolation.

"I am well, Lady Dunston," he lied, inclining his head. "And you?"

Despite Phineas's efforts to ignore the man at her side, Dunston drew her closer with an arm about her waist and interjected, "Busy. Children occupy a good deal of one's time, old chap." The man's eyes flashed hard as steel. "As does keeping one's husband thoroughly satisfied."

"Henry!"

Despite Maureen's warning, Dunston did not look away.

She shook her head in wifely exasperation. "Ignore him, Holstoke. He's forgotten his manners."

"On the contrary, pet," Dunston said softly. "I've forgotten nothing. Neither has he, I'd wager."

The arrow flew straight and true. Yes. Phineas remembered everything. The smell of her hair. The touch of her hand upon his arm. The soft curve of her lips. The despair of discovering something perfect—something he'd never known existed—only to lose it in a single conversation in Hyde Park.

He remembered well. But he did not appreciate being reminded.

Maureen clicked her tongue and waved away her husband's possessiveness like a vexatious insect. "My mother and father are hosting a dinner tomorrow evening. You simply must come," she pleaded. "Mama and Papa are ever so fond of you."

Eugenia had said something similar. Why did the Huxley family have any interest in him at all, let alone feel "ever so fond"?

"I'm certain Holstoke hasn't the time," said Dunston, casually examining his own waistcoat before giving Phineas a mocking smile. "Gardens to tend, you know. Follies to construct. A bride to acquire."

Phineas was not angry—of course not. His stomach might be twisted into thorny ropes and his neck might be hard enough to crack walnuts, but he was not angry. Phineas did not allow anger to control his actions. It was unproductive.

Maureen's expression melted into a soup of maternal sympathy. "Of course, how thoughtless of me. The season can sometimes be ... all too short."

Pity. That was *pity* on her face. Pity for him and his doomed quest to find a wife who neither fled from him in terror nor caused him to contemplate celibacy.

Bloody hell, it was galling. Her pity. Dunston's smugness.

He straightened. Raised a brow and his chin. "When shall I arrive, Lady Dunston?"

Minutes later, as he exited Lady Randall's house and donned his second-best hat, he breathed deeply the cool spring air. His headache yet pounded. His stomach yet churned. Nothing good had come of this torturous night.

But he had not allowed it to defeat him. A small victory, perhaps. Lately, small seemed to be the only size he was permitted.

He blew out another breath and started down the street, passing a pair of young gents conversing beside a waiting carriage. Neither paid him any mind.

"... five daughters in all."

"The youngest is a fair one, I reckon."

The first man laughed and jostled the second man's shoulder. "Fair of face or fair of bosom?"

"Why not both?"

The two men guffawed.

Phineas released another breath and continued on his way.

"I don't know. If she's anything like her sister ... well, I'm loath to wed a chit who might be another Huxley Harlot."

He stopped. Every muscle hardened. He closed his eyes. Reached for rationality. If two vulgar cretins wished to insult one of the Huxley sisters, it was none of his concern.

"Wouldn't mind lifting the sister's petticoats a time or two, I daresay."

"Bit of practice before you offer for Lady Katherine, eh?"

A sharp laugh. One of them leaned toward the other. "The Harlot's tastes run to footmen. Likely she'd be grateful for a change of mount. Do you suppose sisters are the same between their—"

"Gentlemen." Although Phineas's voice was quiet, the word jerked the two cretins around like a shot. Both were young—boys, really.

He should not be doing this.

It was stupid.

Reckless.

"I could scarcely help overhearing your discussion," his anger said softly.

The taller one, who appeared to have imbibed too much of Lord Randall's port, stumbled back into the carriage wheel.

The shorter one—Phineas recognized him as Randall's nephew—swallowed convulsively. "L-lord Holstoke."

He politely fingered his hat brim, keeping his motions smooth and his expression still. "I have seen you at Reaver's, I believe." He glanced at the taller one. "Both of you."

"Y-yes, my lord. We were guests of my uncle. Lord Randall."

"Reaver's serves excellent coffee," Phineas commented casually. "And Lord Randall serves superior port."

The taller one's head began to tremble visibly.

"Curious fact: Either coffee or port—any liquid with a strong flavor, really—makes an ideal vehicle for, shall we say, delivery of medicinal compounds."

The shorter one squinted a bit. Soon, his eyes rounded. "P-poison?"

Phineas slowly blinked. Only once. Then he stared. "If you like."

"N-never cared for coffee. Or port."

"There are other options." Phineas moved his gaze calmly between the two men. "One must be clever when delivering medicine." He took a single step forward, and the shorter one retreated three. The taller one appeared to be having more trouble than his companion. Each breath emerged with the edge of a whimper attached to it.

Phineas stopped. Clasped his hands at his back. "A pity no cures exist for the crassness of youth. Alas, all we have are punishments."

The whimpering grew louder.

"Now, then. I must be on my way. Tomorrow I dine with Lord and Lady Berne and their lovely daughters. Good evening. *Gentlemen.*"

He'd likely damaged his own cause, he thought, as he strolled into the deepening night. Confirming everyone's worst suspicions about him was far from helpful. He estimated he'd worsened his chances of acquiring a suitable wife by fifteen percent. Perhaps twenty.

But he was smiling as he turned the corner toward Holstoke House. Despite his headache. Despite seeing Maureen again. Despite everything, he was smiling.

He'd relished those men's pallor, their palpable fear. It was satisfying. Nearly as satisfying as picturing her reaction. She would laugh, he suspected. Cat-like eyes would spit fire at the cretins. Then, she'd congratulate him for putting his "peculiar nature" to good use.

His smile grew into a grin. He only wished she could have been there to see it.

THE GIRL ALREADY SHOWED SIGNS OF FAILING: WHITE EDGED WITH green. Glassy eyes darting about. Convulsive swallowing.

She clutched at her mother—as plump as she—while the yellow pair climbed into the carriage.

"Once we are home, your father will send for the physician," the mother crooned frantically. "Simply a fever, darling. A bit of laudanum will help." He heard the woman's desperate platitudes continue as the coach door closed.

He covered a grin with his gloved hand, shrinking back into the shadows of Lord Randall's house.

Laudanum would not help. Laudanum would only carry her further along the river of death.

He hunched and leaned a shoulder against the bricks of the house, biting his fist now. His chest shook and shuddered.

Her death was a divine thing. An ordained thing.

And that which had been ordained could not be undone.

Chapter Three

"The rules are simple: Do not awaken me before breakfast. Do not singe my hair. And do not dally with the footmen. The secret to keeping your position, my dear, is to avoid violating all three in one day."

—THE DOWAGER MARCHIONESS OF WALLINGHAM upon dismissing her most recent lady's maid, the eighth in as many months.

∞

BENEATH HER BLANKETS, GENIE'S WORLD WAS SIMPLE. WARM. Dark. A bit close, but that was to be expected. She burrowed tighter as the knocking echoed on.

"Genie! Unlock the door."

Genie sighed, heating her blanketed den further. Tugging a corner, she squinted at the rude white light from the window then glared at her bedchamber door. "Go away, Kate!"

Back into the den. Safe. Quiet.

Bang, bang, bang.

Perhaps not so quiet.

She closed her eyes, drawing her pillow up against her ears. There. Better.

"Dash it all, at least come down to breakfast," came the faint, muffled voice of her younger sister. "Cook served a ham. It is your favorite."

Once again, Genie poked her head into the appallingly bright day. "I don't want any. Now, go away!"

She waited. One breath. Two. Silence. Blessed silence.

Her eyes drifted closed again. Her head dropped back onto the pillow. She didn't bother to tug the blankets back into place.

God, she was tired. Sleep either came in long visitations or not at all. Today, it failed to arrive.

Failed. Much like her, she supposed.

The bitter truth clamped down upon her throat. She gritted her teeth and fisted the pillow. Flopped over and smashed her face into the soft, feathery thing. Screamed until her throat hurt.

It didn't help. Nothing did, really. She was a failure without a future. She would linger at the edges of her old life like a ghost. Annabelle and Jane and Maureen would have a dozen more children. Kate would marry and add to the Huxley numbers. Her brother, John, would soon return from Scotland with tales of mad adventure, then dazzle the ladies of London before choosing one to bear him a half-dozen babes of his own.

And Genie? She would live at Clumberwood Manor. Alone. She would make hats no one would buy. She would avoid speaking with neighbors out of concern for their reputations, avoid appearing friendly with the household staff lest she reignite old gossip. She would grow old. Eccentric. Children would whisper about her in dreading tones, dare one another to approach while she haunted village shops.

The ghost of Eugenia Huxley, ever in search of the perfect red ribbon.

Her chest ached. She glared at the window.

She should have known better. Eugenia Huxley an employee? Preposterous. She could scarcely manage obedience to her doting father. When she was a girl, Papa had called her his "little rebel." He'd always said it with a fond twinkle. Most employers hadn't any use for a rebellious assistant, and Mrs. Pritchard—incompetence aside—was no exception.

Of course, Mrs. Pritchard had waited to give her the sack until she'd wrung every drop of work from Genie's fingers. The morning after the incident with Holstoke, Mrs. Pritchard had entered the workroom with a beaming smile for Fancy Nancy. She'd avoided glancing at Genie, merely placing eight written orders upon Genie's stack and collecting the five gold turbans from the shelf.

Genie had completed the eight orders in the time it had taken Fancy Nancy to finish a sad yellow cap from which all traces of lace had been removed. By late afternoon, Genie had wondered if Mrs. Pritchard might have forgotten her name, or perhaps Holstoke had revealed too much after all, and the milliner debated how to address her. A cold lump had settled in her stomach as she'd watched the woman grow increasingly pinched.

In the end, it had been worse than she'd imagined. Mrs. Pritchard had swept aside the curtain just before six. She'd watched Genie trim her last ribbon. Then, while Fancy Nancy hung her apron in the dimmest corner of the room, Mrs. Pritchard had spoken.

"Miss Huxley, you may consider your work here finished."

Genie had blinked up at her, a bit dizzy after bending over her needle all day. "Yes. I was just about—"

"For good."

The cold lump in her belly had grown. Spread to her muscles and skin. Crystallized and stung. "I—you—"

"Miss Knox will complete any remaining orders."

Genie's eyes had dropped to the capote in her hands. Wool

felt and satin ribbon had blurred into a blob of delicate pink. "None remain," she'd murmured, stunned despite the warnings that this would happen. "They are all complete."

If anything, her answer had angered Mrs. Pritchard further, as though she'd wanted Genie to fall short. "Leave your apron. Leave the tools. I should not like to discover you have stolen from me."

Raising her gaze, Genie had slowly stood, watching the woman's face. Mrs. Pritchard had refused to meet her eyes. The coward.

She'd placed the capote on the shelf, quickly tugged at her apron's ties, and folded it neatly before tossing it onto the worktable. "I should like to bid farewell to Mr. Moody."

"He was dismissed this morning."

A wave of nausea had struck, bringing Genie's hands to her belly. "No. You—you—"

Finally, the milliner had looked at her. Viperous triumph lifted one corner of her lips. "He was caught reading again. Mr. Pritchard does not countenance sloth."

Every sarcastic epithet that had risen in Genie's throat stuck in place. She must help Mr. Moody. He'd been sacked because of her. She could not allow it.

And so, she'd begged. "Please," she'd said hoarsely. "Please do not punish him. He's done nothing wrong. *I* am to blame."

Satisfaction had edged Mrs. Pritchard's unpleasant smile. "Yes. You are." She'd gestured toward the dimmest corner of the room. "Miss Knox and I shall do well enough without you, I daresay. And one of Mr. Pritchard's previous assistants has already agreed to return to his position. Neither Mr. Moody nor you, Miss Huxley, will be given a reference. Now, leave my shop."

Inside, Genie's wrath had blasted Mrs. Pritchard with every scathing truth she'd held in check for nearly a year. The incompetence. The cowardice. The ugly, unpleasant pleasantness. The absurd tea sessions, vapid tittering, and absurdly tight hair. *Nobody is fooled, you vain, talentless peahen,* she'd longed to shout. *Your idiocy is as obvious as your forehead creases!* Unfortunately, Mrs. Pritchard had swished through the curtained doorway and departed the shop before a single word could escape past Genie's tight throat.

The final indignity had been Fancy Nancy, smirking from her dim corner. "No less than you deserve. Conceited bit of baggage."

Fortunately, Genie's throat had loosened. As she'd passed by the bitter lemon, she'd leaned in, braving the stench. "When Mrs. Pritchard claims you and she will do 'well enough,' whom do you suppose will be charged with completing eightfold the orders you ordinarily make in a day? Mrs. Pritchard? Or her last remaining assistant?"

The dawning dismay from dull, muddy eyes had been Genie's only solace that day. She hadn't lingered to deliver further satisfying truths. Instead, she'd rushed back to Berne House and asked their new butler, Emerson, to locate Mr. Moody. Previously, Emerson had been employed by Dunston, and, like most of Dunston's employees, he had a talent for ferreting information. But the process took time. Too much.

Days later, her guilt was making her writhe. She must find Mr. Moody. She must tell him she would secure a new position for him. A better position. One which paid enough that he could purchase his medieval adventures in bookshops rather than circulation libraries.

Perhaps she had been the cause of his misfortune, but she might also be the solution. Being an earl's daughter did have some advantages.

A key rattled and clicked. Her door opened on a rush of air. Soon, a face remarkably similar to her own hovered above her.

"Stop wallowing," the face said. "Come eat some ham."

Genie cupped her sister's cheeks and gently shoved. "For the last time, Kate. Go. Away." She rolled onto her side.

Kate's face reappeared, now hovering above the flowered coverlet. Sparkling eyes shone with determination and—worse—a challenge accepted. "Ham, Genie. Then, you and I are going for a ride in the park."

Genie groaned and rolled toward the opposite side of the bed.

That was when the singing began. Warbling and grandiose, Kate's voice approached her ear as her arrival jostled the mattress.

"In the downhill of life, when I find I'm declining," she sang merrily, *"May my fate no less fortunate be, than a snug elbow-chair can afford for reclining and a cot that o'erlooks the wide sea."*

Genie covered her ears with her palms.

Kate clasped her wrist and drew her hand away. *"With an ambling pad-pony, to pace o'er the lawn, while I carol away idle sorrow."*

"For the love of all that is blessed and holy, Kate. I will make you a new hat."

"And blithe as the lark that each day hails the dawn."

"Ten. Ten new hats."

"Look forward with hope for tomorrow." Kate drew a breath to start a new verse.

"Very well!" Genie sat up and threw her blankets off. "I will eat ham if you will only stop!"

"And ride with me in the park. It has been months since the last time."

Genie hugged her knees and stared down at her bare toes. "You shouldn't be seen with me."

"Rubbish. We are sisters, and we shall ride together. Today."

She was silent a moment too long.

"With a porch at my door, both for shelter and shade too, as the sunshine or rain may prevail. And a small spot of ground—"

"Good heavens. Yes, today. Now, do be quiet."

Kate's arms looped around her shoulders from behind. A

soft cheek touched her own. "Never let that ill-coiffed prig defeat you," she whispered, squeezing Genie into a fierce hug.

"She has already won," Genie grumbled.

"The tartness of her face sours ripe grapes."

"This is no time for Shakespeare's insults."

"Shakespeare is always appropriate. Particularly his insults."

Genie's head hung forward until her forehead touched her knees. Gently, she squeezed her sister's arm and kissed her sister's hand. "Let me dress, Katie. I shall come down in a trice."

"Do you promise?"

"Yes."

Despite feeling she'd aged eighty years in three days, despite having no sleep and less reason to be awake, she gathered her hair into a simple coil, donned her finest blue velvet habit, and went down to breakfast.

The ham was salty. She ate two bites. But she kept her promise.

A half-hour later, as Kate rode at her side recounting her "magnificent performance on pianoforte" at Lady Randall's fete the previous evening, Genie rocked with the motion of her horse and strove to ignore the scornful gazes of Hyde Park passersby.

The hypocrites. Both Mrs. Riley and Lady Baselton were carrying on torrid affairs with a groundskeeper and a butler, respectively. For either of those two supposed *ladies* to cast aspersions in her direction was patently absurd.

No, the feigned outrage of some in the beau monde counted little more than the fly currently buzzing near her right ear. A nuisance, merely. Instead, she raised her chin and savored the breeze upon her cheeks, sunlight fluttering inside busy leaves, birds chirping merrily.

"... quite the most eventful evening in recent memory. There was, of course, the death of Miss Froom. One of the sillier girls this season, I must say. Still, it is a shame. Apparently, she collapsed mere minutes after departing Lady Randall's ..."

Perhaps Kate had been right, Genie thought as warm wind soothed her. This might be better than her blanketed den.

"... reported that he simply stood there, conversing intently with Lady Wallingham. What about, I cannot guess ..."

Now that she considered it, this had been precisely what she needed—a warm day, a pleasant ride, the scent of green and the stroke of sunlight.

And, of course, the chance to display her finest riding hat. It had three cerulean feathers and a touch of white silk braid.

"... until Maureen invited him to dine with us. Heavens. Were I Lord Holstoke, I should find such an invitation rather uncomfortable."

Genie blinked. Glanced sideways at her sister, who wore an elegant green habit and a hat with a plaid ribbon but, sadly, no feathers. "Holstoke?"

Kate shot her an annoyed glance. "Have you listened to a word I've said?"

"I stopped listening when you started singing. What was that bit about Holstoke?"

"He will join us for dinner this evening."

Genie frowned. "But Maureen and Dunston will be there. Won't that be dreadfully—"

"Uncomfortable. Yes." Kate released a long-suffering sigh. "I am not about to repeat our entire conversation because you cannot be bothered to pay attention."

"You are only vexed because I insulted your singing."

"Everyone says I have a lovely soprano."

"Everyone is wrong."

For several minutes, Kate was silent, her lips pursed, eyes trained forward upon the path.

Drat. Regret ate at Genie's stomach, turning two bites of ham into a caustic brew.

Kate fancied herself a performer of some merit. She'd been obsessed with music and theatre since before she could walk, and while her talent was middling, she didn't deserve to have it stomped upon because Genie was having a wretched week. The scandal had made her sister's life difficult enough.

"You would do better to strive for alto," Genie offered. "Your natural pitch is lower."

Kate squinted in her direction. After a long while, she clicked her tongue. "I knew it. That dunderpated tutor repaid Papa's coins with dreadful advice. Why did you not say something sooner?"

Genie shrugged. "Your future consists of planning meals and producing your husband's heir, Katie, not performing the Queen of the Night's aria from *The Magic Flute*. It serves little purpose to offer my critique."

"But you are right, I suspect."

"Of course I am. Now, tell me about Holstoke."

As they exited the park, turning back toward Grosvenor Street, Kate described Holstoke's bizarre effect on marriageable young ladies, turning them into frightened ninnies. She then explained that Maureen had—in Maureen's usual fashion—imagined she was being kind by inviting Holstoke to dine with the Huxley family.

"Hmmph," Genie commented. "More likely, she felt sorry for him. Which is perfectly silly. His troubles on the marriage mart are due to his peculiar nature. He could, if he wished, lower himself to pretend normalcy and thus solve the problem. The ton despises nonconformity."

"Well ..." Kate bit her lip as though biting her tongue.

"Well, what?"

"There is the small matter of his mother."

Genie bit her own lip, reconsidering. "Yes. There is that."

"And his father."

"Most unfortunate."

"And his sister."

Sighing, Genie frowned at Kate. "None of which is his doing."

"No. But you know how gossips like to wag their tongues. Everyone thinks him mad, like his mother. Some speculate *he* was the Primvale Poisoner."

"What a lot of rot. Holstoke is odd, not murderous." She looked at Kate, her curiosity striking again. "Is Maureen perhaps thinking *you* and Holstoke …?"

"Good gracious, I hope not."

Genie glowered in her sister's direction. "Surely you don't believe the gossip."

"No. But I also don't fancy marrying such a humorless man."

"He is not humorless. Exactly."

"Really, Genie. He acts as though laughter would crack his teeth."

"He laughs."

"I have never seen it."

"Then, you have not paid attention."

Kate's eyes narrowed upon her again. "Apparently, you have."

Genie would have scoffed at the implication, but they'd already arrived at Berne House's small stables. Dismounting with help from their grizzled old groom, Genie patted her mare's neck before following Kate into the house.

In the oak-paneled corridor leading to the main staircase, Emerson appeared with a report that lightened Genie's spirits. "I have located Mr. Moody, my lady. Shall I send a footman to deliver a message?" He handed her a small, folded slip of paper.

"No. Thank you, Emerson. I shall go and speak with him myself."

The butler blinked, his eyes saying what his careful expression could not. "The direction is in Cheapside, my lady."

She glanced down at the paper. "Yes, so it is. A hack might be best."

Lingering ten feet away, Kate drifted back to join the conversation. "Are you mad? You cannot go to Cheapside in a hack."

Genie lifted a brow. "Shall I go in a phaeton?"

"Genie! Do not be such a—"

"I am going. I owe him that much."

While Kate ranted that Genie must cease behaving as though her reputation meant nothing, Genie gazed down at the address and wondered whether she should don one of her work gowns before heading to Cheapside. Yes. That would be best. Mr. Moody might be intimidated by her finest riding habit. It was rather splendid.

"... still a chance you could marry one day, you know. Do you wish to toss that chance away, willy-nilly?"

Genie glanced up at her sister, whose hands rested indignantly upon her hips. Even if she'd wanted marriage—which she did not—her chances had evaporated years ago. But she didn't know how to tell Kate such a thing. So, instead, she shook her head and replied, "Let us leave the fairy stories to Shakespeare, hmm?"

Distantly, she heard Emerson greeting a guest at the front door. Over Kate's shoulder, she spied a towering shadow sliding across the entrance hall's marble floor.

Her sister continued arguing, but it was not Kate who claimed her notice. Instead, it was a man's voice, flinty and low. "Thank you, but I shall keep it. Of late, my hats suffer great indignities when they leave my possession."

The seriousness with which those words were uttered brought on Genie's grin for the first time in three days. She brushed past a consternated Kate and strode toward the man who had spoken them.

"Holstoke. Missed me dreadfully, did you?"

He turned, his expression forbidding. "Lady Eugenia." Those pale eyes lingered upon her for several heartbeats before sliding over her shoulder. "And Lady Katherine." His dark head lowered briefly. "A pleasure."

"You are a bit early for dinner," Genie teased, depositing her gloves and the folded paper on the console table near Holstoke, who stood staring down at her like a great, green-eyed raven.

"Not too early to give my regrets, however."

"Regrets?" The spark of pleasure she'd had upon seeing him so unexpectedly in her entrance hall deflated.

"I accepted Lady Dunston's invitation in haste. I'm afraid I must—"

"Do not cry off." She stepped closer, finding it easier to read the subtleties of his expression—tension around his lips, flaring around his nose, shifting of his gaze—at greater proximity. "Come now, Holstoke. You are among friends. We are quite fond of you."

He frowned. "So you have said. What I do not understand is why."

Blinking, Genie opened her mouth to answer and ... nothing. Why, indeed? He was a peculiar man—taciturn, abrupt, and consumed with plants.

She propped an elbow on her wrist and tapped her lips with her finger.

His eyes followed the motion, though his frown only deepened. "You are taking a long time to answer."

"I am thinking."

"Try not to strain yourself."

"The explanation is not so simple. You are far from charming."

"Neither handsome nor charming." His nostrils flared. "A mystery, indeed."

The flare of his nose equated to annoyance—she was now certain of it. He was annoyed with her. She tapped her lips again. His eyes riveted upon her finger and flashed with ... something. More annoyance? She could not be sure.

Drat, the man was difficult to decipher.

She blew out a breath and shrugged. "I cannot explain it. We like you, Holstoke."

"That is irrational."

"Yet true. You must accept our high regard and let us help you."

"I do not require help."

"Nonsense. If Kate's account of Lady Randall's fete is accurate, you need us far more than I thought."

Pale eyes flashed. "Why not help yourself first," he retorted, his voice hard and low. "Leave that rubbish milliner and engage in activities better suited to a lady of worth."

Her head snapped back. Her heart stuttered. Her chest squeezed around an awful, hollow ache. For a few moments, she'd forgotten. She'd seen him in her entrance hall, and they'd begun talking, and reality had disappeared.

The reality of her failures—first, as an earl's daughter whose only task was to marry well and avoid scandal. Then, as a milliner-in-training whose only task was to learn her trade and avoid being dismissed.

Behind her, Kate was murmuring with Emerson. In the distance, she heard footsteps as maids went about their work. She breathed the scents of beeswax and lemon and mint. The wool of his coat, so recently outside. The faint hint of shaving soap.

But all she could see were his eyes, snapping with disapproval.

She swallowed. Raised her chin. "That rubbish milliner is no longer my employer."

"Good," he said with a gleam of satisfaction. "You've seen reason at last."

For a moment, she considered correcting his assumption, but promptly rejected the idea. Let him believe she'd left of her own accord. She hadn't much pride left, but what she did have, she intended to cling to with all her—

"In my opinion, she is well rid of that position," said Kate from behind her. "The cheek of Mrs. Pritchard to dismiss someone of Eugenia's talent!"

Genie's heart shrank. Her skin prickled. She'd long ago ceased flushing at every indignity—there had been too many—but this appeared to be an exception. Because *he* was here. And she wanted him to think well of her. And being dismissed was the most dreadful, pride-sinking experience she could imagine.

Apart from being caught with one's skirts up around one's chin, of course. That had been worse.

"She dismissed you?" For some reason, Holstoke's soft, ice-edged utterance gave her a chill.

Genie answered with a brief nod.

Kate—ever helpful—chimed in, "Her friend, too. Mr. Moony."

"Moody," Genie corrected, turning to address her pest of a sister. "Whom I intended to pay a visit before I was distracted."

"For the last time, you cannot go alone to visit a man in Cheapside," Kate replied. "I shan't allow it."

"Cheapside?" The single word from Holstoke had an ominous ring.

Ignoring the looming lord, Genie focused upon her sister. "I am the reason he lost his position, Kate. Unlike you or me, he hasn't an allowance and a grand house and a high-flown honorific to sustain him. He has been given the sack without a reference."

Kate's chin went up. "I shan't allow it," she repeated.

"I am going."

"Not without the direction."

Genie's eyes flew to the table. No paper.

"I have instructed Emerson to send the carriage and a footman for Mr. Moony."

"Moody," Genie growled.

"Yes, well. Harry is headed there now. He will return with your friend soon, and you may conduct your discussion properly chaperoned."

Genie flattened her palm against her forehead. "He does not know who I am and has no reason to trust Harry. Devil take it, I must catch the carriage and go myself. What were you thinking, Kate?"

Again, Holstoke intruded with a low, ominous lash. "Perhaps Lady Katherine was thinking you'd lost your head. She would be correct in that assessment."

Spinning to face him, Genie found herself stunned breathless. Holstoke was ... furious. About what, she could not say, but for the first time, she could read his eyes without trying. They were afire.

She started to speak, but her mouth had gone dry. He seemed larger, closer, darker. Holstoke in full dudgeon was a sight to behold.

"What did she say?" he uttered, his jaw tight.

Genie blinked and signaled her confusion with a small shake of her head.

His face hovered above hers like a great cloud. "Your employer," he snapped. "What reason did she give for dismissing you?"

"Oh," she said, struggling to catch her breath. "Mrs. Pritchard offered no reason, particularly." She swallowed. "Only that I should leave and not steal anything."

His nose flared. His eyes narrowed.

Drat. Perhaps she should have kept that last bit to herself.

"I shall discuss the matter with your father."

"P-pardon?"

"Everything about this is unacceptable."

"Holstoke." She grasped his arm as he charged past her. The muscled limb slid through her hands until all she held were his fingers. She clung and took hold of his wrist, only to be dragged six feet before he stopped and glared back at her.

"It—it is nothing to do with you," she sputtered.

Abruptly, he tugged until they nearly bumped noses,

dropping his hat and trapping her hands against his chest. "I should have informed her of your proper title. That was my mistake. No one should be permitted to speak to you the way she did."

Her heart gave a queer leap. "You only kept my secret because I wished it."

"As I said, my mistake."

A throat cleared delicately. "Ehrm, Genie?"

"Yes, Kate." Why did her voice sound breathless? And why had she never noticed how defined his lips were? As though they'd been drawn by a newly sharpened pencil.

"Perhaps you would like to release Lord Holstoke's hands. I am certain he needs them for other purposes. Retrieving his hat, for instance."

She glanced down. They were clutching at one another, pressed close enough to be dancing. Or kissing.

What a strange thought. She did not enjoy kissing. And even if she did, she certainly would not be kissing *Holstoke*. He'd once proposed to Maureen, for pity's sake. He might have been family, had Dunston never existed.

Kiss Holstoke? What a ninny-headed notion.

Another throat cleared pointedly. This time, it was Emerson. "I do beg your pardon for the intrusion, my lady, but Lord Berne would be glad to receive Lord Holstoke in the library, now."

Slowly, she untangled her fingers from his.

Holstoke held her fast. "Do not go to Cheapside."

It might have been an order, a plea, or a threat. How would he respond when she refused to comply? She could not be certain. The man had many oddities, which made him unpredictable. He'd taken a good deal more umbrage at both her employment and dismissal than was warranted by their acquaintance.

She raised her chin. "Very well. I shall remain here—*if* you do likewise."

Green eyes narrowed. "Likewise."

"Dinner?" she prompted.

His nose flared.

She smiled in satisfaction.

"Done," he said.

Her smile faded. Drat. Unpredictable, just as she'd predicted. "Maureen will be here," she reminded. "Dunston, too. And their children. They have four."

A muscle moved in his jaw. "I know."

"And let's not forget Lady Wallingham! And my mother—"

His hold upon her loosened. Gently, he lowered her hands and let her fingers slide away from his. "I know," he repeated. "Do not go to Cheapside, Lady Eugenia."

This time, she knew it was neither a plea nor an order. It was a warning, written inside those pale eyes like a sign above a door: Defy the Earl of Holstoke at your own risk.

Silently, she watched him gather up his hat and follow Emerson up the stairs, a tall, dark, looming form disappearing past streaming light and dust motes.

"Well, now," said Kate. "Lord Holstoke, hmm?"

"What of him?"

"Oh, nothing. A bit ... proprietary is all."

"Don't be silly."

Kate's fingers clasped Genie's chin and tugged her around until she focused upon her sister, rather than the empty staircase. Genie brushed her hand away, and Kate grinned like an imp. "Silly or not, had I realized his persuasive talents where you are concerned, I might have invited him here days ago."

Genie snorted. The sound lacked conviction. "Holstoke is mercurial. It is sensible to be cautious."

Kate's grin turned wry. "Sensible, cautious Genie. Yes, nothing unusual about that." Her snort was far more convincing than Genie's. She added an eye-roll for good measure.

"Go away, Kate."

Her sister's laughter stirred the dust motes as she, too, disappeared up the stairs.

Chapter Four

"A past without error is like a library without books—empty and useless. Though, I daresay, every library needs a good cleaning now and then."

—The Dowager Marchioness of Wallingham to Lord Berne upon said gentleman's complaint that Lady Berne's feline companions twice destroyed both his draperies and his waistcoats.

∞

This was the room where Phineas had proposed to Maureen. Blue draperies had since been replaced by gold ones, and he thought the carpet might be new, but otherwise, the library at Berne House remained as he remembered: Wood-paneled and small, it was as cluttered and comfortable as the Huxleys themselves. A winged chair sat between the window and fireplace, the worn, age-crinkled leather beckoning hours of reading. A small sofa sat along the opposite wall, and the large writing desk beside it was littered with papers, an open book, and a teacup steaming beside a pen.

Phineas remembered this feeling—as though he'd wandered in by mistake, a stranger from a frigid, desolate land discovering warmth and chaos and ready affection for the first time. The last six years had changed many things, but this feeling was not one.

"Holstoke." Stanton Huxley, the Earl of Berne, rose from the desk, his smile wide and welcoming. "By God, it is good to see you." The lean, silver-haired man extended his hand.

Phineas shook it, still uncertain why all Huxleys appeared to like him so well. "Lord Berne. Thank you for agreeing to speak with me. My apologies for the early call."

"Nonsense." The man's eyes—a lively hazel none of his daughters had inherited—glinted with humor. "A bit early for dinner, but hardly for conversation."

After offering him tea and inviting him to sit, Berne perched on the sofa, sipped from his cup, and casually stated, "If you think to cry off, I should warn you, Lady Berne will not have it. She would have invited you sooner, had she thought you might agree. We're all rather fond of you, young man."

Sighing, Phineas stroked the winged chair's creased arm. He supposed their fondness must go perpetually unexplained. "No, I shall be here. Your daughter insists."

Berne's smile turned sympathetic, an expression Phineas was beginning to loathe. "Maureen's heart is in the right place."

"Not Lady Dunston," Phineas corrected, his earlier vexation returning in a flood. "Lady Eugenia."

Berne's brows arched. "Eugenia."

"You are aware, of course, that until recently, she was *working*."

"Yes."

"For a shabby milliner near Soho."

"Mmm. She is no longer employed there." Berne's demeanor was calm. Too calm.

Phineas wanted to shout at him, but shouting was the

response of a man ruled by his anger—which Phineas was not. "Because she was *dismissed*," he snapped, "which may be the only thing more offensive than her being employed. How have you tolerated this?"

Berne deposited his tea on the desk and sat forward. "With great patience."

"More than is wise. I would not permit my sister to walk along that end of Oxford Street, let alone—"

"Allow me to explain something to you, Holstoke." Berne's eyes crinkled at the corners. "If I may."

Phineas nodded.

"When you are a father to five daughters, you might realize, as I did, how deuced little you know. Each child is different from the next. Different temperaments. Different interests. Different talents and aspirations. A man who loves his daughters must decide how much pressure to apply in fitting a girl into the mold society demands. Too much, and she will be crushed. Too little, and she will be ruined." Berne sat back and retrieved his tea again, taking a sip before continuing. "Take Maureen, for example."

"We were discussing Lady Eugenia."

"Patience, my boy. I am getting there." Berne took another sip. "Now, then. Maureen never gave me a moment's trouble. Sweeter than the cakes she makes for me at Christmastide, that's my girl. Her fondest wish was to be a wife and mother, and she did not mind following the prescribed path for that purpose."

"I remember."

"Hmm. Yes, I suppose you must." Sympathy flashed again then disappeared. "Eugenia is …" Berne chuckled, the sound affectionate yet sad. "Well, she is quite another sort, isn't she? Like it or not, she speaks her mind freely and goes where her interests take her. Unfortunately, one of those interests was footmen."

Something sharp and dark twisted inside Phineas. It made him restless. Made him want to leave before Berne elaborated further about Eugenia's fascination with the lower rungs of English society.

"Although she'd never done more than admire their handsomeness, her mother and I worried others would mistake admiration for intention," Berne continued. "We pressured her to abandon her prior habits and focus upon landing an appropriate husband. She wished to please us, so she stopped speaking about footmen. She also lessened her fixation on bonnets and the like, and moderated her conversation to appear more ... amiable.

"My daughter is an attractive young woman," Berne continued, stating the obvious. "She turned heads at Almack's. Danced and mingled and conversed in the manner of every young lady making her debut. She shaped herself into what was expected." Berne paused. Dropped his gaze to his cup. Appeared to gather his thoughts. "To put it simply, she disappeared. My little rebel was gone, replaced by a girl indistinguishable from any other. Made her desperately unhappy. She hid it well, for a time. But we knew something was wrong, even before the incident at Lady Reedham's ball."

Again, Phineas wanted to stop him. He did not wish to hear more about Eugenia's "incident." He wished to castigate the man for failing to stop it. But something in Berne's face gave him pause. Regret—deep and pained—etched inside a father's grimace.

Berne's eyes drifted to the window above Phineas's shoulder. "So, you see, my boy, the mistake was not in granting her too much license, but too little. Spirit such as hers does not fit easily into a mold. Before you know what's happened, it's sprung back into its true form and broken everything apart." At Phineas's glare, Berne gave a small smile. "Someday, you may understand. Perhaps you will have a daughter of your own."

Phineas understood quite enough. Berne was far too tenderhearted, and he had lost control of her. "You believe allowing her to work in a third-rate milliner's shop is acceptable, then."

"I believe forbidding her to pursue her aims would be worse."

"I disagree. She should be married. Protected."

Hazel eyes crinkled with amusement. "Are you offering, then?"

Lightning ran from his head to his feet. Offering? For Eugenia Huxley? The very thought was disorienting. Berne's jest caused his skin to pulse strangely. He struggled to ignore the sensation, as he would one of his megrims.

"No," he murmured. "Of course not. I am merely concerned for her and for your family."

Berne smiled. "You are a fine man, Holstoke."

Eugenia's father moved on to other topics—a renovation of the gardens at Clumberwood Manor, a recent bill introduced in the House of Commons, the odds of greater crop yields due to fair spring weather—but all the while, Phineas puzzled away at Berne's explanations for Eugenia's predicament.

He had long admired the Huxleys. They laughed together, teased one another, argued and embraced. He did not remember ever being embraced as a boy. Perhaps that was why it seemed alien.

Eugenia, in particular, often failed to maintain a proper distance. Every time they spoke, she managed to position herself within a breath of him. She brushed his arm with her fingers, grasped his fingers with hers, patted him like a familiar friend. When she wished to make a point, he found her reaching for him.

It was odd. That might have been how she liked to describe him, but in fact, he found Eugenia Huxley and her entire family odd—so outwardly affectionate, he felt like a foreigner.

Perhaps he was. He had trained himself to mimic affectionate gestures for Hannah's sake, and his sister had learned to accept them from time to time. He wanted Hannah to know what a proper, loving family should be. The Huxleys were the best model he'd found.

Except for Eugenia. Little rebel, indeed. She had certainly spoiled the broth.

He frowned. Berne had given up on reining her in, but she faced a bleak path of spinsterhood if someone did not take action—and soon.

"By Jove, you are a good listener, Holstoke," Berne said now, setting down his empty cup. "Most gentlemen prefer to hear themselves talk. Serves them well enough in Parliament, I suppose."

Phineas nodded, realizing their conversation had reached an end. He shook hands with Berne and made his way down to the foyer, only to find Eugenia there, clutching the hands of a plump, freckled young man in rough workman's clothes. Phineas recognized him from the hat shop. She spoke softly, beseechingly, as though they were lovers.

The lightning that had burned through him earlier—such an unusual feeling—struck again, jagged and sharp. His skin prickled. His neck tensed. His stomach tightened.

"... accept my apologies, Mr. Moody. I shall make inquiries on your behalf this very day. You mustn't despair for a moment."

The young man's cheeks were flagged with red. His eyes were near glassy with lust. It must be lust. He'd scarcely looked away from Eugenia's lips.

Phineas understood, of course. She had splendid lips—plump and curved and mobile. But he needed to remove her hands from the other man's grasp. He needed to put distance between them. Much, much more distance. The impropriety was damned risky for her and an insulting overstep for the young hatter.

"Thank you, Miss Hu—I mean, m'lady."

"Oh, pooh. Call me Eugenia. And I shall call you Lewis."

Moody's flush deepened, as did his grin.

Bloody hell. Yes, distance. Now.

"*Lady* Eugenia will send a note round when she has news to report." Phineas's lashing statement had the desired effect—Moody dropped her hands, backed away three steps, and stammered out a "yer lordship," in gratifyingly short order.

Phineas ignored Eugenia's startled glare to stride forward and finish his rebuke. "Until then, I suggest you refrain from touching her."

He'd meant to say, "Recall your proper station." But the more explicit admonishment was better. Specificity left little room for interpretation.

"Lord Holstoke," Eugenia said tightly as he came to stand behind her. "May we speak in the parlor?"

"After he leaves." Phineas leveled a cold warning at Moody, watching with satisfaction as the hatter's color drained to freckled white. "You were leaving, were you not?"

Eugenia's "no" was drowned out by Moody's high-pitched "yes, m'lord!" The portly young man staggered backward, bowing awkwardly and muttering a series of m'lords and m'lady's.

"Mr. Moody—Lewis," Eugenia protested, starting forward.

Phineas shifted to impede her path as the Huxley butler, Emerson, held the door open. Moody fled as though chased by a specter. Eugenia, attempting to sidestep Phineas, came up short when he grasped her wrist. As it had when he'd held her earlier, the fineness of her bones startled him. She was a strong woman. She should not be so small.

With her free hand, she gave his shoulder a bruising shove. "Now look what you've done," she hissed. "You've frightened him away."

He tugged her into the adjacent parlor before releasing her. "Do you really wish to embroil your family in a perpetual scandal because you cannot control your queer fascination with men of the lower classes?"

Her eyes—rich, sherry brown—flashed hot. "How *dare* you?" She stomped toward him, her cheeks flushing, her hands clenching into fists. "You may have sought to become my brother-in-law once, but you have not the tiniest, miniscule iota of authority where I am concerned." She pointed at the foyer. "I ruined that man's life, Holstoke. He did nothing to deserve it, apart from reading *Ivanhoe* and tolerating my presence."

"'Tolerating'?" Surely Eugenia understood, though Phineas could see from her expression that she did not. Baffling, given her predilections. But then, she was not a man. Perhaps she needed one to enlighten her. "Moody's *tolerance* is rooted in lust. It is obvious."

Her hands landed on her hips, drawing his eyes there, just below where her riding habit hugged a surprisingly tiny waist.

"What a lot of rot," she spat.

How could a woman's hips be so beautifully rounded and yet so slender? He frowned, puzzling at the contradiction.

"Lewis Moody is the sole person in either shop to show me kindness, and I will *not* repay him by letting him languish in penury."

Still distracted by his attempt to reconcile the geometry of Eugenia's form, Phineas answered honestly, if a bit hoarsely, "He was kind because he wants you."

Those mystifying hips moved closer, bringing her within reach. His palms and fingertips tingled with a milder version of the lightning. He rubbed his fingers together to stifle it. Such a curious feeling.

"You are an appalling judge of character, Holstoke. You'd do well to confine yourself to plants and leave us humans to conduct our own affairs."

His gaze slid up to meet hers. Her cheeks were blushing pink. Her lips, normally curved like a bird's wing, were both flat and full. Another contradiction. One of many, it seemed.

"I am a man, Lady Eugenia. That is how I know what motivates his actions. The greater mystery is what motivates yours."

"Mine?"

"The risks you take are both foolish—"

"Incredible. Bloody incredible."

"—and destructive to those you profess to love. Your family—your father, in particular—has indulged your unruly nature too long."

Rich, cat-like eyes narrowed to a bristling glint. "Get out."

He raised a brow.

"I mean it, Holstoke. Leave. Before I do something *unruly* and strangle you with your cravat."

"We had a bargain. I shall keep my end."

"You are hereby absolved. Do not return for dinner. I will explain to Mama that you fell prey to an unfortunate ailment." She sniffed. "In deference to her fondness for you, I won't mention the ailment is your personality."

He nearly laughed. The urge was yet another contradiction—one should not feel amused by insults. But Eugenia Huxley was proving the exception to every rule. He lowered his head until he could breathe her in, violets and an elusive hint of fruit. Cherries, perhaps.

"As I have given my word," he murmured, eyeing her lips, "I must return, Lady Eugenia. Apologies." Slowly, he smiled, enjoying her disgruntled frown.

For several moments, she gazed up at him, half bewildered and half infuriated. "You are not a bit sorry, so do not pretend. And why the devil are you smiling?"

His smile grew. Then, he shook his head, uncertain of the answer. "Must be the company," he said. "Rarely am I insulted with such proficiency."

She struggled against it, but soon, her lips quirked at the corners. She gave his arm a stinging swat and pushed him toward the door. "Go away, or I shall demonstrate my proficiencies with great relish."

He gave her a bow. Then laughed.

He was still laughing as he passed an alarmed Emerson,

donned his second-best hat, and descended onto Grosvenor Street, anticipating the evening to come.

∞

The bony woman was almost too easy. Thin and listless, her body took his poison as though starving for it.

"I—I cannot ..." She staggered forward, grasping at her chest. Her lips were already parched.

He smiled.

She dropped her cup into a shatter. Fell to her knees. Bled on the shards.

"Help." Her voice was a hellish wheeze, her hand a desperate claw reaching for him.

He'd given her a swift journey. She should be grateful.

Leaning down to watch as her blood seeped from cut knees through her white gown, he smothered his laughter. "Time to fly, my lady." His voice shook. "Fair thee well."

Perhaps she was too easy. But the sacrifice was what mattered. The flight. The offering. As he left her father's house, blending into the crowds along Brook Street, he looked to the sky.

Yes. His assignment was coming along splendidly. Splendidly, indeed.

Chapter Five

"Children are, indeed, a delight. I find their charm increases with age. Twenty years should do."

—THE DOWAGER MARCHIONESS OF WALLINGHAM to her daughter-in-law, Lady Wallingham, while repairing the quizzing glass damaged by her youngest grandson.

∽∞∽

"SIR EDWIN, I HEREBY DECLARE YOU EMPEROR OF THE Realm!" Genie waved her wooden spoon with a flourish and gently tapped her nephew's shoulders. "Further, I do declare upon this day that your realm shall be …" She paused before pointing the spoon with regal flair toward the corner of the drawing room. "Grandmama's new sofa."

Mama, currently chatting with Maureen and bouncing Maureen's youngest son upon the tufted, armless monstrosity, glanced in Genie's direction. "It is an ottoman, dear."

Genie raised her chin and stirred her spoon in midair.

"Forsooth, Sir Edwin, your realm shall be known as ..." Genie cast a sideways glance at her niece, Sophie, who clapped her hands and hopped in place.

"What is it, Auntie Genie? Tell us!"

Genie gave her a wink and bowed to little Edwin. "The Ottoman Empire."

Sir Edwin collapsed into a heap of giggles. The paper crown she'd made for him slid over dark-blue eyes, and his mother's indigo shawl slipped down one tiny shoulder. He was four years old, so she forgave his lapse of decorum.

One must make allowances.

She felt a tug at the back of her skirts.

"Angie! Angie! Liff."

She pretended confusion. "Who is there?"

"Liff!"

Circling around the little mite several turns, she finally grasped her round-cheeked, ginger-haired niece, Meredith, beneath her arms and swung her up in one motion. Merry squealed and shrieked with laughter as they spun.

"I say, Lady Meredith," Genie said as she stroked the two-year-old's red curls. "You seem to have lost your bonnet." She *tsked* and kissed Merry's cheek. "Where is it, my darling?"

Merry pointed toward the red-draped window.

And there it was—the tiny newspaper bonnet with pink ribbons and two small daisies. It lay near the toe of a polished boot.

Which belonged to the man she was ignoring with all her might. She needn't have bothered, of course. Upon entering the drawing room a half-hour earlier, he'd greeted Maureen warmly—a bit too warmly, in her view. She'd frowned at him, wondering how such a glacial stare could be so affectionate. So ... gentle. He never looked upon Genie in such a way. No, with her, whenever his eyes heated, the cause was outrage or anger or indignation. That green ice snapped and sparked, rather than glowing with admiration.

Dunston had noticed, too. Her brother-in-law had bristled. Tossed out several veiled insults. Glared in deadly fashion.

Ordinarily, Dunston was humorous, witty, and dashing. Genie had always found him great fun, able to discuss waistcoat fashions, Shakespearean tragedies, and Thoroughbred bloodlines with equal aplomb. But he was also dangerous—a man who had secretly hunted his father's murderer for over a decade, working with both the Foreign Office and the Home Office, disguising his darker side even from his beloved Maureen.

Although he'd sought to protect Maureen by diminishing their connection to mere friendship, the pair had been madly in love for years before Holstoke had set his cap for her. Holstoke's courtship had invigorated Dunston's harder, possessive nature, and in the end, Dunston, too, had proposed. Maureen had rejected Holstoke, married Dunston, and had proceeded to bear him four beautiful children.

Naturally, Genie had known her sister's choice long before Maureen had. Anyone with a jot of sense could see Maureen's incessant preoccupation with the handsome, dapper lord. In truth, Holstoke had never stood a chance. Even if Maureen had accepted him, Dunston would have cut Holstoke in two with his favorite daggers before letting her marry anybody else.

And that was *before* discovering Holstoke's mother had murdered Dunston's father—along with numerous others—across decades of criminal treachery.

So, it was not surprising that Dunston needled his former rival. Likewise, Holstoke's reaction was much closer to what Genie expected. His expression neutral and inscrutable, he'd ignored Dunston, given Maureen a dignified nod, and moved away to greet Mama, Papa, Kate, and Lady Wallingham. Then, he'd trained those pale eyes upon Maureen from across the room, observing her sister for long minutes before turning away to converse with Papa.

He'd ignored Genie entirely. No greeting. No glances. No lectures about inappropriate behavior. Which was all just as well. Genie had little desire to further subject herself to Holstoke's high-handed judgment. Still, he might have at least acknowledged her existence. As Lady Wallingham was fond of saying, "Rudeness is an art few have mastered well enough to apply without consequences."

As she played with Dunston and Maureen's adorable band of offspring, she'd felt his gaze turn in her direction more than once. She assumed his scrutiny had one of two purposes: Either he found Genie too unruly for his liking or he was curious about Maureen's children, perhaps even melancholy that they were not his own. The answer was likely a bit of both.

Now, as Edwin and Sophie skipped away to claim Mama's ottoman, and Merry wriggled to be set down, Genie could no longer avoid him. She lowered her niece to the carpet, watching the girl toddle after her siblings. Then, she took a breath and strode toward the window. Toward him.

"Holstoke," she said, feeling a strange rush as his eyes locked upon her.

"Lady Eugenia."

"I am surprised you came."

"Odd. I did promise as much."

She sniffed and gestured toward the paper bonnet. "My niece lost her hat."

Slowly, he crouched and plucked up the creation between two long fingers. After rising to his full, looming height, he examined the thing as he might a new plant specimen. "You made one for each of them, did you not?"

"Give it to me, if you please."

Those eyes moved to her outstretched palm then slid slowly up her arm and bodice and throat and, finally, settled on her face. Such intense scrutiny produced odd sensations: Prickly skin. Heat. Curling chills and gooseflesh.

"I thought you were fond of me," he said, his tone merely curious.

"My family is fond of you. I am vexed with you."

"Still?"

"You were dashed rude, Holstoke," she snapped. "If I wish to help Mr. Moody, that is *my* concern, not yours. For that matter, if I wish to dampen my skirts and promenade down Regent Street singing 'God Save the King,' it should have nothing whatever to do with you."

He tilted his head and stared, his expression intent and unreadable. He was giving her the shivers from head to toe.

"Stop that."

"What?"

"Staring."

Slowly, the beginnings of a smile tugged at his lips. "Does it *vex* you, Lady Eugenia?"

She inched closer so they could not be overheard. Then, she snatched the paper bonnet from his fingers. "Yes," she hissed. "Your eyes are unnerving, as you well know."

His smile grew. "They are simply eyes."

"They give me shivers."

"Hmm. What effect would hands have, do you suppose?"

Her heart stuttered. Good heavens, was he flirting with her? *Holstoke?* She blinked and tried to catch her breath. No. Holstoke did not flirt. And if he did, it would be with Maureen, no doubt. The likelier explanation was that he was curious, a scientist trying to solve a riddle.

Vaguely, she heard her mother announce dinner. She sensed the arrival of servants—the children's nurse herding her flock off to the nursery, Emerson quietly directing the footmen. She heard the rustling of gowns and the shifting of wool and the murmuring tones of her family making their way toward the drawing room doors.

Yet, she stood frozen. Locked inside the strangest battle she'd ever known.

He would not let up. Would not release her.

"We should go," she whispered.

"To the dining room. Yes."

"Holstoke?"

His head lowered. His eyes lingered on her mouth.

"You really are the most peculiar man." Her voice was hoarse and throaty. Perhaps some wine would help. Of course, she was already a bit lightheaded. Tingly. Warm.

Behind her, the trumpeting voice of Lady Wallingham intruded. "Lord Holstoke! I require your escort, young man. Do let's observe some semblance of propriety."

Lady Wallingham was not alone. When Genie turned, she discovered her mother giving her a sharp, distinctly maternal look. Both Holstoke's arm and his ear were confiscated by the dowager, who drew him toward the doors, describing the "proper way to bait one's hook in murky waters, dear boy."

Genie frowned and asked Mama, "When did Lady Wallingham take up angling?"

"Eugenia," Mama said, her tone worried and chiding. "You do understand Holstoke is seeking a wife."

Swallowing her sudden queasiness, she scoffed. "Of course, Mama. I am hardly daft."

Mama clasped her hands in a warm grip, her dark eyes kind but crinkled with concern. Genie hadn't seen her mother this way since before the scandal, when Mama had gently advised her to cease discussing bonnet construction with eligible suitors.

Now, her warning was more direct—and humbling. "He faces a great many obstacles in that pursuit. You mustn't be one of them, dearest."

The reminder that she was, in fact, the Great Burden of Genie struck all the harder for its unexpectedness. Shame burst through her, an old, sick feeling. Heavens, she'd thought herself inured to the pain. It was sharper than ever.

Round, dark eyes shone with regret. "How I wish matters

were different, my darling," Mama said. "How I wish I had done things differently."

Genie clenched her teeth and stiffened against the choking ache. She would not stand here and weep, for it would accomplish nothing but adding to her mother's pain. So, instead, she shook her head and offered an admonishment of her own. "The scandal was my fault, Mama. Not yours. I have told you this."

Mama dabbed her eyes with a lace-edged handkerchief. "Maureen's seasons were so effortless. Everyone adored her—even Holstoke. I assumed your debut would be the same. I should have realized—"

"Stop," Genie said softly, drawing her sweet, round mother into her arms and patting her back. "You are not to blame, and I'll hear no more about it." She gave one last pat and drew back to give Mama a smile. It was forced, but necessary. Mama had suffered greatly because of Genie. A smile was the least she could do. "Now, I don't know what caused your suspicions, but there is nothing untoward going on between me and Holstoke, I assure you."

Mama blinked and sniffed. "You appeared preoccupied with one another, dearest."

"Don't be silly. We were simply having a discussion."

"A rather heated one."

"Holstoke is rude and peculiar. I could discuss strawberry tarts with the man, and he would argue vociferously in favor of apricots."

"I have never known him to be argumentative. More aloof, really."

"Hmm. Perhaps he finds me vexing."

Mama's brow crinkled. She dropped her gaze to her handkerchief and firmed her chin before raising solemn eyes. "I could not bear for you to be hurt again, Eugenia."

"Mama—"

"All I ask is that you exercise caution until you return to

Clumberwood." Mama patted her hand. "I understand a new physician has moved to the village. Quite handsome. A widower with two sons in need of a mother." Mama grinned her matchmaking grin. "It would be rude not to invite him for dinner, wouldn't you agree?"

Genie sighed. Shook her head and nodded toward the doors. "Perhaps we should focus upon the dinner you are currently hosting."

"Oh! Yes, of course." Eyes twinkling, Mama looped her arm through Genie's. "Few things cannot be improved—"

"By a good meal." Genie chuckled. "So I have heard."

For the following two hours, while Genie ignored Kate's prattle, pretended to eat, and drank freely of her wine, she divided her attention between the tablecloth and Holstoke. More Holstoke, really.

Very well, almost entirely Holstoke.

He *was* peculiar. And tall. And, now that she had time to properly look, not unhandsome. His nose, while long and blade-like, was rather regal. His hair, while more severe than stylish, was thick and black. She quite liked his lips, as well. Thin yet defined. They were fascinating.

She frowned and twirled her fork in her hand. Fascinating? What a lot of rot. A man's lips were not *fascinating*. Her eyes returned to said lips for verification. No. They were simply more attractive than one first supposed.

There, that was better. Attractive. Yes, Holstoke was attractive.

Handsome, even. And his eyes were ... riveting.

She sipped her wine, granting herself the luxury of studying him across the table. Such a pale color, that icy green. The rings nearly disappeared into the whites. But they didn't. Rimming the ice was a band of darker color. A shade of blue. Nearly imperceptible, but there.

Fascinating.

"... are not listening to a word I am saying, are you?"

Genie blinked. Turned toward her younger sister, beside whom she was seated. The room continued spinning, causing Genie to list a bit. She straightened and answered, "Really, Kate. Such acrimony is no way to begin a conversation."

Kate snorted and shook her head, gesturing toward Holstoke. "If I specified he was the topic, would that capture your attention?"

Genie drank the last few drops from her empty glass. "Holstoke is rude. I care nothing for him."

"Mmm. Then you won't care that the gossip is worsening."

Frowning, Genie waved the nearest footman forward to refill her glass. "Worsening how?"

"Suspicions are growing, particularly since Miss Froom's death. Her mother claims it was poison. Lady Wallingham reported only this evening that Mrs. Froom is accusing Lord Holstoke of murder, though not publicly. Naturally, Mr. Froom objects to leveling such grave charges at a peer of the realm without proof."

"Hmmph. As well he should. Holstoke is not a murderer. Rude. Strange. But not a killer." And he was staring again. Ignoring Lady Wallingham as the imperious old dragon lobbed unwanted opinions in his direction, Holstoke appeared fixated upon Genie's neck. Blast him, why could he not behave like a normal man? The shivers were getting worse, now accompanied by waves of heat.

His gaze did not leave her until Emerson entered to announce that another guest had arrived. The young woman was ethereally white with raven hair and Holstoke's eyes. She stood in the dining room doorway, gowned in layers of rosy pink gauze. To Genie's eye, Hannah Gray always appeared eerily composed—cold, even—yet fragile as a reed in winter.

The girl had been through hell, of course. And, until Maureen had introduced her to Holstoke six years earlier, she'd survived that hell alone. Holstoke had not hesitated to take her in, protecting his sister with the full force of his title, his fortune, and his devotion. Now, his devotion surged to the fore as Holstoke immediately frowned, shoved out of his chair, and went to his sister.

"What do you suppose this is about?" Kate murmured.

Genie shushed her and listened. Seated near the doors, she was able to hear most of it, though they kept their voices low.

"Phineas," Hannah breathed. "I told him to leave, but he refused."

"Who?"

"The Bow Street man. Mr. Hawthorn. He asked so many questions, and I—I answered before I knew why he'd come."

Holstoke gently braced his sister's shoulders, stilling her trembling. "It is all right, little one. Tell me what he said."

Hannah blinked up at him, her brow puckering with distress. "H-he wanted to know where you were this morning. I said you'd gone out after breakfast. He said Lord Glencombe's daughter was m-murdered today. Poisoned."

Holstoke's shoulders stiffened. "Lady Theodosia?"

She nodded.

Despite obvious tension, he stroked his sister's upper arms and gathered her close. Genie noted how slowly, how carefully he did so, as though Hannah were made of wet paper. Hannah closed her eyes and sighed against his coat.

Maureen rushed from the other end of the table to join them, soothing the girl with a hand at her back. The trio huddled together, murmuring softly. They looked like a family, bonded by past horrors and deep affection.

Genie's insides tightened and twisted. She took another drink of her wine.

Beside her, Kate whispered, "Good heavens. Miss Froom and now Theodosia? I had no liking for either of them, but this is ... dreadful. Do you suppose—"

"No," Genie said, narrowing her eyes upon the huddled trio. "If they were poisoned, it was not Holstoke."

"How can you be certain?"

She looked at the way he held his sister. Noticed the looseness of his arms, as though he never wanted her to feel trapped again. "I just am," she answered. "Besides which, we know who the murderer in the Brand family was. Dunston and Maureen were there when Lady Holstoke came after Hannah. Others witnessed it, too—Mr. Reaver and Sarah Lacey. The magistrate was well satisfied, even when he discovered Hannah was the one who ..."

"Stopped her."

Genie met Kate's eyes and nodded. The incident had further devastated the fragile girl, who'd been sixteen when she'd been forced to shoot a madwoman to save her own life and that of the others in the room. Holstoke, having met his half-sister only that day, nevertheless had protected Hannah ferociously, refusing to allow the magistrate to question her. Subsequently, he'd moved Hannah into Primvale Castle. Then, he'd spent thousands of pounds and several years finding his mother's many victims and offering recompense to their families.

That was how Genie knew Phineas Brand was not a murderer. He was a man of deep honor, peculiarities aside. He deserved better than to be accused of poisoning two young women.

She glanced down the table at her brother-in-law, who glared at the trio, obviously struggling against his darker nature. "Dunston must help him."

"Er, Genie. It might be wise to leave Dunston out of this. He has no liking for Holstoke."

Genie pushed to her feet, bracing herself against the table as the wine made its presence felt. "He must still have contacts at Bow Street."

"Perhaps you should let Maureen ..."

Kate might have continued talking, but Genie was focused upon reaching Dunston without tripping over her own feet. Good heavens, when had the dining room floor developed such a slant?

Raising a single chestnut brow as she arrived beside his chair, Dunston gave her an affectionate grin, despite the turbulence in his eyes. "Enjoying the wine, Brat?"

She waved away his quip. "You must help Holstoke."

The grin faded. "I fail to see why."

"Bow Street suspects him of poisoning a girl. Perhaps two."

Dunston crossed his arms. "I shall give him the name of a good barrister."

She braced her hand on the table. China clinked as she missed her mark. "He is innocent, and well you know it, Henry."

"Probably. But I don't see how it is any of my—"

"You're acquainted with all sorts of shadowy men. At the Home Office. At Bow Street." She waved her hand in a circular motion. "Do whatever it is you do, and make this matter disappear."

"You are asking a great deal, given his prior pursuit of my wife."

"Yes, well. Maureen chose you. Now, do stop being a jealous idiot."

"I have already done you one favor today by securing a position for your friend, Mr. Mudd."

"Moody."

"And now, you wish me to intervene for Holstoke."

She raised her chin. "It is the right thing to do."

He frowned. Glanced past her shoulder toward the trio. Ground his teeth until his jaw flexed. Then, he met her gaze. "Very well," he said softly. "But only because Maureen will reward me generously when I claim it was my idea."

Grinning in triumph, Genie replied, "Your idea entirely, dearest brother. Entirely."

Two more hours and two more glasses of wine later, Genie's head was still swimming, and it was beginning to ache. She sat in the corner of the drawing room on Mama's hideous ottoman.

Beside her sat Lady Wallingham.

Perhaps that was why her head ached.

"This whole affair is rubbish," the old woman pronounced with a sniff. "Holstoke is odd, not homicidal."

Genie sighed. "My thoughts precis—"

"How many times must I remind him, one *hires* gardeners. One does not *become* one. No, no, no. His oddities are numerous; there can be little doubt. The eyes are positively spectral. And if you ever have need of achieving a tedium stupor, ask him which strain of wheat is preferable for coastal winters. Good God, Catholics employ less Latin."

Genie rubbed her forehead with two fingers.

"His mother was vile, of course. Beautiful and vile. I never liked her."

Genie silently counted to three.

"But then, I am cleverer than most."

Yes, indeed. Right on cue. Genie wondered if she might find additional wine in the abandoned dining room. Surely one should be fully sotted if one was forced to endure a Lady Wallingham diatribe.

"She was French, you know. Lady Holstoke. Pretended to be English." Lady Wallingham snorted. "The French always reveal themselves in the end, my dear. Something about their odor, I suspect. They reek of smugness."

True to his word, Dunston had summoned his friend, Mr. Drayton, who had been a Bow Street runner for years. The haggard man had arrived at Berne House five minutes earlier and currently stood speaking with Holstoke and Dunston near the fireplace. A fierce frown creased Drayton's forehead.

Holstoke appeared calm, but Genie noted the flare of his nose from time to time. Somehow, his annoyance gave her comfort. If he'd thought the charges serious, surely he would exhibit signs of real anger, as he'd done upon learning Genie had been dismissed.

"That man, there. Mr. Drayton. He was shot whilst chasing

Lady Holstoke, was he not?"

"Her accomplice. An apothecary, I believe."

"You know, he reminds me of Humphrey."

Genie rolled her eyes. Humphrey was Lady Wallingham's dog, a scent hound with more wrinkles than the dragon herself. The old woman considered him her boon companion and spoke endlessly about the hound's finer attributes.

"Humphrey's nose is unparalleled."

And there it was.

"One of my lady's maids stole a pair of slippers last autumn. Humphrey tracked her through three villages, then delivered the slippers to me, along with a satisfying quantity of the little thief's petticoats."

Genie never knew whether to believe the dragon's assertions, though she'd also never known Lady Wallingham to be wrong.

"Rest assured, Humphrey would ferret out the real culprit in this villainous poisoning, and he would do it with ease." She harrumphed. "Far superior to the feckless Bow Street rabble, I daresay."

Across from Genie and Lady Wallingham, Maureen and Mama sat with Hannah, who appeared calmer than when she'd arrived. The girl sipped tea and nodded through Maureen's reassurances. Kate had gone to retrieve a shawl for the girl. The children had been put to bed. Papa was pouring himself a brandy.

As for Genie, she was wondering how in blazes Holstoke intended to prove his innocence. And she could not hear the men talking while Lady Wallingham sat nearby. It was intolerable.

She stood.

"Don't be foolish, girl."

At the sharp rebuke, Genie blinked and glanced back at the old woman who insisted on two, rather than three, feathers in her blue turbans.

Lady Wallingham arched a brow. "You always were impulsive. When has that ever bettered your situation, hmm?"

Genie returned her gaze to Holstoke. He, too, was frowning now. Scowling, really. Rubbing the back of his neck. He looked ... angry.

"Cannons cannot be unfired, Eugenia," the old woman warned. "Leaps cannot be unleapt. You should understand this better than most."

"I need to know, Lady Wallingham." She turned again to meet sharp, emerald eyes. There, an unexpected bit of empathy dwelt.

Fancy that. The dragon understood.

Genie gave her a small smile. "I'll only be a moment."

"Hmmph. A moment is all it takes, my dear."

Chapter Six

"It is a sad truth, Meredith. Some men choose to hurl themselves haplessly into the arms of failure rather than accept the assistance of a woman. Did I say 'some'? I meant 'all'."

—THE DOWAGER MARCHIONESS OF WALLINGHAM to Lady Berne upon receiving Lord Holstoke's long-awaited reply to an offer of assistance in matters matrimonial.

༻✦༺

"IT'S A PROBLEM, M'LORD. SORRY TO SAY." THE BOW STREET runner had salty whiskers, a weary face, and a grim look in his eye.

Phineas did not like it. "I went riding," he repeated.

"Aye," Drayton answered with a shake of his head. "But who saw you?"

"Nobody. I have a property less than an hour from here. Open farmland. I go there when I wish to be alone."

Drayton slanted him a skeptical glance and scribbled in his notebook. "Just land. No house? No servants?"

Phineas stiffened, his gut going cold. "No. The land is experimental. I use it for testing new crops."

"And the men who work it are ...?"

"Hired seasonally from a neighbor's land. Nobody would have seen me, Drayton. Planting is over."

The runner grunted and stroked his grizzled jaw with his knuckles. "You attended the Randall affair, yes?"

"Yes."

Dunston, who stood with arms folded beside the runner, added, "He left early. I saw him go."

Drayton's mouth twisted. He sighed. "Doesn't bode well, m'lord. Not well at all."

Phineas looked at both men, one a handsome man of privilege and the other a haggard hound, and saw the same hard expression. They both had spent years in this world—the realm of murder and danger and deceit. They'd both been instrumental in discovering his mother's crimes and bringing her to a just end.

They both looked as though the gallows were swaying outside the door, awaiting Phineas's neck.

"I've nothing to do with this," he snapped. "Why the devil would I wish to kill either woman?"

Drayton rubbed his jaw again. "Man I spoke with—Hawthorn. Deuced clever sort. He says both Miss Froom and Lady Theodosia rejected your ... attentions."

Phineas stiffened further, his nape prickling, his right eye beginning to throb.

Dunston smirked. "A point in Holstoke's favor, perhaps. By that criterion, every lady in the upper ten thousand should be poisoned."

"The deaths appear similar to your mother's work. Another thing," Drayton continued, his tone reluctant, his eyes squinting at his notes. "Randall's nephew, Mr. Capshaw, claims you threatened him outside Randall's town house. Same night Miss Froom died."

"Bloody hell," Phineas muttered, running a hand over his knotted nape.

"Aye. Capshaw said you threatened to poison him and his friend."

Damn and blast. He'd let his anger get the best of him, and now came the consequences. "Cretins, both," Phineas said, keeping his voice low. "Their insults toward ... a certain lady were contemptible. I threatened them solely for purposes of motivating discretion."

Dunston raised a wry brow. "Which lady? Never fancied you a man of sentiment."

"It doesn't matter."

The other man tilted his head, his gaze turning sharper. "I think it does."

Phineas ignored him to address Drayton. "If I were clever enough to poison two women without any witnesses, it makes little sense to suppose I would announce my maniacal tendencies to a pair of half-sotted halfwits on my way out the door."

"Come now," Dunston persisted, ignoring being ignored. "Give us her name, old chap. For whom did you act the gallant defender?"

Phineas turned a glare upon the falsely dapper lord. "A member of your family, as it happens."

Everything light and charming left Dunston's eyes, replaced by steel and stone. Phineas had seen the look before—on the day his mother was killed while attempting to kill Maureen. The same day Dunston had held a blade to his throat.

"They insulted my wife?" the other lord now said softly.

"No."

"Then whom?"

"Lady Eugenia."

Dunston blinked. "Genie? What the devil did they say?"

"Nothing I care to repeat."

"Was it the footman thing again?"

Phineas's chest grew hot and tight. "I bloody well don't wish to discuss it, *old chap*."

Slowly, Dunston's gaze turned from hard to assessing to faintly amused. "Ah. They called her Huxley Harlot, didn't they?" He clicked his tongue annoyingly. "In fairness, she did dally with the household staff." He grew another smirk. "Or should I say, the staff's staff?"

Perhaps it was the throbbing pain behind Phineas's right eye. Perhaps it was being accused of murder or being forced to comfort his sister again or simply having to endure Dunston's odious presence for an entire evening.

Regardless, one moment he was rational. The next, Dunston's lapel was wadded inside his fist, and a guttural voice was growling, "Say such a thing again, and I'll bloody that precious waistcoat."

Unfazed, Dunston glanced down at Phineas's fist and grinned. "You are fortunate I left my daggers at home, of course. But all in all, well done."

Drayton cleared his throat. "M'lords." He scratched his chin and pointed behind Phineas.

"Holstoke?"

Throaty, feminine voice. The scent of violets. It was her. Bloody hell.

"Release Dunston before he damages you, for pity's sake."

Reluctantly, he did. Dunston straightened his waistcoat and continued grinning.

"Now, I have waited patiently—*very* patiently, considering I was seated next to Lady Wallingham—and it has been long enough. Tell me what is going on."

"An accusation of murder or two," Dunston replied. "Nothing Holstoke cannot dispel with his winning charm. Or an alibi. What say you, old chap? Better an alibi, I should think."

Phineas didn't bother with Dunston any further. He faced Eugenia instead. She stood with her hands upon her hips, blinking up at him and, strangely, swaying from side to side as though she were on a ship.

"You should lie down," he told her, moving near in case she stumbled. She'd obviously had more wine and less food than he'd thought—and he'd watched her diligently throughout dinner.

Behind him, Dunston chuckled. "Taking the direct approach, eh, Holstoke?"

Eugenia frowned and peered past his shoulder. "Oh, do be quiet, Dunston. This is no time to be amusing."

"Right you are."

Her gaze came back to Phineas. "You require an alibi?"

"No."

"Tell them you were with me."

A shock ran through his body like lightning through a tree. It traveled clear to his roots. "No."

"Don't be a fool. You were here with me this morning. You visited with my father, then—"

"I said no, Eugenia."

"—we were alone together for the remainder of the afternoon. Simple."

Drayton shuffled forward, his limp more pronounced than when he'd entered. "Is this true, m'lord?"

"No."

"Of course it is," Eugenia lied, her chin elevating.

Phineas grasped her elbow as she swayed. "It damned well is not. You are in your cups and speaking nonsense." He wanted to shake her, shut her up, pick her up and carry her to her bedchamber before she ruined herself any further.

"Nonsense is accusing you of murder." She tugged away and addressed Drayton. "I shall swear it to your Bow Street man. Holstoke could not have poisoned Lady Theodosia because he was with me."

Phineas had half a mind to simply clap a hand over her mouth then haul her away until she regained her senses.

Fortunately, Dunston intervened. "Genie, while your offer to sacrifice what's left of your reputation for Holstoke is generous—if a bit disturbing—might I suggest you cease talking? There's a good girl."

Phineas opened his mouth to reinforce the point, only to have Drayton interject, "It would cool Hawthorn's pursuit of ye, m'lord. An alibi, particularly one involving a lady friend, would send him lookin' elsewhere."

Eugenia sniffed. "You see? An elegant solution, I daresay."

"She is not my lady friend," Phineas bit out, grasping the madwoman's slender arm and pulling her into his side to prevent her toppling over. She was obviously sotted.

"O' course, m'lord."

"We did not spend the day together."

"Right."

"I was here to see Lord Berne. Then I went riding. Alone."

Drayton glanced to where Phineas's hand cupped her tiny, curved waist.

"Really, Holstoke," she said, clutching his arm like a rope at sea. "I can stand on my own. Now be the brilliant man I know you to be, and accept my help."

"No." He ordered his hand to release her. Instead, it tightened and pulled her closer.

"I haven't any reputation to sacrifice, for pity's sake. I shall say we were together. They will believe me. Huxley Harlot and all that."

He spun her to face him, using both hands to grip her firmly. "You will do nothing of the sort. By God, woman, if you ever repeat that vile term again, I'll—"

Her bare hand reached for his cheek.

His body jerked, lightning rippling from the contact.

"Sometimes they will only believe a lie," she whispered.

"I will not permit you to lie for me."

Her hand dropped to his shoulder. She patted him softly, brushing at his coat and tidying his cravat. "And I will not permit you to be hanged for murders you did not commit. Besides, I depart for Clumberwood in a few days. If there is a bit of gossip, I shan't hear it."

The bones in his chest tightened. "You are leaving?"

She gazed at his cravat pin, her mouth a wry twist. "Nothing for me here. Perhaps Nottingham will benefit from a bold new milliner. I shall set a fashion. Red ribbons and cerulean plumes upon every head." She released a melancholy chuckle. "Mrs. Pritchard would be appalled."

It was then he heard it—silence, thick and distinct. It layered behind him like a pillow.

He swallowed. Straightened. Forced his hands away from her and slowly turned.

There they stood in a half-circle, all with mouths slightly agape. Hannah and Maureen appeared startled. Kate dropped the shawl she'd been holding. Lady Berne covered her lips with a handkerchief. Lady Wallingham peered at them sharply through her quizzing glass. And Lord Berne, arms crossed, stared at him with a father's wrath.

Damn and blast.

"To be clear, Holstoke," announced Lady Wallingham, "when I suggested casting your line into more desperate waters, I was not referring to the Huxley fish pond."

"Dorothea!" gasped Lady Berne.

Kate giggled.

Maureen turned pink.

Hannah frowned in confusion.

Berne resembled a cumulus cloud, thunderous and dark. "Holstoke," the ordinarily mild man barked. "In the library. At once."

Phineas gathered himself, realizing how intimate their conversation had appeared, how easily it might have been misinterpreted. He moved to place himself between the crowd and Eugenia, shielding her from direct view. "She is in her cups," he explained, clasping his hands behind his back.

"I most certainly am not! The wine made me a bit dizzy, but I am perfectly—"

"I apologize if my attempts to assist her seemed inappropriate—"

"—lucid. If anything, *you* are the one out of your head—"

"—but I felt I must prevent her from making a grave error on my behalf."

"—if you think Mr. Froom and Lord Glencombe will be mollified by—"

"Hush, Genie!" her father said. "Holstoke, I will speak with you in the library. Now."

Seeing no alternative, Phineas nodded and followed the older man out of the drawing room. Perhaps if he explained more clearly, Berne would understand.

He'd only touched her because it was necessary.

He wouldn't mention how his hands still tingled where they'd gripped her, how his cheek still pulsed oddly where she'd placed her palm. He could not explain the phenomenon to himself, let alone to her father.

Berne shut the library door with a firm crack. "I believed you a true gentleman."

"Matters are not as they appear, sir."

"No? So, that was not you clutching my daughter as though you meant to steal her away to the nearest bed?"

Berne's bluntness caught him like a blow to the chest. He needed air and an answer. He had neither. Lust hadn't driven him, but rather, the need to protect the little fool from her own impetuousness. Obviously, Berne had the wrong end of things.

Largely.

Perhaps ninety percent. Seventy-five at a minimum.

"It is ... she is ... my intention ..." Phineas released a breath and rubbed the back of his neck. "Bloody hell."

"Bloody hell, indeed," the other man snapped. "It seems I gave you the wrong impression this morning, Holstoke. Allow me to clarify. My daughter is *not* to be trifled with."

Phineas's muscles tightened, his head throbbing in earnest. "I sought only to protect her, Berne."

The man paced closer, hazel eyes no longer warm but flashing fury. "In her youth, she suffered a lapse in judgment, one for which she has paid a hundredfold. But any man who mistakes her for a lightskirt had best understand the risk he invokes. Never doubt her family will see that she is *protected*, Holstoke. I, for one, am a damned fine shot. Her brother is in Scotland, but he will return soon. And from his letters, it appears he's adopted a full measure of Highland barbarism."

His jaw hurt. Perhaps because he was grinding his teeth.

"You may have no liking for Dunston, but know this—the last man to take liberties with Eugenia was given numerous dagger scars for his trouble. Her other brother-in-law is the Duke of Blackmore. Shall I tell you how many vulgar pups Blackmore ruined when they dared apply that hateful epithet to my precious girl?"

Dunston had defended her? Earlier, he'd taunted Phineas with the "hateful epithet," provoking Phineas's intemperate response. He frowned. Perhaps that had been the point—provocation.

"Another thing, Holstoke. My daughters are not bloody well interchangeable."

His frown deepened, his neck twisting harder. What the devil was the man on about now?

"Maureen and Eugenia are the sun and the moon. Honey and ham. Each is a delight in her own right, but they are not the same."

Good God, was he implying ...?

"To use one as a substitute for the other is the lowest—"

"Enough." Phineas's voice was a quiet snap. Fortunately, he'd managed to control it before shouting the word. Did Berne think he did not understand the difference? What sort of depraved blackguard did he take him for? "Let me speak."

It took a moment, but Berne nodded.

"I swear to you that I have dishonored your daughter in no way whatever." He clamped down upon his anger again, surging and swelling in his chest before he got hold of it. "On the contrary. I admire your family, sir. I seek only to defend it. And her. If we appeared ... familiar, it is because of our long acquaintance. Lady Eugenia has taken an interest in my present difficulties. I am attempting to dissuade her from such notions."

The fatherly fire gradually diminished. Berne took a long time to answer. When he did, his voice was calmer. "As you should." He glanced down at his shoes then back up at Phineas. "She is headstrong."

Phineas nearly laughed at the understatement. Instead, he nodded and kept his expression neutral.

"Very well, Holstoke. If you swear upon your honor this is nothing more than a misunderstanding—"

"It is."

"Then I shall say only this." Berne's eyes, having resumed their amiable light, nevertheless hardened. "At the first hint of impropriety between you—particularly in a public setting—your wife hunt is over, my boy, for you'll be marrying Eugenia." Berne turned and opened the door, waving Phineas forward. "I may not have wanted a footman for a son-in-law, but the Earl of Holstoke?" Berne clapped him firmly on the shoulder as he passed. "You'll do splendidly."

Chapter Seven

"Impulsivity is scandal's boon companion, Eugenia. Invite one, and you might as well set your table for the other."

—THE DOWAGER MARCHIONESS OF WALLINGHAM to Lady Eugenia Huxley upon witnessing said lady's reckless offer to a certain pale-eyed earl.

∞

THE FOLLOWING DAY, SOMEWHERE BETWEEN BOND AND BOW Street, Phineas began to feel better. The previous night had been a disaster, true. He'd never been threatened with both hanging and marriage in the same hour before. But after a morning spar at Angelo's with an old chum from Harrow—who was both a weak swordsman and an excellent Home Secretary—he was beginning to think his circumstances less dire than he'd assumed.

Thirty or forty percent less, perhaps.

As his carriage passed a woman milking a cow, he ignored

the cacophony surrounding Covent Garden and reflected upon his chances. First, he was an earl. This was not an insignificant fact. Even Bow Street would hesitate to level charges of murder at a peer, whatever the suspicions.

Second, he intended to assist in the investigation. If, as Drayton reported, the poisons used in the murders were similar to his mother's, perhaps he could be of use, as he had been previously.

In the years after his mother's death, he'd made an exhaustive effort to identify her victims, unearthing her long fascination with poisons. Dunston, Drayton, and the gaming club owner Sebastian Reaver had all helped. Drayton had even been wounded while tracking the apothecary who had mixed the formulations. But none of them had possessed the necessary knowledge of botanical extracts. Phineas had. The only thing he and his mother had shared in common, in fact—apart from a bloodline—was an interest in plants. She'd employed various formulations over time, tailoring them to her needs.

With his father, for instance, she'd orchestrated a slow, debilitating death marked by a decline in mental faculties. He remembered his father before the "illness" had begun. Simon Brand had been quiet. Thoughtful. Remote but kind. Phineas recalled his father lifting him onto his shoulders to watch a balloon ascension, explaining how heat changed the weight of air. He remembered the day he'd departed for Harrow, how torn his father had looked, as though he'd wanted nothing more than to keep Phineas with him.

Simon had loved his son. He'd loved Hannah's mother, whom he'd met on a trip to Bath. He'd loved his daughter. But he had married a viper. And her venom had been his death.

A woman of exquisite coldness, his mother had targeted his father, a second son, like a serpent with prey. Within three months, Lydia Price had become Lydia Brand. Then, after engineering the deaths of Phineas's uncle and grandfather, she'd become the Countess of Holstoke. She'd craved influence among the aristocracy, pursued it with naked avarice, assuming that a title equated to acceptance. For a time, it had.

Eventually, however, the ton had rejected her. Apart from a smattering of susceptible men who worshipped her beauty, nobody desired to be near Lady Holstoke for long. Most sensed her unfeeling nature and sought to escape it, as Phineas had done.

By all rights, a son should not hate his mother, but apart from birthing him, she'd not been a mother at all. She'd consigned him to the care of nurses and tutors from birth, preferring to host entertainments and cultivate the gardens at Primvale Castle. Even in gardening, she'd had little use for him, often ridiculing his opinions and dismissing his knowledge out of hand.

As their dislike had been mutual, Phineas had managed to avoid her company—and she his—until six years ago, when he'd come to London to begin his search for a wife. Rather inexplicably, she'd insisted on accompanying him. Later, he'd realized her purpose: She'd devised a scheme selling specialized poisons to families who wished to hasten their inheritances. Phineas had been her excuse for establishing the necessary connections and staying in town.

It was hardly her first foray into criminality, of course. His mother's appetite for wealth and power had been bottomless, and she'd spent decades in the effort. Her illicit schemes had ranged from smuggling and thieving rings to brothels and gaming hells. Murder had simply been a means to an end.

Now, as his coach slowed on its approach to Bow Street, Phineas considered the deaths of Miss Froom and Lady Theodosia. His mother was gone, as were her accomplices, but her methods had been salaciously reported in *The Times* and other newspapers. Any madman who'd been capable of reading at the time might have decided to mimic her crimes.

Perhaps after the bodies had been examined by surgeons,

he might deduce whether the poisons were, in fact, similar in formulation to Lady Holstoke's or whether this was all some horrific coincidence.

The carriage halted outside the Bow Street police office. He waited for a market cart laden with flowers and fruit to rumble past before exiting and crossing to the door. Inside the dingy space, he noted the odd assortment of belligerent drunkards, red-waistcoated patrolmen, shame-faced wretches, sharp-eyed newspapermen, and resigned whores. A constable shoved one slovenly woman. The man laughed as she scurried away, tugging at her bodice and spitting in his general direction.

Phineas searched for Drayton within the dark and crowded room, but halfway across the rabble, his eye snagged upon an anomaly.

A small-waisted, proudly postured, distinctly female anomaly.

He weaved through the crowd, drawing closer.

Her walking gown was fine, green wool. Her bonnet sported two miniature pears and three gold feathers. The plumes bobbed as she spoke with a square-jawed, dark-haired officer who paused in taking notes to arch his brows and stifle a grin.

"All night, my lady?"

"All night," her sweet, throaty voice insisted. "Every night. There are no nights when he is not with me. Most mornings and afternoons, as well."

The officer shook his head and lost control of his grin. "His lordship has formidable vigor, eh?"

By God, Phineas should have insisted she be locked in her bedchamber. Now, it was too late for them both.

"Precisely so. *Formidable.* Yes. So, you see, he would have little time to spare on poisoning anyone, as we are together always. Except when he is at his club. Or attending one of his tedious garden lectures." She sniffed. "Mostly, he is with me."

Lightning burned through him, firing every fiber. It cracked and split and devoured until everything disappeared—the whores and the rabble, the barred windows and stench of desperation.

No, there was only this woman and the fate she'd unleashed—Eugenia Huxley would be his wife. No need to calculate likelihoods. This certainty measured one hundred percent.

The knowledge pounded beneath his skin. Quickened his heart, his breath. It tightened his groin until he could scarcely draw air. Automatically, his legs carried him within inches of her.

The officer glanced up. Sharp, world-weary eyes flared. He inclined his head. "My lord."

Gold plumes swiped Phineas's chin as she turned. Rich, cat-like eyes widened beneath a pair of pears. "Holstoke!" Her cheeks reddened. "I—I was just explaining." Her fingers fluttered. "To Mr. Hawthorn, that is. I was telling him—"

"I heard," Phineas snapped, clasping her slender arm above the elbow. "We are leaving."

Eugenia widened her eyes insistently, bobbing her plumed head in the runner's direction. "Perhaps we should ensure Mr. Hawthorn has no further questions."

The officer's gaze fell to Phineas's grip upon her arm, then to the fall of his trousers. The wry grin returned. "Unnecessary, my lady." Hawthorn arched a brow and met Phineas's eyes. "My questions have been answered for now."

"Oh. Well, then. I shall bid you good day, Mr. Hawthorn." She nodded crisply as though she'd passed the Bow Street runner in Covent Garden rather than confessing to spending "every night" being ravished by a man of "formidable vigor."

"Tell Drayton to come see me at Holstoke House," Phineas ordered through gritted teeth.

Hawthorn nodded, tapping his pencil against his notebook.

Phineas tugged his impetuous, maddening, audacious future bride through the throng and exited onto Bow Street.

"Holstoke," she squawked as he hauled her toward his carriage. "I can take a hack."

"We shall discuss it in the coach." He yanked open the door. "Get inside."

Sherry eyes blazed. "Don't be—"

He leaned down. "Get. Inside."

Something of his fury must have conveyed itself at last, for she simply swallowed and climbed inside. He barked an order to his coachman and followed her in.

For long seconds, he breathed and watched her and silently commanded both his anger and erection to retreat. Neither cooperated. Bloody hell.

"Staring is rude, Holstoke." She sniffed. "You should thank me."

"Thank you?" he murmured, incredulous.

"You are welcome."

"Damn and blast, woman."

"Cursing is also rude."

"I warned you not to do this. It is irreversible."

Her plumes bobbed as she raised her chin. "Good. My intention was to irreversibly exonerate you. And that is what I have done."

"What you have done," he said softly, "is force my hand."

"Don't be ridiculous. I rescued your neck from the noose. Further remedies are unnecessary, so long as you do not stupidly contradict me."

"I would have rescued my own neck, you little fool."

She folded her arms and shot him a disbelieving smirk. "How, pray tell?"

"By finding the real murderer."

She blinked. Her smirk disappeared. "Oh." She nibbled her lower lip then propped her elbow on her wrist and tapped that plump lip with a finger. The movement drew his eye like a bee to a blossom. "Still, such an investigation might take weeks. Months, even. By then, you would be on trial before the

House of Lords and reliant upon Dunston's dubious assistance. That would be bad. He doesn't like you. No, my solution is better. Let Hawthorn hunt the killer. By the looks of his attire, he could use the funds."

He offered no reply. At the moment, his body was riddled with lightning, and his hands gripped the seat to keep from reaching for her.

"Furthermore, it might be best for you to leave London. When I return to Nottinghamshire—"

"You are not going to Nottinghamshire."

That mouth—the one causing his blood to run hotter than it should—rounded and pursed. "What are you ...?"

He met her eyes. "I will leave London," he said. "And you will come with me."

Her throat rippled. "No, I—I don't think that's necessary. Hawthorn seemed well persuaded—"

"We will be married within a week."

"Married." She whispered the word. Her chest shuddered and quickened with rapid breaths. Her hands dropped to her lap.

"Then I shall take you to Primvale, where you will be safe."

"Holstoke."

"Hannah will be relieved. She prefers Dorsetshire."

"I do not want a husband. Furthermore, as potential wives go, I am a dreadful prospect. Dreadful. Only think of the humiliation. The scandal."

He leaned forward, struggling not to picture her lying beneath him, those fine lips engaged in a more worthwhile activity than endless arguments. "Perhaps you might have considered such things before you declared yourself my mistress."

She shook her head, golden plumes undulating in agitation. "I shan't agree to it."

"A license will take a few days, but if the church has an availability, there should be no delay."

"Maureen mentioned you wish to join Lord Gilforth's little plant club. A notorious wife will surely diminish your chances—"

He frowned. "The Horticultural Society of London is not a 'little plant club.' It is the foremost botanical organization in England. Its purpose is scientific inquiry."

"And if you wish to become a member, marrying the Huxley Harlot only further taints—"

"I warned you never to speak those words again, Eugenia."

"Denying reality benefits no one. Besides, I've no wish to live in Dorsetshire. Do they even have milliner's shops there?"

"Wishes do not matter. Choices do. You have made yours." He clenched his jaw. "And mine, it would seem."

"Nonsense."

Her pert response, along with her continued denials, inflamed him further. His body ached and throbbed. He forced himself to look away from her. It helped a bit. He noted the day had gone gray.

"Listen to me, Holstoke," she said after a long silence. "You are a man of admirable character."

She obviously knew nothing of his thoughts, for they were as far from "admirable" as thoughts could possibly be. He wanted inside—her mouth, her body. As though the certainty of marriage had opened some heretofore undiscovered gate, he was flooded with the near-uncontrollable urge to claim her.

Eugenia Huxley, of all women. An utterly irrational response to an utterly irrational female.

"If I believed my statement to Hawthorn would harm me or Kate or the rest of my family to any significant degree, I would not have done it," she continued, her voice calm and reasoned, her words nonsense. "But you must understand, all conceivable damage was done three years ago. There is nothing left to salvage."

"Nevertheless, we will marry."

"But ... I am a disgrace. You don't want me, and I don't

want a husband, and—"

"And you will be my wife by week's end." He steeled himself before returning his gaze to her. By God, she was a temptation. Defiant. Rebellious. A curved, cat-eyed provocation. "Accept it."

A perplexed frown crinkled her brow. "How am I to accept something so absurd—"

Between one blink and the next, he moved from his seat to hers. Another blink, and he had Eugenia flattened beneath him, startled and flushed.

"Accept it," he repeated.

Her bonnet slipped down low on her brow. He tugged the thing loose, eyeing her hair. He wanted to see it down. Spread out and shining.

She blinked up at him. "Good heavens, you really are furious with me, aren't you?"

Furious? In part, perhaps. Who could say with all the lust swirling about? Percentages were lost amidst the thunderous tumult, crackling hot and confusing.

He held her waist with one hand, braced himself above her with the other, taking care not to let her feel his hardness. If she mistook his need for anger, so much the better. Perhaps she would be intimidated into acquiescence.

"Accept it," he demanded again.

"You will regret this, Holstoke. There are things you don't know."

He lowered himself until her soft, sweet breasts cushioned his chest and her soft, sweet lips were near enough to kiss. "Accept it."

Her breath panted over his chin, her eyes searching his. "Do not blame me when you lament your decision. Remember this moment."

"Oh, I shall."

"Yes, well. Just recall who allowed chivalrous nonsense to ruin his life and who offered him a way out." She licked her lips and eyed his mouth. "You are him, in this instance."

He did not want out. He wanted *in.* "Say it, Eugenia."

She sighed, her eyes wistful. "At least my family will no longer bear the burden."

"Say it."

"Very well, Holstoke. I shall marry you."

Chapter Eight

*"A hat, however ostentatious, can only disguise
the deficiencies of its perch so long, Meredith."*

—The Dowager Marchioness of Wallingham to Lady Berne in
a moment of vexation at Lady Eugenia Huxley's wayward behavior.

―――※―――

Genie had been certain he meant to kiss her. Those pale eyes had flared dark; his breath had been upon her lips; his chest had pressed her flat against the seat.

By all rights, he should have kissed her.

But then the coach had jolted around a corner, he'd groaned as though pained, and whatever odd emotion had caused Holstoke to behave so unpredictably either dissipated or was brought under fierce control. He'd slowly pushed himself away, pulled her upright, and calmly retrieved her hat from the carriage floor.

She should have been relieved, of course. Kissing was not

her strong suit.

Instead, she wished she knew what those lips felt like against hers. She wished she'd been able to cup his jaw in her hands, breathe in his lemony scent, and discover the source of the heat that had made her heart pound at a thunderous pace.

Now, six days later, she sifted through her basket of red ribbons, hoping this dratted unease would pass soon. "Perhaps white would be better," she murmured. "White flowers, white gauze, white feathers."

"Ugh," Kate scoffed. "White is so ... un-Genie."

"Appropriate, you mean."

"Predictable. You are getting *married*. To Holstoke!" Kate laughed and ambled to the opposite corner of the parlor to pour a cup of tea. "Heavens, everything about this is surprising. Why should your hat be anything less?"

Genie propped her cheek against her hand and stared down at the beginnings of her headdress, which she was remaking for the third time.

Surprising. Yes, she supposed her imminent marriage was unexpected. The biggest surprise would be Holstoke's, of course. The only thing she dreaded more was the journey to Dorsetshire. Three days in a cramped carriage with the silent, fragile Hannah? Heavens, Genie would have to mind her every word.

"You know, it reminds me of a play," said Kate.

Genie snorted. "Of course it does."

"In *The Taming of the Shrew*, Katherina initially battles with Petruchio, yet they share a spark from the first. Their match is a contentious one, but it all ends rather well."

"For Petruchio, perhaps," Genie muttered.

"She even has a fetching younger sister who also marries." Kate plopped down on the chair beside Genie's. "Except the sister's name is Bianca. And *my* name is Katherine. And even if *your* name were Katherine, you would never agree to declare the sun was the moon at your husband's whim." She sipped her tea. "You would sooner bury him beneath your bridal bed, I suspect."

Genie plucked up a peacock feather and a violet ribbon, holding them up to the light. "So, you are saying my circumstances are nothing at all like your play."

"The comparison does fall apart a bit upon closer inspection."

This was why Genie rarely paid Kate much mind. Her sister—lovely though she was—spoke in a terribly circular fashion.

"Come to that, Holstoke would be more apt to cut down a brute like Petruchio than become one, himself." Another sip. "Particularly if *you* were treated roughly. Heavens, can you imagine? He was incensed by Mrs. Pritchard!" Kate chuckled.

"Holstoke is honorable." Genie discarded the peacock feather and replaced it with a yellow ostrich plume. "Too honorable, sometimes."

"He is quite protective of you."

Genie chose not to reply.

"One might say ferociously so."

"Do you have a point, Kate?"

"I think he cares for you."

Her heart twisted tight. "He cared for Maureen."

"That was ages ago. Surely you don't think he is still in love—"

"Holstoke is the protective sort," Genie retorted. "Only look at how he treats his sister. I am certain he would protect a ragged pup he found on the street, provided that pup did not eat his hat. It is simply who he is."

"Hmm. I doubt very much he would offer to marry a ragged pup."

"He has no special feeling for me, silly." Except that he *had* pinned her to the carriage seat and demanded she agree to wed him. She'd scarcely known what to say. Those eyes had pierced through every response, leaving her staggering.

She'd wanted to tell him the truth. Then, she'd thought of Mama and Papa and Kate. Dear, circular Kate with her Shakespeare obsession and sweet, fanciful notions about a love match. Kate deserved happiness untainted by scandal. Mama and Papa deserved to be released from the Great Burden of Genie. For that matter, Dunston and Blackmore deserved a respite from threatening all the rude men who insulted her.

She should have told Holstoke the truth. But after being dismissed from Mrs. Pritchard's employ, her plan to open a shop and achieve independence as a scandalously fashionable milliner had suffered a blow. If she could not even manage to remain employed as a lowly assistant for a full year, how could she expect to run her own shop successfully?

In truth, Holstoke's offer—demand, really—had come at a vulnerable time. She'd seen a way out, and she'd taken it. She would marry him, even though it transferred the Great Burden of Genie onto Holstoke's undeserving shoulders. Even though she might never be the sort of wife any fully functioning man would want.

She would try. That had been her silent vow as she'd gazed up into shockingly heated green ice and given the answer he'd wanted. She would try to be a good wife.

Surely Holstoke would not be *too* demanding. He'd always struck her as rather chilly, more interested in plants than passions. He hadn't seemed cold in the carriage, of course, but that had almost certainly been anger rather than ardor. No, in all probability, Holstoke would require little more from her than what was necessary to beget children.

And children would be lovely, even if the begetting was not.

Kate snorted. "You are daft. After the wedding, you will realize I am right. Whenever you're near, he seems unaccountably feverish. I cannot explain it."

Genie shook her head and dropped the yellow plume in favor of brown velvet ribbon. "Fairy stories again?"

Kate clicked her tongue and leaned across the table. Then, she plucked up a length of coral silk and draped it over Genie's wrist. "The red, dearest. It was red all along."

Later, as Genie pleated satin lining and stitched piping around a tall poke, she contemplated both the pitfalls and benefits of becoming Holstoke's wife.

First the pitfalls: They had little in common. According to Maureen, who corresponded regularly with Hannah, Holstoke spent much of his time pottering about his gardens and glass houses, writing scientific papers which he then submitted to the little plant club that continually denied him entry. Genie could not imagine a more tedious enterprise. She knew nothing about plants, apart from which ones best decorated a lady's coiffure, but surely there were more thrilling ways to spend one's hours.

Additionally, she had not lied about Dorsetshire. Rambling about the coastal countryside with nothing but wind and wildflowers to divert her thoughts from the abysmal loneliness? Good heavens. She must devise some useful purpose, else be driven mad.

As she unwound a length of green ribbon and began wrapping wire to form leaves and stems, she focused upon the more beneficial aspects of becoming Holstoke's wife.

Truly, she did admire the man. He was kind to his sister. Noble. Tall. And, as she'd come to realize, quite handsome in his way. The eyes were extraordinary, of course. The lips ... yes, he had superb lips. She might not even mind kissing if she were kissing Holstoke.

Sighing, she curved her green vine along the hat's brim and stitched it into place. Best not to delve too far into the subject of marital relations. It made her stomach bubble and ache.

She frowned and moved on to more practical considerations. A generous allowance was likely. He was wealthier than any man of her acquaintance—including the Duke of Blackmore. Maureen had described Holstoke's castle as "astonishingly palatial for an ascetic man." Genie wasn't certain she believed her, as Maureen could be overly lavish in her compliments. However, Lady Wallingham had once complained Holstoke was "determined to lay ownership to every grain of English soil." His holdings must be vast, indeed. Surely he would not begrudge his wife sufficient funds to purchase a few millinery supplies.

Her grin grew as she thought upon it. Oh, how splendid her new workshop would be—yards and yards of ribbon, acres and acres of lace. Proper shears and sturdy blocks and a sizable table. Ten—no, twelve feet at least. Yes, a long, beautiful table she need never share. Not with Fancy Nancy. Not with anyone at all.

Good heavens, this marriage might be just the thing. For the first time since Papa had kissed her forehead and shaken Holstoke's hand with hearty approval, she did not feel queasy. She felt ... good.

A tall, handsome, honorable husband whom she admired. Children, eventually—she quite enjoyed children. A generous allowance. The possibility of a truly expansive millinery workshop. This marriage promised to be far more palatable than she'd anticipated, particularly if Holstoke proved an undemanding husband.

She nibbled her lip. Unfortunately, she could not be certain of the last part until they were, in fact, husband and wife.

A knock sounded at the door. It was Emerson. "Beg your pardon, my lady. You have a visitor. Mr. Moody has asked to speak with you."

"Oh!" she exclaimed. "Do show him in."

Red-cheeked and smiling, Lewis Moody entered the parlor with his cap in hand and bowed. "M'lady. Thank ye for seein' me."

She stood and went to greet him. "Don't be silly, Lewis. I am pleased you've come. Tell me, how do you like working for Mr. Smith?"

"Splendid, m'lady. He is a most generous employer. Already, I have learned new methods of feltin' and ..." Lewis swallowed and dropped his eyes to his cap, twisting the thing in his hands. "That is why I come, m-m'lady."

"Lewis, do call me Eugenia. We were once conspirators, you and I," she teased. "Surely we needn't be so formal."

His eyes came up, gleaming and avid. Round cheeks flushed deeper until his freckles disappeared. "Lady Eugenia."

"Hmmph. That will do, I suppose." She gave him a chiding grin. "Now, what brings you here?"

He swallowed again. "I—I wish to thank ye proper, m'la—er, Lady Eugenia." The portly man blew out a breath and glanced to the ceiling before meeting her eyes once again. "Ye've shown me great kindness, and I am most grateful."

"Is that all? Oh, Lewis, you needn't have come all this way—"

He stepped closer. "It is what I most admire. Ye never treated me anythin' other than kind, though ye be a lady and I nothin' but a common hatter."

She tilted her head, acknowledging his thanks with a pat upon his shoulder. "Well, I am pleased you have landed well after I caused your misfortune."

Abruptly, he dropped to his knee and grasped her hand.

"Oh! What in—"

"I wish to pledge m'self to ye, m'lady. Lady Eugenia."

"Lewis, really. There is no need—"

He clutched her fingers and gazed up at her with a worshipful air. "I shall be yer knight, though I am but a humble hatter. And whenever ye have need of me, I shall come to ye at once. Or as quick as I can locate a hack. Assumin' walkin' ain't faster."

She swallowed the bubble of laughter that threatened to erupt. Sweet, silly man. He'd been reading too much *Ivanhoe*. "You are a true gallant, Lewis Moody." She wondered if she shouldn't fetch a wooden spoon and declare him Knight of the Ottoman Empire.

He kissed her fingers and grasped her hand in both of his. "My sword is yers, Lady Eugenia. Now and forever."

From the corner of her eye, she saw a tall, lean shadow move through the open doorway and into the light from the parlor window.

Drat. Drat, drat, drat.

"A man who wishes to continue breathing would be well advised to keep his sword a proper distance from a lady." The low, flinty voice flicked off the oak-paneled walls with an icy snap. Green eyes shone like frost. "Particularly this lady, who is soon to be my wife."

Genie's stomach sank.

Lewis's eyes went ridiculously round. He dropped her hand and scrambled to his feet. Spun to face the towering lord.

"Holstoke," she breathed, quickly stepping between the two men. "It was simply a gesture of gratitude ..."

He ignored her, stalking slowly toward Lewis, pinning the man with his unblinking stare. Heavens, Holstoke did have a talent for intimidation. He halted mere inches from her, straight and tall and cold, his hands clasped behind his back, his eyes boring into Lewis above her shoulder. Softly, he spoke one word: "Leave."

Lewis squeaked. And bowed. And fled. For a portly man, he moved fast.

"Was that really necessary?" she said, watching Lewis scurry away for a second time in one week.

She'd expected Holstoke to thaw after the other man's departure, but he merely transferred that frigid, opaque, penetrating stare to her.

"Why are you looking at me that way?"

Nothing shifted. He scarcely blinked, his neck rigid, his body still.

"Holstoke. Say something."

When he finally did, she wished she hadn't made the demand.

"As we will be married tomorrow, let us be clear, Eugenia." His voice was soft. Cold. "Whatever your prior proclivities, when you are my wife, you will conduct yourself as befits *my wife*."

"Proclivities," she murmured, her belly swooping painfully.

"I will not be made a fool."

It took a moment to catch her breath. "Is that what you think of me? That I have *proclivities*?"

"I am a rational man."

She snorted.

"Rationality means following reason and evidence to a logical conclusion. Where you are concerned, evidence abounds."

She hadn't thought anyone could make her bleed again. But he'd done it. The gash was a tearing pain through her middle. Breathing hurt. Looking at him hurt. Why had she thought he'd be different? Because he, too, refused to conform?

How daft. Even a peculiar man was still a man.

He leaned closer, no signs of annoyance or anger. Simply ice. He smelled lightly of lemons. Otherwise, he was a stranger. "Tomorrow, when you promise faithfulness, I will hold you to it," he said quietly. Carefully. Precisely. "Whatever might have come before is of little consequence. What comes after matters a great deal. Is this acceptable to you?"

She tightened her jaw. Steeled her spine. Opened her mouth to speak.

Lost her nerve.

She nodded.

Calmly, he straightened. "Then I shall see you at St. George's. Good day, Lady Eugenia."

Phineas dismounted onto Park Lane and handed the reins of Caballus to his groom. He took care with his movements. Slow. Steady. He tilted his head a bit to block the glare of the sun with his hat's brim, but also to watch the ground.

He was half-blind at the moment, flashes of white flickering around the edges of his vision. It was but a nuisance.

The knife piercing his skull was worse.

But even that did not compare to what lay beneath it. He'd crushed that black thing as small as he could. He'd wrapped it in logic and forced it down far below the surface.

There, it burned like a coal.

He'd ignored it while finalizing the marriage settlement with Lord Berne. He'd ignored it on the ride home. It did not like being ignored.

Entering Holstoke House, he handed his hat to the footman. The boy's handsome face swam in and out of his vision.

The coal flared bright, and he smothered it harder.

"My lord, would you care for a pot of your tea?"

He breathed until the urge to vomit passed. "Yes. Bring it to my chamber, if you please."

The footman nodded his understanding, a crinkle of sympathy edging his handsome brow. "Straight away."

Phineas moved to the stairs, easing up the first three steps before he heard voices. His sister. And a man.

He frowned, rubbing at his right temple. Climbing to the first floor, he followed the sounds toward the drawing room.

"When did you say Lord Holstoke would return?" the man asked.

"I did not."

"Mmm. I thought you had."

"You thought wrong, Mr. Hawthorn. One has the impression it is not the first time."

"Was that an insult, Miss Gray?" The man's voice sounded amused. Intrigued.

"An observation. The insult is your presence here."

As usual, Hannah's voice was supremely calm, but Phineas knew her well. A thread of apprehension—fear and worry—ran beneath.

He made his way to the open doors. Inside, Jonas Hawthorn stood too close to her, a mere foot away. Little wonder she'd treated him with hostility.

"Hawthorn," he snapped, wincing at his own voice. "What are you doing here?"

The runner turned slowly, as though reluctant to remove his eyes from Hannah. Her cheeks were ... pink. What the devil? Hannah rarely blushed. He had obviously upset her deeply.

Hawthorn crossed the room in a few long strides. He inclined his head briefly as he approached, the only sign of deference to Phineas's title. "Coroner's inquest for Miss Froom is complete. They've concluded murder by poisoning. I expect the results for Lady Theodosia shortly. Froom and Glencombe also have hired surgeons. Reports should come within the week. They remain convinced you're behind their daughters' deaths." A slow grin appeared. "Now, me? I don't believe it. Why would a murderer offer to help catch himself?" Hawthorn shook his head. "You do still intend to cooperate, don't you, Holstoke?"

Glaring light from the windows brightened the halos obscuring his vision. He struggled to bring Hawthorn's face into focus. Brown hair, gray eyes. Square jaw and deep cynicism. Handsome, he supposed, though a bit rough. He appeared to be around Phineas's age, an inch or two shorter—six feet, perhaps. Phineas blinked and examined the man's clothes. Rough, black wool coat. Brown trousers. Plain waistcoat. All were ill-fitting and loose, giving him the appearance of a vagabond.

Eugenia had been right. Hawthorn dressed quite plainly, as though he either couldn't afford better or couldn't be bothered. Bow Street runners typically received a middling salary, but those with ambition supplemented their incomes by claiming rewards offered by men like Froom and Glencombe. A competent officer could certainly afford a decent coat. A talented one could live quite comfortably, indeed. If Drayton hadn't already assured him Hawthorn was "the cleverest of the Bow Street lot," Phineas might assume his skills were as shabby as his apparel.

But he'd seen disguises before. His mother had worn one until the very end.

Narrowing his gaze, he glanced at Hannah, who lingered near the windows, her hands folded at her waist.

"As I gave my word, Mr. Hawthorn, and I am not inclined to break it, you may be certain of my cooperation," he said. "However, should I find you alone with my sister again, you will lose far more than my assistance. Understood?"

The other man raised a brow, cast a glance over his shoulder at Hannah and came back grinning. He chuckled and shook his head. "Understood." His eyes shone with a calculating light. "I also understand you intend to marry Lady Eugenia Huxley tomorrow."

"Yes."

Hawthorn glanced about the room, tapping his pencil against his notebook. "This is a fine house, my lord. Fine, indeed. Will you be staying in London awhile after the wedding? Or perhaps returning to ..." Hawthorn pretended to thumb through his notes. "Ah, yes. Dorsetshire. Primvale Castle. Grand name."

Already, Phineas was growing weary of the charade. Could the man not simply speak plainly? But then, the knife in his skull made him want to gouge out his own eyes, so his patience was short.

Additionally, there had been the incident with Eugenia. The black coal burned bright as his mind touched on the memory—her smile, brilliant with amused affection, aimed down at a man wrongly touching what rightly belonged to Phineas—but once again, he forced it to recede. To be ruled by his pain or his anger or that unidentified blackness was to be rendered weak. He must be strong. For Hannah. For Eugenia. For himself.

"London for several days," he answered the runner. "Then, we leave for Dorsetshire. You may give the reports to Drayton. He will ensure I receive them."

"Oh, I shouldn't like for any important documents to be lost. I shall deliver them personally, my lord."

"Do not trouble yourself."

"No trouble." Again, the man glanced back at Hannah. "None at all." Then, he turned and bowed with a hint of mockery in Hannah's direction before placing his plain, worn hat upon his head. "Miss Gray. A splendid good morning to you." He turned back to Phineas and gave a brief nod. "My lord."

As he departed, Phineas felt as though a wolf had just left the room. Hannah appeared to agree, gliding toward Phineas with a look of relief. It was quickly shadowed by concern. "Phineas," she sighed. "Your tea. Shall I fetch it for you?"

"No." He pressed the heel of his hand into his right temple. It didn't help, but it was something. "It is likely already in my chamber."

She nodded, the little furrow of concern deepening. "You should lie down."

"What did he say before I arrived?"

Her lips tightened. Her nose flared. "Nothing important. He is a very ... irritating creature."

"If he calls again whilst I am not here, turn him away and send one of the footmen to follow him until he is well out of Mayfair."

"He fancies himself charming, I think. I do not find him so."

Phineas lowered his hand. By God, his head was pounding. And the nausea was now constant.

"I find him presumptuous. And vexing."

"Will you be all right, little one?" he murmured, focusing his control upon keeping his breakfast where it was.

She blinked. "Yes, of course." Blinked again. "You should lie down," she repeated.

He nodded and turned, bracing himself against the doorframe. He paused, losing command of the black coal. It burned and reminded and insisted. "Hannah. I must ask a favor."

"Anything."

"I need a list of footmen. All the footmen at Holstoke House and Primvale."

"Footmen? Well, I suppose I could ask Sackford or Mrs. Varney. But you really should be resting."

The coal burned hotter. He clenched his jaw against its power. "I must do a bit of ... rearranging before tomorrow. Will you—"

Her small hand settled on his arm. "Of course I will."

"The grooms, too. Groundskeepers." He frowned, rubbing his temple. "All the male servants, really."

She sighed. "Very well. Go now, Phineas. Drink your tea. Let tomorrow be tomorrow."

He wished he could. But at least that strange, black coal had been quieted. Rearranging. Yes. A highly logical answer to an irrational need.

Entering his bedchamber, he passed the handsome footman again. Pleasant young man. Showing deference and concern for his employer.

William was his name. William would have to go.

Phineas closed the door and then the draperies. His valet helped him remove his coat and waistcoat, his boots and cravat. He drank a cup of his tea, hoping this formulation worked better than the last. His valet took the tray away. Finally, Phineas threw back the blankets and sprawled beneath.

His eyes slid closed. Then, in the darkness, she appeared. Mahogany hair loose and gleaming. Cat-like eyes shimmering a challenge. She was naked, her confounding geometry revealed to his gaze.

His heart kicked as his body hardened, defying the pain in his head. He would take her in the garden, just as the sun broke across the horizon. He would see her bathed in gold.

Let tomorrow be tomorrow, Hannah had said.

He did not know how. For, despite the knifing pain, the thing devouring him now was an infernal, inexplicable hunger. Tomorrow would not change it.

But it would make her his. And perhaps, he thought as he stared up at the ceiling and envisioned her in the sweet light of dawn. Perhaps if he applied logic and rationality to the problem, having her would be enough.

FROM THE FRINGES OF THE PARK, HE WATCHED THE LORD ENTER his house. The man stepped carefully, as though he could not see well. While he was but a dim echo of the goddess who had birthed him, an echo of divinity was better than none at all.

Earlier, a ragged hunter had entered Holstoke House. Polite tip of his hat. Friendly pretense. The Supplicant was not fooled. He'd employed similar tactics, himself. Most people never looked beyond the surface.

Long minutes passed. Before him, Park Lane teemed in the bright light. Gilded carriages and gleaming mounts. Behind him, a parade of vermin displayed their costumes, mimicking gods. They, too, were disguised. Unlike the hunter and the goddess's son, they pretended to be more than what they were, rather than less.

The black door opened. The hunter stepped out, tucking something into his loose coat. He had the look of a worthy *opponent—sharp and savage. Long, swift strides took the hunter along Park Lane. For a moment, the Supplicant considered staying. He must observe Holstoke House with great diligence. A goddess's son required no less.*

But the hunter was of interest. A worthy opponent. Yes.

He adjusted his wig. Gave Holstoke House a final glance. Then, with swift strides of his own, he followed the man in the loose coat. A hunter disguised as a harmless hound. A worthy opponent, indeed.

Chapter Nine

"The promise of obedience means little when it has been so recently discarded in favor of satisfying one's illicit appetites."

—THE DOWAGER MARCHIONESS OF WALLINGHAM to her boon companion, Humphrey, upon said companion's implied vow of obedience in exchange for another bite of ham.

∞

"TO LOVE, CHERISH, AND TO OBEY," THE PRIEST REPEATED FOR the second time.

Genie swallowed and gazed up at Holstoke, looming like a green-eyed raven inside a halo of Belgian lace and ivory satin. Dear heaven, what a glower. She really should complete her vows. But the words lodged in her throat as surely as a fish bone.

"My lady," whispered the priest. "You must repeat this portion as well."

Holstoke's hold upon her right hand tightened. His nose

flared. His eyes narrowed.

"To—to love, cherish ..."

The silence in the church thickened. Her stomach cramped. He refused to look away.

Finally, she forced the words out. "And to obey."

The remainder of the vows came easier, thank heaven. Holstoke slid a rather plain ring upon her hand, and they were declared man and wife. They knelt while the priest nattered on about husbandly love and wifely submission. The latter portion was significantly longer than the former, she noted.

Then, at great length and all too soon, it was done.

She was Lady Holstoke.

As they stood and turned to face the church together, she glanced up at her newly minted husband. Something about his demeanor had changed. It was subtle—a softening at the corners of his mouth, a thawing of the ice in his eyes. She blinked, uncertain what to make of it. He seemed eased, as though he'd been ravenous and now was quenched.

After yesterday morning, she'd half expected him to cry off. His coldness had frozen her through, a seamless, impenetrable shell around the man she'd come to know.

But did she know him, really? They'd spent the past six years apart. Certainly, *she* had changed in that time, and Holstoke had been through a great many hardships. It might explain the odd—and insulting—reaction to Mr. Moody's silly declaration. Perhaps he'd been remembering Maureen's rejection in favor of another man.

Yes, perhaps that was it.

A queer ache squeezed her chest. Her eyes drifted to the pew where Maureen and Dunston sat. Maureen, cradling her youngest son, beamed and brushed a tear from her cheek. Dunston looked amused. Again, Genie cast a glance at Holstoke, expecting him to be similarly preoccupied with Maureen. Instead, she found him staring at her. A shiver rippled across her skin.

Organ music played. Kate handed her the bouquet of violets, rosebuds, ivy, and the extraordinary red lilies Holstoke had sent to Berne House that morning. She clutched the flowers and Holstoke's arm. Took a deep breath and blew upward, rippling her Belgian lace. Silently, she prayed as she'd never prayed before that neither of them regretted their decision. *Please, God,* she begged. *Let him be a passionless sort. For his sake and mine.*

An hour later, seated beside Holstoke at the Berne House dining table, she wondered how best to test him. A kiss seemed prudent. But it might be misconstrued as an invitation to retire early, and she was certainly in no rush. She sighed and searched the room for a prospective advisor on matters of an amorous nature.

She drifted to Papa, then to Mama, who laughed merrily at little Edwin's antics and asked Lady Wallingham, "Tell me, Dorothea. Is Bain clever enough to stand upon his head?"

"Hmmph. He is clever enough *not* to, Meredith," Lady Wallingham replied. "My grandson has better uses for his head than replacing perfectly functional feet."

Genie continued her perusal of the table. Silent and stony, Hannah lifted a spoonful of syllabub to her lips. Holstoke's sister watched Sophie and Merry spinning in their little white gowns and ivy wreaths. A hint of a smile appeared briefly before she dropped her gaze again to the table.

Though Hannah had been papery and lusterless throughout the morning, her gown was lovely: soft, leaf-green gauze with a round, daintily ruffled neckline, white embroidery at the hem, and a white taffeta sash at the waist. Genie had long admired the other girl's taste in gowns. Her choice of hats ran toward the plain, of course, but perhaps with Genie's influence, she could be persuaded to add a few feathers or even some dashing little fruits.

Chewing a forkful of ham, she contemplated her reflection in a silver tureen. Her own hat was a masterpiece: ivory silk,

Belgian lace, coral-red roses, green leaves and vines, and a bit of azure piping the very color of Genie's gown. She glanced down at her bodice, admiring once again the bias-cut blue silk that molded to her shape. Yes, her wedding ensemble had been fully "Genie," as Kate had observed. Even Mama had wept upon seeing her, clasping Genie tightly and whispering what a beautiful bride she made. Genie's throat had tightened, and she'd squeezed her mother in return.

Mama was free now. So, for that matter, were Papa and Kate. She'd made the proper decision for her family.

None of which would help her when Holstoke decided to claim his husbandly rights.

The ham stuck in her throat. She chased it with a bit of tea.

Drat. Both Jane and Annabelle had recently birthed new offspring, so they were busy wallowing in domesticity with their husbands in Yorkshire and Nottinghamshire, respectively. The only married sister in attendance was Maureen.

And Genie would sooner ask Lady Wallingham for advice.

There was Kate, of course, but Kate was both unmarried and far too fanciful. Likely she would quote a Shakespeare sonnet about comparing Holstoke to a summer's day, or some such nonsense.

Genie took another sip of tea as she completed her circuit of the table. She frowned. This was dreadful. Was there no one who might answer a few pressing questions?

"Butter, my lord?" a footman asked.

"Yes. Tea for my wife, as well." The low, flinty voice came from beside her.

She blinked. Set her empty teacup down with a clatter. Turned wide eyes up to him.

And there he was—green ice and black hair and the faintest smile. He calmly buttered a roll and asked, "What has you bothered?"

The footman poured tea, and the children squealed, and

her family chattered away, but all of it faded into nothingness.

"Holstoke," she breathed.

"Eugenia." His smile deepened. His eyes returned to hers.

She shivered, though not from cold. "I have questions."

"For me?"

"I think ... yes. You ... precisely."

He set his roll on his plate. "Ask away."

"Not here."

His smile quirked deeper along one side. "Where?"

After a moment, she suggested, "The library."

He managed to ensconce them in the library—alone—approximately three minutes later. The man was efficient, she would grant him that. He closed the door and came toward her, hands clasped behind his back. "Now, then. What did you wish to ask?"

Swallowing hard and resting her backside against the writing desk, she crossed her arms. "First, you should know I do not regret anything."

He remained silent, though he continued forward.

"Our marriage cannot be reversed. And whilst it was unfair to transfer the Great Burden of Genie into your hands, I nevertheless believe it was right."

He was close, now. Inches away. His eyes gleamed in the shadowy room.

"Well," she continued, wishing the pressure in her chest would ease. "Right for my family, at least."

His eyes moved to her skirts, then to her hat, then to her lips.

"Besides which, you were unlikely to do much better, Holstoke." She wetted her lips to stop them tingling. "Murder is no small scandal."

"Eugenia."

"You were the one who insisted we marry, remember. I was all set to return to—"

"Ask your questions."

She nibbled her lip and nodded. "How—how often will you wish to ..." She paused to clear her throat, as it was unaccountably dry. "That is, what sort of frequency will you require in the area of ..."

He frowned. "Of?"

"Marital congress."

He froze. Right there, before her eyes. Like a lake solidified by a cold snap.

"There is the necessary task of begetting children, of course," she said, hoping for a thaw. "I should like to have children, I think."

Still, he said nothing.

"But you may find my nature somewhat ..." She dropped her gaze to his cravat pin. An emerald, she noted. "Lacking." Her breath shuddered. "I should have told you before now, but this marriage—I do want it, Holstoke. I want it to work. But I may not be a very pleasing wife for a man of ... strong appetites."

Silence fell between them. She was afraid to look up. Afraid of what she might see. Instead, she watched his chest rise and fall in a steady, controlled rhythm.

Finally, he spoke, his voice quiet and a bit hoarse. "Is that a bird perched on your hat, Eugenia?"

Her eyes flew up and found him frowning at her hat's poke. "Yes. 'Nature's splendor' is the motif. Notice I reduced the ostrich plumes to three, so that he appears to be poised amidst a garden in bloom—"

"Would you object if I removed it?"

"The bird?"

"Your hat."

She blinked. "I suppose not." Her hands lifted to grasp the brim.

His hands were there first. "Let me." Gently, he removed her pins and lifted the hat away.

She automatically reached up to smooth her hair into place.

"I should like to see it down," he murmured, eyes intent upon her undoubtedly flattened curls.

"Yes, well. If you find my appearance objectionable, you may blame yourself. A lady's coiffure requires reassembly after—"

"When we are at Primvale, I will show you my greenhouse."

Glowering up at him, she grunted her annoyance. "You are avoiding my question, Holstoke."

"Hmm. What was it, again?"

"You know very well."

"Remind me."

Releasing an exasperated hiss, she snapped, "How often will you wish to bed me?"

His eyes returned to hers. They were glowing. "Often."

Her stomach dropped into her feet, her lower belly aching. A rush of prickling heat was followed by squeezing despair. "What—what of kissing?"

"That, too."

"Oh, God. This is a disaster."

"How so?"

"I am dreadful at all of it, Holstoke," she confessed in a rush. "The kissing. The touching. The ... everything." Once again, she focused upon his cravat pin. She was glad he'd taken her advice. Emeralds suited him.

Several heartbeats of silence were followed by a single, softly spoken word: "Explain."

"I am frigid."

"Not your conclusion, Eugenia. Your evidence."

She shook her head then adjusted the folds of his cravat and chuckled her despair. "My sisters—the married ones, that is—all said the same thing: 'It is wondrous, Genie! The tingles and the closeness and the pleasure,' and on and on." She rolled her eyes. "Hmmph. What a lot of rot." She stroked the emerald pin with her fingertip. "Perhaps for them it is pleasurable. I doubt they lied about it. They do seem to enjoy their husbands' attentions." She sniffed and settled her palm on his chest, just to the right of the pin.

He held his silence, though the rhythm of his breathing quickened a bit.

Her finger returned to stroking his pin. "During my season, I experimented. I let two separate gentlemen kiss me. My sisters had filled my head with nonsense, of course, so perhaps my expectations were too high, but even accounting for that, both occasions were ... well, *disappointing* would be putting it mildly. The first gentleman was reported to be quite expert, but I found his efforts appallingly invasive. A bit like someone forcing a bite of food into your mouth. Firstly, that bite of food had best be ham, not some dry, stringy duck peppered with snuff. Secondly, I should prefer to wield my own fork, thank you."

While she spoke, Holstoke had moved closer. Now, he leaned into her, his hands bracing on the desk beside her hips. She liked this position. It let her rest her forehead against the soft, fine wool of his lapel. She turned her head to keep her eyes on the emerald, her thumb stroking and stroking.

"I assumed I had simply selected the wrong gentleman. So I tried again with another. If anything, he was worse. I've had more pleasurable experiences being mauled by Lady Wallingham's hound."

"What is his name?" Holstoke said softly.

"Humphrey. He is a good dog. Quite lovable, really, if a bit exuberant."

"Not the dog. The gentleman."

"Oh. Preston. Mr. James Preston. Another expert." She snorted.

"And the first gentleman?"

She sighed. "It's of little consequence. He married one of Lord Aldridge's daughters two years ago, and they are dreadfully happy." She smoothed Holstoke's cravat and studied his waistcoat, a fine silver brocade. "No, there is something wrong with me. For a time, I considered whether I suffered from an unnatural distaste for gentlemen of a certain stature. The ton is afflicted with vapidity, you know." She paused, gathering her courage.

Holstoke was her husband. He should know the truth.

"The scandal," she continued, "was another experiment."

He stiffened against her, his shoulders going rigid, his voice going dark. "The footman?"

"I had formed a hypothesis. Is that not what a scientist does?"

He did not answer, holding very still.

"Well, I may not be a scientist, but I needed the answer, Holstoke. I needed to know for certain whether I was ... indifferent."

She closed her eyes, remembering that night. She'd worn a lovely white gown with puffed sleeves and an exquisite shawl of French lace. Her hair had been elaborately plaited and woven with pearls and orange blossoms.

She'd imbibed enough orgeat punch to tip the world sideways. Then, she'd permitted herself to flirt with the handsomest footman she'd ever seen—one she'd likely never see again. She'd paid a second footman for information, gladdened to discover the first footman was known for "dallying with his betters." The ideal choice for an experimental assignation.

She'd lured him to Lord Reedham's conservatory, a glass room turned blue by moonlight. Heavens, he'd been handsome. Tall and strong. Confident in his every movement. She'd invited him to kiss her, certain it would feel different.

It had not. Instead, it, too, had been an invasion, foreign and strange. The footman had touched her, grasped her, stroked her with effortless persuasion. He'd kissed her neck and her shoulders. His breath had been hot and damp. She recalled thinking it felt as though Humphrey were breathing upon her.

She'd wanted to enjoy his attentions. Wanted so badly to

experience what her sisters had described. But she'd felt nothing. No tingles. No excitement. Only vague distaste and hollow despair.

"What was his name?"

Genie blinked. Her eyes widened. *Drat.* Drat, drat, drat. She had blurted out her entire pathetic tale to her new husband. Well, except how it all had ended. The end was the most pathetic part.

"His name? I—I don't remember, really. Thomas, I think. Or Edward. I was a bit tipsy."

Holstoke's chest pumped deeper now with every breath.

She lifted her cheek away from his coat and glanced up, but angled above her as he was, she could not see much—only the lower part of his jaw. The muscles there were flickering.

"You mustn't be cross, Holstoke. The scandal was my doing, not his. Had I imbibed less punch, perhaps I would not have chosen a room made of glass for our—"

"Based on three experiences, you have concluded that you are frigid."

"Well, yes. Rather persuasive evidence, you must admit."

His chest shuddered. He hung his head then shook it. The new position gave her a better view of his face. His eyes were closed, his features unsmiling and carefully still. He blew out a breath and opened those exceptional eyes. "Eugenia."

She searched his face, tracing the lines of his mouth. Her heart gave a restless kick. "Yes?"

"I propose a fourth experiment."

"I fail to see how this will help—"

"We are married now. It is worthwhile to try, wouldn't you say?"

Her belly clenched as she gazed up at her new husband. A good man. An honorable man. And evidently, a man of stronger appetites than she'd suspected. Yes. For his sake, she would try. "So long as you are prepared for disappointment."

"An experiment free of expectation is likewise free from

disappointment," he countered. "Its purpose is to answer a question. From there, we shall refine our conclusions with further experiments until we devise a sensible path forward."

She narrowed her eyes upon him. This sounded like rubbish. But perhaps a man like Holstoke needed to verify things for himself.

"By the sound of it, these 'experiments' might go on for years," she observed dryly.

A tiny tug at the corner of his lips caused a pang in her chest. "Let us begin with this one," he murmured.

"Very well." She closed her eyes and tilted her face up.

And waited.

Nothing.

Her eyes popped open. Holstoke gazed down at her. His face was unreadable, yet she sensed amusement.

"Holstoke?"

"You've already conducted your experiments, Eugenia. This is mine."

"And I have agreed to participate."

"So, you will do as I instruct?"

"I will do what is necessary."

His nose flared as he breathed in. His exhale was scented with lemon and mint. "Here is how we'll begin. I shall touch a part of you, and you tell me how it makes you feel. Are you ready?"

"Why do you always smell of lemons?"

A furrow formed between black brows.

"Lemons and mint," she clarified.

"Does it displease you?"

"No. I quite like it."

"Probably *Melissa officinalis*. Lemon balm. I take it in my tea."

"Oh."

"Stop avoiding the experiment, Eugenia."

She sniffed. "Go on, then. Touch me."

He did, but not where she'd expected. He touched her hair. Lightly. Softly. He smoothed his fingertips down from her center part over the curls near her ear. Then, he traced his thumb along the sensitive line where her hair met her nape.

When he stopped, she could scarcely breathe. Her skin was covered in gooseflesh.

"How did that feel? Be specific."

"Sh-shivery. Little chills everywhere."

This time, his mouth curled a bit. "Good. Let's try another spot, hmm?"

His thumb moved down to stroke the side of her neck. Other men had kissed her there with scarcely any effect, so her expectations were dim. But Holstoke's thumb had some sort of magic in it. The sensations spiraled outward in a burst. His touch was light, like a butterfly landing. Then it pulsed like wings.

Her breath caught. Her eyes slid closed. "What is ... what is that thing you're doing?"

"This?"

"Mmm."

"Only touching you. How do you like it?"

She swallowed. "Feels like a butterfly."

A pause. "Is that good?"

She nodded, too breathless to form words.

He ran a knuckle along her collarbone. Magic followed in a glittering trail. With great effort, she opened her eyes. Wondered how it might be if she touched him similarly. At present, his neck was encased in a stock and cravat, but that shouldn't take long to remedy. Her fingers clutched at his lapels.

"Tell me, Eugenia," he said. "Are you warm yet?"

She paused. Until he'd asked, she would not have used such a description. There were too many chills to think of heat. But now that he mentioned it, she did feel warm. Hot, in fact. Her skin tingled and throbbed as though reaching for him.

"I—I am." A groan escaped her throat. "Why is that?"

His hands fell to her waist. He flattened one palm over her belly, his fingers cupping the lower portion, pressuring just a bit. "And here?"

"M-melting. It feels—I ache there, Holstoke." Eyes flying wide, she panted and searched his face.

He gave her nothing apart from his hands, keeping his gaze lowered upon her mouth.

"I think you should kiss me," she suggested.

Faintly, he smiled.

"Really," she insisted. "I don't mind."

"Let us try something first."

Impatience tightened her grip upon his lapels. "I wish to feel your lips, Holstoke. Now."

Pale green came up glowing yet dark. "You will."

The melting worsened. Her muscles ached. She could not get enough air.

Then, he lowered his mouth to the place his thumb had stroked earlier. Softly, he hovered and breathed. Blew the gentlest stream of air upon her neck.

Without warning, her legs gave way. He caught her waist in his hands, holding her in place effortlessly. His lips touched her skin. A butterfly's kiss. Scarcely there, yet so powerful, she could not bear the showering sparks. They traveled along her skin, spiraling out to her bosoms and down to where he'd pressed her belly. Then lower.

She gasped and gripped and groaned. "What in blazes, Holstoke? I ... you must ... do something."

He did, but it only made matters worse. Those fine lips nibbled. Then suckled. Then moved to her shoulder, where he employed light strokes of his tongue. Finally, he moved his mouth to her ear, where warm breath whispered, "How do you feel, Eugenia?"

Yanking hard at his coat, she flattened her bosoms against his ribs. It only helped a little. "Afire. That's how. I need you to do something."

"What would you have me do?" he murmured, his voice raw in her ear.

In answer, she leaned back, reached down, grasped his hand, and laid it upon her breast. "Oh, heavens." Her eyes drifted closed. "Yes. That's better. Now, kiss me."

His hand slid away, his palm caressing her nipple lightly before returning to her waist.

"No, Holstoke. Put it back. God, please."

"There you go commandeering the experiment again. I shall give you your kiss, but only if you stay very still."

It was then she realized she'd been writhing. Undulating against him in a bid to get relief. She looked up into his eyes. Heat deepened and burned.

She examined his lips, firm and defined. The feverish need to feel them against hers demanded she do whatever was necessary. Gripping his lapels, she forced her hips back against the desk, forced her body to remain motionless. She nodded.

He lowered his head. Breathed against her lips, the delicious scent of lemon and mint and ... him. Something about him was intoxicating. He made her head spin.

Those wondrous lips brushed hers. Once again, his stroke was light as a butterfly. She chased it, wanting more of the sparks he seemed to possess in every inch of his skin. Good heavens, what a thought. She could touch him anywhere on his body and have this strange pleasure bloom wherever the point of contact happened to occur.

At the moment, it was occurring between their mouths. His opened over hers. She tensed, bracing for an invasion. But it did not come. Instead, he breathed into her. Caressed her lips with his. Squeezed her waist and grinned against her.

She frowned. Why was he not invading?

A flicker brushed her lower lip. Warm. Wet. Sleek and slow and furtive.

She ... liked it. Seeking more, she stood on her toes and

tilted her head to fit her mouth more fully against his.

He gave her what she asked, but his tongue was soft and elusive. She pursued it with her own, her heart pounding furiously as she tasted the inside of his mouth. Clean. Delicious. A feast she wanted to devour.

She moaned, enjoying the pleasurable hum. Suddenly, his hands moved to the sides of her neck, cupping and holding and gripping. Oh, yes. That was the way. Her hands clutched wool and pulled hard. Her breasts pressured and pleasured themselves against him. Her hips did a dance of their own.

Their mouths fused. She could not get enough. She would never get enough. Of his kiss. Of his touch. Of his tongue.

Holstoke. Oh, God. She needed more of him.

Her heart pounded—*drum, drum, drum.*

Drum, drum, drum.

He pulled that enchanting mouth away, his breath coming fast and hot against her tingling lips. He cupped her cheeks, stroked her brow with his thumb, then muttered, "Damn and blast."

"Holstoke!" shouted Dunston through the library door. "For God's sake, man. That can wait. This cannot." *Bang, bang, bang.* "Open up!"

Disoriented, Genie blinked as Holstoke brushed his lips against hers one final time before withdrawing his wondrous touch. He turned stiffly, straightened and buttoned his coat, then stalked to the door, unlocking and yanking it wide.

"What the devil do you want?"

Dunston was not smiling, and he was not alone. Mr. Drayton stood by his side, equally grave. Behind them, Maureen had her arm around Hannah's shoulders. Holstoke's sister was even whiter than usual.

Drayton was the first to speak. "There's been two more murders, m'lord. Lady Randall was found this mornin'. Two of her dogs were also killed. Appears she was feedin' the animals from her own cup."

Still reeling from the dizzying heat of Holstoke's kiss and the shocking desolation of his sudden removal, she could only cover her mouth and brace herself against the desk behind her. She watched her husband's shoulders stiffen.

"You said two murders," he said, his voice low and surprisingly calm. "I trust you were not referring to the dogs."

"No, m'lord. Sorry to say, it's your housekeeper. Mrs. Varney."

Faintly, she heard Maureen murmuring to Hannah. The girl's lips were white. Genie noticed an unfamiliar maid with tears on her cheeks hovering in the background. One of the Holstoke House servants, no doubt, come to deliver the dreadful news.

Dunston peered past Holstoke and met Genie's eyes. She'd seen her brother-in-law this grim only once before—when a wealthy young blood had decided to "have a go" at the Huxley Harlot. She'd been working late at Mrs. Pritchard's shop. Dunston and Maureen, who had offered to drive her home on their way back from the theatre, were parked one street over, as Genie usually requested.

When she'd exited the shop, fussing with her reticule, the blackguard had been waiting for her. A short time later, just as the man shoved her against grimy bricks and grasped a handful of her skirts, Dunston and his daggers had arrived to deliver punishment with ruthless precision.

Genie had been grateful for Dunston's darker nature that day. But, in truth, she'd hoped never to see it again, for it heralded danger to her or someone she loved.

"Henry," she said now, her insides going cold. "Why is this poisoner circling Holstoke? And how—how has he managed to get so close?"

He pushed into the room, striding to her and warming her hands in his. "We don't yet know, Brat." It was his name for her, one adopted from Maureen and filled with brotherly affection. Hearing it made her want to hug him. "But we will.

Do you hear? We will."

She nodded and squeezed, her entire body beginning to tremble like jam.

From the doorway, her husband began to order things to his liking with a series of commands. His voice was low, but all the more resonant for it. "Claudette, return to Holstoke House and arrange for my and Miss Gray's belongings to be loaded onto the travel coach. Inform the staff I shall arrive shortly."

The maid curtsied and murmured, "Yes, m'lord," before scurrying away.

"Mr. Drayton," Holstoke continued crisply. "Summon Mr. Hawthorn. And reiterate my intent to assist in the investigation. Perhaps knowing I was in a church standing before a priest and a dozen witnesses when these crimes occurred will turn his attention in a more productive direction." Finally, his eyes found Genie.

She lost a breath then regained it and blew it out. "Holstoke."

His nose flared. His chin elevated as though he resented what he was about to say. "Pack your belongings, as well. We leave for Primvale this evening."

Chapter Ten

"I had my suspicions, you know. One does not discover vile things on one's carpets without realizing something is amiss."

—THE DOWAGER MARCHIONESS OF WALLINGHAM to her butler upon learning of her housekeeper's fondness for gin.

○∞○

CROUCHING BESIDE HIS DECEASED HOUSEKEEPER, PHINEAS did the only thing a rational man could do with unfathomable blackness eating him from inside.

He ignored it.

What had begun as a coal had bloomed into something vast and volatile. Nothing would be solved by giving in. But, if he applied logic to more tangible problems—finding the devil who had murdered his housekeeper and three other women, for instance—perhaps that blackness would diminish of its own accord.

Thus, he turned his attention to Mrs. Varney, who lay

sprawled on the gold carpet of the dining room, her pupils unusually wide. Her lips were wrinkled and parched. One of her hands still clutched the leg of a chair.

"Anybody unfamiliar about?" Drayton's question was directed to Holstoke House's butler, Sackford. "New servants?"

"No, sir," Sackford replied, his voice somber. "In preparing for his lordship's departure, Mrs. Varney and I had begun reducing the household staff."

"What about visitors? Deliverymen and the like?"

"Not to my knowledge. But I shall make inquiries." Sackford's voice grew thin. "She often took her tea whilst gathering his lordship's herbs each morning. She loved the garden, did Mrs. Varney."

Beside Phineas, Dunston knelt with an elbow propped on his knee. The other lord pointed to the woman's eyes. "See that?"

"Yes," Phineas replied. "*Atropa belladonna*, most likely."

"Nightshade. Your mother never used it, as I recall."

"No. For her purposes, the appearance of a natural death was paramount."

"Yet, this blighter seems determined to be caught."

"Not caught, perhaps." Phineas eyed the woman's hand, still curled around fluted mahogany. "But acknowledged."

Dunston nodded. "He has managed to capture your attention."

Yes, he had. And that had been an error. The blackness Phineas struggled to contain wanted many things, but nothing more fervently than to eliminate the abhorrent creature who had done this. He held his breath as the blackness expanded and threatened to take hold.

A hand clapped him on the shoulder. "Try not to cast up your accounts, old chap. The stench is rather pungent, but think of the mess. You are without a housekeeper at present."

He blew out his breath and rubbed at his brow. "Bloody hell, you are perverse."

"Occasionally. Maureen rarely complains, however. I am a fortunate man."

Phineas supposed the comment was meant as a taunt, but it didn't land. He frowned and examined the other man. Relaxed yet focused, Dunston scanned the room methodically, first the body then two overturned chairs.

This was the man who had hunted Phineas's mother for a decade, chasing a woman who had fooled everyone—including her husband and son. By using accomplices and intermediaries, she'd managed to elude capture for many years. But no one had come closer than the Earl of Dunston, and no one had been more dogged in his pursuit. Later, one of her accomplices confessed Lady Holstoke had long been terrified of him. She'd thought him a phantom haunting her every move.

Phineas must protect Eugenia and Hannah. Thus, he required help from a man like Dunston. He turned and met eyes like sharpened steel, gratified to see his own resolve reflected there. "I need men," he muttered. "Enough to keep her safe."

A faint smile appeared. "To which 'her' are you referring, Holstoke?"

Blinking, Phineas paused. He hadn't meant to speak aloud. The blackness had spoken for him.

Dunston chuckled. "Never mind. You shall have five by tonight."

"Seven."

"Very well. Seven. Though, I should warn you, there will never be enough men to ease that vise round your chest."

Bloody hell. That was it precisely. He was being crushed. Suffocated.

Phineas shoved to his feet and rubbed his neck. Strode past Dunston and paced the room. Searched for something. Anything to ease the pressure.

Yet, he saw only Mrs. Varney, vacant and cold.

The vise tightened until he wanted to tear something apart.

Hawthorn entered just as Drayton finished questioning the maid who had discovered Mrs. Varney's body. As usual, the Bow Street runner looked as though he'd fallen from his bed into a vagabond's clothes.

"What the devil took you so long, Hawthorn?" Phineas snapped.

The runner busied himself digging his notebook from his pocket. He gave Phineas a seemingly friendly grin before patting his chest and withdrawing a pencil. "Ah, here we are. Forever misplacing them, it seems." He approached Mrs. Varney, taking in the overturned chairs and signs of poison. "Apologies for the delay, Holstoke. Lord Randall was a mite distraught. He was quite fond of one of the dogs that perished, you see."

Phineas glared at the man, who bent forward to peer at Mrs. Varney's face.

"Dicky, I believe the animal was called," Hawthorn continued. "Randall mentioned an incident involving your hat."

Rubbing his brow, Phineas bit down on the urge to strike Hawthorn and instead replied, "I did not bloody well murder a dog because it damaged my hat."

Hawthorn used his pencil to pry open Mrs. Varney's mouth, cringing at the stench. "Haven't claimed you did." He opened his notebook and began writing. "Still," he said absently before grinning up at Phineas. "Would be interesting if the dog were the target of a vengeful plot, no?"

What was it about men like Dunston and Hawthorn and this perverse humor in the midst of horror? Phineas found nothing about this amusing. Not one damned thing.

Drayton approached from across the room, his limp worsening with the passing hours. "Accordin' to the maid, Mrs. Varney was actin' most strange when she came in from the garden. Quarrelsome and laughin' by turns. Then she began stumbling about and complaining of needing to lie down. The kitchen maids assumed she'd been at his lordship's brandy. She made it far as the dining room when the girl heard the clatter. Must have been the chairs toppling. She says when she entered, Mrs. Varney was lyin' where you see her, clutching the chair tight as can be." Drayton glanced down at his notes and scratched his head. "Curious thing, m'lord. Though she was several feet away at the time, the girl says she could hear the woman's heart beatin' and that it sounded like horses at a gallop."

Tendrils of unease began at the back of Phineas's mind. It was a familiar sensation, one he often felt when he was conducting experiments or working through a new theory and a part of the pattern failed to align properly.

He glanced again at Mrs. Varney's hand. It lay curled around the chair, even in death.

"Did Mrs. Varney say anything?" Phineas asked. "At the end."

Again, Drayton examined his notes. "Just nonsense. Flyin' apart, she said. Mrs. Varney complained she was flyin' apart."

There it was. The piece that hadn't fit.

"So she grasped the nearest thing," Phineas murmured. "It was not *Atropa belladonna*. Or, at least, not merely *Atropa belladonna*. The poisoner also used *Hyoscyamus niger*."

All three men turned to him with similar hard focus.

"Speak English, Holstoke," said Dunston.

"Henbane. Same family as belladonna—*solanaceae*. Similar effects when ingested, except that henbane gives one the illusion of flying or, in some, of flying apart." He frowned and glanced again at Mrs. Varney. "The dose had to have been quite high for her to die so rapidly. Odd."

"What's odd about it?" asked Hawthorn.

"The first taste would have been bitter and, indeed, malodorous. Henbane is rather unpleasant, as plants go. Tea would not have disguised it."

Hawthorn straightened, dispensing with his earlier affability. "Would gin?"

Phineas considered it. "Possibly. Though the required concentrations still preclude the use of the plants themselves, in my estimation. The poisons must have come from medicinal grains one finds at—"

"An apothecary," Dunston said, dark and silken. "Like the one your mother employed."

Drayton shuffled forward, rubbing his thigh as though it pained him. "That one's dead. Watched him suffocate from the inside, I did." The Bow Street runner shuddered and ran a hand down his haggard face. "Still have nightmares sometimes."

"Lady Randall had a fondness for gin," Hawthorn commented. "She drank it in lieu of her morning tea. And, incidentally, shared it with her dogs."

"How quickly did she perish?" Phineas asked.

"Not as quickly as Dicky." Hawthorn grinned. Again, the runner's dark humor made Phineas frown, though Dunston appeared amused. "But within a quarter-hour of finishing her morning 'tea' she collapsed. We've examined the cup. It smelled of gin and orgeat."

"Orgeat." Phineas's neck prickled. "You mean almonds."

Hawthorn nodded.

Mrs. Varney's cup had been washed by one of the scullery maids before anyone had realized something was wrong. But Phineas would wager every one of his Suffolk properties that her cup would have mirrored Lady Randall's. The scent of almonds had been a common description in the murders his mother had engineered.

Dunston appeared to follow his thoughts. "Multiple poisons, then. Similar to—"

"My mother's methods. Yes."

"We are back to apothecaries."

Phineas shook his head. "Not necessarily. It could be

anybody with enough coin to purchase the medicines and enough time to perfect his formula, though he would need subjects for experimentation. Animals, perhaps."

"Or patients," countered Drayton, once again rubbing his thigh. "Who would question a surgeon's stock?"

"There are no reports of surgeons visiting any of the victims prior to their deaths," Hawthorn interjected.

"Who'd they have in common, then?" Drayton asked.

Hawthorn looked pointedly at Phineas.

Phineas glared back at him.

"Well, let's see," said Dunston casually. "Miss Froom and Lady Theodosia both attended Lady Randall's soiree. That's three of your victims right there. And Miss Froom was, in fact, poisoned at that very event. Suggests it was someone present in Lord Randall's home that evening."

Drayton grunted. "Scores of guests that night, m'lord."

"Indeed. Myself included. And Lord Randall, who apparently had more love for the late, lamented Dicky than his wife. Alas, much as I should enjoy seeing Holstoke hauled away to the gallows, he departed fully two hours before Miss Froom's collapse." He waved toward Mrs. Varney. "As we've seen, the effects appear within a quarter-hour."

Hawthorn turned to Phineas again. "Lady Holstoke sold her formulas to her victims' complicit relatives. She was miles away when the poison did its work. Is that not so, my lord?"

Phineas's patience evaporated. "Your suspicions of me waste time we do not have," he snapped. "This blackguard has managed to kill four women inside a bloody month without leaving a hint as to his identity. He could be anyone. And, for some ungodly reason, he has trained his sights upon me." His voice lowered until the blackness turned it rough and gritted. "I will not countenance the threat to my wife and sister, Hawthorn. With or without your assistance, that threat will be found and eliminated. I suggest you do not stand in my way."

The other man cocked his head. He glanced at Dunston

then Drayton then back to Phineas. "How do you intend to protect them, Holstoke? As you say, the murderer could be anyone."

"We are leaving London tonight."

"For Dorsetshire."

"Yes."

Hawthorn nodded. "Miss Gray, too?"

"I would hardly leave my sister behind."

"You have men?"

Phineas blinked. Frowned. "Dunston is providing some."

Another nod. "How many?"

"I offered five," Dunston answered. "He insisted on seven."

For a moment, Hawthorn's mask disappeared, and Phineas had a glimpse of the true man.

His original instincts had been correct. Hawthorn was a wolf.

"Watch for new faces," the runner warned, voice hard and jaw harder. "Anybody comes near her that you haven't known longer than six months, get rid of him. Servants. Visitors. Physicians or bloody parsons. Trust no one, Holstoke."

Phineas weighed the need to have a wolf's aid against the need to warn him away from Hannah. The divide was roughly fifty percent. But the warning could wait. For now, a wolf was willing to join the hunt, and Phineas was not fool enough to turn him down.

"I will keep my family safe," he vowed. "Have no doubt."

The wolf grinned. "Then go to Dorsetshire, my lord. And leave London to me."

Chapter Eleven

"Finished? Are you mad, girl? A long and arduous journey demands full preparation, the extent of which you have clearly failed to comprehend."

—The Dowager Marchioness of Wallingham to her lady's maid in reply to the assertion that a shawl would suffice for an evening at the theater.

∞

"Drat," Genie muttered, tossing aside her third-favorite half-boots in favor of her fifth-favorite bonnet. "Where is Harry with the spare trunk?"

Kate sighed and reached for a pair of spangled crimson slippers. "I have always adored these."

Shoving hard at the pile of gowns and shawls and bonnets and reticules inside the overstuffed trunk, Genie straightened and threw up her hands as the lid popped open. "How can he expect me to pack everything in one afternoon? This is madness." She blew upward and turned toward Kate, who sat on Genie's bed admiring Genie's slippers—on her own feet. "Kate!"

Kate looked up.

"I already gave you my green pair."

"But these will match my new tartan gown."

"Stop coveting my possessions and come help me close this trunk."

She scooted off the bed, and together, they sat on the lid. After Genie managed to lock it into place, Kate grinned and patted her knee. "Whatever will you do without me?"

The flood came without warning, rushing in and rolling her flat. Her eyes filled until Kate's face—so like her own—swam and swirled.

"Oh, Genie." Her sister's slender arms grasped tight and held her close.

"I don't know," Genie rasped, swiping away dratted tears and clutching Kate in return. Her throat hurt. Her eyes leaked. Worst of all, her chest felt as though someone was sitting upon it. "What does one do without one's dearest friend? Languish, I suppose." She swiped more tears and laid her cheek upon Kate's shoulder.

"You have Holstoke now."

Genie gave a damp snort.

"And Hannah. She seems ... pleasant."

"Oh, God."

"I shall come for long visits. And we shall write all the time. Every day."

"I hate writing."

"Send me sketches instead. Hats upon hats."

"I'll miss you dreadfully."

"Even my singing?"

"Yes, even that."

Kate giggled, the sound wet and choked.

Genie gathered in a sigh and straightened. She brushed the tears gently away from Kate's cheeks and gave a trembling smile. Then, she nodded and slid off the trunk. "Never let your modiste persuade you to wear yellow again, dearest. Only Maureen looks lovely in it. The rest of us look like lemons."

This time, Kate laughed fully.

Outside, the sound of carriage wheels echoed along Grosvenor Street. Genie moved to the window and drew aside the draperies.

"Drat!"

"He is here already?"

The travel coach was large but plain. Well-sprung and probably expensive, but it sported no crest, no ornaments. It was simply a mode of transport, pulled by six stout horses.

"Drat, drat, drat. I am scarcely half finished."

"I shall go and find Harry and Bess. They must have located the trunk by now."

Genie waved her fingers in Katie's direction, but she kept her eye upon the carriage. He climbed out a moment later, tall and lean and darkly handsome in his black coat and silver waistcoat and emerald cravat pin. Her heart thudded and swooped. Her belly heated as it had earlier, when he'd kissed her.

Oh, heavens. How he'd kissed her.

Her fingers drifted to her lips. She could feel him there, even hours later. What did *this* man's lips have that other men's did not? It was Holstoke, for pity's sake. Chilly, peculiar Holstoke.

He spoke to the coachman and nodded to the two footmen who came out to begin loading the carriage. Three strides toward the front door, he paused. Glanced up. Those pale eyes flashed bright in the late-day sun.

Found her.

She drew in a breath. Turned her fingertips against the glass.

His gaze sharpened until her middle went soft as warm butter. His nostrils flared, and he removed his hat. But he did not look away.

"Apologies, my lady," Harry said behind her. "The trunk was buried beneath a pile of old draperies."

"Aye," concurred Bess, who served as lady's maid to Genie and Kate. "Appears an animal got to 'em. Claw marks everywhere."

Genie swallowed and finally managed to turn away from the window. "My mother's cat," she said, remembering the near-feral creature. "He was a menace."

Bess, a pleasantly round young woman with blonde curls and a dimpled smile, grinned and replied, "Oh, I adore cats."

"Yes, well. Unfortunately for Papa, so does my mother." Genie chuckled and traced the fine scar on her right hand, a memento of the irascible creature. "Papa insisted she keep the draperies as a reminder of her last attempt to bring one into the house."

The cat had been consigned to the stables shortly after Maureen had declined Holstoke's proposal and married Dunston. She could still recall Holstoke's reaction to the animal—he'd been bewildered by Papa's indulgence of Mama's feline fixation.

Once again, Genie felt a flood of useless, unwanted sentiment press in upon her. Dear Papa with his cat-induced sneezing and boundless patience. Sweet Mama with her problem-solving luncheons and her long, fierce hugs. How Genie would miss them.

With a firm effort, she stilled her trembling lip. She blinked away maudlin tears, grasped a pile of stays and drawers and stockings, then placed them inside the spare trunk. "Help me, Bess. We must hurry. Lord Holstoke has already arrived."

A short while later, it became obvious she could take *some* of her hats, but not all.

"Drat." She tossed a lace cap beside the handkerchiefs Maureen had embroidered for her and eyed the pink bonnet she often wore with her rose carriage dress.

"That one might be easiest to remake, my lady," Bess commented while tucking Genie's gloves into the crevices of a bulging valise. "It has fewer adornments."

"Mmm." Genie tapped her lips. "But the color is an unusual shade. Who can say whether I shall ever achieve it again?"

Behind her, she heard Harry huffing as he entered. She glanced over her shoulder then grinned her delight as she saw what he delivered. "Oh, how marvelous!" She rushed forward to throw open the small trunk. At least now, she'd be able to take her pink bonnet. The rose carriage dress was simply less lovely without it. "I would kiss you, but that might start rumors neither of us want."

The footman flushed.

Genie patted his arm and laughed. "A jest, Harry. Thank you. This is precisely what I needed."

"It has been five hours, Eugenia," came a frigid snap from the doorway. "Why are you not yet ready?"

She spun to see Holstoke looking as though a blizzard had turned him into ice-encrusted stone. She blinked, unsure what had changed in the few minutes since she'd felt that strange charge of heat flash up three stories and melt her through paned glass. Despite the freeze, she planted her hands on her hips and answered, "Packing takes time, Holstoke."

"You have had a week."

"Not to plan for Dorsetshire. Have you any idea how many trunks are required to—"

"Haul whatever trunks are ready down to the carriage. We depart in ten minutes."

For a moment, she thought the icy command was meant for her. But Harry snapped his heels together and uttered, "Yes, my lord," before Genie could muster a reply. The footman left carrying one of the smaller packed trunks.

"Ten minutes, Eugenia. Whatever is not loaded onto the coach will remain here."

She snorted. "Including me?"

He took two steps into the room as though propelled by a force beyond his control. Then, he stopped and rolled his shoulders. "You go where I go. Whether you are ready or not." His gaze flickered to her gown. "Is that your carriage dress?"

She looked down at the blue bias silk. Inside, a sharp pain stabbed between her heart and stomach. "This is my wedding gown, Holstoke." She'd been reluctant to remove it, wanting to hold on to the memory of their kiss for as long as possible. Every breathless, tingling, shivery moment. For him, by contrast, the encounter had clearly been a trifle, meaningless and forgettable. "Perhaps if I were a plant, you would find these details of greater interest."

Frowning fiercely, he took another step forward. "There is only one detail I am concerned with—that is putting distance between you and a murderer. You do recall the murderer lurking about and poisoning housekeepers, do you not?"

"I am not a halfwit, Holstoke, despite what you seem to think of me—"

"We must leave. Now, Eugenia."

"I am nearly finished. Miraculous when you consider how little warning you gave me."

Another step closer. His shoulders were rigid with tension. "You are done," he said softly. "Fetch a wrap. We are leaving." Those pale eyes bored into her as though he could glare her into compliance.

She sniffed. "An hour here or there will make no—"

"Ten minutes. Delay any longer, and I shall haul you outside myself."

She opened her mouth to reply.

"Do not try my patience, Eugenia. This has been a bloody wretched day."

She flinched. Blinked away a sudden sting in her eyes. Swallowed a sudden tightness in her throat. Wretched? That was how he regarded the day of their wedding, their first kiss? *Wretched.*

"Leave," she said quietly, breathing away the hurt.

He did not move, his eyes on her mouth.

"I'll be down shortly." She brushed past him to hold open the door. "Leave me to finish."

He did as she asked, but his movements were stiff and reluctant. He glanced back at her, a furrow between his brows.

She closed the door on him and stiffened her spine. "We have ten minutes," she said to a wide-eyed Bess. "Let us make them count."

Precisely ten minutes later, Genie climbed into Holstoke's plain, black traveling coach and nodded to Holstoke's still, silent sister. Inside, the carriage was plush and roomy. Genie took the seat opposite Hannah's, piling her blanket and basket of supplies beside her.

Holstoke could sit elsewhere, as far as she was concerned.

"Phineas asked me to inform you he will ride separately," Hannah said in her customary serene tone. "He suggested you try to rest, as our first stop will be hours from now, and we shall depart again at dawn."

Examining the girl, Genie frowned. They were of an age, she and Hannah, both two-and-twenty. And yet, the other girl seemed both much younger and much older.

Innocent and ancient. That was Hannah Gray.

Of course, her life had been horrid until she'd discovered her half-brother. Maureen had changed that—given Holstoke his beloved sister, given Hannah a family with whom she felt safe. Maureen had been a friend to them both.

Genie, on the other hand, was a virtual stranger. Now, seated across from Hannah, she felt it more keenly than ever. The girl was her sister by marriage, and yet her expression was closed. Composed. Cold.

Even if Holstoke and Hannah had not inherited those distinctive eyes, she would have seen a resemblance. They both had a gift for wearing winter as a mask.

The coach jerked into motion. The late-evening sun angled

low and red through the window. It shone on Hannah's bonnet.

Her unremarkable straw bonnet.

"Have you considered adding flowers to your hats?" Genie inquired, hoping to pass the time in a way that might be useful and perhaps induce a thaw.

Pale, familiar eyes blinked and examined her like an insect. A loathsome insect. "No."

"You should."

Silence.

"Nothing too bold, mind you. Daisies, perhaps. A touch of ribbon to match—"

"I like my hats as they are." Winter had clearly set in with no thaw in sight. "I like most things as they are." The girl turned her head to watch out the window. "Or were."

The last two words were a whisper.

But Genie heard quite clearly.

She sat back and folded her arms. Narrowed her eyes and tapped her lip. "Things rarely stay the same, you know. We are all like toads riding in a decrepit old cart. Just when we settle in to live our comfortable little toad lives, the cart runs out of a rut and into a hedge, and we all go flying." She'd used the same analogy with her nieces and nephews, who had subsequently demanded to know what became of the toads, whether they'd found new homes beside a lovely pond or in a grove of trees. Children were quite literal, she'd found. "One is well advised to learn how to leap and how to land, however predictable the road appears."

Again, silence.

"Now, about your hats. I have some ideas, but I concede you may have to see them in practice before you agree they are brilliant." Genie tapped her finger against her lips again. "Which they are."

Hannah's gently sloped jaw tightened. Otherwise, she did not respond.

Genie dug through her basket and withdrew her sketchbook and pencil. "Your gowns are exquisite. It will not take much to improve the overall ensemble. Flowers or greenery here and there, perhaps. I am fond of feathers, but"—she squinted at Hannah's soft features and pale skin—"not for you, I think."

She began sketching, letting the girl sit and stare and sulk because life was changing more than she liked.

"I prefer my hats as they are," Hannah repeated, keeping her eyes to the window.

It was going to be a long night, Genie thought as she sketched the beginnings of a new creation. A long night, indeed.

HE DID NOT CLAIM HIS WIFE THE FIRST NIGHT. THE INN WAS rough, and he spent the few hours of their stay speaking with Dunston's men. There were seven, and all had a similar look to Dunston and Hawthorn and Drayton—hard and vigilant.

Their presence eased his mind perhaps ten percent.

Neither did he claim his wife the second night, for they pushed on, traveling straight through.

Mid-morning, they stopped at a coaching inn twenty miles from Primvale. Caballus was exhausted. Phineas could scarcely see, his vision weary and blurred. He needed a bath and a shave.

He needed to claim his wife.

By God, that blackness had grown thorns. It wound around his insides and infected his mind. If he'd understood it, he might have some chance of controlling it. But he did not. So it grew.

And it wanted certain things. It wanted to kill the man who threatened her. It wanted to punish footmen and hatters upon whom she bestowed her smile. It wanted to lay her out upon a bed or a bench or the blasted grass and thrust until she looked at him the way she had in the library.

With wonder. Desire. Discovery.

The lust was vaguely familiar, though it was a bit like comparing a tuft of grass to a towering oak. He'd had mistresses. He'd made a study of them, in fact. He liked exploring a woman's pleasures and textures and idiosyncrasies until the mystery disappeared. That often took years. So, he'd had four mistresses in his life, the most recent lasting the shortest duration at two years.

All of them had been lovely women and pleasant companions. None had evoked the kind of need he felt for Eugenia. It clawed and demanded. It dug in and cut deep.

Likewise, he'd never contemplated physically attacking other men over a woman. The very notion was primal nonsense. Irrational.

But the blackness was defined by its irrationality. And although he'd used his time on the journey to Primvale to work at the problem, those bloody wants had only hardened.

Now, as he patted Caballus's neck and dismounted in front of the inn's stable, he stretched weary legs and glanced back at the two coaches pulling into the small courtyard. One entire carriage had been required to haul Eugenia's load of trunks. Fortunately, he'd anticipated the necessity. He hadn't realized quite how many new gowns Hannah had purchased during the season, but that, too, made him glad to have arranged it.

The lead coach rolled to a stop near the inn's door. Hannah exited first. She looked as exhausted as Caballus, with dark rings beneath her eyes and pale, pinched lips.

Phineas crossed the small courtyard and approached his sister. "Go inside, little one," he said, gently cupping her elbow as she navigated piles of muck. "Purchase something to eat. It is a couple of hours yet to Primvale."

She sighed and leaned against him briefly. "I shall. Would you care for anything, Phineas?"

He began to answer, but his attention wandered. Riveted. To the woman climbing out of the coach. Her bonnet appeared first—it was delicate pink, like the inside of a seashell. Next, he could see her bodice, a deeper, redder shade of the same color. He'd produced a rose that hue once. She emerged from the coach like a painting of Venus—at least, that was how it felt to him, for she glowed like a goddess.

"Phineas?"

Her skin was ivory and her eyes sherry in a shaft of sunlight. What would she say if he simply lifted her back into the coach and showed her what pleasure could be?

"Phineas." A tug at his arm.

He looked down.

Hannah appeared annoyed. "Do you want anything?"

Yes. He wanted a bed and Eugenia. Or merely Eugenia. The bed was preferable, but secondary. He could take her standing up in a stable, if necessary.

Swallowing, he watched his wife step down and wrinkle her nose. She settled her skirts, tilted her chin, and wove her way to the inn's door without once glancing in his direction. Meanwhile, his heart thundered. His vision sharpened upon her perfectly confounding hips.

"Phineas!"

"Nothing," he answered, his voice down to a thread. "I'll be along in a moment."

He heard what sounded like a snort or a huff, but thought it must be one of the horses. Hannah did not make such noises.

No, that was more of a Eugenia trait.

He nearly smiled at the thought. When she was vexed or dubious or simply impatient, Eugenia made all sorts of little sounds. She rolled her eyes and delivered sharp rebukes. She shoved and swatted and breathed fire. He never had to wonder whether she was angry. Eugenia did not mince words.

Regrettably, he'd upset her on their wedding day by

cutting short her packing, and she hadn't spoken to him for the entire journey. Good God, the woman had more hats than sense. Didn't she realize how dangerous the situation was?

Perhaps he'd been abrupt. But what did she expect? She'd been jesting about kissing a footman, of all things, then had *touched* that same footman and flashed a grin dazzling enough to turn a man inside out.

Eugenia needed barriers. She needed a firm hand and clear rules. She needed to cease touching other males.

"Eh! You, there. Make way!"

Phineas blinked and glanced behind him. An old man glowered down from atop a crate-loaded wagon. The man's wife, tucking her knitting into a basket at her feet, also frowned.

Damn and blast. He'd been standing in the middle of the inn's courtyard staring at the door through which his wife had disappeared. This blackness had muddled his mind.

He rubbed his neck and went inside the inn, wondering whether she would speak to him if he bought her some ham.

Eugenia sat beside a weary Hannah, drinking from a wooden cup with a hearty appetite. She plunked down her cup and chattered at his sister, who glared down at the scarred tabletop with a stony expression.

Phineas searched out the innkeeper and requested some ale for himself, then approached the ladies and sat on the bench opposite them.

"Feathers add height, you know. Now, for some, that is a crucial feature. Lady Wallingham, for example, never goes about without a feather or two. I also enjoy their grandeur."

Hannah heaved a great sigh and turned her glare to the filthy courtyard window.

Phineas looked from one lady to the other and frowned. Something was amiss, but he could not be certain what it was. "I assume the discussion is hats," he ventured.

Eugenia pretended he hadn't spoken. "Ordinarily, I would

not recommend feathers for you, but in the case of a riding habit—"

"I do not ride," Hannah snapped.

His frown deepened. What the devil?

Sniffing, Eugenia took another drink of her ale. "You should," she told Hannah. "It helps clear the mind."

"My mind is perfectly clear."

"Improves one's disposition."

This time, Phineas heard the snort clearly. Fancy that. Hannah snorting.

"I daresay riding might well be the cure for an intractable sulk. In my experience, it is far more enjoyable than stewing in self-pity." She took another drink. "Though, that does have its merits."

Phineas cleared his throat.

"I shall teach you," Eugenia continued. "Assuming Primvale possesses an adequate stable, and you possess a modicum of capability, I would guess you'll be riding for pleasure at least once every day. Mornings are best."

"I do not ride."

The seething hostility in those words stunned him. He'd never seen his fragile, gentle sister behave this way.

Blithely, Eugenia retorted, "You do not ride *now*. That is why I must teach you."

"I don't wish to learn."

"Well, that much is evident." Eugenia's wry utterance was accompanied by an eye-roll.

The innkeeper set a large tankard of ale in front of him, but Phineas could not look away from the bizarre interchange between his wife and sister, neither of whom had yet bothered to acknowledge his presence.

"Many wishes go unfulfilled, sadly," Eugenia continued. "I wished to bring along four additional capotes and three bonnets, for example. Yet I was forced to leave them behind. Now, I shall require twice the allowance Holstoke originally planned." She *tsked*. "Remaking hats is costly, as some designs require specialized materials."

His frown deepened. At last, she was speaking to him, albeit indirectly. He elected to answer her charge with a helpful explanation. "We had to leave when we did, Eugenia. Delays would have increased the chances of the poisoner—"

"So, how much does Holstoke grant for your allowance, Hannah?"

"That is none of your concern," came Hannah's reply.

"Perhaps not, but I should like to know. Come now, tell me honestly. It is astonishingly generous, is it not? Yes, it must be. Those gowns of yours are divine. Madame Legrande's work, if I am not mistaken. An unparalleled talent—grand, indeed." She chuckled again at her own pun. "I have several of her creations. Papa was not as generous as Holstoke." Eugenia blinked and tapped her lips with her finger. "Now that I think upon it, even Holstoke is not as generous as he is *going* to be." This time, Eugenia's message was sharpened and aimed exclusively for him.

Bloody hell.

He made an attempt to intervene. "Eugenia, this is a topic best reserved for—"

"Now, then. Once we arrive at Holstoke's little castle, and we've had a chance to settle into our comfortable little routines, we shall assess your skill in the saddle."

"I prefer walking."

"Hmm. Yes. Oddly, preferences are much like wishes. Another excellent example: Holstoke prefers not being accused of murder. And yet, that is precisely what happened. Had it not been for certain timely interventions, he might yet stand accused with nary an alibi in sight."

He sighed and drank his ale. It was weak and flat. Perhaps he should return to the stables.

"In the end, one would assume a bit of gratitude might be in order. Timely interventions do not come along every day."

Eugenia tipped back the last of her own ale and thudded her cup onto the table with some force. "Alas, whilst one might *expect* gratitude, one may never receive the merest jot. And whilst that is dreadfully rude and disappointing, it is not unexpected."

The innkeeper delivered a basket of bread and a plate of sliced ham.

Thank God, Phineas thought. Perhaps food will improve matters.

It didn't. Hannah promptly gathered up a hunk of bread and a slice of ham before rising from the table and heading for the door.

"Hmmph," Genie muttered before shrugging and doing likewise.

Phineas grasped her wrist as she brushed by. "Eugenia."

She stopped, but she did not look at him.

He stroked her fine-boned wrist with his thumb, again struck by how small she was. "I know you are … displeased with me."

A snort.

"Granting you more time would have put you in greater danger—"

"It was not the hats, Holstoke." Her voice was unusually low and even.

He stood. Turned her to face him. Tugged her closer until he could smell violets. "What, then?"

She kept her eyes lowered upon his coat. Her lips were tight. If he wanted the faintest chance of kissing them later—and he did—he assumed discovering what he had done to vex her so thoroughly would be to his advantage.

He pulled her closer. Lowered his head. "Tell me."

"You demanded I agree to marry you. And so I have."

He frowned. "To preserve your reputation after you announced to all and sundry—"

"You demanded I let you kiss me. And so I have."

"An experiment you quite enjoyed, if I recall—"

"You demanded I leave my home and my possessions and everything familiar with less warning than you would give your cook when requesting kippers for breakfast. And so I have."

She still refused to meet his eyes, and it was stoking the blackness inside him. He did not like this Eugenia—calm and flat and, somehow, wounded. He wanted the woman who laughed and touched him without thinking.

"You demanded I follow you to this land of grass and cows and nothingness." She finally raised her eyes to his. They were snapping fire. "And so I have."

He didn't understand. He'd explained everything. Rationally and reasonably. Hadn't he?

"The least you might have done was notice that I still wore my wedding gown and not a *carriage dress*."

She was furious. Hurt. He could see it, flashing there in her eyes. But her reasons made no sense. He eyed her rose-hued ensemble. No, it was not the same as the one she'd worn at their wedding. That one had been blue. Truly, it never mattered what she wore. Everything lit him like a torch when she was near. Even a foolish little bird perched within a forest of ostrich feathers.

Frowning, he attempted to regain his footing. "A member of my household had just been murdered."

"Yes. And?"

"And we still do not know who the killer is. It might be anyone." He sighed and rubbed his nape. "Anyone who knows how to formulate poisons, that is."

"Such as an apothecary."

His gaze sharpened upon her. Ordinarily, he would not consider burdening Eugenia with talk of poisons and murder, but his frustration was making him desperate. "Yes, though the apothecary my mother used is long dead."

She sniffed, her chin tilting. "What of his assistants?"

Phineas blinked. "The guild listed no apprentice."

"I did not say apprentice. I said assistant. Many shopkeepers prefer to avoid arrangements in which they are obligated to train someone for several years. Instead, they favor a simple exchange of wages for labor. No contract. Easily hired, easily dismissed. Mrs. Pritchard, for example, claimed to do all her own work. In truth, she did very little, though she did enjoy taking credit for that of her assistants. I suppose she considered it an employer's privilege." She shrugged. "A common enough practice."

The blackness hated the reminder of how Mrs. Pritchard had mistreated Eugenia. Phineas forced it to recede, soothing himself by stroking her arm with his thumb.

She continued with calm hauteur, "Whoever the poisoner is, I doubt very much he would have scaled the walls of Berne House and served me my death whilst I completed my packing."

He frowned. "I could not take such a chance. I needed you to stop frittering about and get in the blasted coach."

She yanked her arm from his grasp.

Evidently, his explanation was unsatisfactory.

With a tilt of her chin, she said tartly, "As you have never before had a wife, and no doubt your closest companions all have leaves and stems, I concede you may require training, Holstoke. A great deal of training. Until then, I suggest you ruminate upon the benefits of generous allowances." She pivoted on her heel and made for the door.

"How long?" he asked, watching confounding hips sway.

She paused. Raised an inquiring brow over her shoulder.

"Until I am forgiven," he clarified.

She didn't answer, instead sweeping out the door and returning to the coach.

He went back to the table and drained his tankard. Nothing sensible had happened here. But at least she was speaking to him again. That was something.

He looked down at the crumbs remaining in the basket and retrieved the last, small piece of ham. Then, he paid the innkeeper and made for the stables.

Women. They were bloody confusing.

He sighed and took a bite of ham. A bit dry and oversalted, but it would do. On his way across the courtyard, he glanced toward the coach where his wife and sister engaged in some foreign, female battle he could not possibly comprehend. Finally, he went to find Caballus—a creature with sanity. He spoke briefly with the groom tending Caballus—also a creature with sanity. Finally, he gave instructions to seven weary-yet-vigilant men, who all possessed distinctly high levels of sanity.

And he formulated a hypothesis that females were saner when not confined to cramped spaces for long periods. Proximity to other females seemed especially problematic.

Eugenia's complexities were greater than he'd first suspected. He still did not understand what he'd done, apart from rushing her a bit. But, no matter how labyrinthine her thinking, he intended to master his subject.

A long, thorough exploratory process. Yes, that was precisely what was needed.

The blackness was pleased with his plan. So was Phineas.

He finished his ham and rubbed Caballus's neck. His grin slowly widened. Once they reached Primvale, he would begin unraveling the mystery of his wife. And that meant experiments. Numerous experiments. A true scientist must be diligent, after all.

Chapter Twelve

"Something must be done. We simply cannot have poisoners running about Mayfair reducing the population of marriageable ladies one by one. Who will be left for Lady Gattingford to gossip about?"

—The Dowager Marchioness of Wallingham to the Home Secretary, Robert Peel, regarding the need to address criminality in a more sensible fashion.

∞

The ugly, bald giant plunked down a tankard on the table. Jonas Hawthorn gave him a wry grin. "My thanks, Rude. Haven't had a decent pint in months."

Rude Markham grunted and scratched his cauliflower-shaped ear. "Aye. Been some time since I last seen ye. Off chasin' the muslin, eh?"

Jonas drank his ale and sighed, slumping back in his chair.

"Nothing so fine. Thieves and knaves, mostly."

Rude nodded and clapped his shoulder with bruising force. "Tha's what pays, I reckon."

Indeed it did. Jonas spent his waking hours hunting rich men's trinkets and the pathetic wretches who stole them—so he could one day afford to stop hunting rich men's trinkets and the pathetic wretches who stole them. Rich men paid rich sums to find their gold watches and silver ladles. Pathetic wretches paid with their necks.

It had been years since he'd given a damn about the imbalance. More since he'd relished the chase.

Now, as he watched the ugly, bald giant return to the bar, he wondered at all the ways hunting a murderer felt different. Curious thing, that.

It was a worm in his gut. Acid and fire. He wanted this poisoner more than any thief. More than anything in a long, long time.

He'd thought Holstoke was his man. The pieces had fit. But the itch along his neck hadn't eased, no matter how many ways he argued where the evidence should lead.

Then, there had been the problem of ... her.

He closed his eyes and took another drink, warm exhaustion sliding like fog into a valley. No sense in thinking about her. That was one bit of muslin he would never see, let alone touch.

"Fine time for sleepin', Hawthorn."

Jonas opened his eyes and gave Drayton a half-grin and a tip of his tankard. "It comes when it comes."

As Drayton yanked out a chair for himself, the deceptively dapper Lord Dunston removed his hat and took the seat opposite Jonas. The man's eyes were sharper than his old moniker—Sabre. "What have you found?"

Sighing, Jonas sat up. Leaned his elbows on the table. Pulled a folded scrap of paper from his pocket. "Of Randall, Glencombe, Holstoke, and Froom, only one hired new servants in the past two months."

Dunston unfolded the paper and nodded. His waistcoat shone bright green in the firelight. "Randall. Do you suspect he was involved?"

"Unlikely," Jonas replied. "He benefitted more from keeping his wife alive. Their arrangement served him well."

Drayton frowned. "Arrangement?"

"Mmm," answered Dunston. "Lady Randall long tolerated Lord Randall's affection for male companions. Some wives would not be so understanding."

"I interviewed every member of the four affected households," Jonas continued. "Randall's butler hired two additional footmen to serve guests at the ball where Miss Froom was poisoned."

"You spoke to these men?"

Jonas nodded and pointed to the paper. "The names are there. One was ... occupied with Lord Randall for most of the evening."

"And the other?" asked Drayton.

"Fell ill a week prior. His mother and two cousins claim he was in bed with a fever the entire day and night of the Randall affair." Jonas glanced at Dunston, who, apart from his waistcoat, exhibited few signs of the dandy he pretended to be. "They also claim he was never employed by Lord Randall."

Dunston's gaze narrowed. "Never?"

"Not hired. Not employed. Not contacted. The boy says he worked for an army captain until the illness came on, and that he hadn't been strong enough to search out a new position."

"An imposter, then." Dunston rubbed his jaw and shook his head.

"Bloody, bleeding hell," muttered Drayton. "Appears we 'ave ourselves another ghost, m'lord."

Jonas reached inside his greatcoat and withdrew a second folded sheet. "Perhaps not," he said, offering the square to Dunston, who unfolded it. Blinked. Sharpened his gaze.

Jonas grinned and took a drink of Rude Markham's fine ale. "Ghosts don't have faces, do they?"

He knew what Dunston saw—he'd drawn it. The slim nose. The mild brow. The round, gentle eyes. It was a man, but one with such banal features, he'd had a devil of a time prompting maids and other servants to give him sufficient descriptions. Still, it was a face. That was something.

Dunston handed the paper to Drayton. "Recognize him?"

"No. Looks harmless."

Dunston met Jonas's eyes. "The cleverest ones do."

Jonas raised his tankard and saluted the true statement before taking another drink. "Glencombe's butler said one of Randall's footmen delivered a message to Lady Theodosia the morning she was killed."

"Let me guess," said Dunston, sliding the sketch across the table. "He was the messenger."

Jonas nodded and set his near-empty tankard on the table, gesturing to Rude. The proprietor slung a towel over his shoulder and retrieved a pitcher. "That's as far as we're likely to get by questioning the households. Randall knows nothing. Froom and Glencombe want Holstoke's head on a platter. And Holstoke claims he knows of no reason why the poisoner would desire his attention, apart from a fascination with his mother." Jonas folded the sketch and list before tucking them into his pocket. "I need to know more than what I know," he continued, nodding his thanks to Rude, who slapped his shoulder and poured for all three men.

"That there's the truth, ain't it, Hawthorn?" Rude said, wiping the pitcher with his towel. "I said as much to Reaver last week." The bald giant glanced around The Black Bull with both pride and nostalgia. "Would that I'd known at the start what I know now. But I were just a fighter with a bit of blunt. Reaver taught me some when I bought the place from 'im. But I ain't no Reaver, that much is certain."

"You do fine, Rude. Just fine."

"Ah, ye're a staunch cove, Hawthorn." Another bruising clap of his shoulder, along with a booming laugh. "A mite clutch-fisted from time to time, but a good sort."

As Rude wandered away, Drayton sat straighter and squinted at Jonas. "Reaver might remember somethin'. He helped me track Lady Holstoke when 'is lordship married and …" Drayton cast a sidelong glance at Dunston and raised a shaggy brow. "Gave up the chase. For a time, at any rate."

Dunston murmured his agreement.

Sebastian Reaver was the owner of a gentlemen's gaming club occupying an entire square off St. James. The quality liked to frequent the place, or so Jonas understood. As he wasn't quality, he wasn't a member. He'd never met the man. But knowing Reaver's reputation, Jonas would guess he'd been both relentless and effective.

"What might he recall?" Jonas asked.

Drayton finished his swallow of ale and shook his head. "Could be he knows somethin' of the apothecary." The older man rubbed his own leg beneath the table.

"What do *you* remember of it?"

"Well, as I told ye, we'd tracked the Investor's—that is, Lady Holstoke's—poisons to an apothecary shop near the Strand. When we entered, the place was wrecked. The apothecary wore nothin' but a shirt and drawers. In a bad way, he was." Drayton ran a hand down his face and took a long pull of ale before continuing. "Shakin' and droolin'. His eyes were too big."

"Too big?"

"Bulgin'. The centers were big, too. Like Mrs. Varney's." Drayton took a shuddering breath. "Anyhow, Reaver picks up the poor bugger and tries to get a name. Nothin'. The man was chokin' on his own throat. Reaver sends me out to search the garden behind the shop. High walls. A gate leadin' out to an alley." He rubbed at his leg again. "The shot came sudden. Scarcely turned round before the scrawny bastard slipped out the gate."

Jonas's neck itched. "Scrawny?"

"Aye. Thin as a girl, but moved like a boy."

"Did you see his face?"

"Nah. Only caught a glimpse of his back. I took him for the apprentice. After the surgeon pulled the ball out of me, I attempted to find him, but the apothecary had no apprentices registered with the guild."

"We concluded the boy had been paid to dispose of Lady Holstoke's partner," Dunston said. "She had a penchant for hiring young men to rid her of her difficulties."

"So, you never learned what became of the boy who shot you."

Drayton shook his head. "He disappeared. After a few years, I reckoned he returned whence he came or landed in a grave like many others who'd done tasks for Lady Holstoke." He shrugged. "Perhaps Reaver remembers more."

Jonas looked again at Dunston. "Care to make an introduction?"

The lean lord smiled. "Why not?"

A short while later, Jonas and Dunston stood inside a third-floor chamber in one of the most exclusive gentlemen's clubs in London. Jonas took in the surroundings, noting the neatness and sturdiness of the furnishings. The room was less lavish than the rest of the club, but spacious and comfortable, for all that. Rising from behind a massive oak desk, a man more muscled and two inches taller than Rude Markham removed a pair of spectacles.

Dunston introduced him as Sebastian Reaver.

Jonas could see where the black-haired giant had acquired his reputation. He looked like he might break a man with a single blow.

"Hawthorn," he rumbled, coming around the desk. Black eyes focused upon Jonas. "I've heard the name. And the complaints."

"Thieves." Jonas chuckled. "They cluck worse than a thousand hens."

"Aye. Particularly when there's a wolf in their midst who never fails to catch his supper. What brings you here?"

Jonas withdrew the sketch and handed it to the giant, who retrieved his spectacles and gave it a look. "Have you seen him?"

Reaver glowered down at the sketch and shook his head. "Who is he?"

"Another poisoner," Dunston replied softly. "An admirer of Lady Holstoke's work." Dunston described the murderer's deeds, his apparent fixation upon Lord Holstoke, and their suspicions about his methods.

Reaver's eyes flashed and narrowed. "The formulations are different than hers, eh?"

"So says Lord Holstoke," said Jonas.

"He would know." Reaver grunted and shook his head. "Bloody brilliant, that one. Relentless, too. Went after his mother's accomplices like a demon for several years after her death. Found her victims by matching descriptions of their deaths to her methods."

Jonas knew that to be true. Holstoke had coldly explained his reasoning, his exhaustive process. He'd appeared emotionless, but after seeing the earl's reaction to Lady Eugenia Huxley, Jonas tended to believe it was more a mask than his true nature. "Based on Holstoke's analysis, it appears the killer's formulations more closely resemble the poison used upon Lady Holstoke's apothecary. You were there. What do you recall of that day?"

The giant ran a hand through his hair and rolled his massive shoulders. "It was no easy death. By the time we arrived, the man was insensible. Strangling."

"Were you in the garden when Drayton was shot?"

"No. I heard the shot and ran out there. Saw a figure fleein' out the gate."

"Male or female?"

"Male. Wore a brown hat, coat, breeches. Moved like a boy."

Drayton had said the same thing. Jonas pointed again to the sketch. "Could that have been him?"

Reaver looked again. "Never saw his face. I gave chase, but he disappeared quick as rum from a sailor's flask. You believe the boy who shot Drayton is the killer?"

Jonas's neck itched. "Perhaps. How tall was he?"

"Bit shorter than you. Thin. Fast."

Jonas leveled a hand across the bridge of his nose. "About this tall?"

"Taller."

Jonas moved his hand to his forehead.

"Aye."

Bloody hell. Too tall. The killer had been described by Randall's staff as around five-foot-eight. If Reaver's memory was right, it could not be the same man.

With a grim scowl, Reaver looked to Dunston. "Does Miss Gray know of the blackguard's fixation?" Reaver asked. "Is she safe?"

Everything inside Jonas shot to attention. His neck prickled. His hands itched. His hair nearly stood on end. Admittedly, his reaction was extreme, but the last topic he'd expected hear out of Reaver's mouth was ... her.

"Curious how Miss Gray was your first thought," Jonas said softly, keeping his tone mild despite the odd urgency running through him. "Why is that, Mr. Reaver?"

Dunston cleared his throat. "Perfectly reasonable, my good man. Being Holstoke's sister puts her within the killer's sights—"

"But why her, specifically?" Jonas moved closer to the giant. "Why not the woman Holstoke married? Or Holstoke, himself?"

A hard, black gaze scoured and scanned, flashed and calculated. Finally, Reaver replied, "Because if this whoreson admires Lady Holstoke, he must surely despise the girl who shot her."

Shot her. Sweet Christ. The cold, untouchable Miss Hannah Gray? He could not picture her deigning to lay her delicate fingers upon a gun, much less fire one. Jonas looked to Dunston, unaccountable fury rising in his chest.

Dunston glared at Reaver. "There was little need to tell him."

"Every need," the giant retorted. "She'll be in danger. Again. If he's to stop this blighter, he must know that."

Danger *again?* Why the hell had she been in danger at all? "I need to know everything, Dunston." Jonas snapped. "Everything."

The other man sighed. "Hawthorn, all you need know is the girl suffered mightily because of Lady Holstoke. She shot the countess in defense of her life and that of others in the room, including me and my wife."

"The records from the magistrate in Dorsetshire made no mention of this."

Reaver answered, "We all vowed to protect her, and so we have. Bloody, bleeding hell, she's been through enough, eh? Dunston is right. You needn't know details. Just know she may be a target again."

"Was it because she was a by-blow? Did Lady Holstoke—"

"It doesn't matter," Dunston said flatly.

It mattered. Enough to make him want to pummel answers out of both men. Why, he could not say. Hannah Gray was the haughtiest of haughty females. Beautiful, of course. Cream-white skin. The most stunning eyes he'd ever seen. But from the moment they'd met, she'd treated him like the leavings of an ill-bred mount—repulsive and best avoided.

He should not give a damn whether she was in danger. He should not care that she'd "suffered mightily," and had "been through enough."

Just like he should not be dreaming of her at night and waking hard as stone.

Life was full of should.

They were interrupted by Reaver's wife, who entered without knocking. She was tall. Auburn hair. Confident and regal. She swept toward her husband, one gloved hand resting upon her round, swollen belly. "Bastian, your sons have decided to steal Mr. Duff's boots and ride them like a pony. Perhaps you can—oh!" She blinked. Glanced from Jonas to Dunston. "Lord Dunston. And ...?"

Reaver moved to her side. The giant slid his arm around her, bracing her fully. "This is Hawthorn. He works at Bow Street."

She inclined her head in queenly fashion. "A pleasure, Mr. Hawthorn." Then, she gave a regretful smile. "Gentlemen, I fear I must steal away my husband."

A deep, rumbling chuckle sounded. "Are the boys givin' ye that much trouble, Gus?"

She gazed up at her husband with flagrant adoration. Then, she patted her belly. "This one is. He has dreadful timing."

Reaver's heavy muscles went rigid. Black eyes went wide. "No. Not for another—"

"Two weeks." His wife sighed, her expression sheepish. "My calculations may have been off slightly."

"Bloody, bleeding hell."

"I do apologize, gentlemen."

"Never mind them. We must get you home. Where is the coach?"

"The same place it was before. I asked Duff to collect the boys. They were not particularly cooperative."

"Time to leave." Reaver, looking panicked, bent and scooped his wife into his arms.

"Bastian! I am neither an invalid nor a valise. And this is the hardly the first time—"

Without another word to Jonas and Dunston, Reaver strode out of his office carrying his wife, who appeared to be on the verge of delivering him another babe.

Dunston retrieved Jonas's sketch from the floor and

handed it to him with a wry grin. "That will be the extent of his assistance, I'm afraid. Reaver is single-minded when it comes to his family."

Jonas tucked his sketch into his pocket and gave Dunston a hard glare. "Which leaves you to answer my questions. A bit more fully this time, if you don't mind."

The dapper earl grinned. Then chuckled. "Come, Hawthorn. It so happens I am a member here at Reaver's. Let us drink brandy and pretend we are civilized."

Jonas did not smile. "I will have answers, my lord."

"I do not doubt it, my good man." Dunston clapped his shoulder with force rivaling Rude Markham's. "Civilization first. Plenty of time for hunting hens later."

Chapter Thirteen

*"Gardening is not a gentlemanly pursuit, my dear boy.
No lady wishes to discover the hand leading her
through a waltz has soil beneath its fingernails."*

—The Dowager Marchioness of Wallingham to Lord Holstoke
in a letter explaining the proper role of an earl and the improper
nature of dirtying one's hands in tasks best left to servants.

∞

Genie's first glimpse of Primvale Castle came long after its surroundings had rendered her both speechless and breathless. And that came long after she'd begun to despair that she might perish for want of civilization.

The landscape of Dorsetshire was rolling, the air cool and breezy and faintly marine. In short, it was much like other parts of England she had seen before, though less populated—unless one counted cows.

Her apprehension had grown as she saw fewer and fewer

villages among the wind-waved grass. The last had been at least five miles back, little more than a cluster of white, thatch-roofed cottages. No shops. No other carriages. Not even an inn. Here, where the land emptied out, long, shallow valleys resembled rolling water, the grass itself rippling like a splash. It felt as though she were embarking on a long sea voyage with few supplies, fewer comforts, and disagreeable company.

She'd begun silently mourning the nothingness when the coach topped one of the swells, and she gasped. Genie reserved her gasps for only the most extraordinary sights. This was one.

Ahead, along a great, looping drive was a living fence in full bloom. Blushing pink and white, the blossoms were beginning to drop, showering the drive in a profusion of white petals. They sprinkled upon the coach like a nature goddess's blessing.

But she had little time to contemplate the effect, for everywhere, tall trees and leafy shrubs and jewel-bright blooms formed spectacular, painting-like scenes along each bend in the winding drive.

Genie wondered if she would run out of gasps before they'd reached their destination. Then, slowly as they rounded a particularly gnarled and ancient oak surrounded by dazzling orange lilies, the green of the trees and hedges gave way to a half-moon clearing bordered by a low stone wall. A bench sat cradled inside the curve. That was where the sea appeared. Blue and infinite, it merged into the sky, the only distinction being the shimmer of light upon water. Wondrous blue was framed inside an arch of drifting white petals and great, arm-like branches.

The coach rolled by, but Genie's heart remained within the spot, idling away an afternoon sketching glorious, sea-inspired hats.

As they continued along the drive, she experienced the same sensation—of leaving a bit of her heart in each small alcove or cleverly designed scene—again and again. Truly, it was a series of wonders.

Then, the drive forked. To the left, she glimpsed a sprawling, square brick structure centered by a massive arch. Through the arch was a courtyard with a fountain and more lush plantings. The coach house and stables, perhaps? The carriage continued along the right fork, rounding a statue of a dragon and a knight at least twelve feet tall. Genie sighed, wondering how Mr. Moody was faring. The coach topped a rise and, at last, the castle came into view.

It might not be as large as Lady Wallingham's gargantuan Grimsgate, but then, few castles were. Still, it was massive—five splendidly symmetrical stories of smooth, gray stone. Square and perfect, Primvale boasted a round tower on each corner, a multitude of windows, and a long series of steps leading up to a terrace partially covered by a portico with a pointed arch. Inside its shadow was a set of enormous wood doors.

"Good heavens," Genie breathed, noting yet another fountain at the center of a circle drive. "Is that a griffin?"

"Battling a sea serpent, yes," came Hannah's reply.

Genie had nearly forgotten the girl was there. Through sheer persistence, she'd managed to coerce a few civil sentences over the past two hours. It was progress, but Genie anticipated difficult days ahead for Hannah, who had little notion of how determined her new sister-in-law could be.

As the coach neared the fountain, she squinted. The two creatures at its center were twisted up together, spiraling into the sky. Wounded and at the edge of death, the griffin's wings were bound inside the serpent's long coils as the serpent sank its fangs into the creature's feathered throat. It was a savage, compelling portrayal of death and dominance.

"Lady Holstoke commissioned it," Hannah commented softly.

For a moment, Genie thought the girl might be digging at her, implying Genie's new title made her as poisonous as its previous owner.

But Hannah's expression was neither petulant nor resentful. It was haunted.

Her heart twisted. It took a moment to answer casually, "Hmm. Beautiful work, but a rather grim welcome. Why did Holstoke keep it?"

"I do not know."

Knowing something of what Hannah had endured at the previous Countess of Holstoke's hands, Genie's heart fairly squeezed into a knot. She considered giving up her self-assigned task then and there.

But the last thing Hannah needed was more coddling.

"Well," Genie replied, brushing at her skirts. "It is ghastly. Primvale will be much improved by its removal."

Hannah offered no reply, but a thoughtful crinkle appeared between her brows.

The carriage stopped at last, and Genie breathed a loud sigh of relief. "I do hope the offerings for luncheon are better than this morning's ham. Dreadful stuff."

Blinking slowly, the girl answered, "We do not serve luncheon."

Genie clicked her tongue. "Don't be silly. Of course we do. A good meal soothes many, many ills. And after the vagaries of a long journey? It is a requirement."

Hannah once again frowned.

"Trust me. This is one change you will enjoy."

Before Hannah could protest that she didn't want any changes, Genie threw open the carriage door and stepped down onto smooth, wedge-shaped stones laid in a radius pattern. Once again, she sighed. What a magnificent place. Maureen had been right to dub it palatial, although Genie thought even that word a bit weak. Perhaps she should have listened more closely, but Maureen did tend to natter on about gardens to a tedious degree.

She strode toward the ghastly fountain and turned in a circle. Everywhere—positively *everywhere*—were gardens the likes of which she had never seen. Walled gardens and sunken gardens and watery gardens and flowery gardens. Acres upon acres of them. She gasped when she spotted a peacock strutting beneath a nearby tree. To the west, she spied the peaks of glass houses glinting in the sunlight. To the east, an expanse of ornate hedges gave way to vividly green pastures dotted by cows and wildflowers in orange, white, and indigo.

And she could smell the sea on every breeze. She could not see it while standing on the drive beside the fountain, as the castle was set hundreds of yards inland, but she wondered if it might not be visible from the first floor.

Hurriedly, she climbed the steps to the entrance and spun about. There it was—a ribbon of blue at the southern horizon, framed by gently rolling land and leafy trees. Between the castle and the sea, yet another series of gardens stretched outward in winding fashion. She suspected the vistas grew more spectacular as one approached the water or ascended the castle's floors.

Coming up the drive from the direction of the stables was the man who had engineered this splendor. Something in Genie's chest pressed outward. Made her breathless. Made her heart pound.

He was weary—she saw it in his stride, which was more careful than usual, and the squint of his eyes. For all his exhaustion, however, his gait was agile, his demeanor calm.

She surveyed her surroundings again then returned her gaze to him. She'd long known he was honorable. And everyone knew he was brilliant—one need only converse with him a handful of times to be intimidated by his intellect. Yet, she'd not comprehended how impressive her husband was until this very moment.

The weary, tall, brilliant man now rounding the ghastly fountain was her husband. Fancy that.

Heavens, could admiration infect one's heart and lungs like a disease? She was full to bursting inside. She wanted to dance down the steps and kiss him again. It was true he was frequently oblivious to the nuances of sentiment, trampling her feelings without realizing it. And he ordered her about in the most abrupt, high-handed fashion.

Nevertheless, he'd married her. Protected her. Kissed her in a way that made her long for another experiment.

Her heart sped into a thundering patter. She shook her head and dropped her eyes to the stones of the castle's terrace. She must stop mooning over the man.

Her eyes returned to him as though tugged by strings. He did look tired. She'd noticed it at the inn, when he'd been so perplexed by her anger. Nibbling her lip, she began planning. A good meal and a bath would serve as a start.

He climbed the steps, his eyes finding her hips and rising to her bosom then finally landing upon her face. "Eugenia." His voice cracked as though it, too, was spent.

She managed to smile, though inside, that expanding pressure now sparkled and bubbled and made her breathless. "Holstoke," she murmured. "Show me my new home, won't you?"

Subtle lines of tension along his brow eased. He sighed as he reached the terrace and offered his arm. "With pleasure, Lady Holstoke."

Glimpsing Hannah at the base of the steps, frozen and staring up at them, she paused. Turned. Waved the girl forward. Hannah frowned, and Genie clicked her tongue. She descended the steps to Hannah's side and gently tapped the girl's elbow. Hannah jerked at the contact, but Genie paid the reflex no mind. "It has been a long journey, I daresay. Shall I ask one of the footmen to carry you?"

Hannah's long glare was her answer.

"Oh, pooh. Do come along. I shall need your help."

"For what, pray tell?"

Genie flared her eyes. "Planning luncheon."

"We do not—"

"Yes, yes. But the correct phrasing would be '*did* not.' Past tense. One must never become so attached to what has been that one cannot imagine anything better." She offered her arm. "Come along."

Hannah sniffed. Glared. Tilted her chin stubbornly. But she started up the steps toward the door and clasped one arm of a thoroughly baffled Holstoke.

Genie grinned and followed, taking Holstoke's other arm as they waited for the giant wooden doors to open. A white-haired butler bowed deeply. "My lord. And Miss Gray. Welcome home." His eyes—blue and gentle—fell upon Genie. "My lady." Another bow. "We are honored to welcome you to Primvale Castle."

Holstoke introduced the butler, whose name was Walters, before leading both Genie and Hannah forward into the entrance hall. Which was enormous. The floor was white and gray marble squares. The walls were velvety gray stone. The arches all had points. And at the far end were five sets of glass doors leading out into a central courtyard.

"Heavens," she breathed. "Is that a third fountain?"

"Mmm," Holstoke replied. "Would you like to see it?"

She glanced up at him. Noticed the redness around pale green eyes, the dust on his hat and coat, the lines of weariness around his mouth. "Not just yet," she murmured before turning to the butler. "Walters, I must ask a boon, I'm afraid. Miss Gray informs me Primvale rarely serves luncheon, yet I find I am famished after our journey."

"Of course, my lady. It will be my pleasure to arrange a tray, if you like."

"Thank you, but I think a proper luncheon will serve best. Whatever you have on hand should do. His lordship and Miss Gray will benefit from the refreshment, as well."

Hannah sniffed. "Nothing for me."

"Nonsense," Genie replied, peering past Holstoke to meet Hannah's challenge. "You must eat, as it is the only way I shall feel content to let you alone." She grinned, knowing she had won.

With narrowed eyes, Hannah huffed. Spun on her heel. Stomped from the hall through one of the arches without another word.

"Walters, arrange luncheon, as Lady Holstoke requested." Holstoke's voice was low and calm—until the butler left. Then, it was low and angry. "What in blazes is going on between you and my sister?"

Genie slid her hand from his arm and wandered away to sniff the beauteous orange lilies decorating a marble table. "I don't know what you mean," she lied.

"Yes, you do. Explain."

"These are cut from that spot beneath the giant oak, are they not?"

"Eugenia."

She spun to face him. He wore an intimidating scowl. Her spine rippled with shivers. "Trust me. It is for the best."

"You haven't the faintest notion what she has endured—"

"Actually, I do."

"I'll not allow anyone to do her further harm."

She rolled her eyes. "As though I would wish to. Cruelty was your mother's favorite sport, Holstoke. Not mine."

He released a breath and rubbed at the back of his neck. "She is fragile."

"Not as fragile as you might—"

"Damn and blast, Eugenia. You are a bloody scythe."

She blinked, reeling at his harsh tone.

"When will you realize you cannot swing wildly about, catering to every passing whim, without cutting those around you to ribbons?"

Swallowing, she dropped her gaze and tried to absorb the sharp, burning ache. She tried to remember that he'd had little sleep and nothing decent to eat in the last two days. She reminded herself that minutes earlier, she'd been overwhelmed by admiration for the man, and that his protectiveness toward his sister was one of the reasons.

He stalked toward her until the toes of his riding boots entered her vision. "It is well past time for you to curb your impetuous nature. Boldness of your sort is not charming. It is brazen and destructive."

"Are you through?" she asked.

Silence, long and tense.

"Well, then," she said to his chin. "I suggest you ask your valet to arrange a bath, as it may improve your mood. Luncheon will be served in forty minutes. Until then, I will show myself about the castle." She started past him.

He grasped her arm.

"Let go," she said softly.

"I will not," he gritted.

"This is becoming a tiresome habit. Let go, Holstoke."

He pulled her closer. "Tell me why I am wrong."

"We haven't that sort of time. At most, I will live only another seventy years."

His hands moved to her waist and drew her hips hard against him. "Tell me." His face hovered near hers now, his breath hot against her chin. "Please."

"You despise my boldness."

One of his hands slid up the center of her back. The other loosened and removed her bonnet. His jaw came down beside hers as his nose nuzzled her temple.

"But without it, I would not be here." She stiffened against mutinous tingling as he nibbled her earlobe. "Stop that."

"Your boldness makes mistakes, Eugenia."

"Once in a great while."

"It causes you to speak without thinking."

"Hmmph. That only shows how little you know of me. I rarely speak without thinking. My thinking is simply faster."

"Look how often you lay your hands upon people." Holstoke's own hands had returned to her waist. Now, they squeezed as though he were agitated. "It is impulsive. Inappropriate." His lips caressed her neck. His nose nuzzled and drew her in.

The tingles swarmed her senses. Weakened her knees. "Strangely, you don't seem to mind when my brazen hands land upon you."

"I'll not have you touching other men, Eugenia." His whisper fell hot against her ear. "Not ever again."

"Hmm," she murmured. "Anything else? Shall I refrain from speaking out of turn? Would you prefer I wear yellow?"

His chest pumped now, his eyes darkened and heated and riveted upon her mouth.

"No answer? Then, I have a suggestion, if it is not too *bold*."

Hands gripping her hard, he squeezed his eyes shut and lowered his forehead to rest against hers. Gently, she cupped his chin. He jerked then pressed into her like a cat, his whiskers rough against her palm.

"Nobody knows my faults better than I, Holstoke. Not you. Not anyone. It is impossible to eliminate them, for if it weren't, I would have done so already. One does not endure the biggest scandal of the past three years without wishing one were differently made."

He opened his eyes. Held hers.

"Do not ask me to change my fundamental nature," she whispered. "It won't work, and you'll only make us both miserable."

Frowning as though she'd said something bizarre, he opened his mouth. Lifted his head away from hers. "I—I don't want you to change."

"No?"

"I want you to promise you will not touch other men."

Her mouth quirked. She let her hand drop to his chest and gave him a pat. He really was a most peculiar man. "If I give my promise, you must grant me something in return."

"What?"

"Trust me with your sister."

His frown deepened.

"That is my condition. I shall even promise not to harm her. See how reasonable I am? I have offered you two promises for only one small bit of trust."

"Why should a condition be necessary? A wife's obedience should be—"

"I have already promised obedience. Perhaps you missed it. No doubt distracted during the vows. My hat was breathtaking, I admit."

"Eugenia—"

"Now, you are demanding my assurance that I will not incidentally touch other men. Rather unreasonable, even by your standards, and yet I am willing to accommodate you." She sniffed. "You have married a very generous woman."

He looked tormented. There was no ice, no barrier. Simply a dark, private battle. "She is precious to me, Eugenia."

"I know." She waited, holding her breath.

His hands squeezed her one last time, his fingertips digging in. It didn't hurt, but it spoke of the intensity inside him. Trust could not come easily to the son of Lydia Brand. His throat rippled on a swallow. "Very well," he said. "Grant me your promise, and I will grant you my trust."

Her admiration, temporarily dampened by his dark mood, swelled again. She managed to keep from kissing him, but just barely. "You have it."

Once again, his eyes slid closed. He gathered her in and pressed his lips to the top of her head then to her temple then to her neck.

She thought she heard him whisper either, "Sank cod" or "Thank God," several times, but she could not be certain. Her heart was pounding too loudly to hear much of anything.

Holstoke's valet, a wiry man with a neat ring of hair around a bald head, entered the hall. "I do beg your pardon, my lord. My lady. Mr. Walters has asked whether her ladyship would care to visit her chambers before or after luncheon."

"Before," answered Holstoke.

"After," answered Genie simultaneously. She blinked up at her husband, who glared down at her. "Why are you vexed?"

"It is too long to wait."

"To see a chamber?"

He released a breath. Withdrew his hands. Turned and paced away from her while rubbing his neck. He whispered either, "Bloody hell" or "Flooding yell," several times. She assumed it was the former, though his frustration made little sense. What difference would an hour or two make?

She approached the valet, whose name she could not remember, then smiled and nodded.

"Ross, my lady," he said quietly, inclining his head. "At your service."

Thank heaven for kindly, understanding servants. She nearly reached out to touch his arm. Just as her fingers lifted to do so, she folded them at her waist. "Thank you, Ross. Please tell Walters I shall enjoy seeing my chambers after luncheon. And, if it is not too much trouble, would you arrange a bath for Lord Holstoke?"

Ross smiled. "Of course, my lady. May I do anything for you?"

She waved and grinned in return. "Oh, do not trouble yourself. I shall be contented with a good luncheon and a chance to walk about this magnificent place." She leaned closer. "I have only seen the entrance hall, so far."

Ross chuckled. "Might I suggest taking it slowly, my lady? Beauty is best when one has time to absorb it."

"I agree entirely. Why, as we were coming up the drive—"

"Thank you, Ross. That will be all." Though the abrupt command was aimed at the valet, Holstoke glared at her.

She set her hands on her hips. "What now? I kept my promise."

"You smiled at him."

"Honestly, Holstoke." She held up her hand as he started to speak. "No, I will not promise to refrain from smiling. For pity's sake, go and have a bath. I shall see you at luncheon." She shook her head, retrieved her bonnet, and selected one of the pointed arches before leaving her husband to his own devices.

For the remainder of the afternoon, she explored the castle and spoke with servants. First, she encountered the housekeeper, Mrs. Green, in a drawing room near the entrance hall. The walls were swathed in soft yellow silk, and the furnishings were all gentle blues with the occasional spot of white. The windows were tall and looked out on the courtyard.

Mrs. Green was lovely. Genie sipped tea with her for a half-hour while learning everything she could about the household. Then she gave the housekeeper a list of changes, starting with luncheon. It would be served every day at precisely two, with dinner at eight.

Of course, their first luncheon was less than auspicious. Holstoke glowered from his end of the table in the cozy morning room, while Hannah refused to speak, stabbing at her plate with resentment. Genie did note, however, that both of them ate every bite of the delicious herbed lamb, pillow-soft bread, and honey cakes that were presented. The asparagus and cauliflower, she noted, were received with less enthusiasm.

Later, she roamed the remainder of the castle, ambling from room to astoundingly lovely room. In each chamber, she spoke with servants she passed, all of whom appeared capable, efficient, and best of all, kind. Every one had a gentle way about them. From the laundry maids to the under-butler to Mrs. Green and Mr. Walters, each spoke respectfully yet with sincere warmth that was noticeable.

Genie assumed it was Holstoke's doing. He would not have haughty servants around his sister. Rather, he would only hire those who treated her tenderly.

Still, she'd noticed one befuddling theme in regard to the

male servants, the footmen in particular. To a man, they were ... well, rather plain. One might even say unattractive. She counted at least three whose teeth scarcely fit in their mouths. Another two were spotted or pockmarked. And the rest lacked a discernible jaw or had too much forehead or ... drat. They were ugly. There was no way around it.

Ordinarily, a peer's footmen, particularly in a household of Primvale's grandeur, would be both tall and handsome. It was very nearly a rule, and Genie knew how well Holstoke liked his rules. Ugly footmen were rare and short ones scarce, indeed. Yet, all of Holstoke's footmen matched either one description or both.

How very peculiar. But, then, Holstoke was a peculiar man. Only hours earlier, he'd demanded she never touch another man. Strange, indeed. This penchant for unattractive servants must be another of his many idiosyncrasies.

She shrugged away the observation as she continued her tour of Primvale Castle. It was magnificent, of course, from the two-story, walnut-paneled library to the thirty-foot-long dining room painted an unusual shade of amber to the master bedchamber with its emerald-green velvets and silver silks.

Chatting with Mr. Ross, who demonstrated how his lordship preferred his lamps lit low in the evenings, Genie discovered Holstoke suffered headaches. Dreadful, debilitating headaches, by the sound of it. Fortunately, the friendly Mr. Ross assumed she already knew—an assumption she did not bother to correct.

Next, she wandered through connecting doors into the mistress's suite, which was now hers.

It was yellow.

The same yellow silk that dressed the walls of the main drawing room decorated the bedchamber reserved for Holstoke's wife.

Yellow was not Genie's favorite color. But it was Maureen's.

Slowly, she wandered deeper into the room, running her fingers across the sky-blue damask of the coverlet, tracing the golden-mahogany posts of the canopied bed. The carpets were French, the designs swirling in shades of blue and rose. The windows were large and arched. The center one was a set of glass doors that led onto a terrace overlooking the sea.

It was a bloody masterpiece. Every carved feather of the marble cherubim flanking the fireplace, every feminine whorl of the writing desk, every blasted tassel on the little cerulean pillow that lay waiting to comfort its mistress on a rolled-armed sofa.

It was perfect.

For Maureen.

A moment passed in which she was certain she would collapse in upon herself.

She'd known. She'd known he'd loved Maureen once. She'd realized the risk that his feelings might not have changed. But she'd hoped a man as rational as Holstoke might understand how fruitless his feelings had been, particularly after six years.

Yet, here was the truth, dressed in yellow and cerulean blue. He loved Maureen still. He'd kept an entire room for her with feathered marble and tasseled pillows. He'd likely designed his gardens for her and amassed his wealth for her and gone to London for her.

The hollow filled with pain. It grew roots and seeped into the crevices until she thought she might crack open.

She tightened her fists and stared out toward the sea. Evening approached. The sun's rays had turned golden. Slowly, she forced herself forward. Opened the glass doors. Stepped out onto the terrace.

The breeze nearly blew her back into the chamber. But she needed it. Wanted the wind's strength. She gripped the cold stone balustrade and leaned forward, keeping her eyes on shimmering water.

It was better that she knew now. This way, she would never

expect more than he could give.

She watched a gull swoop in an arc, white and gray and graceful. It blurred, and she swiped at her cheek.

Silly, girlish fancies were daft, anyway. Ladies indulged their husbands far too much when they were in love. Genie would not be daft. She would be firm. Practical.

Swiping at her cheek twice more, she swallowed the burning constriction in her throat.

She would know he did not love her. *Could* not love her. And she would know it from the start. It was an advantage, really. Knowing meant she would not stupidly imagine a kiss meant anything at all.

"My lady?"

She sniffed and blew out a breath before turning and giving the pretty, red-haired maid behind her a polite smile. "Yes?"

"I am Harriet, my lady. Mrs. Green suggested I might act as your lady's maid, if it pleases you."

Genie nodded. "That would be fine."

The girl stepped forward. "Would you—may I fetch you a handkerchief, my lady?"

Swiping at her cheek with impatient fingers, Genie shook her head. "It is only the wind. A shawl would be lovely, though. And my bonnet. The pink one with the flowers."

Harriet retrieved a soft white shawl and the bonnet, and Genie left the chamber she now regarded as Maureen's room. Then, she set out to explore the wonders Holstoke had created outside the castle. For the next several hours, she meandered through garden after garden, beginning with the northern side of the castle, which featured a broad terrace leading down to a parterre. Orderly, formally arranged squares were filled with flowers. Between the squares were graveled paths dotted with benches. At the center of the design was a fourth fountain surrounded by yet more flowers. Good heavens, she'd never seen so many flowers. Beyond the formal north garden was a lake surrounded by leafy trees, irises, and flowering shrubs so vividly red, they appeared silken.

Slowly, she explored each garden "room," working her way from north to west, the latter of which included two connecting walled gardens, one dedicated entirely to herbs and the other to vegetables. While these functioned as the castle's kitchen garden, even they were aesthetically pleasing, with everything from cabbages and cucumbers to thyme and lavender arranged in an ornamental spiraling pattern. Each section of the spirals was neatly and discreetly labeled with little wooden signs staked into the soil. When she wandered past a pretty herb labeled "balm," she reached down and plucked a leaf, rubbing it between her fingers and breathing it in.

Ah, yes. Lemons.

She took a nibble, enjoying the light, cooling flavor.

Continuing her explorations, she noticed the air turning the same color as the lavender she now stroked between her fingers. Dusk was approaching. Dinner would be served shortly.

She breathed in the scents of the herbs and lavender. Gathered her shawl closer. Made her way to the iron gate nestled into one of the garden's lower walls.

Drat. She'd exited on the wrong side. She spun about, searching for an easy path back toward the castle. It was then she saw the shadow. A tall, dark shadow moving about inside a long glass house.

Her heart flipped and tumbled painfully. She squeezed her shawl between her fingers. Perhaps she should simply return to the castle and see him at supper.

He moved again, and this time, she could see him fully through glass and fronds. Tall. Serious. He examined something on the table before him then rubbed his neck as though he were tired.

Heart pumping out a rapid rhythm, she started to turn

back to the kitchen garden. Then stopped. Pivoted. Made for the glass house.

As soon as she entered, the blast of warm, humid air surrounded her. She draped her shawl over one arm and removed her bonnet. Glancing around, she could see Holstoke in every aspect of the place—the neat, labeled shelves filled with plants both familiar and exotic, large and small. The long table strewn with several stacks of paper.

And there was Holstoke.

Her hand drifted to her belly. She paused to catch her breath.

He was in shirtsleeves. No waistcoat, no cravat, and certainly no cravat pin. Just a white linen shirt and dark trousers.

She hadn't thought he could be more handsome. She'd been wrong.

Drifting toward him as though caught on a Holstoke-bound breeze, she peered at his hands, which penned tidy, organized notes arranged similarly to his most formal garden—in squares.

Good heavens, how his squares made her smile.

"What are you doing in here, Eugenia?"

Her eyes flew to his, which were stern and remote. "Exploring the gardens. And you?"

A muscle flickered in his jaw. "Research."

"About?"

"Plants which might mitigate the effects of *Hyoscyamus niger*."

"High what?"

His eyes were darkening, flickering down to her mouth repeatedly. "Henbane."

She set her shawl on the table between his notes and an odd-looking potted plant. She ran her fingers over the thick, waxy spikes. "What is this?"

"Aloe."

She traced her fingertips over the page where he'd divided his notes into squares. A smile tugged. "You are peculiar, Holstoke."

His hand covered hers. Gripped her fingers. Refused to let go. "You should leave," he murmured, his voice rasping as though he were parched.

She wetted her lips and wondered at the sensations he evoked wherever her skin touched his. "I should like to conduct research of my own, I think."

"Eugenia." Her name was nearly a groan. "This ... this is not the time."

Letting her gaze linger upon his hands then rise up his chest to his throat and then to his mouth—that defined, handsome mouth—she moved closer. "I like your gardens, Holstoke. Very much."

"Bloody hell." The two words were scarcely a whisper. He braced his free hand against the table and bent at the waist as though he were in great pain or having trouble standing upright.

Her smile grew. The shivers went everywhere, from her toes to her scalp to the tips of her breasts. Her skin felt alive with them, especially the place where his hand gripped hers as though she were holding him at the edge of a precipice.

"Perhaps tomorrow you can show me everything," she said, her own voice acquiring a bit of rasp, too. "For now, however, I should like another experiment. Our first was quite successful, wouldn't you agree?"

Those pale green eyes lowered, his lofty cheekbones flushing. Was he looking at her bosom? She thought so.

She wasn't very good at kissing and such, and Holstoke was always a bit difficult to read, but she recognized lust when she saw it. His pleased her greatly. While he might not love her, she could make him want her. Perhaps that would be enough.

"You should leave," he repeated. "I don't have ... I am not altogether ..." His chest heaved before settling into a fast, roughened pattern. "It has been a long day."

Glancing at the glass around them and the darkening twilight beyond, she asked, "This is where you conduct your experiments, is it not?"

"Eugenia."

She tossed her bonnet on the table beside her shawl. "I experimented a bit, myself, earlier."

Holstoke went rigid. His hand tightened on hers. "Did you?"

"Mmm. I was roaming about your herb garden and spotted a lovely plant labeled 'balm.'" She managed to free her thumb and stroked the back of his hand. "Tender leaves. I like the texture, rough and nubbly."

His grip eased. "It is part of the mint family."

"I recalled you saying you take it in your tea. So, I thought I might have a taste."

"Bloody hell, woman," he breathed. His other hand came up to squeeze her waist. He drew her into his hips until a hard ridge pressed her belly.

Oh, yes. He wanted her.

She grinned up at him. "I liked it, Holstoke. Almost as much as I like your gardens."

"Take down your hair." His eyes were molten and dark, the black centers nearly swallowing the green.

"Is this part of the experiment?"

He did not smile. Instead, his face lowered until his lips hovered a breath from hers. "This is me telling you to leave for the third bloody time. Because if you stay, I will take you, and I want your hair down while I do."

Chapter Fourteen

"The question is not whether the thin veneer of civilization will hold against the barrage of primal instinct. The question is what precedes the downfall of the former and the reign of the latter. For some, it is a tide. For others, a whisper."

—The Dowager Marchioness of Wallingham to Lady Dunston in response to said lady's intention to limit sweet indulgences to a more sensible quantity.

∞

Nothing was left of rationality. Only blackness. He scarcely recognized his own voice, let alone his thoughts.

Eugenia was his tormentor. Pert and glowing. Soft and strong. Sweetly gowned in rose silk and dusk's light. It hurt to look at her. It hurt to touch her hand. The grinding need had sharpened into incessant pain sometime during luncheon, when he'd realized she intended to tour the castle on her own rather than retire to her bedchamber or his or any bloody place where he could claim her and ease the maddening ache.

Now, she stood before him in this place—*his* place—and seduced him with an imp's smile. God, he'd never felt this kind of arousal. There was only one explanation: His wife knew precisely what she was about.

How else would she know complimenting his gardens might turn him harder than stone? Even he hadn't suspected it. How else to explain the sheer incitement of telling him she'd tasted lemon balm and found it to her liking?

The only thing she hadn't guessed was how much he longed to see her hair. It was not full daylight. It was not rosy dawn. But if she was determined to seduce him, he would gladly take what she gave.

"My hair?" she asked, blinking slowly and swaying into him.

Her breasts brushed his chest. Her belly pressed against his cock. He groaned. It sounded more like a growl, but his control was frayed to a thread. Only one thing prevented him from taking her like a brute—the thought of those who had been there before.

His wife might not be pure, but she was now his. And he wanted her obsessed with the pleasure only he could give her.

"I thought you might kiss me again," she murmured, her lips forming the faintest pout.

"I will. Take down your hair."

She reached up and plucked out her pins, then ran her fingers through the thick mass. Gleaming and rich, mahogany satin tumbled in waves over her shoulders and back. One curl circled the center of her right breast. This was the vision that had plagued his dreams. Except that she'd been naked. She was not now, but she could be.

And he could be inside her.

"Bloody hell," he muttered. His heart was going to beat him to death. His cock was going to explode. "I'll obsess you later."

A puzzled pucker formed between her brows, but he

couldn't stop to explain—not that he would wish to. His lack of control where she was concerned was humiliating enough.

"I am going to lift you onto the table now."

"I suppose that would be—oh!"

There. That was better.

He drew his shirt over his head.

"Oh. H-Holstoke? This is most"—she swallowed—"unexpected." Her fingertips stroked his chest, lingering over his nipple and leaving streaks of lightning behind in a glittering trail.

He cupped her jaw and kissed her fully—no playful laps of his tongue or teasing hesitation. He was claiming her. Now. His wife.

Her lips were soft and her mouth delicious. She hadn't lied. She tasted of lemon balm. God, he wanted to devour her whole.

She, in turn, cupped his neck, her thumbs stroking the hinge of his jaw. "Mmm." She panted against his lips. "I'm too hot. I need ..." She licked her lips and gazed up at him with transparent arousal. "Kiss me again."

He did, but he did not stop with kissing. Rather, he put his hands to work, finally able to touch her mystifying hips and tiny waist and bountiful breasts. His palms skimmed her nipples. They were hard and likely painfully swollen. They needed his attention.

His fingers flew down the front closures of her gown, unfastening three before he lost patience and tugged, not realizing how much force he'd used until he heard something tear.

She didn't complain. She'd busied herself kissing his chest and returning again and again to circle his nipples with her thumbs.

He shoved her corset lower and reached inside to lift out her breasts until they perched high and round. Her skin flushed the prettiest pink. Her nipples, on the other hand, were red—the red of her gown. Like a midsummer rose, the hard points bloomed and flushed with her desire.

He took one in his mouth and suckled hard.

Eugenia squeaked, the sound rusty. But her fingernails dug into his scalp, and her hips worked against the table, and her arm wrapped forcefully around his nape, pulling him closer.

Everything about her drove him deeper into obsession. Her nipples against his tongue, her hands upon his face and neck. Her panting breaths and little needy grunts. He wanted more. More and more and more.

He suckled harder. Used his thumb to stroke the ripe little tip he hadn't yet tasted. He would save it for when he was inside her—which had to be soon if he didn't want to embarrass himself. Seconds later, he gripped behind her knees and spread her thighs. Then, as steadily as he could manage, he raised her skirts. He didn't want to release her nipple, but to see her thighs and the place where he would claim her, he must. So, reluctantly, he did.

She was panting. Trembling. Every breath shook those round, heavenly breasts. He raised her skirts past her hips and glanced down.

White thighs trembled, too. She wore stockings but no drawers, only petticoats. And between those thighs, which he'd spread quite wide, were the wet, shimmering petals of Eugenia. Red as her nipples. Ready for him.

He spread her with his thumbs, exposing her sweet, swollen bud. She glistened there, furiously aroused and needy. With a whispery touch, he teased her with his fingertip. Watched her beautiful red petals quiver and flush darker. Eugenia's entire body undulated as she threw back her head and moaned. He'd never seen anything so exquisite. He would taste her. Devour her. Spend hours making her bloom for him. God, how he wanted that. But he was dying. And he could not delay any longer.

It took only a moment to release his fall, grip his cock, and place himself there. On the precipice. He paused. Met her eyes. They were wide and oddly startled, but she reached up and drew his mouth down to hers before he could ask why.

He kissed her. Plunged back into her mouth and gripped her mystifying hips. Slid his hands down to grasp her thighs, yanking her forward into his thrust.

The sound she made should have stopped him—a smothered cry blended with a gasp. The way she stiffened should have stopped him, for her fingernails dug into his nape and her back went rigid.

But she was so. Bloody. Tight.

And he'd waited so. Bloody. Long.

And his skin thrummed and drummed and hummed like lightning.

So he thrust again, not yet far enough inside her. He felt the tightness give beneath his pressure. He needed to be deeper.

Her arms encircled him, her breath panting against his throat.

Tight, hot silk. Tighter than anything he'd ever ...

Nothing had ever fit him so ...

Something was different. But he couldn't place it.

He was burning. He needed to go deeper. So, he did.

Eugenia clung to him, her moans muffled against his skin.

He pulled her closer. Closer. Sank deeper and thrust higher. Felt her nipples drag against him and slid his hand between them to raise the neglected one to his mouth. He suckled and thrust. Suckled and thrust. Pulled her hips tighter and suckled and thrust.

This time, her moan was longer and punctuated with a gasp. Her gasps increased to match his tempo, and her sheath squeezed until he thought he might die from the pressure.

She wriggled, her thighs gripping his hips. He braced a hand on the table and went deep. Hard. Buried his face in her neck, breathed violets and the sweet, unmistakable scent of his woman. He needed her pleasure. He needed to see it and feel it rippling around him.

He slid his hand to where they were joined. Found the little swollen bud amidst her petals. Sank in fully and stroked her there, hoping he could last. She gazed up at him, cat-like eyes soft and black at the centers.

"Come for me," he panted.

Again, a crinkle of confusion.

By God, if she did not come soon, he was going to leave her behind. He pressed and stroked, moderating the angle of his thrusts to give her more. The pressure building from his spine and into his cock was winding like a spring, tight enough to drive him mad.

A small ripple was his only warning. Then, Eugenia threw back her head and let out a startled yelp followed by a sobbing groan. Thereafter, he lost his mind.

Her sheath seized him in a slick, silken grip, demanding over and over that he give her everything he had. And so he did.

The explosion came in a repeating flood, launching him past glass walls and into the star-filled sky, where the pleasure pounded over and over like waves battering rocks. And Eugenia was with him, holding him so tightly, he could scarcely breathe. For a moment, he wondered if he'd lost consciousness, for he'd never experienced anything like this. The release. The relief. Filling his wife. Taking her and being taken in return. Even now, minutes after his peak, the tension of his lust had not fully dissipated.

He shuddered and breathed into her neck. Felt the satin of her hair catch against his jaw then slide away. His spine tingled, especially at the base. His hands clutched at her still, afraid she would disappear.

"Hol—Holstoke?" The tremor in her voice, the uncertainty, gripped something deep and low inside him and twisted hard. "Was that ... normal?"

No. Far from it. But the fact that she had to ask chilled him. She'd been so tight. And now that he considered it, less practiced than he'd imagined. He swallowed, his blood going colder, his suspicions digging in.

Slowly, he drew back until he could see her eyes. They were lit with the question she'd asked, part wonder and part worry. God, she was beautiful. He ran his knuckles over her brow. Kissed her lips gently.

Then he withdrew, and the moment he felt her wince, he knew the truth. The small smear of blood on her thigh merely served as his accuser.

His wife, the woman everyone thought dallied freely with footmen, the one they called the Huxley Harlot, had been a virgin. And he had taken her like a man starving.

Which he was.

Damn and blast. The blackness wanted her now more than ever. It preened and roared its triumph. Demanded he take her again.

Instead, he lowered her skirts. Tucked himself away. Donned his shirt. Raised her bodice and helped her down.

"Why did you not tell me?"

She shook her head. "Tell you what?"

"That you never lay with a man."

She scoffed. "Really, Holstoke. I already explained that I do not enjoy the attentions of other men. Did you suppose I would complete the act, despite being repulsed? So much for your vaunted logic."

He rubbed his nape, turned, and paced to the end of the table.

"You know, I'm feeling a bit drowsy," she said. "And my legs are not altogether steady. I will ask Mrs. Green to serve supper on trays this evening. Also, a bath would not go amiss."

Bracing himself against the wood, he squeezed the edge and focused on regulating his breathing. "Tell me what happened, Eugenia."

Silence. Then, a sniff. "Well, I have done a great deal of walking today. And, as you've discovered—albeit a bit *late* for a man of your intelligence—I am unaccustomed to such intimacies as we engaged in here."

He gripped the wood until it burned against his palm and fingertips. "What happened with the footman?" His voice was harsh. Guttural. He could not soften it, for the blackness had regained command.

Behind him, he heard her approach. Then, she circled around to face him, her hands on her hips, her chin tilted at a challenging angle. "I told you already. What in blazes is the matter with you?"

Her hair—that lustrous, dark mahogany hair—cascaded upon her shoulders and breasts. Her lips were swollen, her cheeks still blushing.

"Tell me again," he rasped.

She released an exasperated breath. "I lured him to Lord Reedham's conservatory."

"How?"

"We flirted a bit. I suggested he help me repair my hem. Honestly, I don't remember everything. I was in my cups at the time."

"You let him kiss you." He gritted his teeth. "Touch you. Then what?"

"Well, you know how drink sets me off balance. Within minutes, I had decided my experiment was a failure, and so I began to push at him. He ignored me, so I shoved harder, and he let me go, but it was sudden. I remember falling backward and grasping something. His shirt, I think. Next thing I knew, I was on my back, he lay atop me, and my skirts were ... higher than they should have been. Evidently, he'd mistaken my little topple for passion. Once I'd regained my ability to draw air, of course, I told him in no uncertain terms that I wanted him off of me, but by then, we'd been spotted from the garden by Lady Gattingford and her band of fellow gossips." She glanced at the glass surrounding them. "Next time, I should like proper walls, Holstoke. And a bed, preferably."

He gazed upon this woman who rarely hid her thoughts yet frequently surprised him—and wanted her. It was not lust, after all. It was deeper. He wanted to hold her. Before he could think better of it, he reached out to do just that. Took her in his arms. Gathered her close. Sank his hands into her hair. Raised it to his nose and breathed violets and a faint hint of cherries.

"Er, Holstoke?" Her hands patted his back.

He held her harder, his arms fully around her now, pressing her softness against him. Taking comfort in her warmth, in the contact from her hips to her shoulders.

"Are you all right?" Her voice was muffled against his shirt. "It's one of your headaches, isn't it?"

He sifted his fingers through her hair, savoring the satiny texture. "You said they saw you through the glass, but rumor suggested Lady Gattingford and the rest entered the room whilst you were—"

"Indeed." She shivered against him and fisted the linen at his back. "Dreadful night. I don't like to remember it."

"They humiliated you. Purposely."

"Yes. Too delicious to resist, I suppose. Catching a Huxley girl with her skirts up round her shoulders vastly improves one's standing among other gossips."

He closed his eyes and struggled not to see it. She was his, now. Only his. He cupped the back of her head and drew her up into his kiss, ignoring her squeak of surprise. He claimed her mouth and lips, loving her softness, coaxing her sigh. He reveled in the knowledge that she had never belonged to anyone else, and she never would.

"What ..." Her lashes fluttered as he drew back to gaze upon her beautiful, blushing face. "What was that for?"

"It will not stand, Eugenia. They must be punished."

Her eyes flared wide. "No. Do not start this. My family already tried, and it only made matters worse. Lady Wallingham—"

"Did nothing," the blackness growled. He stroked her hair to calm himself. Strangely, it helped.

"Because she realized what would happen. Lady Wallingham is no fool. She understands this game better than anybody."

The blackness could not bear it—the thought of Eugenia being mocked and scorned. Being called a harlot and shunned from polite society. Forced into *employment*, for God's sake. He wanted to ruin them all. Everyone who had hurt her.

"Listen to me," she said, her hand lifting to cup his jaw. Increasingly, her touches were less startling. More natural. "It was the worst decision of my life, one I made in desperation. It cost me dearly, Holstoke. Damaged my family and put Kate's happiness at risk. I should not have done it, precisely because I knew the price I would pay if I were caught. What came after was ... dreadful." She swallowed and stroked his cheekbone with her thumb, as though it comforted her as much as him. "But the mistake was mine. So the punishment was mine."

He could see she believed what she was saying, though it was perfect rubbish. Which meant he must proceed without her knowledge. So, rather than argue his point further, he settled for part of the truth. "You did not deserve what they did to you."

She smiled up at him, her eyes glowing. "Thank you for saying so, Holstoke," she whispered.

It was then he realized how mussed she was, noting the wrinkles in her gown, the looping tumble he'd made of her hair. She was sensual. Intoxicating. And small. His fingers overlapped where they gripped her waist. Why had he not taken more care with her?

"A bath," he rasped, looking down to where his hands held her, loving the warmth of her caress upon his cheek. "Then supper." The lightning moved through him as it had before, but now it seemed to travel into her, returning tempered yet stronger in an endless loop. "Then walls and a bed."

For a moment, disappointment flickered in her eyes. Her hand fell away from his cheek. Her eyes dropped to his chest.

She nodded. "I saw my bedchamber this afternoon. It is ... lovely."

He frowned. "You may enjoy it tomorrow."

Cat-like eyes flew back to his. "Tomorrow? You're saying ... oh." She swallowed. Stared at his mouth. "*Your* walls. *Your* bed."

"I shall take better care of you this time," he assured her. "No more pain."

"It wasn't so terrible, really. Especially at the end. Is—is that a usual sort of thing, Holstoke? You never did answer."

He lowered his head until his lips hovered over hers. Skimming. Touching. Whispering, "With me, you will find it the most usual of usual things, Eugenia. Only with me."

Chapter Fifteen

"Yes, indeed, Humphrey. A stroll through the gardens would be just the thing."

—The Dowager Marchioness of Wallingham to her boon companion, Humphrey, after a rousing breakfast.

∞

Across a steaming stack of succulent ham, Genie examined her husband carefully. Black hair, short-cropped and rather severe. Cheekbones that might be regarded as exotic, they were so high and prominent. Dark, level brows. Vivid, pale eyes. A long, distinguished nose. And lips that could wring screams of ecstasy from her throat for hours.

Hours. Not minutes. Not brief or passing or demure. Loud, long screams for hours. Begging, too.

She propped her elbow on the breakfast table and tapped her lips with her finger.

Wearing a calm, neutral expression, he sipped his tea and

read his newspaper. Like any standard gentleman on any standard morning, he went about his business with casual grace. As though this were routine.

To devastate his wife with pleasure then hold her tightly through the night while his heartbeat lulled her to sleep. Then, awaken her periodically for more. Finally, just when she'd thought the storm was over, he'd awakened her one last time with his mouth. Between her ... Upon her ...

Good heavens. She tapped her lips and narrowed her eyes. Best not to recall too precisely. The fire would only reignite, and then where would she be? Flat on her back with a pile of ham for her pillow, that's where.

"You've been staring for twenty minutes, Eugenia." He calmly turned the page of his newspaper without glancing up. "Do you have a question?"

"No." A lie. She did have a question. More than one, actually. But she could not very well ask them at the breakfast table. Could she?

His eyes came up. He arched a brow. Took a sip of his tea and returned his cup to its saucer with a light clink.

She now found herself examining his hands. Long, sensitive, elegant fingers that held some dark form of magic. He had proved himself capable of producing shivers in the most extraordinary places. She rested her chin against the back of her hand and contemplated his shoulders, which were lean but quite muscled, as she'd discovered when he'd stripped off his shirt the previous day. His nipples had been lovely. She'd enjoyed them almost as much as he'd appeared to enjoy her attentions.

But, for all that he had extraordinary eyes and lips and hands, he was an ordinary man. Tall. Certainly attractive in his way. Blindingly intelligent. Very well, perhaps ordinary was the wrong word. But she'd encountered men one might expect to produce the kind of transcendent response he produced in her. The Marquess of Rutherford, for example, who'd been a rake of some renown before his marriage. Lord Atherbourne was another. To this day, she'd yet to clap eyes on a handsomer man. Truly, had she married either of them, her reactions might not have surprised her so.

But she had married Holstoke.

Holstoke.

This was Phineas Brand, the Earl of bloody Holstoke.

He was studious and serious. Brilliant and cold. Honorable and unreadable.

He was not the sort of man a woman begged to touch her.

And she wanted to. After last night and this morning, she should not have the energy to contemplate it. She was doing more than contemplating. She was all but melting into the butter dish.

"I could show you the rest of the gardens today, Eugenia." His eyes found hers. His tongue swiped away a drop of tea from his lower lip. Then, his mouth quirked up at one corner. "If you like."

Oh, dear God. She would not survive this.

She looked at her plate. Well, she would survive, strictly speaking. She'd eaten three slices of ham and two eggs. She never ate so heartily.

This could not possibly be normal. She opened her mouth to tell him so, but he was already folding his newspaper and rising from his chair.

He held out his hand. "Come. I shall show you the gardens, and you may ask me your questions."

Drat. She could not resist him. She slid her hand into his.

He pulled her to her feet then lightly rested his magical fingers on her waist. "Don't forget a bonnet," he murmured, another smile playing with his lips.

Drat, drat, drat. He made her forget everything except him. No, this was not normal in the slightest.

She asked Harriet to fetch her green bonnet with the white flowers, and then clasped Holstoke's arm as he led her through the morning room doors into the courtyard. This fountain—which, she noticed, was pleasingly formed of simple, flower-shaped tiers—must have been his addition. All around were potted plants and little benches and statuary. It was a marvel, really. Five stories of stone walls surrounded them, yet all around were windows and doors leading back into the castle. The sky was their ceiling, yet she felt sheltered.

He led her through another set of doors then out onto the north terrace, which stretched the length between two of the castle's round towers. From this vantage, one could see the sunken garden stretching northward at least two hundred yards. Sloped sides bloomed in swaths of red and purple and yellow, divided by the occasional set of stone stairs. On the floor of the long rectangle, neatly squared boxwood hedges formed a stunning parterre filled with all manner of roses, lilies, and other delights. The only relief from the squared symmetry was the round fountain carved out of the center and ringed by concentric circles of flowers in varying shades of purple and blue. The rings resembled water. At the top of the fountain was a mermaid embraced by a fierce, protective Neptune. The sea god wielded a trident against unseen creatures.

Genie sighed, as enchanted as she'd been the day before. "I love this garden." It was everything Holstoke was—complex and contained and beautiful, yet at its heart, overflowing with valor.

"I have submitted thirty-five new varieties of lily and seventeen new roses to the Horticultural Society," he said. "All exhibit superior resistance to common blights and pests. In some, I have extended bloom times by up to fifty percent."

She had no idea what any of that signified, but it sounded impressive. "Any new colors?" she asked.

He frowned. "Four."

"Well, show me, then."

He took her down into the sunken garden, pausing here and there to explain about pollination. His voice was low and serious, so she assumed his descriptions were meant to be educational. If she'd comprehended half of it, she might have found it so.

Instead, she only wanted his hands upon her again. His mouth upon her. His eyes glowing as he gazed up past her belly and breasts with the closest thing to possession she'd ever seen in a man.

It should not be this way. She felt out of control.

Perhaps another subject would help. She interrupted just as he was going on about "the receptive nature of the pistil," to ask how the fountain was fed.

"The lake," he replied after a pause. "We laid pipes there beneath the ground." He nodded toward the northernmost end of the sunken garden, which bordered the lake with the red-blooming shrubs. "Because the lake is higher than the fountain, gravity creates pressure, which forces the water upward."

She watched his mouth as he spoke about chambers to control the pressure and the basin's advanced drainage system and the ways in which the water was used for the gardens during dry spells. By heaven, it did not seem to matter what he said. Those well-defined lips obsessed her. *He* obsessed her.

Next they strolled along the lake, where ducks swam with their ducklings and the red-flowered shrubs—rhododendrons, according to Holstoke—shown like rubies beneath large willows and small pines.

Holstoke described how, after inheriting the title, he'd purchased a house for his mother in Weymouth and sent her to live there. Then, he'd begun digging. First, he'd excavated the gardens Lady Holstoke had designed, forming the sunken garden. Then, he'd created the lake from two underground streams. Over time, he had replaced every bit of ground his mother's hand had touched.

Except the fountain at the castle's entrance, of course. She noted he did not mention that.

"You rarely discuss her," Genie observed. "Your mother. I presume the two of you did not get on. Before you discovered her murderous tendencies, I mean."

He stiffened as they made their way toward the west gardens. They entered the orchards before he answered, "No."

He went quiet for a time while they walked past fruit trees of dizzying variety—apples and apricots, pears and plums. By the time they entered the section with the walnuts and chestnuts, her curiosity had reached a crescendo.

"What ..." She glanced up at him, noticing how he kept his eyes southward, toward the sea. "What was it like? Being her son."

He did not answer. His face remained expressionless, though they continued on toward the south gardens.

"I met her once, if you'll recall," she continued, hoping to ease his tension. "Astley's. Do you remember?"

A nod.

"I must confess I didn't care for your mother, Holstoke. No, not a jot. She was rude while pretending not to be. Oh!" Genie rolled her eyes. "And what dreadful taste in hats. Plain, plain, plain. Dull, dull, dull."

A long blink. The muscles of his arm relaxed beneath her hand. But the strain around his mouth remained.

"Had she been my mother, I would not have sent her to live in Weymouth. Rather, I should think Greenland more appropriate. The cold suited her."

This time, his jaw relaxed. He even glanced down at her briefly.

"Yes, Greenland. No one to bother except the whales." She clicked her tongue. "Poor whales. Perhaps, rather, a hut somewhere inland. Yes, ideal. She could wear her dull, dull bonnets and live in the darkness and the cold with nothing but her own company. A fitting solution for a mother like yours."

His lips quirked up at one corner. "Fitting, indeed."

She grinned in triumph and listened as he began explaining

how he'd formed the divide between the orchard and the south gardens with a technique called espaliering, in which the branches of trees were trained to grow sideways into a living fence.

"Oh, my!" She squeezed his arm as they traveled through an elaborate arch formed of leaves and branches and little, pebble-sized fruits. "That is what you did on the drive."

His grin was wide now. "With apple trees. You liked it?"

"Goodness, Holstoke, it is a marvel. White and pink blossoms everywhere. I felt as if I'd entered heaven itself."

His eyes glowed as he guided her onto a path winding past leafy shrubs and several vine-wrapped obelisks. "You may find heaven whenever you wish, Eugenia. You've only to ask."

Blast. Her dratted lust returned with a whoosh as powerful as the sea she could now hear crashing onshore. When he looked at her that way, all she could think about was lemon and mint and how it felt when he thrust inside her, his glorious eyes blazing down into hers. A breeze came up, bringing the scents of the sea and his shaving soap.

She forced herself to look away. Cleared her throat. Focused on the next wonder ahead. She did not have to wait long, as the path soon took them into a tunnel of arched wooden trellises covered in vines. She blinked. Stopped. Released his arm to examine the leaves more closely.

"Grapes," she murmured. "You've trained the grapevines into arches. How beautiful."

"Beautiful. Quite." His voice was strangely hoarse. "Harvesting is a simple matter, really. Wait for everything to ripen. Then it all but falls into your hands of its own accord. Plump. Succulent. Delectable."

She spun about to find him eyeing her backside. "Holstoke!"

He raised a brow. "Yes?"

"Stop that."

"What?"

"You are comparing me to fruit."

He licked his lips. "Only in the most complimentary fashion."

"And you are trying to seduce me. In the garden. Again."

"Strictly speaking, you seduced me, Eugenia."

"Perhaps the first time. And I'd little idea what I was doing."

He eyed her bodice with stunning intensity, as though he might burn it away with his eyes alone. "I know."

"Stop it."

A slow smile. "What should I stop now?"

She groaned, her hand hovering over her belly, where the heat bloomed and ached. She wanted to undress for him. She wanted to lie down beneath leafy arches and let him ravish her. "What have you done to me?"

Frowning, he tilted his head.

"Do not give me that puzzled look. You know very well how I feel right now."

Slowly, his frown disappeared, replaced by a subtle smile. Those pale eyes painted her from knees to bonnet, leaving a trail of tingles.

This was not normal.

"Tell me what you've done," she demanded.

He lifted a brow. "I can do it again, if you require reminding."

She stomped toward him. "I am frigid. This is not normal."

His hands clasped at his back. He narrowed his eyes, examining her like a specimen. "Some mysteries may only be solved through experimentation."

"That is not an answer."

"It is the only one I have to offer."

Raising her chin, she said, "Then, here is my experiment. We will no longer engage in intimacies until you explain what you've done."

A deep glower moved across his brow, darkening his eyes like a cloud over the sun. "Don't be foolish, Eugenia."

"It is the lemon balm, is it not? The leaves produce a lustful madness. Tell me truly."

He blinked. His glower turned disbelieving. Then, he laughed. The sound burst out of him, deep and flinty, as he rubbed his brow between thumb and finger. "No." The laughter lightened to a chuckle as he shook his head. "Balm has no stimulant properties. Quite the contrary. That is one reason it is called 'balm.'"

She felt her cheeks heat. "Something else, then. Another herb. Or your shaving soap."

"I am not poisoning you with aphrodisiacs. Good God, you have more thorns than a briar, woman."

"A briar, am I?" She sniffed. "Well, then, perhaps you should avoid kissing me. You wouldn't wish to—"

"You are being irrational."

"—injure those fine lips. And no touching, either. You'll need your hands—"

"Eugenia."

"—for pottering about with your little plants—"

He stopped her words with his mouth, taking hold and sliding his tongue inside in one swift move. Predictably, her body lifted toward him—every fiber, every part. It wanted to merge, to climb, to feel his skin. She moaned at the pleasure of his lips. Clutched at woolen lapels and clawed at a linen-bound neck.

This heat. It could not be natural. She'd never felt the like—aching emptiness only he could fill, tingling shivers only he could spark. These were the strings of madness. He tied her so tight, she lost her breath.

She tore away, pulling his hands from her waist and backing up until grape leaves brushed her skirts. Her heart drummed the bones of her chest in a desperate rhythm.

He stood still. Dark. A green-eyed raven watching her carefully. "You've nothing to fear from me," he said hoarsely.

But she did. The fear filled her like the incoming tide as she held his gaze. Examined those fascinating lips. The long nose. Proud cheekbones and level brows.

His beloved face.

This beloved man.

No. No, no, no, no. She could not love him.

Because he would never love her while he still loved Maureen.

Love without reciprocity made one a slave to endless desire and futile hope. It made one a fountain with no lake, just dry, empty stone.

She refused to fall into such a trap. She would escape it. All she needed was a plan. This was Holstoke, after all. Surely it could not be that hard to keep herself from falling in love with Holstoke.

"Sweetbriar," he murmured as though speaking to himself. "That is what you are. A single blossom is worth every thorn."

Dear God. Resist. Resist. She must resist. "If—if you call me briar again, I shall start calling you ..." She scrambled to think of something, but her mind was swimming in lustful inebriation. All she could manage was another of his names. "Phineas."

His eyes fired. His shoulders went rigid. His head tilted and he licked his lips. Good heavens, he looked predatory. "We have a bargain, Briar."

Oh, no. Her belly was heating and fluttering in a most ominous manner. She shook her head. "That was not a bargain."

He came toward her, hands clasped at his back. "Sounded like one to me."

"Holstoke. Phineas. Honestly." She swallowed and held up her hand. "I am frigid. I am."

Her hand met his chest as he closed in upon her. He leaned down and blew a gentle stream of air on the side of her neck.

Shivers took hold. Gooseflesh rose. Her nipples went painfully hard.

"Not with me," he whispered. "Remember that, my Briar. Perhaps other flowers bloom readily for any hand. You require mine."

Chapter Sixteen

*"Hmmph. Even the finest men have flaws, my dear.
A lady is wise to identify them early so that training may
commence in a timely fashion. Husbands require careful
handling, you know."*

—The Dowager Marchioness of Wallingham to Lady Katherine
Huxley upon said lady's declaration of admiration for a
suitor's fine baritone.

∞

She felt his heart beneath her fingertips. Stunningly, it galloped nearly as fast as hers. He always appeared so calm, so unaffected by her proximity.

But his heart told a different story.

Sighing, she leaned into him. Breathed lemon and mint and shaving soap.

His lips nibbled at a spot just beneath her jaw.

She tilted her head to give him better access, even as she struggled against losing her heart. "Holstoke. Phineas."

"Phineas will do."

"I—I think you've done something to me. Something wicked."

"Not yet. But I intend to."

She squeezed her eyes shut. "I cannot think clearly when you kiss me."

"Thinking is not required."

Gathering every ounce of will she could muster, she pushed at him. He stopped kissing her neck, but he did not back away. "Phineas," she groaned.

Calmly, he tugged at the ribbons beneath her chin and removed her bonnet, plopping it onto the gravel. "Briar."

She met his eyes. Summoned her fortitude. "Tell me something dreadful. About you."

His expression did not change—steady resolve and scalding intensity. He ran his knuckles lightly down her cheek to brush her lower lip. "Why?"

"I like to be informed."

"Hmm. Well, my patience runs short when those I care for are insulted or threatened."

"That is natural, not dreadful. You must have undesirable qualities. Everyone does."

"Some accuse me of tedious conversation."

"No, no. Worse."

He shook his head. "Such as?"

"I don't know! Diseased, putrid feet. Or cruelty to kittens. Or a secret yearning for raw onions."

The corners of his mouth twitched. "My feet are quite healthy, I'm afraid. And I prefer my onions cooked." His grin went wide with a teasing glint. "Roasted kittens with onions—my favorite dish."

She swatted his arm. "Do be serious."

He chuckled. "Very well. Here is the truth: At the moment,

my only secret yearning is for Briar. Sweet, wild Briar."

"Oh, God." Fluttering panic set in. "Please, Phineas. Tell me something bad. Something you wouldn't wish me to know."

His eyes sobered. He turned his face toward the sounds of the sea. For long seconds, she thought he might not answer. Then, he did.

"I hated my mother." His voice was distant. Quiet. "I still do."

She breathed through the pain in her chest. Forced her hands to clench rather than reach for him. "Everybody hates her—"

"Not like this. Long before I knew the things she'd done—before I can remember, in fact—I wanted ..." He heaved a shuddering breath. "I wanted her to die." Within wondrous green was the pain of his confession. The battle he'd fought and lost. "A son should not wish such things."

And there it went. Her last, faint hope for keeping her heart. She felt the tether unravel. Slip from her grasp.

She closed her eyes, but all she could see was a boy. Black hair. Pale, solemn gaze. Intelligent beyond his years. Small as Edwin but much, much quieter. That boy had sensed the evil in his mother. And, being the protective sort, he'd wished her dead.

He'd thought this the worst secret he might reveal. Even now, she sensed he expected her to feel disgust. But she felt only shivers. More and more until they became bubbles of glowing light and heat and expansion. The sensations traveled through her veins to pulse and stretch every inch of her skin.

By heaven, she loved him. Perhaps she always had. For, now she understood how well she knew him. She *knew* him. Down to the bottom of his valiant soul.

How could she hope to keep her heart safe? The answer was obvious: She could not.

"Phineas," she whispered, opening her eyes. Beloved face. Beloved man. "Kiss me."

A flicker of surprise. A blaze of desire. Then, his arms enfolded her, half lifted her. His lips were upon hers. His chest worked against hers. He pleasured her mouth and backed her against the leafy trellis and ground his hardness against her. "Bloody hell, Briar," he panted. "How do you do this to me?"

Her? This was him. Tall and fascinating with sorcery in his touch. He obsessed her. Possessed her. She was a vine upon his trellis, her form permanently altered by his presence.

He cupped her cheeks and kissed her again, deep and long and pulsing. She stroked his arms and wrists. Frantically unbuttoned his coat. Slid her arms inside and around his waist so she could feel his heat against her.

Soon, he was tugging at her skirts. Lifting them just as frantically but with far more precision. Then, his fingers—those sorcerous fingers—were upon her. Inside her. Sliding and circling.

She spread her legs for him, holding herself up with fistfuls of his waistcoat.

Gently, but with increasing firmness, his fingers generated a storm. Sliding. Sliding. Sliding. In and out. Around and around. Skirting the place that ripened to bursting.

"This belongs to me," he whispered against her lips, his breath hot and fast. He inserted a second finger. "Your need is mine. Your nectar is mine. You flower only for me."

Her head fell back, cushioned by leaves and vines. The pleasure was roiling, rippling, rushing like steam. It billowed out and up. Swelled toward his touch. "No, Phineas." She twisted to force his thumb closer to where she needed him. "There."

He slid deliberately past the center while stroking inside her with his other two fingers. The pressure grew inside, but not where she needed him.

"Please," she begged. "God, please." This was how it had been last night. He'd pleasured her with his fingers and his lips and his tongue and his staff. Relentlessly, he'd coaxed her toward unimagined heights, delaying each explosive, repeated peak until she'd pleaded for him. Now, again, he drew out the pleasuring, his eyes glowing down at her with a feverish light. Hard, long fingers pressed harder and deeper. His talented thumb stroked near, yet not upon, the center of her need.

When the peak came, it shocked her into a long, gasping moan. Hard, powerful surges forced her onto her toes as he whispered in her ear, "That's right, my sweet Briar. Bloom. Let me feel it."

Rings of pleasure concussed through her, one after another, as he squeezed her tightly and kissed her throat. The ripples shivered outward even after he withdrew his beloved, pleasure-giving hand and let her skirts fall.

Even after he bent and scooped her into his arms.

She gasped again, scarcely able to make sense of her new position. She clasped his neck, trembling with the echoes he'd left inside her.

With swift urgency, he carried her around a bend in the tunnel. She spied a small opening cut into the trellises—a window to the sea—before he lowered her gently back onto her feet. He stroked her cheek tenderly then shrugged out of his coat and laid it over a stone bench beneath the window.

She stood swaying and watching, not understanding what he was about until he sat upon his coat and pulled her forward between his knees. Then, he loosened his fall. Raised her skirts. And without a word, he positioned her straddling him with her knees resting on his coat and her backside resting on his thighs.

She sighed and hugged his neck. Buried her nose in the linen. Beneath her, she felt his hard staff pressing where she was still slick and sensitive. She blinked. Drew in a sharp breath as the sensations started up again. She moaned and leaned back to see his face. Cupped his jaw and ran her thumb across his splendid lips. "Phineas," she whispered, loving how near he was in this position. How she could see the blue rings around heat-darkened green. How she could kiss him so easily.

She brushed his mouth with hers. Ran her tongue across his lip.

He was saying something, but her blood was pounding and the sea was pounding and everything was pleasure.

"... lift you up. Just relax."

She felt his arm strong about her waist. Felt the blunt tip of his staff, hot and separating. Stretching and full. Sliding and deep and ... "Oh. That ... it is almost ..."

Too much. It was almost too much. As he lowered her down upon his staff, he sank all the way to the root. Her earlier pleasure eased his passage, eliminating most discomfort, though some soreness remained from the previous night and morning.

But, God, how he filled her. How his eyes blazed and consumed her.

"Take me," he murmured.

Yes. Yes, she would. She would take him inside and let herself love him. Because she did. She loved him. Her heart was going to explode with the joy of it. As it was, she felt on the edge of weeping.

She loved him. Phineas. Her Holstoke.

She leaned her forehead against his. Held those stunning eyes. Saw a reflection that looked like ravenous hunger. Felt him brush something from her cheek. "Phineas," she whispered, aching now. Between her thighs. In her belly. In her chest and heart.

His hands gripped her hips. A pained frown darkened his brow. "I cannot wait any longer, my sweet one. I need you now."

She kissed him. Nodded. "What do you need me to do?"

"Move," he uttered, his voice a thread. "You know how to ride. That is the rhythm. Take what you can. And move."

It took her a few moments to puzzle out the angle, but once she braced her hands upon his shoulders, she was able to rise on her knees. Her eyes flew wide at the friction of the withdrawal. Then they drifted closed as she sank back down. Oh, to be filled again. The pleasure of it. The rightness.

"Bloody hell, Briar. You are killing me."

"Oh." She grinned teasingly. "Is that you, Phineas? I was having such a pleasant ride."

Muscles in his jaw flexed. "Quicken your gait, or I shall take the reins."

A little thrill moved across her skin, zinging between her thighs and into her breasts. "Perhaps you should." She leaned forward and tested a theory, whispering against his lips, "I am but a novice, you know. A master rider would have much to teach me."

He groaned, deep and pained. Dark light exploded in his eyes. His arm braced around her lower back while his hand gripped her thigh. Then, he thrust. Drew her down upon him and thrust deeper. Rougher. With every stroke, he filled her fully then withdrew to the tip. Again and again and again. His rhythm was nothing like hers. This was hard and fast and uncontrolled. Heat built inside her sheath, the friction stoking a renewed fire. Soon, she was helping him sustain it, grinding her hips into his, kissing his delicious mouth.

The hand that had been on her thigh moved in and touched her lightly just above where they joined. She jerked. Gasped his name. Seized upon him. Felt the culmination rise up suddenly in a burst of ecstatic pressure.

God, it was painful to feel this much pleasure. She screamed through gritted teeth, clawed at his shoulders and gripped him inside, trying to hold him in place.

He did not comply. He continued his pounding rhythm, his touch against her swollen center harder now, forcing her higher until her voice shredded and her body coursed with rhapsodic waves. Behind closed eyes, she saw nothing but light. Bright bursts of light that were but a dim reflection of her pleasure's pulsating brilliance.

When she opened her eyes again, she saw something even more beautiful—her husband's eyes fixed upon her, near mad with the pleasure she was giving him. And, in that moment, her longing deepened. Widened. Grew to include a new aim: She would give him pleasure he'd never imagined. She would become *his* obsession, as he was hers. Her reward would be to see this every day. Phineas in a state of ecstatic bliss. She would feel this every day. Phineas's release exploding inside her.

Ah, yes, she thought, smiling and stroking his hardened jaw, cupping his neck as he clutched her waist and groaned his release against her throat. If this was all she might have of him, if he could never love her, then she would take every bit. His pleasure. His need. His name and his babes.

She brushed away a stupid tear as she caressed his back and neck, kissed his ear and stared out at the incoming tide.

Maureen might have his heart, and that was surely torment. But everything else belonged to Genie. And, come what may, she intended to keep what was hers.

Chapter Seventeen

"Bah! Arrogant Bow Street rabble. I daresay this matter might have been resolved weeks ago, had he simply accepted your assistance. A good hunter knows the advantages of a superior hound."

—The Dowager Marchioness of Wallingham to her boon companion, Humphrey, upon receiving Mr. Jonas Hawthorn's reply to a most generous offer.

The prostitute was not poisoned. She'd been discovered inside a house in Knightsbridge, her throat cut open, her face beaten so badly she'd been unidentifiable. Pinned to her gown, however, had been a flower, shriveled and dry. Henbane. Jonas had known it on sight, thanks to the botanical sketches Holstoke had sent him.

Now, as he tapped his pencil against his notebook and

watched a constable haul a drunkard to stand before the Bow Street magistrate, Jonas rubbed his eyes and silently cursed. In the two days since a watchman had discovered the body, he had not slept. Something about this murder deepened the itch along his neck.

Poison was a refined weapon, distancing and clean. Fists were personal. Enraged.

He'd scoured the area around Knightsbridge, asked neighbors what they'd noticed. Nobody had heard or seen anything. The house had sat empty for years, and Knightsbridge was not known for its prostitutes. But she'd been dressed like one, her body showing signs of her profession. That was all he knew.

"Sleepin' again, Hawthorn?"

Jonas glanced up to see Drayton limping toward him. "Tell me you found something."

Drayton tossed his notebook on the desk in front of Jonas and slumped into a chair, rubbing his leg as though it pained him. "She was a lightskirt, name of Mary Bly. Her bawd, Old Sally Sawyer, claims she went missin' a week ago."

A week. Jonas sat forward, his skin prickling. "What else did Old Sally say?"

"Not much." Drayton looked as tired as Jonas felt, his eyes drooping even more than usual. "Miss Bly had been at it a year or so. A right popular dove."

"Popular?"

"Aye." Drayton winced and rubbed harder at his leg. "The gents called her Midnight Mary, on account of her hair. A real beauty. That was all the bawd would say. You know Old Sally. Cares more for 'er gin than 'er girls."

Jonas shot out of his chair and retrieved his greatcoat and hat.

"Hawthorn! Where the devil are you goin', man?"

"To speak to Old Sally." He had a sick feeling in his gut. This murder was different. It was a message. He just hadn't deciphered it yet.

Drayton groaned and shoved to his feet. Ignoring the older man, Jonas strode out of the Bow Street office and headed for Castle Street, where Old Sally resided. He was halfway there when he felt it. The itch on his neck intensified, running down his spine like a trickle of water. He glanced over his shoulder. Saw Drayton loping to catch up, yet falling behind. He scanned the shouting peddlers and indolent wretches who frequented the outskirts of Covent Garden. Little pickpockets darted between pedestrians. Carts full of pottery and fruit and chickens lumbered by. A young girl sold a handful of daisies to a couple fresh from the country. The girl's accomplice lifted the man's purse as deftly as Jonas shaved his whiskers.

Bloody hell, his nerves were ablaze. He walked faster, disguising his speed with a slouched posture and lengthened gait. Night was coming. Gray light gradually thickened into dusk.

He found Old Sally leaning against the wood-framed corner of her lodging house, arguing price with a withered man thrice the age of the girl whose arm he clasped.

"Go on with ye!" the bawd shouted, yanking the girl's other arm. "'Tis two-pound-five or nothin', ye old sod." She shoved the man hard. He stumbled back into the path of a hack. The driver shouted and veered, narrowly missing him.

Ignoring the fracas, the young whore adjusted her bodice and grinned prettily at Jonas as he approached. "Ooh, ye're a 'andsome one, ain't ye? Care for a tumble?"

Old Sally glanced up from the coins she'd been counting. "Eh. Don't bother, gel. 'Ee's got more'n 'is share without payin' for it. Ain't that so, Hawthorn?"

"Tell me about Mary Bly, Sally."

The bawd sniffed. "She's dead. What's to tell?"

As he moved in closer, he could smell the gin on her breath, the sweat of summer's heat. She was a fleshy woman, her hair a blend of orange and gray, her nose red and shiny, even in the dwindling light. "More than you told Drayton," he uttered, pulling his notebook and pencil from his pocket. "Who hired her last?"

"Already told Drayton, I's indisposed. She took payment 'erself."

"What did she look like?"

The bawd shrugged. "Black hair. Flat bosom."

"Tell me about her face."

A scowl settled deep into the woman's creases. "Comely enough to fetch four guineas."

Tilting his head, he let her have a glimpse of his impatience. "Details, Sally. Now, if you please."

The bawd shifted nervously, shot him a wary squint, and swallowed. "Light eyes. Fair skin. Good teeth. Like I said, four guineas. Would've been five if not for the bosoms."

The sick feeling he'd been battling sank deeper. Grew colder. Apart from one feature, she might be describing Hannah Gray.

"Eh!" the bawd shouted, shooting past him to shove at the man who'd almost met his end beneath a hack. The man was pestering another of Old Sally's girls.

Jonas released a breath, attempting to calm the bloody itch. He needed more answers. He needed to know who had hired Mary Bly and then murdered her in the most brutal fashion.

"Mr. Hawthorn?"

He turned.

The young, yellow-haired whore with bruises forming on her arms gazed up at him with a puckered frown. "Ye're lookin' for the man what killed Mary?"

"I am."

"I—I might'a seen 'im."

Bloody hell. "When?"

"A week past." The girl's brown eyes gleamed with tears. "Poor Mary. Is it true she were b-beaten?"

Gently, he took the girl's elbow and drew her deeper into the shadows of the lodging house. "Just tell me what you remember. Can you describe him?"

The girl sniffed and swiped at her nose. "Mary 'ad the loveliest eyes. Like moonlight, they were. Drove the lads mad."

Inside, he went colder. He reached into the lowest pocket of his greatcoat and withdrew a sketch he hadn't meant for anyone's eyes but his own. Carefully, he unfolded the paper. "Did she look something like this?"

The girl peered at his drawing. A frown tugged. "Aye. She were a bit 'arder, ye understand. Not as lovely as that one. But similar."

He folded the sketch, tucked it away, and offered the girl a handkerchief.

She took it and blew her nose.

"I need to know about the man Mary left with. What did he look like?"

The girl made a show of dabbing her eyes. Sniffed again. Wiped away a tear. Then, she calmly held out her palm.

He glanced down at the small, empty hand. Came back to meet young, jaded eyes.

Devil take it. How he despised this world.

He dug out two pounds and five shillings and dropped the money into her open hand. "Now," he said softly. "Tell me."

"'Ee were shorter than you."

He held his hand level with his nose.

She nodded. "Pleasant to look upon. 'Is eyes were soft, understand. Round, like 'ee were a green lad. But 'ee weren't that. There were a coldness in 'im. I told Mary not to go. But 'ee offered five. Nobody does that."

"Five guineas?"

She nodded again. "Last I saw of Mary Bly, she were climbin' into a 'ack with 'im."

He reached into his upper pocket and unfolded the now-careworn sketch. "Is this the man you saw?"

Her eyes widened. "Aye. Tha's the one."

His urgency increased a hundredfold. The blackguard was

going to attack Hannah Gray. He did not know why, but it bloody well didn't matter. All that mattered was reaching her. Keeping her safe.

"Ye missed 'is scar."

He frowned and glanced down at the sketch. "What scar?"

She traced a finger along the side of the man's neck. "Ear to shoulder. A long, white scar. From a blade, I reckon. Healed jagged, though."

"He wasn't wearing a neckcloth?"

"Naught but a shirt and waistcoat. Plain. Bit like yours. Tha's why I took notice. Looked too poor to offer five shillings, never mind five guineas."

Jonas did not understand the man's game. He'd dressed in a footman's livery to invade Randall's house—complete with the powdered wig. An effective disguise if a man wished to blend into the scenery. Then, he'd solicited a prostitute wearing plain, humble clothes that exposed a distinguishing scar. No wig. No disguise.

Why change patterns with Mary Bly? Why not poison her and leave her somewhere near Covent Garden, where she was known to ply her trade?

Knightsbridge was a fair distance away. The blackguard had paid for the hack. He'd paid five guineas for Miss Bly. He'd managed to enter a vacant house and murder a woman without the neighbors noticing.

And he could be anywhere.

Once again, Jonas glanced around, taking in the rabble of Castle Street. The workhouse. The lodging house. The withered man arguing with the bawd.

He nodded to the girl and tucked away his notebook and the sketch. Then, he began to move. He needed to go to Dorsetshire. He needed to be where Hannah Gray was. The prickle in his neck and the fire in his spine screamed it until his pace neared a run.

He rounded the corner off of Hart Street and felt his neck

catch fire. Sheer instinct drove him to dart left.

A searing pain speared his shoulder.

He blinked, disoriented by the force of the blow. It jerked him sideways into a wall of brick.

Blood pounded. Drumming and drumming. His hand went numb. Dripped.

He looked everywhere, but dark had fallen while he'd talked to the yellow-haired whore. Nobody in sight. A single light. It glowed gold in a window on the second story. The window was open.

His breathing sharpened. He shoved away from bricks. Staggered forward toward the gold glow. A figure appeared in silhouette. Tall. Different than he'd drawn. He blinked, the gold and shadow blurring.

A quiet *thwick*. Another streak of agony. His right thigh.

He went to his knees hard. His blood drummed and drummed. Seeped and pooled. Whatever had struck him made his vision blur. He could scarcely see his own hands gripping cobbles and dirt.

He'd met death before. Old friends, they were.

This was not how things would end.

He needed to get to the gold window. That was all. He needed to kill one man before that man killed ... her.

Bracing his hand on the bricks, he forced himself to rise. Forced his feet to plant and his hand to shove and his left leg to carry his full weight. The filthy street tilted. Undulated and duplicated. He shook his head. Took a step.

An explosion of anguish cannoned through his right leg. He looked down. Twin feathered arrows protruded from his thigh. No, not twin. There was one. One in his leg and one in his shoulder.

Christ, his blood kept drumming and drumming. He had to get to the window. Had to kill one man.

Another step. Another burst of anguish. A third. And a fourth.

"Hawthorn!"

A fifth. His breath sawed in and out. He focused upon the door that led to the second story that led to the blackguard who meant to kill ... her.

"Bloody, bleeding hell, man. Are those arrows?" It was Drayton.

He fell to his knees again as the other man reached him. "W-window." He gripped Drayton's arm, shaking it. "Second story. Go." He shoved, but he was weak. Too damned weak.

Drayton attempted to pull him up.

"Go!" Jonas roared, pointing toward the gold window.

A cursing, limping lope carried the other man away.

Jonas tried to convince the ground to steady. But it was only growing wetter.

His blood drummed and drummed. The darkness came, gray at the edges.

Breathing was shallow now. He blinked. Sound faded. A woman passed by, her skirts swishing away from him.

A woman. Pale skin. Eyes of moonlight. Hair of midnight. Miles above him. Leagues. Cold and pristine as a winter lake.

"... will hurt like bleeding hell, Hawthorn. Must be done ..."

Fire. In his shoulder and leg. Bursting white behind his eyes, then dark and gray and blurred. Then rocking. Pulsing green gaslights.

"... see Dunston's surgeon. Hold tight, man. Nearly there."

For a moment, his vision sharpened. He saw Drayton above him in a coach. A hack, perhaps. The wheels clattered on the pavement at a furious pace.

"Catch him?" Jonas wheezed.

Drayton ran a hand over his whiskered, haggard face. "No. He was gone. Left the bow behind, though. Generous fellow."

Jonas reached up with his uninjured arm and carefully clawed a fistful of Drayton's coat. He drew the older man down so that he would hear him well. The green gaslights were dimming. Blurring.

"Must go to Dorsetshire."

"Hawthorn—"

"Dorsetshire," he shouted, though it came out as a threaded wheeze. "She is in danger."

Drayton glowered, his eyes flashing in the passing light. "Who?"

"Gray," he whispered. "Hannah Gray."

"You're out of your head. Once the surgeon has a chance to—"

"Swear it to me," he growled, shaking Drayton with as much force as he could muster, which was not much. "Must go to Dorsetshire. Warn Holstoke. Protect her."

"Aye. Dorsetshire. I'll leave at first light."

"We," he corrected, the green lights graying. Blurring. Disappearing.

His grip slipped loose as he heard Drayton's rough crack of laughter. "… daft, Hawthorn … been shot … bleeding arrows, for Christ's sake."

Jonas's eyes drifted closed until the only thing he saw was … her. "I am going," he whispered, wondering if he'd only spoken the words in his mind. "This is not how it ends."

Chapter Eighteen

"When I advised you to take up new gentlemanly pursuits, perhaps I should have been more specific: Riding, archery, fencing. These are all quite appropriate. Notice I did not mention ladies' fashions."

—THE DOWAGER MARCHIONESS OF WALLINGHAM to Lord Holstoke in a letter of reply to said gentleman's request for a list of periodicals best suited to those of a feminine persuasion.

∽∽∽

TWENTY DAYS AFTER ARRIVING AT PRIMVALE, PHINEAS received his third report from Drayton. He shoved away from his library desk and tossed the missive aside.

Damn and blast.

Rubbing the back of his neck, he moved to the window, glared out at the sunken garden, and shook his head in disbelief.

Another woman had been found dead. This time, the victim was not an aristocrat or even a servant. She was a prostitute. Her body had been discovered inside a house in Knightsbridge. The house had sat empty for years.

Natural, he supposed. Few people would wish to live where a demon had been righteously slaughtered. The demon was Horatio Syder—once his mother's partner and Hannah's captor. Syder had been pure evil, which might explain why Lydia Brand had been drawn to him in the first place. To discover another victim in the very place where Syder had died left no remaining doubt about the poisoner's intentions: The blackguard had fixated upon Phineas's mother and, by extension, Phineas.

Scarcely anybody knew of his mother's connection to Horatio Syder. Dunston, of course. A handful of others. But the fact that Syder had been her solicitor and business partner for years had remained secret, partly because Phineas had paid large sums to key officials and newspaper publishers. He'd also leveraged every connection he'd acquired at Harrow and Cambridge, including the current Home Secretary.

He would have done more to protect Hannah. Anything. Fortunately, his measures had been enough. Until now.

Somehow, the poisoner knew. About Syder. About his death and his association with Lydia Brand.

Phineas, on the other hand, knew precious little of the poisoner. He'd sent Drayton numerous theories, including Eugenia's insight about the apothecary having an assistant. Drayton had questioned surrounding shopkeepers and discovered a young man named Theodore Neville had worked there for several years before the apothecary's death. He'd vanished thereafter, rumored to have fled north. Drayton, Dunston, and Hawthorn had soon ruled him out as the poisoner, since the descriptions did not match the man who had infiltrated Randall's household.

Yet, the poisoner must be tied to Phineas's mother. He

must know how to produce the poisons, and he must be acquiring his ingredients from druggists. The concentrations were too high for it to be otherwise. According to Drayton, Hawthorn had drawn a sketch of the poisoner and carried it to virtually every apothecary shop in London. Nobody had recognized him.

Phineas had spent weeks puzzling it out, his only result frustration.

A light knock sounded at the door. Before he could say a word, the door opened.

"There you are," said the woman who never left his thoughts. "I intend to persuade Hannah to ride farther than a few paces this morning. We shall be practicing in one of the east pastures, provided she does not attack me with her riding cane. Do not be alarmed."

He smiled. Turned. Lifted a brow. "Is that an acorn?"

Eugenia tilted her chin and fingered the wide straw brim of her hat. "Why, yes. Yes it is. The theme is 'Plant a seed and lo, it grows.' Do you approve?"

Grinning, he stalked toward her. He'd been grinning for weeks. He'd never laughed or smiled or outright guffawed so much in his entire life. It was her. She made him ... light. Just seeing her lifted him ten feet off the ground. Perhaps twelve.

"Yes, Briar. I approve."

"You don't think it is too much?" Her smile remained teasing, but an odd thread of uncertainty ran underneath. He'd sensed similar doubts when she'd shown him her new workshop—a sitting room near her bedchamber that she'd transformed with tables, shelves, hat blocks, and enough feathers to construct a castle-sized ostrich sculpture. As she'd chattered away, describing all the reasons why he should not be alarmed by the bills soon to arrive at his door, he'd watched her hands. The nervous fluttering had surprised him. He'd asked about her plans, whether she still intended to open a shop one day.

She'd been startled, that uncertainty clouding her eyes. "No," she'd said quietly. "Countesses do not open shops any more than Huxleys do."

He'd begun to argue that countesses—particularly his countess—could do as they pleased, but she'd distracted him with kisses and tugged him away to luncheon with her and Hannah beside the lake.

That very day, he'd begun his research. She did not yet know, and perhaps he should wait to tell her until he had completed his inquiries. But her doubts ate at him. His Briar should be fearless, growing in whatever direction her heart directed. That was her nature, though something had obviously shaken her confidence. Mrs. Pritchard's dismissal, perhaps.

Now, eyeing her broad-brimmed hat with its leaves and acorns and ribbons, he felt the compulsion to replace the uncertainty in her eyes with her customary spark of boldness.

He cleared his throat. Clasped his hands at his back. "I have seen a hat similar to yours."

She blinked. Shook her head. "Where?"

"A recent edition of *La Belle Assemblée*."

Her mouth rounded. She frowned. "Why, may I ask, are you reading a publication valued primarily for its fashion plates?"

Again, he cleared his throat. "The articles are edifying."

"Phineas."

"Research."

"About?"

"Ladies' fashions. Hats, specifically."

Silence and a perplexed stare.

"My findings are preliminary. The degree to which one may be certain of one's conclusions in matters of ephemeral preferences in headdress is subject to—"

"Phineas." This time, his name emerged throaty and soft.

"Your creations, so far as I can determine, are quite the

first stare of fashion. Should you desire to establish your own shop, I've little doubt you would find success."

Although he had simply stated the truth, her breathing quickened. A gloved hand settled above her bosom.

Her response was most encouraging.

"*Great* success," he emphasized, once again moving toward her. He thought she was pleased. Perhaps even feeling amorous. This had been an excellent idea. "I like your hat, Briar."

"Oh, heavens." Her eyes went soft the way they did when she stroked his cheek or when he caught her gazing at him while he worked in his greenhouse. "How many publications did you—"

"Enough."

"How many?"

"Five. Several years' worth of issues." He cleared his throat. "I noted a marked increase in both size and ornamentation in the past two years. Ladies appear to be favoring such styles more and more."

Her grin started slowly and grew. It grew until she laughed and beamed. "And you like my hat."

He nodded. Helplessly, his eyes fell to her breasts, round and full beneath gold silk. "I also like your dress."

She closed her eyes and laughed again, her hand falling to her belly. "Oh, Phineas."

God, he loved hearing his name on her lips. He loved her silly, elaborate hats. He loved to strip them off her and unpin her hair and breathe in violets and sweet, dusky cherries.

Her eyes opened.

He closed in upon her, wanting more. More of her laughter and her shine.

She sighed then put her hand on his chest and moaned. "Drat. I cannot spend the day in bed with you, much as I should adore it. Your sister's lessons have been far too sporadic. At this rate, she will be in her dotage before she learns to canter."

He bracketed her between his arms, trapping her against the door. Then, he swooped beneath her brim and captured her mouth. Sweet. Beautiful. Luscious mouth.

"Phns. Muz top. Mmm." She pushed at his chest, and he drew away, gratified to see her eyes heated with longing. "Well, perhaps ... if we are quick ..." Eugenia pressed a palm to her belly and moaned. "No, I cannot stay. Your sister is waiting for me. It took an hour at breakfast to persuade her to accept another lesson."

"Why are you so determined she should learn to ride?"

She sighed. "At times, I ask myself the same question." She shoved away from the door, kissed him all too briefly, and spun to leave.

"Stay within sight of the men," he warned.

"Of course." She pulled open the door and gave him a mischievous smile over her shoulder. "I am ever the obedient wife, am I not?" She adjusted her hat and sauntered away.

He had to lean against a bookcase and shake his head like a dog shedding water before rational thought returned. His erection took several minutes longer to subside.

Nothing had ever been like this. His desire for her was a tide with no ebb. Certainly, it might be temporarily quieted after an explosive release. In those moments, when her slender arms clung and her hands stroked and her silken heat engulfed him, the peace was unlike anything he'd ever imagined.

But his hunger surged again at the slightest provocation: a glimpse of her naked hips. A breath of her violet scent. A thread of her sweet, throaty voice telling him it was time for breakfast.

He was three-and-thirty, for God's sake. Yet, whenever Eugenia was near, he might as well be seventeen again. No, worse than that. He remembered being seventeen. His first mistress—a few years older and worlds more experienced than he—had indulged every fantasy a randy youth could concoct before demonstrating a few he'd missed.

His need for Eugenia was unfathomably stronger.

Rubbing the back of his neck, he crossed to the desk and sank into his chair.

He was confounded by his own obsession. She was not the sort of woman he'd imagined marrying. Rather, Maureen had been his ideal match. They'd had much in common—Maureen's interest in gardens and landscapes nearly equaled his. He'd found her kindness and maternal nature soothing. She'd spoken lovingly about her family, and once he'd met them, he'd wanted such a family for himself. He'd known she would be an extraordinary mother. And she was.

He hadn't been wrong. Maureen made far more sense than Eugenia. Had she accepted his proposal rather than Dunston's, he suspected they would have been quite content together.

With Eugenia, he was not content. He was consumed. She stoked the blackness inside him until it spoke for him, thought for him, demanded he possess her again and again.

He closed his eyes and rubbed a hand over his face. He needed to regain control. The blackness drove him hard, and though she hadn't complained, he often wondered whether she knew how mad he was.

Releasing a breath, he picked up his pen and withdrew a sheet of paper. Then, he began to reason. He drew squares. He made lists. He built arguments for why he should not be obsessed with Eugenia. They were sensible arguments based upon evidence. Rationality. When he finished, he sat back in his chair and reread what he'd written.

Words faded. In their place, the blackness showed him a vision of Eugenia—his beautiful Briar—making paper bonnets for their babes. Beaming that mischievous grin as she plucked pins from her hair and explained how very stimulating she found the flavors of lemon and mint. Gazing up at him in open-mouthed wonder as she stood beneath a drift of white blossoms.

He rubbed his eyes, trying to force the visions away. But, in the end, they remained, satisfying the blackness's cravings. He tossed his list onto the desk. Left the library and asked Ross to retrieve his hat.

First, he went to the stables. Asked his head groom which mount Hannah had selected for her lesson. The groom assured him Lady Holstoke had insisted upon a sedate mare he'd purchased six years ago in anticipation of a wife. He nodded then, as he entered the stable courtyard, he paused. Turned. "Which mount did her ladyship take, George?"

"None, m'lord. She said as she'd be teachin' Miss Gray, she 'ad no need for one."

Frowning, he continued on his way toward the east pasture. Eugenia intended to teach Hannah herself? He'd assumed she would employ the help of the stablemaster or one of the grooms, all of whom were excellent riders. Of course, none of them were female, whereas Eugenia certainly was. Every curved, impudent inch of her. And she knew her way around a sidesaddle.

He shook his head as he passed the fountain at the south entrance of the castle and headed toward the orchards. Regardless, he still did not understand why Eugenia would take on such a task. Over the last fortnight, Hannah had recovered her manners, but she'd remained stubbornly opposed to Eugenia's overtures. The pattern had grown predictable: Eugenia suggested teaching Hannah how to make silk flowers, and Hannah politely declined. So Eugenia demonstrated her technique at the breakfast table. Eugenia offered to go along on Hannah's daily walks, and Hannah protested she enjoyed the solitude. So Eugenia accompanied her every other day. Eugenia asked if Hannah might teach her to play chess, and Hannah advised her to learn from Phineas, as he was a superior player. So Eugenia declared she would watch them play one another.

All of it was baffling—Eugenia's dogged pursuit, Hannah's coldness, and the fact that neither of them would discuss the matter with him. Maddening female nonsense.

He topped the rise where cherry trees rustled in surprisingly gusty winds. Clouds had moved in, turning the day darker. He glanced south, toward the sea. Rain was coming.

He looked back toward the pasture. In the distance, he saw them. They were halfway across the valley, Eugenia in her wide acorn hat and Hannah clinging to a saddle atop a gray mare. Eugenia led the way, stopping every few feet to look up and chatter away at Hannah, who appeared both fearful and displeased.

He stopped beneath a cherry tree. Leaned his shoulder against the trunk. Watched his wife and sister negotiate the pasture—and their battle. He was gratified to see three of Dunston's men positioned at intervals along the north and west boundaries of the pasture. They, too, kept watch.

For a long while, he observed the ladies, admiring Hannah's courage and Eugenia's patience. The wind came up and blew away his Briar's acorn hat. She did not stop leading the horse. As they approached the southeast corner of the pasture, Hannah glanced up and started speaking frantically. That was when the horse sidled away from Eugenia, who stumbled and lost her grip upon the mare. The animal danced sideways. Even from this distance, Phineas could see Hannah gripping the reins too tightly, yanking hard in an effort to regain control. Eugenia dashed toward the pair, attempting to take the reins from Hannah, who jerked away. The mare moved into his wife, knocking her petite frame flat.

Phineas's body flushed with ice. He shoved away from the tree the moment she hit the ground. And when the horse danced dangerously close, the air crystallized inside his lungs. He headed toward her at a dead run. But even as he leapt the rail fence, he knew. He was not fast enough.

There was nothing he could do to stop it. The blackness roared. And finally—finally—tore free.

The day had begun in such a lovely way. Genie had awakened to bright, golden sunlight and cloud-tufted blue skies and her husband's mouth nibbling her throat while his hands cupped her breasts. As they lay in his bed, her back to his front, she had gazed through the window to the sea and savored the wondrous pleasure of his thrusts.

Heavens, how could any day have a better beginning?

Then had come Phineas's reluctant revelation about his "research" into ladies' fashions, obviously an effort to understand Genie's preoccupation with millinery arts. Watching his proud-yet-boyish expression, her heart had gone hot and soft. She'd wondered whether, one day, he might care for her as she did for him.

No. Never that. Her love was all-consuming. Surely that was too much to hope. But friendship. Companionship. Caring. These were possible.

Unfortunately, pleasure and possibility had turned to muck and mire in short order.

First had come breakfast. The tea had been over-steeped, and Mrs. Green had informed her they were running low on ham, offering eel instead. Eel. She would sooner eat the platter it was served upon.

Then, Hannah had argued for an hour against another riding lesson. Genie had been forced to use threats of joining her walks every day rather than every other day. Grudgingly, Hannah had conceded.

Their lesson, too, had started inauspiciously. Through much coaxing, Genie managed to get the girl to mount the horse. She'd also helped her achieve a proper seat, and they'd circled much of the pasture without incident. But resentment had made Hannah tense, which made the placid mare nervous.

Genie attempted to reason with her, but the girl was clearly running out of patience with her new sister-in-law, turning waspish in a bid to defeat Genie's efforts.

"This hat does not suit me."

Glancing up beyond her own hat's wide brim, Genie eyed the dashing little confection, a simple riding hat covered in the darkest green felted wool. It featured a lighter green silk ribbon and small, twin white feathers neatly stitched to the poke.

"Oh, pooh. You look lovely. Now, do stop pretending dislike. It is partly your design, after all."

A fortnight earlier, Genie and Hannah had ventured to the market town of Bridport, which lay a few miles east of Primvale. Relieved to discover civilization was much closer than she'd thought, she'd spent an entire day persuading Phineas that she would perish if she did not soon acquire sufficient millinery supplies. Likewise, she'd been forced to promise Hannah a full-day reprieve from her company before the girl agreed to go with her.

Surrounded by six of Dunston's sharp-eyed men, they had both felt a bit conspicuous, but as soon as they'd entered the haberdashery, Genie's excitement had dwarfed her discomfort. Hannah, usually opaque and quiet, had warmed considerably as Genie demonstrated how they might use this ribbon or that box of spangles. By the time they'd left the shop for the nearby draper's, Hannah was chattering away, telling Genie her ideas for a new reticule to match her leaf-green gown. Those pale eyes had lit, and the girl had forgotten to be rude for the entire outing. Genie's heart had soared at the change, seeing that her efforts were, at long last, gaining ground.

She'd been further heartened when, at luncheon a week later, Hannah had conceded that she felt better for having a midday meal.

"It has improved my walks, I believe," the girl had confessed. "And my sleep."

Genie had disciplined her smile and nodded. "I have noticed you are a bit like me, in that you tend not to eat very much at a sitting. Dining more frequently steadies the constitution."

Hannah had agreed, then asked the footman beside her to fetch another slice of bread. Oddly, she'd called him by the wrong name.

Genie had leaned in and whispered, "Ned."

"Pardon?"

"His name. Ned, not David."

A little frown had puckered her brow. "Oh. I do sometimes confuse one for the other. Phineas insisted on rearranging so many."

This time, it was Genie who frowned. "What sort of rearranging did he do?"

"He sent two dozen servants to other properties and brought a similar number here as replacements. I am still uncertain as to his reasons."

Genie, too, had been puzzled. But, then, Phineas was a peculiar man. She and Hannah had finished their afternoon together with a pleasant stroll along the beach. They'd conversed for two hours without a single disagreeable moment.

Now, however, as they trudged together through the pasture, Hannah clung to her resentment as tightly as she clung to the gray mare's reins. "I do not like this hat, and I do not like you."

Genie sighed and stroked the mare's neck as she led them forward through ankle-high grass and a patch of purple wildflowers. "You realize you are two-and-twenty, not twelve."

"What has my age to do with anything?"

"Your behavior is childish, Hannah. Others may be afraid to say so, but I am not."

A long silence. Then, resentment sharpened to bitter point. "Marrying my brother granted you a title, Lady Holstoke, not guardianship over me. Two-and-twenty entitles me to manage my own affairs. I have no need and less desire for your guidance. Or your frivolous company, for that matter."

Genie gritted her teeth, squelching her irritation and trying to remember her aims. "Marrying Phineas made me your sister. Sisters help one another—"

"Maureen is far more of a sister to me than you," Hannah hissed. "Would that Phineas had married her instead. Everything would be better."

The dig caught Genie like a kick to the chest. Hannah had meant to wound her, and she had finally found her weapon. For long minutes, Genie could not speak. A gust of wind came and tried to take her hat. Absently, she held it in place and blinked away the blur in her vision. She would not cry. She would not.

After a time, she swallowed the pain in her throat and instructed, "Loosen your hands a bit. Remember to use your legs to grip the pommels."

"Maureen understands why I do not wish to ride. She would not have demanded I do so."

Genie did not answer, keeping her eyes upon the nearing rise.

"Unlike you, she is kind. Good."

"Relax your grip upon your cane. Your mount reacts to the pressure."

"I detest this bloody cane, Eugenia," the girl snarled. "I hate it."

Once again, Hannah's words hurt, though in a different way. Genie's heart longed to give in. Pull her down from the horse and hold her tightly until her past went away.

"I know," she murmured instead.

The wind came up again. This time, it succeeded in ripping Genie's hat free. Genie let it do what it would and continued forward.

"We—we should stop and retrieve your hat," Hannah said.

Loosened hair streaked across Genie's cheek. "It is not important."

"It is. You spent hours on it."

"I shall make another."

Once again, silence fell, broken only by the mare's snuffling, the saddle's creaking, and the wind's increasing howl.

"I stole his horse once, you know." Hannah's voice was a thread, scarcely audible above the gale. "I waited until he came inside the house. I could always hear when he arrived. His walking stick. It t-tapped."

Genie did not have to ask who "he" was. Horatio Syder had managed to plague the girl long after his death. She drew a breath, pushing past the sudden pressure in her chest. "A horse would do you little good, as you did not know how to ride."

"True. I fell as I was trying to mount. Then, the horse bolted. I chased it for a mile or so."

The mare sidled nervously. Genie gave the animal's warm neck gentling pats, wishing she could soothe Hannah with similar ease.

"He found me not long after. He was very cross."

Genie nodded, keeping her eyes forward as they started up the rise. "It was brave to try, Hannah."

"It was stupid to try. I should not have done it."

"Brave," Genie insisted. "By now, you know I would not lie to spare your feelings."

Hannah snorted. "No. You do not often spare my feelings."

Genie hid a smile. She liked the snort. She liked the sentiment, wry and familiar. The victory was small, but it was progress.

As they neared the rail fence at the corner of the pasture, Hannah said, "We should retrieve your hat. You will wish to wear it when next we visit Bridport."

Genie's smile grew. She nodded and led the mare up the rise. As they reached the top, she glanced up and noticed Hannah's frown. It was deep and alarmed.

"Dear God," Hannah whispered. "They are dead. They are all dead."

Genie followed her gaze. And saw a horror. Cows—two-dozen, at least—lay motionless amidst the grass and wildflowers of the neighboring pasture.

"We must return, Eugenia. We must tell Phineas."

Hannah's agitation caused the mare to sidle into Genie. She stumbled backward, her boots sliding on the hillside. Just as she regained her footing, she saw Hannah struggling to bring the horse under control. In her fright, Hannah yanked too hard at the reins, and Genie reached for her hands, trying to help.

She scarcely knew what happened next. Hannah pulled away from the contact. Her cane must have whapped against the horse's opposite flank, because moments later, the half-ton animal had knocked Genie flat on her backside, wheezing to catch her breath.

The horse whinnied. Danced. Hooves pawed and dug at the soil near Genie's head. One hoof caught a piece of her hair beneath it, and she felt a horrid, tearing pain as she rolled away. She tried to stand, but she only managed to get up on her knees and crawl toward the fence. Her skirts hampered her. Her hands dug and clawed at the pasture's grass and mud.

A warm trickle traced from her temple to her jaw. She grabbed hold of the lower rail. Dragged herself to her feet. Turned. Saw the mare rearing. Saw Hannah drop the cane and cling to the horse's mane. Saw the girl turn a frightened horse just enough to prevent Genie's head from being crushed.

"Eugenia!" Hannah cried. "Get away!"

The girl did not beg for help. She wanted Genie to avoid harm. Genie's heart was both full and pounding when she found her chance. She watched the mare's hooves come down once more, then rushed forward to grasp the bridle. Fractious and nickering, the mare's sides quivered. But she stayed on the ground. She did not bolt or struggle.

"Come, Hannah," Genie said gently, turning the horse's side to the fence. She gestured to the stark-white girl still clutching fistfuls of mane. "I will help you dismount."

Hannah shook her head. Her dashing little hat had slumped to one side.

Genie grinned up at her. "You did it, dearest. You did it. You stayed mounted. You kept this big girl from landing upon me." She patted the mare's neck. "Well done for a novice, I daresay."

Tears glossed pale eyes. "Y-you were nearly—"

Genie reached for Hannah and motioned her forward. "Come. Turn her mane loose. It is time to get down."

Finally, after a wrenchingly long process of loosening her fists, Hannah let go of the reins and mane. Between Genie and the rails, she was able to climb down from her perch. She trembled so badly, her legs nearly crumpled. Genie automatically wrapped an arm around her waist to brace her. Hannah flinched away. Then, without warning, the girl's arms enfolded her. A dashing little hat plopped onto the ground. Her cheek settled against Genie's, cool and shivering.

"I thought," Hannah whispered, "I thought I had killed you."

Genie squeezed her tightly and smiled. "No. You only kill those who deserve it."

Another flinch. Hannah drew back, searching Genie's face. A tremulous hand brushed at the red, wet trail along Genie's jaw. "Lady Holstoke *was* deserving." A hard glint entered her eyes, reminding Genie of Phineas in his darker moods. "She killed my mother. And Papa."

Genie nodded. "That's right. And when you saw your shot, you took it."

"Yes. I did."

"And when that monster held you against your will, you took your shots then, too."

A lovely brow crumpled. Lovely, pale eyes closed. "But I could not escape."

Genie held her tighter. "You endured. Do you know how much strength that requires?" She sniffed. "Far more than climbing on a horse or defying the gossipy matrons on Rotten

Row. Everyone treats you like wet paper. Hmmph. You are stronger than anybody I know."

"You have torn your hair, Eugenia."

"It will grow back."

A long silence amidst the gusts. Then, a tiny whisper. "I won't."

"Yes. You will. If you let yourself." Genie gave her a squeeze. "Bit by bit, dearest. Bit by bit."

Distantly, she heard men shouting. Hannah's eyes flared. "Oh! We should tell—"

"Phineas," Genie said, though there was little sound. Her air had gone.

Hannah spun and saw what Genie had seen—Phineas striding up the hill, dark as the devil himself. Genie patted Hannah's waist. "Take the mare to that pleasant fellow with the pistol, won't you?" She nodded toward the closest of Dunston's men, who had evidently sprinted across the pasture when the horse had reared. "I shall speak with Phineas."

Why Phineas should be out here in the east pasture, too, she could not say. He must have been watching. Ever the protective brother, she supposed. Shakily, Hannah bent to retrieve her riding hat then did as Genie asked.

Phineas stalked toward her with black fury in his eyes. She braced herself for a lecture about putting Hannah at risk. By the time he reached her, his chest was heaving. Perhaps from exertion. More likely from anger.

She held up a hand. "Before you start—"

"Not another word, Eugenia." His voice was a rough, growling bite. He cinched her upper arm inside an unforgiving grip and promptly dragged her toward the castle.

"Wait! For pity's sake, Phineas." She stumbled after him. "Let go! You must see—"

"I see more than enough."

"What does that mean?"

He dragged her halfway down the hill before stopping. He

pulled her close. "Reckless woman," he gritted. "Do you realize what almost happened?"

"Almosts do not matter. Let go of my arm."

"You are a bloody disaster."

"Reckless *and* a disaster. Your flattery quite turns my head, Lord Holstoke."

"You never listen."

"No, *you* are the one not listening!" She turned her arm in a wide circle until his grip loosened. "Let. Me. Go."

His shoulders rippled as though he were a horse restrained from bolting. But he released her.

Immediately, she started back up the rise, pausing briefly to shout, "Well, come along. I am not climbing this hill again because I wish to relive the glory."

At last, he followed, glowering all the way. When she reached the fence, she pointed out to the adjacent pasture, where one of his herds had obviously been poisoned.

He slowed as he came up beside her. Looked out across the next valley. His face blanched. Hardened to ice-encrusted stone.

"He is here, Phineas. I do not know how or why, but he is here."

For several breaths, she thought he might not say anything.

Then, he did. And his words, murmured as though to himself, sliced her heart wide open.

"I should never have married you."

Chapter Nineteen

"Inebriation is more often the cause than the consolation for one's troubles. Perhaps if one relinquishes the bottle for a blessed hour, one would arrive at this most obvious conclusion."

—THE DOWAGER MARCHIONESS OF WALLINGHAM to her nephew during a discussion of said nephew's lamentable losses at the hazard table.

⁂

THE CORRIDOR'S MARBLE FLOOR TILTED AT AN ODD ANGLE. Genie staggered and nearly lost her hold on the bottle. Fortunately, the doors to the drawing room were there. She caught her sore shoulder against them and righted herself.

"This room. Ah, this room was made for my sister, Mr. Ross. She simply *adores* yellow silk." She threw the doors wide and stumbled in. Outside, in the courtyard, rain pattered against the windows. "Whilst I, on the other hand, do not." She drank again, the room spinning, yellow and blue, yellow and blue.

"My lady, perhaps you would like to sit—"

"No." She shook her head and sank onto cerulean cushions. "Oh. Yes. Perhaps I would."

"Shall I fetch you a pot of tea?"

"No." She held up the bottle and smiled. "Here is to you, Mr. Ross. A fine valet. A true gentleman." She drank until the wine warmed her stomach. "Perhaps you could instruct Holstoke. A gentleman should not tell his wife ..." A hole opened. She closed her eyes against it. Breathed until she could speak again. "Where did Harriet go?"

"She is arranging a bath for you, my lady."

Genie glanced down at her gown. Ruined. The gold silk was stained with rainwater and the pasture's muck. A tuft of grass was caught in one of the frog closures. "Some things never come clean, Mr. Ross."

The valet knelt beside her. His plain, bald head reflected stormy light from the windows. "Some things do, if you work at them."

She laid her cheek on the arm of the sofa. "I forgot I am the Great Burden of Genie. I should not have. He remembered. Or perhaps he's always known." She closed her eyes. Opened them again. "I do not care for this room. Though it is lovely. Too much yellow." She pushed herself upright, waiting for the spinning to stop—yellow and blue, yellow and blue. Then, she surged to her feet. Mr. Ross caught her arm, helping her maintain her dignity. Not that it mattered. Dignity had abandoned her years ago.

"Thank you, Mr. Ross." She tugged loose and made for the doors. "His lordship may not thank you for touching me, but I shall. You are a *gentleman*."

"You are too kind, my lady."

She thought amusement laced his voice, but everything was

spinning, and she could not pin it down. Weaving back along the corridor and through a set of glass doors into the courtyard, she turned her face up to the rain. She liked it. Cool drops on her skin.

"He made himself a paradise," she said, throwing her arms out and closing her eyes. "Magnificent place. She loved it, you know. Called it 'palatial.' How true."

"... perhaps a shawl ..."

The rain washed over her. Cooling and wet.

She circled the fountain and sidestepped a potted plant. Found another set of doors. Another corridor. It was chasing her, the pain. Chasing and chasing. She did not want to be caught. She drank wine and shook her head. Slammed into a wall with her sore shoulder. Winced.

"... my lady, please. Let me help you ..."

Must keep on, she thought. It chased and chased. Another door. She opened it and found wood-paneled hush. Through the window, she glimpsed the sunken garden stretching out toward the lake. At the center, Neptune fought the gale. She sank onto a table beneath the window. Took another drink.

"I shall ask Mrs. Green to prepare tea, my lady. A lovely, warm pot of tea."

The hush grew when he left. On this side of the castle, she could see the rain more than she heard its tumult. She touched her forehead against the glass, which fogged with her every breath.

The rain had come while she'd stood on the rise with Holstoke. Fat drops had splattered on her nose and cheeks. She'd been numb for a minute or so after he'd said ... what he'd said. Then the pain had come, a crack down her middle. She'd called him vile names and shoved him hard. She'd charged down the hill, ignoring his shouts. He'd sent one of Dunston's men after her. She'd accused that man of having a whore for a mother.

Later, she must apologize. She did not even know his mother.

Now, hours on, she drank again. Sighed. Before the wine, her temple and shoulder had hurt terribly. The mare's panic had done some damage. But neither pain compared to Holstoke's cut. That was what chased her.

She closed her eyes. Held her stomach. Perhaps she should have known. He hadn't wanted to marry her. Not really.

Not her.

Breathing came fast now. She slid off the table, knocking a candelabrum to the floor. The clatter echoed in the hush. She ignored it. Moved to a chair. Set the bottle on the desk. Laid her arms beside the bottle and her head upon her arms.

Paper rustled as she shifted. She saw squares.

And words.

Slowly, slowly, she raised up. Read the words inside the squares.

A crack widened into a chasm. It filled with Holstoke's words—sentiments she'd long suspected but hoped weren't real.

God, what a blind, besotted fool she was. Hope was a vicious poison.

On one side of the paper, beneath Maureen's name, were pleasant and true statements: Attractive. Interest in gardens. Pleasurable company. Widely admired. Excellent mother.

On the other side, beneath the word "Eugenia," the ledger weighed decidedly in the opposite direction: Vexing. Irrational. Too bold. Invites scandal. Displays little understanding of botany. Needlessly argumentative. Too familiar with staff. Stubborn. Provokes worst male instincts. Unruly.

The lists were lengthy, going on in a similar vein for several pages. Eugenia's, in particular, took two additional sheets of paper on its own. He'd even noted her "preposterous hats."

Little wonder he regretted marrying her. Reading this list, she could scarcely abide herself.

The pain she'd been fleeing found her. Rushed into the chasm and howled its triumph.

She could not breathe.

She could not breathe.

The pressure built and she could not breathe.

When she finally did, it was gasp. Then a sob.

The chasm yawned wider. Filled deeper.

"Eugenia?" Gentle hands settled on her shoulders.

She could not answer. Only gasp and keen. She covered her mouth with both hands.

Gentle arms wrapped around her from behind. A cool cheek pressed her own. "Do not cry, Eugenia. Please."

Hannah held her and rocked her for long minutes until the shudders slowed and she regained control. Genie did not know when the girl had taken Holstoke's list from her fingers, but it was gone. She sensed a fine tension just before Hannah drew away, commanding Genie to use her handkerchief.

The white scrap of cloth blurred before her, but she took it. Blew her nose. Wiped her eyes. Felt empty and sick.

Hannah took charge, her arm bracing Genie's waist as she helped her upstairs to her bedchamber.

Maureen's bedchamber.

The world spun in shades of yellow and blue. Yellow and blue. Then, she lay down upon the bed she hadn't spent a single night in since arriving at Primvale. Distantly, she realized Hannah had helped her disrobe down to her shift, that the girl was now washing Genie's face with a warm, wet cloth.

Genie looked up at her lovely sister-in-law, whose cheeks were streaked with glistening trails.

"I am sorry," Hannah whispered, those pale eyes glossed and bare. "I am sorry for ... saying those things. About Maureen. About you. I never meant them. I never did, Eugenia, I swear it."

Genie closed her eyes. Nodded. Opened them again and looked out upon the sea. The waves peaked white with fury.

"I—I wished to keep things as they were. After ... the bad

time, Phineas became a home. He is my family. My friend."

The cloth stroked her cheek again, gentle and warm.

"I was wrong to think you might take him from me. That is not what happened at all."

When Genie offered no reply, Hannah began plucking her few remaining hairpins and gently stroked Genie's hair. She went away then returned to brush the curls, taking care not to tug near Genie's wound.

"You are my friend now, too, Eugenia. And I am yours."

Genie closed her eyes again. The sounds of the storm faded and for a time, she slept. When she awakened she was alone. The skies were darker, the sea rougher. The pain was the same—sharp and grinding and unbearable. She rolled over to escape it, but it chased and chased and chased. She threw off the bedclothes and went to the charming little sofa with its charming tasseled pillow.

Fury swept over her like the waves. She destroyed the tassels. Tore them off. Ripped the fine silk down the center and threw the unstuffed mess across the room. She threw open the glass doors and walked out onto the terrace, flinching as the doors slammed closed. The stones were slick and cold beneath her bare feet. The rain plastered her shift to her skin in seconds. She tasted salt. Heard the sea roar its rage.

Gripping the balustrade, she leaned forward and closed her eyes. Out here, on the precipice, the pain chased and chased and chased. Running gained her nothing. It always found her. Filled that chasm to the top.

She looked down. Saw the fountain. A serpent and a griffin battled for dominance. Rainwater fell from her hair down several stories to the circle. She watched the drops descend, wondering how something so beautiful as love could hurt so badly.

Behind her, the door clicked open.

And fury from another source growled, "What the devil are you doing?"

For the first time in weeks, his head pounded. He'd rarely gone so long without one of his headaches. But, then, he'd lived a bloody nightmare that day. Watching Eugenia—fierce but so very small—knocked flat by an uncontrolled horse, then seeing her come within inches of ... God, he could not bear it. The very thought of her being harmed, let alone crushed, sent him into a killing rage.

He would do anything to keep her safe. Anything. Even if it made her unhappy for a time. Eugenia had to remain safe and alive. This was what mattered.

After their argument, he'd spent hours with his farmers and dairymen. They'd discovered *Cicuta virosa* roots amongst the parsnips used as supplemental feed for the dairy cows. Someone had poisoned his cattle with bloody cowbane. These were the cows whose milk and cream and cheese fed his entire household. He'd had to assume every bit of food in the larder was tainted, so he'd disposed of the lot. Next, he'd sent Cook and ten footmen to Bridport to restock. He'd set Dunston's guards the task of questioning everyone who had access to the cattle. Then, he'd ordered seventy percent of his remaining staff to search the castle and grounds for signs of intrusion.

They'd turned up nothing. Bloody nothing.

Worst of all, Phineas knew it was a feint. The blackguard wanted him frantic and distracted. It was working. His body hummed with the need to kill.

Earlier, he'd angered Eugenia when she'd misunderstood something he'd said. By the time he'd realized how his words must have sounded, she'd already informed him—loudly—that he was an "addlepated lobcock" too "bloody dull" to tempt a sheep, much less a woman. She'd further scorned his manners, his matrimonial shortcomings, and his manhood in increasingly vicious terms.

His thoughtless, murmured statement had been aimed at himself, not his wife. Marrying her had been selfish, the act of a man possessed by the blackest enchantment. In claiming Eugenia as his own, he'd put her in danger, which was intolerable.

But he also should not have said what he said. He'd hurt her. Unintentionally, perhaps. His Briar had thorns aplenty, but she was also formed of sweet, tender petals and soft, downy leaves. She could be bruised. *He* had bruised her. Therefore, he must repair the damage.

He'd sent one of Dunston's men to protect her, intending to explain himself once he'd dealt with the cattle. Now, hours later, he discovered she'd raided the wine cellar, led his valet on a merry chase, and was currently ensconced in her bedchamber. He sighed, rubbed his nape, and walked through the door connecting her chamber to his.

The room was cloaked in blue light and gray shadows. He searched for her, seeing the bed disturbed but empty. Strangely, a small pillow lay on the floor, shredded into pieces. Then, he caught a glimpse of white. And wet. And Eugenia—his precious wife—bent forward over the balustrade in the midst of a summer storm.

Bloody hell. Fear and blackness and rage merged. Exploded.

He bolted toward her. Threw the glass doors wide. The blackness spoke before he could think. "What the devil are you doing?"

She straightened and turned. The thin, fine linen of her shift was wet. Clinging. Transparent.

Good God. She was incomprehensibly beautiful. Her waist and hips and breasts—everything was exquisitely curved. He shook away his fascination and started forward. He needed to get her inside before she caught her death.

"Get out."

The coldness of her voice stopped him. Eugenia was many

things—fiery and thorny and blunt—but never cold. Her skin was white, her lips drained of color. And her eyes. God, her eyes were killing him. "Eugenia—"

"I said get out. Leave me, Holstoke."

Holstoke. Not Phineas. He must have hurt her worse than he'd realized. "I will never leave you."

Her head tilted at an inquisitive angle. "Why not?"

Because you are mine, the blackness roared. He refused to speak it. He dared not reveal his madness to her. Instead, he moved closer, ignoring the cold rivulets running down his nape. "Come inside, Briar."

"Stop calling me that." Her face was blank, her words calm. This was not his Eugenia.

"What I said earlier today—that I should not have married you—it was a mistake."

"No." She shook her head slowly. Smiled without smiling. "It was the truth."

"In one sense, and one sense only. As my wife, you are in danger." He struck his own chest. "I put you in danger. Had I been thinking of anything apart from how much I wanted you, the risk to your life from this poisoner would not exist. That risk tears me apart, Eugenia."

She blinked, the rain flying from her lashes. She took a shuddering breath and began to shake. Thunder sounded. Wind shoved. Rain sheeted.

"For God's sake, woman. Come inside."

"Inside where?"

"Your bedchamber, for a start."

"It is not mine. Just as you are not mine."

He frowned. She made no sense. "You are in your cups."

Again, the smile that was not a smile. "Would that I were."

"What do you mean the chamber is not yours?"

"It belongs to Maureen."

This snapped his head back. What the devil? "Maureen has not been here in six years. Apart from which, she is married to

Dunston and mother to his five children."

"Four."

"Five. I have it on good authority." He shook his head and stepped closer, but she retreated to the balustrade, her hands gripping the stone on either side of her hips. "It doesn't matter. *You* are married to me. One day you will be the mother of my children, Briar."

"Do not call me—"

He stalked closer. Leaned down. Braced his hands alongside hers. "It is who you are. My wife. My Briar. Perhaps I was selfish in claiming you. So be it. What's done is done. Now, I must keep you safe." He inclined his head, breathing in rainwater and violets. "And I will, my sweet one. I promise you, I will."

She was shivering now. Her teeth clenched against the chill. Shudders wracked her tiny frame. "I—I never doubted it. Protecting is what you do."

"Come inside."

"Not there." She nodded toward her bedchamber. "It is not mine."

Frustration ate at his gut. "Of course it is."

"No. It is yellow. I hate yellow."

He sighed and rubbed his nape. "Then, we will change it. Bloody hell. All this over a color."

"*Her* color." Her throat rippled. Her brow puckered. Her eyes glistened. "Perhaps you should have added that to your list. 'Eugenia hates yellow.'"

List. Ice ran through his body in a wave. Damn and blast. She'd seen his daft, desperate list?

Her arms folded across her middle. Her shoulders hunched.

Intolerable. He bent and scooped her into his arms. It was a measure of her state of mind that she did not protest, merely dropped her head onto his shoulder. Cradling her precious weight close, he strode through the chamber she'd somehow decided had been designed for her sister and shouldered his way into his bedchamber. Carefully, he set her on her feet beside his bed. Next, he retrieved a pair of towels, using one to squeeze rainwater from the mahogany silk of her hair. Then, he stripped her shift from her body and used the second towel to dry her skin.

By the time he finished, he was wildly aroused, but his body could bloody well wait. He'd injured her. His wife. His Briar. Deeper and more grievously than he'd ever thought possible.

He tossed back the blankets, scooped her up again, and laid her gently on the mattress. After stripping off his own clothes, he climbed in beside her. She rolled away, but he caught her waist and drew her back against him. Her skin was chilled and covered in gooseflesh. He gave her his heat. Wrapped her up tight.

"Listen to me," he whispered in her ear. "Do you know what that list was?"

"Yes," she rasped.

"I don't think you do."

"You were sorting things out. In squares. Such a peculiar man."

His heart thudded. She knew him quite well. Better than he'd realized. "I was giving myself reasons, Briar." He braced himself. Clutched her tighter. God, he did not want to tell her. He did not want anybody to know. But her pain was more important than his pride. "Sensible reasons why I should not be obsessed with you."

Her body jerked against him. A mewling gasp emerged. She shook her head. "Do not lie to me."

He kissed her ear. Her neck. "How I wish it were a lie, my sweet Briar."

"It is. Your obsession is with Maureen—"

"No. Six years ago, I wanted to marry her. She made sense to me. A highly logical choice."

"She was your ideal."

"At the time, perhaps. I had never before realized a family like yours was possible. Maureen opened my eyes. Made me want something for myself that I'd never experienced. More than simply a marriage. A different path, diverging far away from what I had known."

"That—that is why you kept the chamber for her." Eugenia's voice was thin.

He sighed and flattened his palm on her belly, drawing her backside harder into his hips so she could feel what she did to him. "The chamber was decorated two years before I met your sister."

"That cannot be true."

"Ask Walters. Or Mrs. Green. The gardens were not the only places where I wanted all remnants of my mother erased. The drawing room had previously been blue. I changed it to yellow, which my mother disliked. We had sufficient silk to clad the walls in your bedchamber. That room was once hers. Yellow seemed ... appropriate."

Tentatively, her hand slid over his. She sighed and trembled. "But it suits Maureen so perfectly."

He kissed her cheek. Her ear. "Close your eyes." He waited until she did so. "Picture the chamber." He nuzzled her neck. "Do you have it?"

She nodded.

"Now, picture it with red walls. The same shade as the lilies I gave you for our wedding."

Her breath caught.

"For whom is it perfect?"

Her breath quickened. She squeezed his hand, interlacing their fingers.

"Open your eyes."

She did.

"Look about."

"Phineas."

"What do you see?"

"Emerald. And silver."

He breathed her in. Violets and cherries. Sea and skin. Gently, he kissed her bruised shoulder. "There was only one room I changed because of a Huxley girl. Shall I tell you which one?"

"No. That cannot be."

"It is."

"I was only a girl then."

"A girl who cared nothing for boundaries. Who treated me as a friend from the first, telling me I should laugh more and wear emerald pins with my silver cravats because they reflect my eyes to advantage."

"They do," she whispered, turning her cheek toward his mouth. "You have wondrous eyes, Phineas."

"I hadn't the faintest notion what to make of you, even then." He smiled. "I only knew your advice was correct and given without expectation. How rare that is, Briar. For someone to see so clearly, to offer her insights not as currency but as a gift."

"I—I don't understand. Your list." Her voice twisted. "Pages and pages, Phineas."

His chest tightened. His arms tightened. The blackness tightened its grip upon the only thing it gave a damn about—her. It wanted acknowledgement. It wanted to possess her again, to stake its claim. His cock swelled with the demand.

She stiffened against him as she felt the change against her backside.

"Do not be frightened," he said, though his voice was more guttural than he would like.

"F-frightened? I—Phineas." She huffed nervously. "I don't understand."

"I shall tell you. But you must stay. Stay with me."

Her fingers dug into his arm.

"Promise," he rasped. "Please."

She breathed. Clutched his hand with hers. "I promise."

He closed his eyes. And told her the truth. "There is a kind of ... madness inside me."

She waited. Breathed. Patient and soft.

"It wants you very badly, Eugenia."

Her belly rippled beneath his palm. Her hips shifted entrancingly, sliding her flesh along his length. "I did have that impression."

"You don't understand."

She clicked her tongue. "Well, that is what I told you. Go on, then. Help me."

"It wants to take you, yes, but it wants more. Much more. It wants you all to itself. No touching any other man. Bloody hell, it hates when you *smile* at other men. It wants to kill the one who threatens you. Tear him to pieces. It rages when you are hurt." He kissed her injured shoulder again, needing the contact. "It is savage. Uncivilized. I have constrained it, but it has grown until I can scarcely think." He swallowed. "The blackness has command of me now. Ninety percent, at least. It will not be confined. I've tried. God, Briar. How I tried. That is why I made the list. I needed to temper the obsession with logic. You are the obsession, to be clear."

She was silent for a long while. Had her body not remained soft, her thumb tenderly stroking the back of his hand, he might assume she was appalled. Rightly, she should be. But, instead, he concluded she was thinking. Putting things together in her labyrinthine way. After an interminably long wait, he was proven correct.

"Phineas."

"Yes, Briar."

"I love you."

His heart stopped. Then it started again, thudding painfully against his bones. "You do?"

"Yes. I love your gardens. And your hands. And your eyes. And your brilliant mind." She tugged at his arms until he loosened them enough for her to roll onto her back, where she gazed up at him from glistening, cat-like eyes. "I love your peculiar nature and the thing you do with your tongue when you wish to be particularly persuasive." She grinned. Laughed. Glowed up at him. "I thought you should know." Her hand stroked his jaw tenderly. "It might make what I am about to tell you easier to bear."

Now, his heart stopped again. His insides iced until he could scarcely feel her skin. Numb. He was going numb. No. She could not leave him. She'd promised to stay. "Briar." The word was airless.

Her eyes filled with tears. She smiled and stroked his cheek with her thumb. "The madness is not separate from you, my darling. The madness *is* you."

Chapter Twenty

*"Husbands are prone to error.
That is why God invented jewelry, my dear."*

—The Dowager Marchioness of Wallingham to Lady Dunston
upon said lady's complaint about Lord Dunston's
uncivilized behavior.

∞

Genie gazed up at the beloved face of her beloved man, who looked as though she'd plunged her shears into his chest. Pale green flashed his denial before he spoke a word. "You are wrong."

She waited, watching his confusion, his incredible mind puzzling through what she'd said.

"This bloody blackness has no rationality."

"Hmm. So, it must be separate from you. Is that what you mean?"

He blinked. "Yes. I have long preferred reason to impulse

and emotion."

"Eminently sensible. You are a scientist."

His eyes dropped to her lips. "Quite right. Rationality requires rigor. One must examine one's logic down to the roots. The degree to which one strays from such examination is highly correlated with errors and, consequently, deleterious outcomes. Reasoning in this fashion has been my practice since I was a young boy at Harrow." He shook his head. "If I were mad, consistent rationality would not be possible. Apart from which, others surely would have noticed lapses. My tutors. My instructors. Friends at Cambridge. No, this blackness is recent. It began shortly after our conversation in the hat shop. I suspect the headaches are related somehow, as they have improved markedly since our marriage. Perhaps if I develop a proper formula, as I have for my tea, it will abate. I must conduct further research."

"Kiss me."

His nose flared. His eyes darkened, sharpened upon her lips.

"You want to, do you not?"

"I want more."

"Of course. But let's start with a kiss. Consider it research."

His hand slid beneath her nape, cradling her and bringing her mouth up to his. Heavens, how she loved his mouth, hot and sliding. His tongue, sleek and sensual. His hands, strong and gentle.

Her moan hummed against his lips as she wrapped her arms around his neck and dove deeper. Her nipples went tight. Sent sizzling pleasure straight to her womb as they brushed his chest.

All too soon, he drew back. Panting. Flushed. "What was that intended to prove?"

She ran her hands over his shoulders and down onto his chest. "Nothing. I wanted you to kiss me."

He huffed out a chuckle. "Minx."

"I will, however, propose an experiment."

"To what end?"

"I shall demonstrate that this 'blackness' you speak of is nothing more than your peculiar nature, which I have known about for some time."

His shoulders stiffened. His breathing stopped.

She settled her palm in the center of his chest, enjoying the feel of his skin and black, springy hair, the solid thud of his heart. "Will you trust me?" she murmured, kneading his hard muscles, lightly skimming his nipples.

He did not answer.

"Phineas." She ran her hands over his ribs, then his hips. "Will you let me conduct my experiment?"

After a long silence and a deep sigh, he nodded.

"Good. I shall touch you, and you tell me how the blackness—isn't that what you call it?" She waited for his nod. "You tell me how the blackness responds."

A fierce frown creased his brow. "This is not a good idea, Briar."

"Of course it is. If I recall correctly, you agreed to trust me, Lord Holstoke."

"Damn and blast."

"Now, then. Let us begin. Lie on your back, if you please."

Reluctantly, he rolled onto his back. She followed and propped herself above him, her mouth hovering near his. His hands went to her waist. Squeezed.

"I shall start here." She brushed his mouth with her finger. "Your lips are ..." A heated chill ran through her. "Fascinating."

"I could put them to better use."

She grinned, rejoicing that she had been wrong. He hadn't loved Maureen. Maureen had made *sense* to him. Genie, on the other hand, had driven him mad. Mad was much better than sense. Fortunately, with Phineas, she could have both. She only had to help him see it.

"Later," she replied. "For now, tell me how you feel."

"Aroused."

"Phineas."

"Highly aroused. You do realize you are naked."

"And?"

"I cannot think when you are naked."

"Tell me what the blackness thinks, then."

His eyes lit. "It thinks I should be inside you."

"Do you agree?"

"Bloody hell, Briar. Yes."

She rewarded him—and herself—with a kiss, long and sensual and sweet. As shivers and tingles played over her skin, she kissed her way down his throat. Then his chest. Then his belly with its hard muscles and hot skin. "What does the blackness want now?"

He groaned. The muscles of his jaw and belly rippled and flexed. "Take me in your mouth."

She stroked the long, hard stalk with her hand first, enjoying the silken texture, the flagrant need. With her cheek on his belly, she gazed into his eyes. Glowing green was nearly swallowed by black centers. "Do you concur, Phineas? Do you also wish me to take you in my mouth?"

"Yes," he growled, his hips driving his manhood harder into her grip.

Smiling her approval, she answered his need and hers by first licking then gently suckling the rounded tip.

"Sweet, bloody hell." His hand tangled in her damp hair.

She squeezed him firmly at his root while gripping his muscled thigh with her other hand. How she adored his flavor—salt and musk and lust. How she needed the reassurance of his desire for her. Every writhing motion of his hips caused heat to swell inside her, filling her like a cloud. It thrummed beneath her skin, flushed in her breasts, pulsed in her core, as she teased him with playful laps of her tongue and long pulls of her mouth.

"Enough, Briar," he growled, his belly trembling, the hand

in her hair gripping and releasing. Gripping and releasing. "Enough. I need to be inside you."

She gave him a final, lingering stroke of her lips, then found the hand that clenched the sheets and laced her fingers with his. "You or the blackness?" Her own voice was raspy with her arousal.

Before she could blink, he had dragged her up along his body and rolled until he lay atop her, his eyes ferocious and blazing. Just as quickly, he spread her legs and pulled her knees up alongside his hips until she was wide open and pleasurably trapped beneath him.

"Both of us," he breathed. His nostrils flared. He notched himself at the mouth of her core, the tip hot and insistent. "Let me in."

She gripped his neck, her fingers digging into his nape. The need to comply was a towering ache, a pulsating burn. But this was not merely lovemaking. This was a demonstration—one she must complete.

"I will," she whispered. "But first, answer a question. Does the blackness like knowing you are the only man who has ever been inside me?"

His head dropped forward onto her shoulder. He groaned and kissed her neck. "Yes. Bloody hell, yes."

"Why?"

"Because you are mine. Only ever mine."

"Whose wife am I?"

"Mine."

"I belong to Phineas."

"That's right."

"Do *you* like being the first?" She kissed his ear. "Do you like knowing you are the only man whose touch makes me want him until I ache?"

His hips jerked, forcing several inches of thick, hard Phineas inside her. This time, his groan was nearly a shout, tortured and grinding.

She wriggled her hips deeper into the mattress until he slid out of her. "Answer me."

He propped himself above her, the muscles of his arms and shoulders rippling with fine tension. His face was flushed, his eyes molten. Savage. "Yes," he gritted. "I do."

She slid her hand along his jaw. Ran her thumb across his lips. "Then, it is not merely the blackness."

"No."

"Do *you* wish to keep me all to yourself, Phineas?"

"Yes."

"Do *you* want me to avoid touching other men?"

"Yes."

"Do *you* want to kill the man who threatens me?"

"I want to tear him to pieces and scatter those pieces into the sea."

She wrapped her legs around his hips and her arms around his neck. Then, she placed her lips against his and whispered, "Take me."

His first thrust was hard and deep. His second even harder, the third and fourth deeper, forging and filling until her sheath felt stretched. As his movements quickened, the friction grew scalding. Tight rings of pleasure rippled outward like water. His hands gripped her waist and clutched her hair, controlling her movements and holding her still for furious, pounding thrusts. His hips battered hers, his thick staff setting a brutal pace while his chest chafed and pleasured her breasts.

God, how she loved this man.

The mere thought set everything he had kindled inside her ablaze. The flames built in a wild, surging crescendo, licking into the sky. In a burst of showering sparks and booming combustion, her body seized. Arched. Cried out against the skin of his neck. She clawed at his back and his nape, unable to bear the intensity. She sobbed his name again and again as it broke over her. Heat and light. Heat and light. Heat and light.

In the aftermath, she felt his peak approach—the

impossible hardness of his muscles, the urgent tempo of his thrusts, the heated vibrations of his groans against her neck. Caressing his shoulders and back, she tightened her legs around him, her body around him. She held him as strongly as she could then whispered, "It is not madness. It is you. All the blackness. All the rationality. Every part is you, Phineas. The man I love."

The explosion came upon him suddenly, hard and wracking. Her name was a desperate growl. He shuddered and jerked and groaned as his body filled hers.

She would give him whatever he needed—her mouth and her body and her heart. She did not know if it would be enough. She only knew he had somehow separated his fundamental nature into two parts, and the part he wished to deny was the part that loved her.

That would not stand.

She gripped him tightly, stroking his hair and his shoulders, kissing his ear and whispering her love as she took his pleasure with unseemly greed.

He was hers. Hers alone. And she would have all of him. The scientist. The husband. The blackness. The man.

Now that she knew he wanted her—Eugenia, not Maureen, not any other woman—she would have all of him, and nothing less would do.

Chapter Twenty-One

"Very few circumstances require such extreme measures. But this, I daresay, is one."

—THE DOWAGER MARCHIONESS OF WALLINGHAM while dismissing her most recent lady's maid, the second in a single day.

∞

NIGHT FELL EARLY, THANKS TO THE STORM. NO THUNDER, but plenty of wind. It howled and rocked Jonas in angry blasts. He attempted to resettle himself in the saddle and nearly screamed at the white flash of pain. Rain had soaked him through hours ago. The wet helped ease the heat in his skin, which throbbed and fogged his mind. His shoulder and leg were bleeding again.

But he was here. By God, he was here.

He pulled his horse up short beside the castle's fountain, breathing and blinking as his own hands wavered in his vision. Rain cascaded from his hat's brim. He knew he should move, but he could not remember how.

On his right, he heard the creak of Drayton's saddle as the other man dismounted. "Bloody suicidal fool."

In front of him, he watched Dunston dismount and approach. The dapper earl scowled. "I do hope this was worth your death, Hawthorn."

He opened his mouth to tell him it was. That he would have gone farther and suffered worse to save her. But nothing emerged. His throat was dry. His face was hot. Slowly, he blinked.

"This will hurt." Dunston's warning came a second before he and Drayton yanked Jonas from the saddle. Pain exploded. Not merely in his limbs, but everywhere.

Blackness. Weakness. Dripping. Pain and pain and pain.

Dunston, who had looped his uninjured arm across his shoulders, held Jonas upright and dragged him before wooden doors. The doors opened. A white-haired man asked a question.

Jonas could scarcely hear for the wind and the rain and his pounding head.

The entrance hall echoed, but there was no more rain. Just more heat. Other men arrived. Footmen, he thought. Vaguely, he heard Dunston and Drayton talking. Two footmen tried to take his weight.

He groaned as pain radiated outward from his shoulder and leg.

"Mr. Hawthorn?" It was her voice. Pure and soft as snowfall.

Blinking, he forced his eyes to focus. Gray and white squares refused to un-blur.

"... has happened to him?" Her voice sharpened. She sounded distressed. "Fetch Lord Holstoke's physician. Now. Go!"

He blinked again. Tried to raise his head. Christ, he was weak. Hot and weak.

Her face appeared before him, paler than usual but even more exquisite than he remembered. That smooth brow puckered with fret and fear.

For him? No. Unlikely.

He needed to tell her something. How beautiful she was.

Those rosebud lips were moving. Demanding. "... him upstairs. The blue chamber. He is not permitted to die." Moonlight eyes riveted to his. Delicate nostrils flared. "Is that perfectly clear, Mr. Hawthorn? You will *not* die."

Her command was his last memory for a long while. Next thing he knew, he lay naked and screaming in agony. No sound. The screaming was in his head. Firelight flickered on blue walls. Heat pulsed. He dragged his eyes open.

Saw ... her. Dark smudges marred the skin beneath moonlit green. Wisps of midnight curled against creamy white cheeks. She sat beside his bed, hands folded and wringing. "Keep him alive, Phineas," came her cool, soft voice. "Do as you must."

Somebody poured a bitter brew down his throat. He choked and fought, but to no avail. Then came pain unlike anything he'd felt before. This time, his scream was real, ripping from his throat, echoing off blue walls.

The room went dark. When light returned, she was there. Moonlight eyes were rimmed red, gazing at the fire. She rocked herself back and forth in the chair as though she needed comfort. He tried to stretch out his arm toward her, but it weighed twelve tons.

He was hot. Bloody hot and thirsty. His head pounded. Hell, everywhere pounded. He wanted to speak but managed only a croak.

Her gaze flew back to him. She stood and hovered close, though her hands continued wringing at her waist until her knuckles blanched. "Rest," she admonished. "You've done yourself quite enough damage already."

"D-danger," he said, his breath short on the single word.

"I know," she replied with a fierce frown. "Lord Dunston

informed us about your findings. What I do not understand is why you would undertake this foolish journey after you were ... shot." Her lips went tight and white. Briefly, she closed her eyes. "You could have died."

"He is here." Jonas panted. Gathered strength. "So, I must be here."

She paced away, her shoulders trembling with agitation. He watched her retreat, but struggled to focus when she entered the shadows at the edge of the room.

"The—the sketch," he rasped.

"Ruined," she said quietly, keeping her back to him. "Your b-blood soaked it."

His eyes closed. Blast. He would have to draw the blackguard again when he could lift his hand.

She turned. Glided toward him. Stood beside his bed with seamless composure. "Rest, Mr. Hawthorn. My brother and Lord Dunston will ensure our safety."

"*Your* safety," he said, the words nearly a growl as they rattled in his dry throat. "Yours."

Her blinking grew rapid, as did her breathing. Those fine, delicate hands twisted together until he could not bear her distress any longer.

He forced his muscles to respond. Stretched out his arm. Reached for her hands. He was shaking by the time his fingers brushed hers.

As though he'd scalded her, she jerked violently and stumbled back several steps. She folded her arms across her middle, tucking her hands away. Her eyes flared wide as a hare's when flushed by a hunter. Her bosom rose and fell at a panicked pace.

His arm dropped to the sheet. He couldn't hold it up any longer, and she obviously did not want his loathsome hands upon her.

Haughty woman.

Haughty, exquisite, haunting woman.

In the silence, the pain softened. His thoughts grew heavy and slow, though his body floated above the bed.

Soon, he let his eyes drift closed, but he could still see her—cold as a winter lake. So bloody beautiful, she was both pain and pleasure. Heat and ice. Strength and fragility.

Darkness moved in. He slid into it gladly, numbness coating the pain. As it blanketed him, he imagined he felt a tickle against his lips. Delirium, probably. The fever or the laudanum. But it seemed real.

Then, a whisper fell, soft and achingly sweet. "Rest now, Jonas Hawthorn," it said. "I am not so easy to kill."

Chapter Twenty-Two

"A beach on a clear day is a fine place to ramble, Humphrey. In a downpour, however, it is only a fine place to drown."

—The Dowager Marchioness of Wallingham to her boon companion, Humphrey, in reply to his expressed preference for beaches and rambles and rain.

∞

The fourth plume was the key ingredient—Genie was certain of it. She sketched the addition. Squinted. Wrinkled her nose.

Drat. Now, the hat looked silly.

Sighing, she closed the sketchbook, clasped it to her chest, and gazed out the library window. Five days after the storm arrived, rain continued its drenching. Where had summer gone? Washed away to a county other than Dorsetshire, that much was certain.

She hated being stuck inside. Boredom swallowed her,

thick as mud. Of course, she would not have been bored if both Phineas and Hannah were available. Particularly Phineas. She sighed and tingled, remembering how not-bored she'd been last night.

But Phineas was spending his days investigating. Following the arrival of Dunston and Mr. Drayton, along with the nearly dead Mr. Hawthorn, Phineas had trained all his considerable focus upon finding the poisoner. He'd positioned men at every castle entrance. He'd insisted that Genie and Hannah must remain inside. Along with Dunston and Mr. Drayton, he'd visited Bridport to question shopkeepers and mail coach drivers and proprietors of public houses, coaching inns, and taverns.

Day by day, Phineas grew increasingly grim and silent. They all waited for Mr. Hawthorn to awaken. Hannah had scarcely left the man's side in five days. Eugenia had been bringing Hannah supper each evening, sitting with her for several hours and chatting, mainly to herself. Much like Phineas, Hannah had withdrawn into silence and a relentless focus upon a single task—keeping Mr. Hawthorn alive by force of will.

Several times, when Mr. Hawthorn grew restless, Genie had noticed Hannah leaning forward as though she wished to touch him. Genie's heart ached for her sister-in-law, who appeared both desolate and torn.

In London, Dunston's surgeon had removed the arrows that had pierced Mr. Hawthorn before stitching the wounds closed. According to Dunston, the surgeon had been pessimistic even before Mr. Hawthorn had insisted on traveling from London to Dorsetshire on horseback. Phineas's physician, too, had doubted the Bow Street runner's odds.

"Mad, besotted fool," Dunston had muttered, shaking his head. Genie had elbowed him and pointed out that if Maureen were in danger, he would have taken similarly foolish chances. "Perhaps," he'd admitted. "Brat."

She'd rolled her eyes and clicked her tongue.

Then, he'd wrapped her in a tight hug and told her he would keep her safe, as Maureen would never forgive him if he did not. Genie hadn't felt uneasy until that moment. Henry Thorpe rarely spoke in such a way.

Rising from the desk, Genie wandered to the window and gazed out upon the sunken garden. The Neptune fountain spewed high into the air. She frowned, curiosity piqued. Tossing her sketchbook on the desk, she went in search of answers. Ordinarily, Genie preferred creating to reading, but after climbing the spiral staircase to the library's second level, she found a book with both answers and illustrations. Genie liked illustrations. She traced her finger softly over the exquisite feathers and the proud beak, the fierce musculature and the deadly talons. She sank down onto the floor, laid the book open upon her lap, and read as though she were Mr. Moody or her sister Jane—with complete absorption.

Consequently, she could not say how long she'd sat there before voices out in the corridor drew her attention. It was Hannah and Phineas ... arguing? Genie closed the book and frowned. Yes. Hannah's tone was strident, Phineas's exasperated. Quickly, Genie slid the book onto the shelf before rushing down the circular stairs and out into the corridor.

Hannah was shaking, clutching papers in her fist and glaring up at her brother with something approaching fury.

"You are overwrought," Phineas unwisely observed. "Perhaps one of my teas will help. *Valeriana officinalis* has a distinct calming effect, particularly for females suffering ... untimely discomfort."

Genie nearly groaned. Ordinarily, she was on the receiving end of Phineas's maddening male rubbish. To see him treat his sister with similar bewilderment was almost relieving, though not for Hannah. She watched the girl's eyes flare wide.

Oh, dear.

"Curse you, Phineas! I will not be dismissed with idiotic assumptions and valerian tea."

Perhaps Genie should intervene. She cleared her throat. They both ignored her.

"I have already explained the list to Eugenia."

"But you have not asked her forgiveness."

Phineas glowered. "We discussed the matter days ago, and the matter has been resolved. Now, if you will simply hand the papers to me—"

Hannah jerked her fist away. "Her hats are not preposterous!"

He rubbed his neck. "Hannah."

"And she may be blunt, but she is honest and true."

"I do not need you to tell me about my wife."

Hannah shook the papers near his chin. "This indicates otherwise!"

Genie's heart twisted. Hannah was defending her. Like a friend would. Or a sister.

"Give me the list, and I will burn the deuced thing," Phineas said.

"That is no solution. You must apologize."

He blinked. "I have."

Finally, one of them noticed Genie. Hannah turned to her with red-shot eyes. "Did he?"

Genie hesitated before answering. "He explained why he wrote it."

Phineas sighed. "You see? This overreaction is completely unnecess—"

"But he did not apologize." Genie finished. "Not in so many words."

Hannah nodded and approached Genie, extending the crinkled pages with a shaking hand. "As I thought. He should, Eugenia. It is the least you deserve."

Genie took the list, but she kept hold of Hannah's fingers. They were cold and trembling. "Thank you, dearest." She squeezed and smiled. "How is Mr. Hawthorn?"

Hannah's nostrils flared. Her lips went as white as her skin. "He—he has not yet awakened. The physician is with him now. He says if the fever does not break soon, he will likely ..."

Genie examined her sister-in-law's disheveled hair and wrinkled gown. Hannah was more mussed than she'd ever seen her. "Have you eaten?"

Hannah shook her head, her eyes dazed. The slender girl began weaving with exhaustion.

Gently, Genie pulled her closer and braced her elbow. "Well, that is the problem, then. Everything is improved by a good meal."

A small huff. "You always say that."

"Only because it is true."

Sighing, Hannah brushed at the black wisps that had fallen along her cheek. Then she glanced down at her green-sprigged muslin skirt—the one she'd been wearing for two days. "Perhaps a bath, too."

Genie gave a noncommittal "hmm" and nudged her sister-in-law—no, her *sister*—in the direction of her lady's maid, who had been hovering discreetly behind a large urn for the last minute or two. "Go on with Claudette, now. Eat. Rest. Let the physician do his work. I shall speak with Phineas."

Hannah nodded and left.

"I bloody well do not understand."

At her husband's muttered complaint, Genie turned. "Which part?"

"Any of it."

She paused. Listened. Smiled. "The rain has stopped."

"She scarcely knows Hawthorn. They've spoken a handful of times. She is behaving as though his death would be—"

"Phineas. Let us take a walk together."

He glowered at her, the strain around his eyes and forehead signaling his frustration. "I must return to my research."

She looped her arm around his and tugged him toward the entrance hall, pausing to retrieve the bonnet she'd left on a table outside the library. "No. You must take a walk with me. I need to escape this castle."

He let her lead him outside, albeit reluctantly. "Where are we going?"

"To the beach."

His sigh spoke of impatience. "Give me the list."

She tucked the now-folded square into her long sleeve. "No."

"Bloody hell, woman."

Arching a brow, she tied her bonnet's ribbons beneath her chin and tugged him past the fountain at the castle's entrance. "We have matters to discuss."

"I do not want to *discuss*. Nor do I want to walk to the beach. I would, however, very much enjoy taking you to bed."

"Perhaps later."

His nostrils flared. "Give me the list, Eugenia."

"No."

"I want to burn it."

"Sometimes what we want is not what should be."

He fell silent, but he kept walking. They traveled through the south gardens, along the tunnel of grapes and out to where the wet grasses grew high on the bluff. Phineas braced Genie's waist as she started down the cliff trail. Although worn by rain and wind and time, it had been carved into alternating slopes and steps winding down the cliff's face to Primvale Cove. Wind buffeted her, dragging her skirts sideways against her legs. But Phineas was always there, his hands steadying her, his surefooted strides a reassurance.

She braced her hand against the stone as a damp breeze caused her skirts to tangle and shorten her steps. "The first time I visited the beach," she began, nodding her thanks for his help over a slick spot, "I thought it must have taken years to carve these steps."

"It did," he replied. "Before then, the way was treacherous, indeed."

She halted. They'd traveled perhaps two-thirds of the way down. Hugging his arm, she sighed and gazed out at the Channel, shimmering gray beneath clouded skies. "So very beautiful."

"Yes."

She glanced up to find his eyes upon her, burning with intensity. She swallowed. Felt her cheeks heat. Forced herself to keep to the path she had set for them. When they finally stepped down onto the beach, she ran toward the water's edge and spun, laughing. "How could anyplace be more splendid than this, Phineas?" she called above the crash of the waves.

He did not reply, merely gazing at her, unsmiling.

She cast off her bonnet. Unpinned her hair. Extended her arms out to her sides and spun in circles, tilting her face to the sky.

"What are you doing, Briar?" His voice was nearer now.

"Wallowing, Phineas. I am wallowing."

"Could you not wallow in my bed?"

She stopped. Laughed breathlessly. Looked at her husband.

He was not laughing, nor even grinning. Instead, he appeared ravenous. Lost.

"I love you," she called softly.

His brow furrowed in what looked like pain. Yet, he said nothing.

She crossed soft sand and round pebbles, brushing long strands of hair out of her face. When she stood within a foot of her husband, she saw the battle he was waging. Felt the turmoil shining in pale, glorious green. "I love you," she said again.

His chest shuddered, his eyes growing desperate.

"All of you."

He turned his gaze to the water. "You shouldn't."

"Why?"

Again, he fell silent, his jaw tight.

Sighing, she grasped his hand and pulled him to where

waves clawed at the shore. "I did a bit of reading earlier." She chuckled. "I know, I know. A bit unusual for me, but I was curious about something." She shook his arm. "Ask me what."

"What were you curious about?"

"Griffins."

He froze. Stiffened. His hand loosened its hold upon her, but she refused to release him.

"Do you know what they are?"

His breathing quickened. Long muscles in his neck resembled ropes. He blinked down at her as if she'd planted her fist in his belly.

"The eagle and the lion, the noblest of two breeds, united in one extraordinary creature."

"Stop, Briar." His words were airless, carried away by the wind.

But she heard. "Griffins are protectors," she continued. "Ferocious and valiant. Best not to challenge them, for they will savagely kill those who attempt to harm whatever or whomever is in their care."

A tormented stare was her only answer.

"They also mate for life, or so legend has it." She smiled and pulled him closer, aligning their forearms and wrists as she threaded her fingers through his. "I liked that bit especially well."

Water washed across their feet, saturating her slippers. Genie did not care a whit. Her husband needed to stop fighting himself. It was tearing him apart.

She held his eyes, refusing to release him. "You gouged out every trace of her, Phineas. Her gardens. Her blue silk walls. But not her fountain." She tilted her head. "Why is that?"

"I should have stopped her."

She waited.

"I should have seen what she was and stopped her."

"But, you did see it."

He shook his head, clearly confused.

"You wanted her to die. Isn't that what you told me? As far back as you can remember. That means even as a boy, you sensed the evil inside her."

"No, I ... I hated her."

"Of course you did. You are a protector, Phineas. That is your nature. Protectors cannot abide threats in their midst."

"How can you speak of my nature with such certainty? You've no idea of the darkness inside me."

His pain tore at her. She raised his hand up to her lips, kissing his knuckles and stroking his arm, giving him what comfort she could.

"I doubt my own sanity, Briar." The whispered confession broke her heart.

"Never doubt it," she said fiercely. "You asked how I can be so certain of you. The answer is that I have *known* you from the first. What did you think I meant when I referred to your peculiar nature?"

He gave her a blinking frown. "My interest in plants, I suppose."

She snorted. "Lord Gilforth has an interest in plants. So does Maureen, for that matter."

"Then, what did you mean?"

She reached up to stroke his jaw, collecting her thoughts before she explained, "You are two parts in one man. The first part is the head—clear of vision, precise and focused. That is the part you prefer to show the world." She laid her hand upon his chest. "But here is the other part, my love. The very heart of you. The protector. The warrior. The one who recognizes evil and longs for its death."

"The blackness."

She smiled. Stroked his chest with her hand. "Yes."

"It is uncivilized."

"Very."

"Irrational."

"Oh, yes." Her grin widened. "And it—no, *you* are

magnificent."

For long minutes, he gazed down at her. Then, his jaw eased. His neck slowly relaxed. He sighed, long and deep. "As a boy, I came here often." He turned his gaze past her head toward where a large rock arch curved into the sea like a dragon taking a drink. "She demanded that I stay out of sight when my father was away." His fingers tightened where they twined with hers. "I dreamt of her death over and over. I dreamt of being the griffin. Tearing apart the serpent and scattering it at sea."

"Such dreams would frighten anybody, let alone a child. But she was deserving of that fate, Phineas. What you think of as blackness is simply your natural instinct."

"I should be able to control it."

"You do control it. It is *you*, for pity's sake." She clicked her tongue. "If you would stop trying so hard to deny your own nature, you might find instinct serves you rather well." She sniffed. "It certainly has for me."

"You."

"Indeed. What do you suppose led me to you?"

"It also led you to *experiment* with a bloody footman."

She shook her head. "That was not instinct. That was precisely what I am warning you about."

"How so?"

"I denied my own nature. Everyone expects an earl's daughter at age nineteen to make her debut, have a season, dance and deliver pretty compliments and mind every propriety." She rolled her eyes. "Does this resemble me in the slightest?"

His mouth quirked. "No. Well, perhaps the dancing."

"I tried desperately to be what everyone expected. Another Huxley girl who marries well and settles down into domestic bliss. But I was never the same as Annabelle or Jane."

"Or Maureen," he said softly, his thumb stroking the back of her hand.

She sniffed and raised her chin. "Quite right. I was different. And rather than stand firm in that knowledge, as I should have done, I patterned my life after theirs. That was my mistake. The scandal was simply the consequence."

His eyes turned curious. "What would you have done differently, if you could have?"

She shrugged. "What I was doing when poor Lady Randall's pug ate your hat."

He frowned. "Working."

"Learning. Discovering how to run a shop of my own." She moved closer, aligning their bodies so she could feel his heat. "Now, it is your turn. What would you have done differently, Phineas?"

Pale green blazed. "I would never have written that bloody list."

She released him to pluck the list from her sleeve. "You mean this one?"

"Damn and blast." His nose flared as he eyed the paper. "I am sorry, Briar. The thought of how I hurt you is—bloody hell, it is agony. Please forgive me."

"Oh, I have."

"You have?"

"Yes. I am a very generous woman. I might have mentioned this before." She waggled the folded square. "Now, then, when you wrote this list, what was your aim?"

A frown. "To control the blackness."

"There!" She tapped his chest with the list. "You see? That is it precisely!"

He shook his head in puzzlement.

"The attempt to stifle your true nature made you act in a way that you have come to regret."

"But I must control it. If I do not, then you will never leave my bed." He appeared genuinely confused, which was how her laughter started. "I am quite serious."

She held her middle and tried to stop, but she couldn't.

"Eugenia. What the devil are you laughing about?"

"You," she gasped, knuckling away a tear. She took several deep breaths and released one final giggle. "That is like saying, 'Because I am hungry, I shall eat an entire ham in one sitting.' Which may sound lovely, but a sensible person knows how to manage such impulses so that one does not cast up one's accounts onto the dining table."

"You clearly have no idea how much I want you."

She *tsked*. "What a lot of rot."

"Or the lengths to which I will go to keep you all to myself."

She propped her hands on her hips. "Such as?"

"The day before our wedding, I rearranged the entire male staff at Primvale."

She blinked, recalling Hannah's mention of such a measure. "You—you did that for ..."

He nodded.

Her eyes widened. Oh, dear. "You hired ugly servants for me?"

"No. I relocated them from other properties. I have many."

"Servants?"

"Properties."

"Hmm." She narrowed her eyes upon him. "And you chose ugly males for what purpose?"

He looked distinctly uncomfortable. "To keep your eyes where they belong."

She raised a brow.

"Upon your husband."

"Which, to be clear, is you."

The intensity she'd seen in his eyes when they made love gleamed there now. "Yes," he gritted. "And you are mine."

Slowly, her grin started. Then, it grew. "Well, this is all rather primal, is it not?" She inched toward him, her feet sinking into the wet sand. "You are a very possessive man, Lord Holstoke."

"Only with you."

"And I reserve my lustful gazes for only you, so surrounding me with ugly footmen was rather unnecessary, wouldn't you say?"

"I did not know that at the time."

She squinted up at him. "Do you trust me, Phineas? Do you believe that I love only you?"

He nodded. His eyes were an extraordinary blend of heat and possession.

She dangled the list near his chin. "What would you like to do with this?"

Deep, flinty, and unhesitating came his answer. "Tear it to pieces."

She grinned wider. "And?"

"Throw it into the sea."

She offered up the paper in her open palm. "Then do it, Phineas."

He blinked. A heartbeat later, he plucked up the pages and tore them into shreds. Then, he walked deep into the waves and hurled the tiny scraps into the water. His shoulders were heaving by the end. Perhaps from the cold. Perhaps because he'd made a decision.

She'd felt it. Seen the shift in his eyes. She walked out into the waves to stand beside him then laced her fingers with his. "Well done, my darling."

His chest heaved several more times. "It is impossible for me to explain how much I love you, Briar." He looked down at her, his eyes blazing. "Impossible."

She smiled up at him with all the love that shone inside her, an entire sun burning bright and hot. "Then you will simply have to offer evidence until I am thoroughly persuaded. A man of science should do no less."

The next wave struck her knees as he cupped her face and kissed her with exquisite tenderness. Perhaps that was why she could scarcely stand when he was through. Or perhaps it was him—Phineas—and his fascinating lips.

"I shall take you to bed now," he whispered.

Incapable of speech, she nodded. Suddenly, he bent and scooped her up out of the surf before striding swiftly toward the cliffs, her skirts dripping seawater. She was laughing and telling him to put her down, as he could not possibly carry her all the way up the trail, when something caught her eye. A shadow among the grasses at the top of the bluff. It looked like a man, tall and lean, holding something long and thin and curved.

"Phineas?"

He frowned at her tone and set her on her feet.

She blinked. And the figure was gone.

He glanced up in the direction she'd been gazing. "What is it?"

A chill settled in. "N-nothing, I suppose. Only a shadow. Perhaps one of the gardeners."

Phineas's jaw hardened. He took her hand and pulled her up the slope of the trail. By the time they'd completed the long climb to the top, Genie's damp skirts and slippers had sapped whatever warmth she'd felt in Phineas's arms. He drew her swiftly through the tall grass, but as they passed the spot where she'd seen the shadow, she couldn't help tugging him to a halt.

"Is this where you saw him?" Phineas asked quietly.

"Yes." There was nothing but grass now.

Phineas went to examine the spot. "No footprints in the mud," he noted. "No trampled grass."

She frowned. Had she imagined it? "Perhaps it was simply an odd shadow. The breeze does move the grass about in strange ways sometimes."

"Come, love," he said, returning to her side and offering his hand. "Let us return to the castle and get you warm and dry."

She looked at her husband, whose eyes and hands remained steady. Strong. And she knew that, whatever she'd seen—a gardener, the poisoner, or a shadow—Phineas would protect her. He would protect everything he considered his.

Slowly, her smile returned. She took his hand. "Walls and a bed, hmm?"

"Mostly a bed."

She stretched up on her toes to kiss her magnificent griffin, lingering for a long, sweet while. "With such a tempting offer, how can I refuse?"

Chapter Twenty-Three

"As I have previously noted, husbands require careful handling. But if a wife goes about her work with diligence and cleverness, a man may find himself reshaped by her hands before he realizes she's removed her gloves."

—THE DOWAGER MARCHIONESS OF WALLINGHAM to Lady Katherine Huxley at a weekly luncheon filled with sound advice and womanly wisdom.

∞

FROM ACROSS HIS BEDCHAMBER, PHINEAS EXAMINED Eugenia's naked form. She slept on her belly amidst rumpled bedclothes, pale shoulders and curved back bare and lit by the morning sun. Her confounding hips were covered by silver silk and emerald velvet. One small foot peeked out from beneath the blanket.

His heart was still raw. The previous day, when she'd led him down to the beach, he'd thought himself mad, despite her assurances to the contrary. With her usual stubbornness, she'd refused to accept his conclusion. Instead, she'd systematically cracked him open and forced him to examine himself more thoroughly.

Perhaps it had been the setting or Eugenia's persistence or the anomaly of arguing with Hannah, but as he'd stood at the sea's edge with the woman he loved, he'd felt as though time had reversed. Once again, he'd been a boy, sitting amongst sand and stone and water, attempting to trap blackness inside boxes. But this time, he hadn't been alone. Eugenia had been there, assuring him there was no need for boxes, because the blackness was not weakness but strength. His strength.

He was a protector, she'd said. It was his nature, just as it was the nature of leaves to seek the sun or water to wash things clean or roots to anchor and branch. Nature had patterns. His had been set long ago.

He bent now and laid a kiss upon her cheek, near the spot where her hair had been torn. Her skin there had already healed. Her hair would grow. He kissed her shoulder and savored her soft warmth against his lips. His precious woman.

Yes, he was a protector. He felt the knowledge surge inside him now, like steel at his core. Whatever it took, he would keep her safe. That was the reason he'd been born.

He gave gleaming mahogany silk one final stroke then forced himself to leave the bedchamber. Downstairs in the morning room, he found Dunston and Drayton eating baked eggs and discussing Drayton's examination of the bluff.

"No signs of a man," Drayton said after greeting Phineas. "Groundsmen all claim they were nowhere near the cliffs when you and Lady Holstoke were on the beach." Drayton took another bite and swallowed before continuing, "You certain of what she saw, m'lord?"

"Yes," Phineas replied without hesitation. "My wife saw a man. I have no doubt of it."

Drayton merely nodded, but Dunston shot Phineas a wry look. "Eugenia has been known to make mistakes from time to time, Holstoke."

Phineas shook his head. "Not in this. She is not a fanciful sort, and her instincts are sound."

Dunston's grin was approving. "So, this is you in love's thrall, eh, old chap?"

Nodding, Phineas drank his tea and smiled in return.

"Good." Dunston's eyes grew serious. "Take care of her."

"I shall." Again, he felt the rightness of his words, how they resonated through him like music.

"Now, then," Dunston continued. "The blackguard must be nearby. Where haven't we looked?"

"Are there caves about?" asked Drayton.

Phineas shook his head. "None I haven't already searched."

In truth, they'd searched everywhere—the entire Primvale estate, the surrounding cottages and farms, the two villages within walking distance, inns and lodging houses in Bridport. They'd found no trace of the poisoner, even with Dunston's description of the man, recollected from Hawthorn's sketch.

Phineas gazed down into his tea. Saw the few bits of herbs—lemon balm and mint and feverfew—floating on its surface. He'd formulated the tea to treat the headaches that had plagued him since he was sixteen. The alarming pain and partial blindness of the megrims had, in part, prompted him to research medicinal applications of plants, so in one sense, they had driven him down a path he might not otherwise have taken. But plants themselves intrigued him. They always had.

Now, as he considered everything they'd learned of the poisoner, he wondered if they'd gone about this all wrong.

The poisoner, too, had a motivation. A nature. His attacks had centered on Phineas, but Phineas himself had not been targeted. Rather, it seemed the poisoner wanted his admiration. Why, he could not say. All the victims had a connection to Phineas, apart from the prostitute. And her death had been the most violent of all. She had resembled Hannah, who had been hated and hunted for years by Lydia Brand, and who had stopped Lydia forever with a single shot.

Phineas frowned. The poisoner's pattern aimed in a direction, like leaves growing toward the sun. It aimed toward Phineas, yes. But its nature best aligned with Phineas's mother. He looked at the side of his teacup. Flowers and vines. Stems growing in the same direction. Similar plants. Similar patterns. The answer emerged from inside him as though it had been waiting there, trapped in a box that was now open.

"He is in Weymouth," Phineas murmured, certainty resonating through him like music. He raised his eyes to meet Dunston's, which were now alert and steely. "He would want to be where she lived before her death. Not here at Primvale, but at her house in Weymouth."

Dunston did not ask if he was certain. He sprang from his chair, clapped Phineas's shoulder, and said, "I shall ask Walters to prepare our mounts. If you own a pistol, Holstoke, I suggest you bring it along."

"I prefer swords."

Dunston grinned. A flash of eagerness entered his gaze. "By all means, a good hunter should use the weapon that suits him best."

They rode out of Primvale as morning sun painted damp grasses in yellow light. Before they left, Phineas ensured Dunston's men would remain on guard while he was away, and he'd charged Ross with informing Eugenia about their plans.

Weymouth, a seaside town favored as a summer retreat by kings and lords, lay twenty miles east. Riding hard, they arrived at his mother's former residence in less than two hours. Lydia Brand's house sat at the end of a row of fashionable terrace houses along Weymouth Bay. It was several stories high, white and symmetrical, with a garden on two sides surrounded by a high brick wall. He'd kept the house for a year after her death. Then, he'd sold it to a baron who'd used it for his mistress. Phineas did not know who owned the house now, but as they pulled up two houses away, he saw it had been poorly maintained. The paint on the door was peeling, the iron fence on either side of the front entrance had rusted, and grass grew high around the garden walls.

"Appears empty, m'lord," Drayton noted, rubbing his thigh as though it pained him. "Any idea how many might be livin' here?"

"No." Phineas dismounted then closed his hand around the hilt of his sword. It fit his hand as beautifully as the curve of Eugenia's waist. The long, thin blade fell along his thigh past his knee. "Perhaps no one does."

They paid a lad to mind their horses then advanced on the house from three directions—Drayton at the lower side entrance, Dunston at the front door, and Phineas through the garden gate.

Phineas struck the rusted latch on the old wooden gate with a rock, then opened it slowly, flinching at the loud groan of the hinges. He glanced left and right as he entered, taking in the brick planters overflowing with greenery. Unlike the exterior, the garden had been not only maintained but also cultivated. Everywhere he looked were herbs and flowers growing in abundance. Cold settled into his bones as he spotted a heavily veined, dark-throated yellow flower in the rear corner of the enclosed garden. *Hyoscyamus niger.* Henbane. Even breathing its foul scent could produce intoxication.

White, lacy hemlock bobbed nearby. Tall spires of foxglove. He recognized several other toxic varieties, as well, all neatly contained and thriving inside pots and beds.

It was a bloody poison garden.

He withdrew his sword from its sheath, the weapon an old friend in his hand. Slowly, he worked his way toward the rear entrance, pausing briefly to pluck a leaf or two from several varieties, thankful for the protection of his gloves.

Just as he grasped the door's knob, he heard Drayton give a shout. He charged through the door into a dark, damp interior, moving through the scullery and small kitchen toward the sounds of thudding feet and male shouts.

He rounded a corner and discovered Dunston crouched outside the entrance to the dining room. The other man signaled silence with a finger to his lips.

Slowly withdrawing a dagger from the sheath strapped to his thigh, Dunston placed it on the floor at the center of the entrance. He stood, keeping his back to the wall. Then, he called into the room, "Release him, now, my good man. No sense killing anyone when we may all depart with our necks intact."

Laughter—high, rapid, and mad—was the answer. The sound chilled Phineas's blood.

"He wants to fly, my lord. I can set him free. He shall fly and fly."

Dunston shook his head as Phineas tensed. "Let him go, and we'll leave here straight away. No harm done."

"Oh, but you serve his lordship. And his lordship seeks my end."

A hard, steely gaze settled upon Phineas. "Perfect rubbish. Everybody knows I despise Holstoke. He tried to steal my wife."

"He is the son of a goddess. Why should he not take what he wants?"

Dunston's face was grim. He mouthed the word "mad" and gestured to indicate that the poisoner had a pistol directed at Drayton's head.

Phineas nodded and carefully positioned himself on the opposite side of the doorway.

"Tell me your name," Dunston called out.

"The Supplicant."

"No, my good man. Your surname."

"I serve a goddess. My name is nothing." The voice, oddly pitched and jittery, sounded closer. Boots scraped across wood. "She only requires tribute. Sacrifice. She offers great power to those who serve her. Life which begets death. Her beauty sends a man to the sky."

Phineas wrapped his gloved hand around his blade and drew the length slowly through. Then, he met Dunston's eyes and nodded to indicate his readiness.

Dunston nodded in return, unsheathed his second blade from inside his coat, and called through the door, "Drayton would make a poor sacrifice, indeed, limping as he does. Why,

I doubt he could even grasp another man's ballocks with sufficient force to—"

The loud, piercing squeal was their signal. Dunston moved in first, but only by inches. Inside, Drayton clutched the smaller man in two places. One was his wrist. The other made Phineas wince. Dunston charged forward and removed the gun from the young man's hand.

Phineas looked him over from head to toe. Hawthorn's description had been eerily accurate—round, blue eyes, bland features. There was but one difference—the scar, long and jagged along the man's neck. The poisoner was slight of build with every appearance of harmlessness. And he'd obviously been partaking of nightshades, probably henbane, for his pupils were unnaturally wide. Now on his knees clutching his damaged groin, the young man gazed up at Phineas with something approaching wonder. "My lord," he said, his voice ragged from the pain Drayton had inflicted. "I have done well, haven't I?"

Tilting his head, Phineas examined him, wondering how such a pathetic wretch had managed to do what he'd done. The young man was listless. Thin. Weak as watery porridge. Apart from which, he was clearly mad. Not in the same way as Phineas's mother, who had been soulless and calculating. He was uncontrolled. Intoxicated by his own poisons.

"Holstoke." Dunston's tone was cautious, as though calming a fractious horse. "Perhaps you should wait outside, old chap. Mustn't deprive the hangman of his rightful due."

The tip of his sword drew a drop of blood from the poisoner's throat. He scarcely remembered raising the blade. "How did you know her?"

A wide, beatific grin. The young man closed his eyes briefly. "She found me here."

"In Weymouth."

"Along the promenade. She invited me in. She made me fly."

"Bloody, bleeding hell," Drayton muttered. "The boy could not have been but fourteen."

"That *boy* murdered five women," Dunston gritted.

"Not murder," the young man said, his eyes rounding. "Offerings."

Everything inside Phineas went cold and dark. Even his fury felt like frost. "How many?"

"Never enough. The goddess should have more."

Phineas bent down near the young man's face. He could smell death on him. "Tell me how many you have killed," he said softly.

An odd giggle. "More than five by now," he taunted. His chest shuddered as though he could not control his laughter. He turned his jagged scar toward Phineas. "Tried to offer myself once. But the goddess needed my hands. The goddess is greedy."

"The goddess is dead," said Phineas. "And so will you be, soon enough."

He laughed. Loud and high. He laughed until tears rolled down his cheeks. "She—she will never die, my lord. So long as there are Supplicants to serve her." He stifled one last chuckle. His chest shuddered. A small frown marred his smile. "Did you suppose I was the only one?"

Chills streaked his spine, setting his skin afire.

In the silence, Dunston cursed.

Drayton muttered, "Two of 'em? Bloody, bleeding hell."

Phineas straightened. Tightened his grip upon his sword. "Who else?"

The young man whispered, "He will avenge her, my lord."

"Who?" Phineas bellowed.

"I shall be a final offering." He smiled. Shook. "A journey into the sky." He closed his eyes.

Jerked forward.

And forced Phineas's sword through his own throat.

Genie stabbed the bit of ham with her fork. "He might have waited until I'd awakened."

Ross cleared his throat. "Yes, my lady."

"Or, he might have awakened me himself. He has shown remarkable talent in that regard."

"Certainly, he might have done so."

She chewed her ham then sipped her tea. It was oversteeped again. Another annoyance. "In any event, he should not have asked his valet to convey the message."

"I am certain he did not wish to worry you, my lady."

"Well, I am worried. So, that idea is rubbish. It has been hours since he left."

Ross inclined his half-bald head. "He did wish me to convey his most humble apologies."

Her glare was her answer, but she elected to add, "What a lot of rot." Tossing her napkin down upon her plate, she pushed away from the table and stood. "Deliver his messages if you must, Mr. Ross, but do not lie. Holstoke only apologizes under the severest duress. I wager he would prefer to be baked like a ham."

A movement in the morning room doorway caught her eye. It was Hannah. Her eyes and cheeks glistened with tears. The sight sent a dreadful ache swooping through Genie's belly. She rushed to the girl, who threw her arms around her and clung.

"What is it, dearest? What's happened?"

"He—he ..."

Oh, God. It could only be Hawthorn. Had he died in the night? "Take a breath," she murmured. "Then tell me."

Hannah released two sighs before she managed to choke out, "He is awake."

"Oh!" Genie drew back and cupped the girl's shoulders.

"But that is wondrous news!"

Hannah nodded, her tears continuing to flow. "He has asked for paper and—and a pencil. He wishes to sketch the poisoner again."

"Of course." She looked to Ross, who nodded and murmured that he would fetch them straight away. Then, she examined Hannah's eyes. Saw grief and joy battling there. "Come." She drew her sister toward the table then handed her a napkin. "Dry your eyes."

Hannah dabbed at her cheeks.

"Did he say anything to you?" Genie ventured. "Apart from his sudden desire to sketch, I mean."

Pale eyes dropped to where the napkin twisted in delicate hands. "He asked about the poisoner. Whether I had been attacked."

Genie nodded. "Go on. You obviously told him no."

The girl's lip trembled. "H-he asked why I was there with him."

"And you said?"

Her eyes lifted to Genie's. "I did not have an answer, Eugenia."

She ached to see Hannah's turmoil. The girl's seamless shell of indifference was the only thing protecting her. Yet, she could not discard it to reach for what she most wanted—love. Genie had been forced to batter the shell relentlessly to crack the thing open. She'd been rewarded with a new sister, so it had been worth the trouble. But trouble it had been. Genie did not know if a man would have that sort of patience.

"He took my silence for ... I'm not certain. A slight, I suppose. He suggested my purpose was to ensure he lived long enough to provide an image of the man who threatened my life. He requested the paper and pencil." Her hands twisted the cloth tighter. "Then he asked me to leave."

Genie swallowed the lump in her throat and raised her chin. "Perhaps he needed to use the chamber pot."

Hannah blinked. Her lips tightened. Eyes widened. Then, she burst out with a gulp of laughter.

Genie grinned and giggled with her. "Well, the man has been asleep for days, you know."

As tension drained from Hannah's shoulders, Genie insisted she eat. Then, while they sat together at the table, she complimented Hannah's gown, which was a fetching icy-pink frock with little red rosettes at the hem. She discussed plans for a new cap to match her blue gown. The silk, not the velvet. No, the other silk.

She waited until Hannah had eaten everything on her plate before revealing that Phineas, Dunston, and Drayton had left for Weymouth, suspecting that was where the poisoner had been hiding.

Hannah paled. Carefully, she placed her fork beside her plate.

Footmen entered and began clearing trays from the sideboard. Clinking china and the cry of gulls outside were the only sounds for a long while.

Then, Hannah reached for Genie's hand. "You fear for him," she said softly. "As do I." Vividly bright green eyes lifted to hers. "Phineas is strong. Brilliant and strong. I have never won a game of chess against him. Not once. And I am an excellent player."

Genie nodded, tears springing to her own eyes. "I know. But he is the very heart of me, Hannah. So long as that is true—and it shall always be true—I will suffer for his absence."

Ross returned to the morning room twenty minutes later with Hawthorn's new sketch in hand. Genie took it from him and examined the face. She frowned. "Do you recognize him?" she asked Hannah.

"No. I don't like his eyes."

"What about them?"

"They are bad pretending to be good."

Hannah had seen enough bad in her life that Genie

accepted her assessment without hesitation. "Indeed. The worst sort of eyes, I daresay."

More china clinked as one of the footmen sorted his tray. Genie's attention snagged upon him. He wore the Primvale livery, of course. A wig. Blue coat with green facings and gold breeches with white stockings. But he was tall. Six feet, perhaps.

She frowned. Hadn't Phineas "rearranged" all the tall footmen?

The man turned. He was not ugly. Rather pleasant-looking, in fact.

A shiver ran up her spine and across her scalp.

His eyes met hers. And she saw again what Hannah had described. Bad pretending to be good.

Cold washed through her like icy lake water through a fountain. She needed to alert Dunston's men. She needed to get Hannah away from him.

He bent to lift Hannah's plate. Genie grasped her sister's arm and yanked her to her feet. That was when the floor tilted. The walls spun. She pulled harder, dragging Hannah with her to the doorway. She blinked. The door was closed.

Time was slow now. Her movements were awkward and stumbling. Her heart thrashed inside her chest. She shoved Hannah behind her, spinning to face the bad man pretending to be good. And just before the gun appeared, she saw him smile.

Chapter Twenty-Four

"Now, listen closely. Hounds are nothing like wolves. Wolves are born feral. They go a bit mad when they are wounded or starving. And they only play when they're taking your measure for battle."

—THE DOWAGER MARCHIONESS OF WALLINGHAM to her oldest grandson, Bain, in reply to his complaint that Humphrey plays too rough.

∞

PHINEAS HEARD THE MAD BELLOWING FROM OUTSIDE THE castle. The guard at the entrance was missing. The doors stood wide open. He slid from Caballus while the heaving horse was still moving and sprinted up the steps. Ran into the entrance hall.

Found Jonas Hawthorn, naked but for bandages and a torn pair of breeches, staggeringly white, thin, and unshaven. He was leaning against a wall, snarling orders at one of Dunston's men.

"Every man you have. Send them all. Find her, damn you!"

Phineas rushed forward. Hawthorn's eyes came up. Desperate. Near deranged.

Phineas felt the floor disappear. Heard nothing but wind booming in loud, rhythmic gusts. Hawthorn was speaking now. Phineas shook his head. He needed to think. He needed to listen.

"... took them both, Holstoke. Nobody knows where."

God Almighty. Both. Hannah and Eugenia. Gone.

His sister. His wife. Gone.

No. He must think. He must find them.

He closed his eyes for a heartbeat. Pictured Eugenia as she'd been yesterday—wind-whipped hair, arms outstretched, shining love through cat-like eyes. He would find her. He would. But only if he could control his own derangement long enough to think.

He opened his eyes and noticed a sheet of paper crumpled in Hawthorn's fist. Without asking, he snatched it out of the other man's hand. It was a duplicate sketch of the man Phineas's sword had dispatched less than two hours earlier.

"This is not him," Phineas said, his voice hard as ice. "This man is dead."

Hawthorn shook his head. "No. That is the poisoner."

"There are two of them."

Hawthorn went the color of ash.

Dunston and Drayton raced into the entrance hall, Drayton limping heavily and Dunston holding one of his daggers. "Is it true?" Dunston demanded. "Both women are missing?"

Hawthorn nodded and sagged against the wall. His head hung forward. "We must find them. He will kill her."

"How did he get in?" Phineas asked. Once again, the coldness of his own voice surprised him. The fear was there, dark and devouring. But his mind was working, analyzing what he already knew, acquiring what he didn't.

Hawthorn explained Phineas's physician had visited early that morning, bringing along an apothecary-surgeon from Weymouth to assist him with Hawthorn's treatment. But Hawthorn had awakened before their arrival, and the apothecary had soon departed.

"Or so we thought. One of the men found his horse wandering about the orchard. We suspected the poisoner had attacked him. Then, your man, Ross, said he couldn't locate the women. We've been searching ever since."

Phineas held up the sketch. "For the wrong man."

Hawthorn grunted, looking tormented.

Phineas turned to Dunston. "An apothecary from Weymouth."

Dunston nodded. "It fits."

"Can you sketch him?" Phineas asked Hawthorn. "Do you remember his face?"

Hawthorn nodded. "Tall. Six feet. Lean." His eyes narrowed on Drayton. "Like the man who shot you."

"Then let us find the blackguard," Drayton growled, moving to Hawthorn and looping his arm over his shoulders. "You draw 'im. I'll shoot 'im."

While Drayton helped the other runner into the library, Dunston approached Phineas with a grim stare. "Why take both women?"

Phineas shook his head. In truth, his mind could scarcely touch the thought without stark horror devouring him whole. "We must find them. That is all I know."

He spent the next quarter-hour questioning Ross and Walters and Mrs. Green, maids and footmen and guards. He needed every fact he could gather—where had Eugenia and Hannah last been seen? The morning room. Had the castle been searched, top to bottom? Yes, my lord. Which segments of the estate had been searched? The west and north gardens.

The east and south were in process. His mind automatically cataloged every bit of information, seeking threads to lead him in a direction. Toward her.

One of Dunston's men entered and handed Dunston a scrap of cloth. "We found it in one of the east pastures, m'lords, tied to some wildflowers and grass."

The silk was sheer and pink and torn. Running its length was a twin row of crimson roses.

Lightning sliced through him. It was her. His Briar.

"We found more, m'lords."

Phineas looked up, heart pounding with frantic urgency.

"What?" Dunston demanded.

"Blood." The man swallowed, his vigilant gaze sorrowful. "A great deal of blood."

HER HEAD WAS SWIMMING. ACHING. SHE DID NOT KNOW HOW Phineas managed to endure his megrims, for headaches were a wretched distraction. Her eyes hurt. And her heart was about to pound through her chest. Everything was too bright, and her mouth was dry as dust.

Then there was the arm across her throat. Tight. Choking. Her body felt like it wanted to fly apart.

She looked down at her hand. It floated in her vision. Separated from her wrist.

No. She squeezed her eyes closed. This was not real.

The arm across her throat was real. The pain in her head was real.

She was being dragged. Down and down. Past damp rock and loose stones and tufts of grass.

The wind was real.

His voice was real. "Forward, Miss Gray." Smooth, strange

placidity was punctuated by rough panting. "We've an offering to make."

He'd taken them from the morning room. He'd held a gun to Genie's heart and spoken with perfect calm. Hannah would offer herself to the goddess, he'd said, or Lady Holstoke would join her namesake in death.

Clever Hannah. She'd taken her fork with her, hidden in the folds of her skirts.

The pleasant-looking man had forced them to wait inside the castle then exit past a guard who ran to see a horse nibbling cherry trees.

He'd forced them to hide. To move from place to place like rabbits evading traps. First the walled garden. Then the trees around the lake. Then to the farthest east pasture, beyond the rise.

Where the cows had died. Poor cows.

It was there that Genie had been certain *she* would die. The pleasant-looking man had screamed when Hannah plunged the fork into his shoulder.

His hold had loosened. Hannah had seized Genie's separating wrist and shouted, "Run!"

Genie had. But her feet had separated, too. They'd fallen together in the purple flowers and green grass, tangled and confused. Hannah's hem had been there.

Genie had known she must tell him.

Phineas. Her love. Her heart.

She must tell him she'd never leave willingly.

So, she'd torn a strip and knotted it tight, even though the pleasant-looking man had regained his footing. Held a pistol to Genie's head. Forced Hannah to her feet with a brutal shove.

Now, they traveled down and down. Past golden rock to golden sand. Round, gray pebbles poked at her slippers. Her feet were separating.

No. No, she was walking. The beach was real. The water

was real. The cry of gulls and bright, blue sky was real.

She breathed salt and sea. Remembered Phineas's eyes when they'd stood here together. He was her griffin. He would come.

He would tear this serpent to pieces.

She blinked. Focused upon Hannah, whose lip bled red onto delicate white. Pink gauze wafted in the breeze as she backed toward the waves. Eyes like Phineas's gleamed with incandescent power. "He will find you. He will kill you," her sister said. "Never doubt it."

The arm across Genie's throat tightened. "Not before I have made my offering." Something round dug painfully into her rib. "Into the sea, now," he said. "She always favored the sea."

Pink gauze dampened. To her ankles. Then her knees. Then her thighs.

"No, Hannah," Genie called, her frantic heart beating her to death. Choking her to death. "You will ruin your gown, dearest."

Eyes like Phineas's smiled back at her. "Tell Mr. Hawthorn I stayed because I ... I could not bear to do otherwise. Tell him ... I did not want to leave."

The panting breaths grew louder as the man who choked Genie drove them both forward, closer to her sister. The water reached Hannah's waist. Waves shoved her until she stumbled.

Genie could not let her ruin her gown. Hannah looked so lovely in pink.

She saw a wrist. Not hers. It looked like ham.

She took it in her hands and bit.

A shout.

A shot. Fire streaked her hip.

She shoved away the choking arm. Spit the serpent's blood from her mouth. Ran toward her sister, whose skirts were dragging her deeper into the sea.

Hannah sobbed her name. Staggered toward her. Genie's

feet tried to reach her, but they kept sinking into sand and pebbles.

Oh, God. She was coming apart. The pain in her hip burned. Her feet were gone. Only her knees remained. Her hands clutched at deep, soft sand.

She looked to Hannah, who stood in the waves like a wrathful sea goddess, condemning a man she would soon destroy.

Genie twisted to see him—the bad man pretending to be good. Tall and lean. Holding something long and curved. His arms dripped blood. His mouth spoke of offerings. And as he drew back his bow to send his arrow into Hannah's heart, he glanced to the sky.

"For you, my lady," he said. "All for you."

FINDING THE BLOOD NEARLY BROKE HIM. IT SOAKED THE MUD of the pasture. It dotted white daisies and purple cranesbill. It trailed past the rail fence.

It smeared the wood.

Phineas had long passed sanity. Nothing remained but need. The need to find her. The need to kill.

He held on by remembering. How she'd played with his emerald cravat pin and dared him to pleasure her as no man ever had. How she'd glowed when he'd kissed her bare belly and opened her like a flower. How she'd laughed and spun while the wind played with her hair. How she'd waded into deep water and held his hand. How she loved him—every part of him—as though he'd been hers forever.

Eugenia held him. Focused him. Led him along the rail fence toward the sea.

Dunston followed, as did three of his vigilant men. Drayton

followed, too, pistol in hand, haggard face starkly shadowed in the bright sun. He'd recognized the man Hawthorn had drawn—he'd spoken to him at an apothecary shop in Bridport.

Drayton wanted the man's death. But Phineas would have it. This was his task. His.

As they neared the cliffs, Phineas broke into a run. He could feel her. He did not know how. But she was here. Near. He ran faster. Behind him, he heard Dunston warning his men to be ready. He heard gulls crying and waves breaking.

He heard his own heart. Pounding, pounding, pounding.

Ahead, thirty yards from the top of the beach trail, an object caught his eye. There, near where Eugenia had seen the shadow figure the day before, the grass had been trampled into a nest. At the center of the nest lay a wooden bow and a pile of arrows.

Breaths sawed in and out, his lungs burning after running hundreds of yards. He stopped as he reached the nest. Bent and took up the bow. It was well made. Wood and horn. He looked at the arrows. Picked one up. Noted it, too, was quality.

"The blackguard likes archery, I take it," said Dunston from behind him. "I prefer blades."

"As do I," Phineas murmured, weighing the bow and arrow in his hands.

"Swords. Yes, I do recall." Dunston prowled the area around the nest. "No sign of blood here. Are you certain this is the way they came?"

He needed to think. He needed to keep his head so that he could save his heart.

Phineas looked toward the sea. "Yes."

"Then where to next, old chap?"

Before Dunston had finished speaking, Phineas was moving. Striding. Running toward the head of the beach path. He stopped when he reached the edge of the bluff.

There. Two figures. No, three.

Hannah stood hip-deep in the water.

And Eugenia. Oh, God. Eugenia was being held—dangled and choked—by a bloody madman. Her hair was half down. Her gown was muddy. Bloody.

Nearby, he heard Dunston talking in low tones. Then, Drayton was there, limping to the spot beside him. The Bow Street runner held a hunting rifle, probably borrowed from one of Dunston's men. He brought it to his shoulder and aimed it down at the beach.

"No," Phineas growled, grasping the barrel in his fist and forcing it up. "If the bullet goes through him, you will kill her."

Drayton's haggard face winced. "Bloody, bleeding hell." He lowered the gun to the ground.

"I will kill him," Phineas promised. "But I must get closer. Stay here. Keep his head in your sights."

Without another word, he started down the path, moving as swiftly as he could without sliding. He needed the blackguard not to notice him. Not until it was too late.

Hannah was speaking now. The man dragged Eugenia forward with him, closer to the water's edge. Hannah stumbled as a wave hit her.

Then, everything happened slowly, yet all at once. He saw the man's shoulders jerk in what looked to be agony. A shot fired. Red bloomed on Eugenia's hip. Phineas watched Eugenia toss the man's arm aside then spit out his blood onto the sand. She had bitten him. By God, she had bitten him. And she'd been wounded. She staggered forward toward Hannah. Fell to her knees in the sand.

He ran. His heart was pounding, pounding, pounding. He needed a better position. The man was retrieving something from near a rock. Another bow.

Bloody hell. No time. No time to get a better shot.

He stopped on the next step. Nocked the arrow. Exhaled. Aimed for the blackguard's head.

A gunshot rang out. The other man crumpled as the bullet struck his thigh.

Drayton. Bloody hell.

The blackguard took aim again, this time from his knees. He pointed his arrow at Hannah.

Phineas pointed his arrow at the serpent. Then, he breathed. And let it fly.

It pierced the man's throat, jerking his aim high. The other man's arrow soared into the sea. Behind him, he heard cheering. Above him, he heard gulls.

But Eugenia was now lying on the sand, reaching out for Hannah.

By the time he reached her, Hannah was cradling her head in her lap. Both women were weeping.

"Phineas!" Hannah cried. "Thank heaven. She's been hurt. Not too badly, I think, but she is talking nonsense."

He fell to his knees beside his wife. Scooped her into his arms. Held her as tightly as he dared without knowing the extent of her injuries.

He breathed in her scent. Violets and cherries. Felt her arms twine about his neck. Rocked her back and forth.

"My griffin," she whispered in his ear. "I knew."

He groaned into the skin of her precious neck. Kissed the skin of her precious cheek. Ran his hands over the whorls of her precious ears. "What did you know, my sweet Briar?"

She cupped his jaw in her hand. He drew back to meet cat-like eyes. The enlarged, black centers spoke of nightshades. Nevertheless, these were Eugenia's eyes. And she was alive.

"I knew you would find me."

He smiled. "Did you?"

She nodded, perfect assurance beaming. "It is your nature, my love."

Chapter Twenty-Five

"You surprise me, dear boy. I have only ever heard you speak of your wife or your waistcoats in such glowing terms."

—THE DOWAGER MARCHIONESS OF WALLINGHAM to Lord Dunston at said gentleman's unexpected praise for Lord Holstoke's numerous talents.

∞

A WEEK LATER, DUNSTON WAS STILL CROWING OVER Phineas's shot. "Why did you never say you were an archer, my good man? I thought you favored blades."

Phineas lifted a brow. "A preference for one does not imply incompetence with the other."

He withdrew one of his daggers. The blade gleamed in the light of the morning room. "True. When you are next at Fairfield Park, we must test your facility with knives."

"Henry," Genie chastised. "Do put that away. The only knives we should be discussing at my table are those required to slice ham."

Her brother-in-law gave her a wink and returned his blade to its sheath.

She finished her eggs and pushed aside her ham. She still could not bring herself to eat it. Once the memory of biting into a madman's arm diminished, perhaps ham would seem palatable again.

Around her, Dunston and Phineas and Mr. Drayton all ribbed one another. Mr. Drayton was inexplicably proud of the wound he had delivered to the poisoner's leg.

"Serves 'im right." Mr. Drayton shifted in his chair. "He shot me first."

In fact, the recipient of Mr. Drayton's rifle shot was the very same man who, six years earlier, had fired upon Mr. Drayton to escape capture. Theodore Neville had owned an apothecary shop in Weymouth for the past four years. Before that, he'd been Lady Holstoke's associate, using his position as an apothecary's assistant in London to craft her formulations. He'd poisoned his employer when Drayton and Mr. Reaver had drawn too close. Then, he'd fled London and wandered from city to city for a time. Eventually, he'd been drawn to Dorsetshire, where Lady Holstoke had last resided. He'd established himself as an apothecary. Everyone had thought him a rather pleasant fellow, including Phineas's physician, who had expressed horror upon learning of the man's murderous insanity.

Indeed, Neville's obsession with Lady Holstoke had driven him mad. He'd purchased Lady Holstoke's former home and subsequently taken in another of her former associates, Edgar Erwin. Edgar's family had thought he'd drowned or run away while they visited Weymouth, as he'd simply disappeared without a trace. Instead, Lady Holstoke had recruited him. Drugged him. Seduced him. Used him.

A young boy of thirteen.

Genie had wanted to vomit when she'd learned that bit.

Soon after Neville had moved into Lady Holstoke's house, he and Erwin had begun some very strange habits. They'd experimented with poisons, particularly plants, using both themselves and the livestock from local farms to test new formulations. They'd amassed sheaves and sheaves of detailed notes, chronicling their findings.

They'd also regularly sacrificed rabbits, chickens, and several goats to the woman they came to regard as a goddess. Perhaps it had been the substances they imbibed or the warping influence of evil or simple madness, but Neville and Erwin had worshipped Lydia Brand. Murder had been their "offering."

In addition, they'd kept records. Stacks and stacks of records. Phineas had found Neville's vast collection of notes and journals on shelves lining the house's entire second floor. Neville had tracked his sacrifices and experiments with greater care than a rector keeping a church register. Strange, indeed.

It was Neville who had mixed the poisons and Erwin who had delivered them to their victims. In the case of the poor woman who resembled Hannah, Erwin had brought her to the house in Knightsbridge, where Neville had delivered her death.

Phineas had found explaining matters to the magistrate rather trying. Another string of sinister occurrences and poisonous murders. Another death on Primvale land. And this time, the killer had not merely been shot with a pistol. He'd been stabbed with a fork, bitten like a ham, shot with a hunting rifle, and speared through the neck by an arrow. Good heavens, it was a miracle the magistrate had only demanded Phineas surrender Neville's journals.

Now, days later, Dunston and Mr. Drayton were preparing to leave. And so was Mr. Hawthorn. The Bow Street officer remained weakened from his injuries. Mr. Hawthorn sat across the table from Hannah looking grim as death, his square jaw hard, his interest in breakfast slight.

But, then, Hannah had not eaten more than a bite or two,

either. She was coldly composed and beautifully gowned. She sipped her tea and refused to look at Mr. Hawthorn for any reason.

He refused to take his eyes from her.

Genie ached for them both, but she'd done all she could. Hannah had shuttered her heart to the man. Understandable, she supposed. Having suffered deep, permanent wounds, Hannah's past distorted the shape of her future in much the same way as Edgar Erwin's. Charging forth into love, risking her strong-yet-fragile heart, was simply out of the question.

"One day, you will want it enough," Genie had told her gently the previous night. "And then, you'll be brave. Because you are. Though you may not be ready."

A single tear had slid down Hannah's cheek. She'd tilted her chin to a proud angle. "I will learn to ride, Eugenia."

Genie had grinned. Squeezed her hand. "Splendid. We shall start there, dearest."

Now, as breakfast ended and the men prepared to depart, Hannah retreated to her bedchamber while Mr. Hawthorn eyed her with visible hunger. Dunston had arranged for a coach to take him back to London. As soon as she was out of sight, he climbed inside without another word.

Genie looped her arm through Phineas's as they stood on the castle steps watching the men disappear down the drive. "I quite like Mr. Hawthorn."

Phineas frowned. "He was helpful, I suppose."

"You should attempt to like him, too."

"I fail to see why. The probability that I shall ever set eyes upon him again is low. Five percent. Perhaps ten."

"Oh, I'd put it higher than that."

His eyes met hers. "I prefer to contemplate the probability that you'll be naked within the hour."

She chuckled. Drew him down for a kiss. "Easily one hundred percent, I daresay."

He sighed and touched his forehead to hers. The scents of

lemon and mint washed over her. His eyes closed for a moment. "I need to touch you again, Briar. I need to see that you are ... well."

Grinning, she stroked his jaw and gazed up into glowing green. "I rather thought you had verified my improved health several times last night."

"A man of science must be diligent."

"And this morning."

"Inconclusive."

"Twice before breakfast, if I recall."

"Additional experiments are needed to ensure full rigor."

She moaned, her belly heating. "I do enjoy your rigor."

He bent and scooped her into his arms. She clung to his neck, kissed his jaw, his ear, the corner of his fascinating lips. Every part she could reach. By time he laid her upon his bed, she was trembling with heated shivers. Sliding amidst the emerald velvets and silver silks, she propped herself on her elbows to watch him disrobe. His eyes shone brightly as they lingered upon her breasts and hips.

Slowly, she tugged her skirts up her legs. "How naked should I be for your experiment, my lord?" She paused at her knees. "This naked?"

"More."

Her thighs. "This naked?"

He discarded his trousers and climbed into bed, propping himself above her. "More."

"Show me," she whispered against his mouth.

He stripped away her stockings. Her skirts. Her bodice and corset and petticoats and shift. He stroked his palms across her nipples. Took the hard tips into his mouth—first one, then the other. He kissed his way down her center, pausing to linger, as he often did, upon her belly.

"Our babe will grow here, Eugenia." He nuzzled her navel. "Our family will grow here."

She smiled and stroked his hair. "How right you are, my love."

Next, he traced a finger along her hip, near where Neville's bullet had grazed her. The injury still smarted a bit, but she was healing remarkably well, thanks to Phineas's teas and salves. He laid the softest kiss above and below the bandage.

"How do you feel?" he asked.

"Feverish."

His eyes flew to hers, crinkled with concern.

"Your touch sets me afire." She stroked his cheek, her hips undulating into the mattress. "Now, do get on with it."

He laughed, low and flinty. The sound was wicked pleasure.

He kissed her belly. Lower. Then lower.

His fingers stroked her thighs. Higher. Then higher.

"Your petals are soft, Briar. Eager." His fingers parted her folds and slid with maddening strokes around her swollen center. His eyes devoured her there, almost another touch. He dropped his head. Teased the little nub with his tongue. "Sweet, sweet nectar," he whispered, his hot breath another stimulation. Two fingers slid easily inside her while his tongue worked and worked and worked.

The bright burst of heat and light expanded endlessly like a thundercloud over the sea as she lifted herself into his mouth. Writhing and clutching at silver silk, she demanded, "Now, Phineas. Oh, please, my love. Now."

Within seconds, he was filling her. Hard and deep and true. She held his eyes. Kissed his lips. Held him tight and gave him every ounce of pleasure she could.

Because he was hers. Every part of him. The scientist, the husband, the protector. The man. Whole and wondrous.

"God, how I love you, Briar."

"Phineas," she breathed. "My heart."

When her peak came, his body thrust inside hers with mad fury. His eyes blazed, desperate and devouring. She held them as long as she could, wanting him to see her ecstasy. To know that his touch was the only one that could deliver it. And, as his name broke from her throat with a wrenching sob, she could see that he knew.

She was his and he was hers.

She would make him laugh when he grew too serious, and he would strengthen her when her confidence was shaken. Their family would grow. Their love would grow.

Genie knew it as surely as she knew red silk roses looked dashing with indigo plumes.

For, while their marriage might have been sown in the soil of scandal, their roots were now forever entwined.

Epilogue

"A griffin? Why, it is part eagle and part lion. Interestingly, legend has it the creature selects one mate for all its life. Quite similar to dragons, in that regard."

—THE DOWAGER MARCHIONESS OF WALLINGHAM while reading to her oldest grandson, Bain, on a peaceful winter morning.

∞

FROST GLITTERED ON THE STONES OF THE DRIVE. FROM above, Primvale's landscape appeared painted in iridescent white. The sea sighed in the distance. The sun shone bright and pure.

Phineas plucked up a blanket from Eugenia's sofa and walked out onto the terrace.

He wrapped the soft, red blanket around his beautiful wife's shoulders. Then, he wrapped her in his arms. "What do you think?" he murmured in her ear.

She leaned back into him then propped her elbow on her

wrist and tapped her lips with her finger. "It took a very long time."

"Yes."

"And a great deal of expense."

"There is that."

"I shall never regain the sleep I lost from being awakened every morning by hammers and chisels and overly jocular craftsmen."

He chuckled. Kissed her neck. Felt her shiver. "But?"

"It is perfect, Phineas. More perfect than I ever imagined."

Elation filled him. Pride and pleasure moved through him like lightning.

He'd not allowed her to see his design until yesterday, when the last chisel had finished its work. And her initial response had been wordless—tears. Kisses. A passionate afternoon spent demonstrating her appreciation with her mouth and hands and delicious body.

But he'd wanted to hear her say it. And now, she had.

His mother's fountain had been transformed. The griffin remained. But where the serpent had once coiled, now branches and leaves and flowers twined. The sweetbriar's thorns protected the griffin, and the griffin protected the precious blooms. They tangled skyward, strengthened by their embrace.

"I am glad you like it, Briar."

She drew his palm to her newly rounded belly and laced her fingers between his. "I love it. And I love you." She sniffed. "I also love my new bedchamber." They had replaced the yellow silk with crimson in September. "Though I do not see why we keep a bed in there, as I cannot sleep anywhere but with you. Perhaps I shall turn it into a sitting room. Or a workshop."

"Another workshop?"

"If I am to bring the latest fashions to the ladies of Bridport, I must have room to create, Phineas."

He sighed. "I should think two workshops sufficient—"

"Do you have merely one garden?" she asked pertly.

He opted for silence.

"Quite right. Besides, Hannah has suggested expanding my offerings into Weymouth. She is quite brilliant, your sister. I'd no idea she had such a head for profits and percentages."

He kissed the top of Eugenia's head and savored the feel of their babe beneath his hand. "Come inside, my sweet one. It is too cold to stay out here much longer."

"I have no worries on that score."

Smiling, he murmured, "No?"

She smiled, too, her eyes glowing with love as she turned in his arms. "You always keep me warm, Phineas."

He touched his forehead to hers. Breathed her in. Violets and cherries. He kissed her tenderly, then whispered his promise to the woman he loved. "And I always will, Briar. I always will."

More from Elisa Braden

It's far from over! There are more scandalous predicaments, emotional redemptions, and gripping love stories (with a dash of Lady Wallingham) in the Rescued from Ruin series. For **new release alerts and updates**, follow Elisa on Facebook and Twitter, and sign up for her free email newsletter at **www.elisabraden.com**, so you don't miss a thing!

Plus, be sure to check out all the other exciting books in the Rescued from Ruin series, available now!

THE MADNESS OF VISCOUNT ATHERBOURNE (BOOK ONE)
Victoria Lacey's life is perfect—perfectly boring. Agree to marry a lord who has yet to inspire a single, solitary tingle? It's all in a day's work for the oh-so-proper sister of the Duke of Blackmore. Surely no one suspects her secret longing for head-spinning passion. Except a dark stranger, on a terrace, at a ball where she should not be kissing a man she has just met. Especially one bent on revenge.

THE TRUTH ABOUT CADS AND DUKES (BOOK TWO)
Painfully shy Jane Huxley is in a most precarious position, thanks to dissolute charmer Colin Lacey's deceitful wager. Now, his brother, the icy Duke of Blackmore, must make it right, even if it means marrying her himself. Will their union end in frostbite? Perhaps. But after lingering glances and devastating kisses, Jane begins to suspect the truth: Her duke may not be as cold as he appears.

DESPERATELY SEEKING A SCOUNDREL (BOOK THREE)
Where Lord Colin Lacey goes, trouble follows. Tortured and hunted by a brutal criminal, he is rescued from death's door by

the stubborn, fetching Sarah Battersby. In return, she asks one small favor: Pretend to be her fiancé. Temporarily, of course. With danger nipping his heels, he knows it is wrong to want her, wrong to agree to her terms. But when has Colin Lacey ever done the sensible thing?

THE DEVIL IS A MARQUESS (BOOK FOUR)

A walking scandal surviving on wits, whisky, and wicked skills in the bedchamber, Benedict Chatham must marry a fortune or risk ruin. Tall, redheaded disaster Charlotte Lancaster possesses such a fortune. The price? One year of fidelity and sobriety. Forced to end his libertine ways, Chatham proves he is more than the scandalous charmer she married, but will it be enough to keep his unwanted wife?

WHEN A GIRL LOVES AN EARL (BOOK FIVE)

Miss Viola Darling always gets what she wants, and what she wants most is to marry Lord Tannenbrook. James knows how determined the tiny beauty can be—she mangled his cravat at a perfectly respectable dinner before he escaped. But he has no desire to marry, less desire to be pursued, and will certainly not kiss her kissable lips until they are both breathless, no matter how tempted he may be.

TWELVE NIGHTS AS HIS MISTRESS (NOVELLA - BOOK SIX)

Charles Bainbridge, Lord Wallingham, spent two years wooing Julia Willoughby, yet she insists they are a dreadful match destined for misery. Now, rather than lose her, he makes a final offer: Spend twelve nights in his bed, and if she can deny they are perfect for each other, he will let her go. But not before tempting tidy, sensible Julia to trade predictability for the sweet chaos of true love.

CONFESSIONS OF A DANGEROUS LORD (BOOK SEVEN)

Known for flashy waistcoats and rapier wit, Henry Thorpe, the Earl of Dunston, is deadlier than he appears. For years, his sole focus has been hunting a ruthless killer through London's dark underworld. Then Maureen Huxley came along. To keep her safe, he must keep her at arm's length. But as she contemplates marrying another man, Henry's caught in the crossfire between his mission and his heart.

ANYTHING BUT A GENTLEMAN (BOOK EIGHT)

Augusta Widmore must force her sister's ne'er-do-well betrothed to the altar, or her sister will bear the consequences. She needs leverage only one man can provide—Sebastian Reaver. When she invades his office demanding a fortune in markers, he exacts a price a spinster will never pay—become the notorious club owner's mistress. And when she calls his bluff, a fiery battle for surrender begins.

A MARRIAGE MADE IN SCANDAL (BOOK NINE)

As the most feared lord in London, the Earl of Holstoke is having a devil of a time landing a wife. When a series of vicious murders brings suspicion to his door, only one woman is bold enough to defend him—Eugenia Huxley. Her offer to be his alibi risks scandal, and marriage is the remedy. But as a poisonous enemy coils closer, Holstoke finds his love for her might be the greatest danger of all.

About the Author

Reading romance novels came easily to Elisa Braden. She's been doing it since she was twelve. Writing them? That took a little longer. After graduating with degrees in creative writing and history, Elisa spent entirely too many years in "real" jobs writing T-shirt copy ... and other people's resumes ... and articles about giftware displays. But that was before she woke up and started dreaming about the very *unreal* job of being a romance novelist. Frankly, she figures better late than never.

Elisa lives in the gorgeous Pacific Northwest, where you're constitutionally required to like the colors green and gray. Good thing she does. Other items on the "like" list include cute dogs, strong coffee, and epic movies. Of course, her favorite thing of all is hearing from readers who love her characters as much as she does. If you're one of those, get in touch on Facebook and Twitter or visit **www.elisabraden.com**.